S0-CFA-653

Heidi Rittenhouse

Andrew Pyper is the author of the novels *Lost Girls* (which was a *New York Times* and *Globe and Mail* Notable Book of the Year) and *The Trade Mission,* as well as *Kiss Me,* a collection of stories. He lives in Toronto.

www.andrewpyper.com

Livonia Public Library
ALFRED NOBLE BRANCH
32901 PLYMOUTH ROAD
Livonia, Michigan 48150-1793
(734)421-6600
LIVN #19

FICTION

ALSO BY ANDREW PYPER

Lost Girls

The Trade Mission

Kiss Me

ALFRED NOBLE BRANCH
32901 PLYMOUTH ROAD

ADDITIONAL PRAISE FOR

The Wildfire Season

A *Globe and Mail, Vancouver Sun,* and *Calgary Herald*
Best Book of the Year

"A hugely impressive and utterly compelling thriller… moody,
thought provoking, and altogether remarkable."

—*The Independent* (UK)

"With its tortured hero and fast-paced action, *The Wildfire
Season* is a true Yukon potboiler. Andrew Pyper has talent
galore and sure hands, ratcheting up the suspense to the very
end."

—Stewart O'Nan, author of *The Good Wife* and *Snow Angels*

"Pyper knows how to whirl a complex plot into motion…but
exceeds the demands of the suspense-thriller genre….A liter-
ary craftsman who knows what he is doing at all times."

—*The Globe and Mail* (Toronto)

"An edge-of-the-seat thriller."

—*Booklist*

"A novel of true haunting loneliness and isolation, plus a gripping
story that scorches off the page. This novel of extraordinary
power combines the supernatural, edge-of-your-seat suspense,
nature in all its wondrous ferocity, and scars—visible and invisible. The writing is a dream, demonstrating that indeed the past
can kill. This is a novel that blazes with all the ingredients of the
best literature."

—Ken Bruen, author of *Calibre* and *The Dramatist*

"A thriller that no reader can afford to miss...Pyper is able to bring out both the excitement of the wilderness and the claustrophobia of a small desolate town.... Certain to keep readers on the edge of their seats."

—*Richmond Times-Dispatch*

THE
WILDFIRE
SEASON

ANDREW PYPER

Livonia Public Library
ALFRED NOBLE BRANCH
32901 PLYMOUTH ROAD
Livonia, Michigan 48150-1793
(734)421-6600
LIVN #19

PICADOR

THOMAS DUNNE BOOKS · ST. MARTIN'S MINOTAUR · NEW YORK

JUN 11 2008

FOR HEIDI

THE WILDFIRE SEASON. Copyright © 2005 by Andrew Pyper Enterprises, Inc. All rights reserved. Printed in the United States of America. No part of this book may be used or reproduced in any manner whatsoever without written permission except in the case of brief quotations embodied in critical articles or reviews. For information, address Picador, 175 Fifth Avenue, New York, N.Y. 10010.

www.picadorusa.com

Picador® is a U.S. registered trademark and is used by St. Martin's Press under license from Pan Books Limited.

For information on Picador Reading Group Guides, please contact Picador.
E-mail: readinggroupguides@picadorusa.com

Library of Congress Cataloging-in-Publication Data

Pyper, Andrew.
    The wildfire season / Andrew Pyper.
       p. cm.
    ISBN-13: 978-0-312-42767-2
    ISBN-10: 0-312-42767-0
    1. Wildfires—Fiction. 2. Fire fighters—Fiction. 3. Arson—Fiction. 4. Fathers and daughters—Fiction. 5. Yukon Territory—Fiction. I. Title.

PR9199.3.P96W55 2006
813'.54—dc22

2006047495

Originally published in Canada by Harper Perennial,
an imprint of HarperCollins Publishers Ltd

First published in the United States by St. Martin's Press

First Picador Edition: April 2008

10 9 8 7 6 5 4 3 2 1

3 9082 10804 8417

a boy with a head stuffed with nothing but bleached teeth and a Stanford MBA, had asked him while lifting a glass of white wine— *white wine!*—to his lips, and Bader had silenced the pup by growling, "Thought I'd go up to Canada to bag me one of those Boone and Crockett Kodiaks." Three years passed without his mentioning it again. Then, one morning this past November, he had abruptly muted the rec-room big screen—an unheard-of interruption of a Vikings vs. Redskins game—turned to his wife and said, "You want to go hunting with me in the spring?" It had been so long since her husband had surveyed her wants that she had said yes and giggled with an overflow of pleasure before she wondered if she actually wanted to witness somebody kill a bear or not.

Miles watches Jackson Bader look about him distractedly, pale and string-necked, and has the impression that the old man isn't sure what he's doing here. It's not the confusion that comes with age or with discovering oneself in unfamiliar surroundings. Bader is simply the kind of man who finds the company of strangers slightly absurd, useless, an expenditure of energy on those who, in all likelihood, you will never see again. Miles meets the man's eyes and wonders if Bader has identified the same distance in him.

Now that he thinks of it, Miles has to concede that everyone here likely sees him as Bader does: the near-silent burn victim, friendless and grotesque. What people wonder about more than anything else are his scars. The muddy splotches that spill down the one side of his neck, his rib cage, and disappear below his waist. All anybody is sure of is they have reason not to ask him about it. Within months of his arrival, Miles earned a reputation as a merciless barfighter on the nights when the drink goes down him the wrong way, or if provoked, or if merely spoken to in what he interprets to be an unfavourable tone. Currently, he is one victim short of sending an even half-dozen down to Whitehorse on free medevac rides.

On these occasions, Miles spends the night under Terry Gray's watch in the single cell of the RCMP office, apologizing for keeping

Terry up late, and Terry telling him that he's a lousy sleeper at the best of times and that he'd rather type up the assault charges against Miles than lie awake all night in his trailer. Most recently, it concerned a visiting miner who had affronted Ross River's meagre charms by saying of Bonnie, "There's better-looking barmaids back in the goddamn hole," referring to the all-male open pit mine in which he'd spent the last three weeks. For this offence, Miles had beaten the man into a long and dreamless sleep.

Terry Gray has started getting calls. "Hear you've got a real wild man on your hands up there, Sheriff," the superintendent down in Whitehorse will joke with him, but Terry knows it's getting less funny all the time. He also knows about the stories. Tales of a monster whose rage has pursued him to the end of the world. He killed a pregnant woman in Prince George. He scarred his face blowing up a Hells Angels clubhouse in Edmonton, and a pack of murderous bikers have been spotted as far north as Carcross, asking after a guy with a fucked-up face. And a dozen other improvised myths. In fact, the Welcome Inn has become as famous in the rest of the territory for the brooding fire ranger who drinks in its bar as for its mouldy, overpriced rooms.

Mungo Capoose sees his boss differently.

"Miles McEwan? He's not so mean," is how Mungo likes to conclude any conversations concerning his boss's character. "He's just running away."

"From what?" someone will ask.

"From his face."

"But you *can't* run from that."

"That's why he's gone as far as he has."

There is also a figure visible to Miles alone. Standing in the shadows on the far side of the pool table that's been too slanted to play an honest game on since Miles piledrived Wade onto it the first and only time he called him Scarface. Miles couldn't say how long the figure has been there. It's only when he stares at the one spot for a while that he can make out the outline of a person at all. The slumped shoulders. The pale reflection of unblinking eyes.

It stays where it is long enough that Miles wonders if it is only his own idle creation. Yet the figure is too inarguably *there* for him to pretend it couldn't be. Its stillness prevents it from being wholly alive. This is what Miles tries to tell himself. The man in the shadows will remain a shadow until it can move.

And then it moves.

As it slides toward him, Miles counts the ways the shadow takes on colour. Khaki work pants splashed with what looks like machine oil. Eyes showing themselves to be unnaturally wide and red-rimmed. The head so bald it's missing ears as well as hair.

Miles watches the man emerge from where there was nothing before, as though stepping out of the wall itself. When the tips of his boots slide into the light cast by the bare bulb nearest him, he stops.

Although the figure is tall, Miles can see that it belongs to a young man. A kid stretching his neck to show a face burned black. And smiling. His teeth long and shining as ivory keys.

With a spastic lurch Miles swings around on his stool. He pounds his fist against his chest to show the room it's only a swig of beer that's gone down the wrong way. Even when the others return to their conversations Miles refuses to look beyond the pool table.

"Nice one."

"She is."

"Where'd you get her?"

"Come up on a flatbed to Carmacks."

"Used?"

"They're all used. But this one's not as used as others."

Without asking, Miles knows that Wade and Crookedhead are talking about trucks. Men speak of half-tons up here in the same covetous, technical way that others might speak of power tools, laptop computers or women. Everything else that happens in Ross River might ultimately boil down to a tale of foolishness or mild humiliation to cling to its subject for years, but trucks alone are taken seriously. If he closes his eyes and listens selectively to the drinkers around him, Miles can pick out the names of the Big Three manufacturers, each brand spoken with reverence, as though ancient gods. Dodge. Ford. Chevy. Once, and only once, a Toyota made an appearance so scorned that its owner, Crooked-head James, was compelled to drive it to Whitehorse and sell it, coming home on the once-a-week bus with a hangover that made his nose run, four hundred dollars, and a gym bag of newish skin magazines.

"Nice truck," Wade says again, although this time about a new arrival in the parking lot.

"Wade?" Margot calls. "Bring me and the Baders here another round, would you?"

After a time long enough to let Margot know she will later pay for addressing him in this way, Wade turns to the bar and leaves Crookedhead to follow whatever movement there is outside.

"*Thank* you, Wade," Mrs. Bader gushes. "I'm not sure when I last had so much *beer* to drink. I mean, usually I just have a single gin, and that's only at *functions!*"

Jackson Bader says nothing. Everyone in the room except for his wife has heard someone at the door, and they have shifted in their seats to see who will open it.

"Oh, Margot. You're so *lucky* to live way up here, where you can do things like this all the time—not just drink beer, but enjoy the *real* things. The wilderness. Cowboys and Indians! Good heavens. You're not supposed to say *Indian* anymore, are you? And most of *you* are—well, I only meant—"

Elsie Bader's face is slashed by the light coming in through the open door. It is against this illumination that two strangers appear. A woman in her late twenties holding the hand of a little girl.

The two of them come inside but the door remains jammed on a raised crack. The woman lifts her sunglasses. Without a change in either of their expressions she spots Miles and, after the most brief of pauses, the two step toward him.

The Welcome Inn patrons are a transfixed audience to their march. Everyone hopes, no matter what is about to take place, that the woman doesn't ask Miles about the mottled burns that, in the sudden light, look like crimson ink splashed from his temple to his shirt collar.

Miles's eyes won't leave the little girl holding the woman's hand. Her just-brushed hair shining blue against the twilight. A summer dress patterned with strawberries down to her mosquito-bitten knees. Maybe five. Maybe six.

He doesn't recognize the woman next to her. Not at first. But although Miles is certain he's never seen the girl in the strawberry dress before, she smiles his way, and without thinking, without touching his scar, without the ongoing work of forgetting that demands to be remembered, he smiles back.

The girl smiles at him and he smiles back and he knows.

Less than fifteen miles away, where the even ground outside Ross River gives way to the first sloping of the St. Cyr foothills, a cold rain falls windless and straight on the deadfall. For the past three weeks there has been little other precipitation than this. Dark clouds that cluster and begin their low murmurings, and within seconds the air drops three degrees, leaving a bristling anticipation in the spruce needles. When the rain comes, it does not fall so much as collapse. The air crushed with white noise in which anything from whispered voices to gunfire can be heard.

And then it's over.

The rain had soaked the bear through to the skin, but her fur is already dry, porcupined in dark spikes. She has marched close enough to town to detect traces of the man-made: diesel exhaust, woodsmoke, the sugary temptations of the dump. It keeps her nose low. Inhaling the clean, mineralized scent of soil turning to mud.

Behind her, two male cubs follow. They are no more than twenty months old but are already bigger than sheepdogs. And yet the length of the sow's stride requires an awkward half-run of the cubs to keep up. Two sulking brothers with ears standing atop their heads like a pair of children's mittens.

Faraway sheet lightning casts its shadows across the wall of pine trunks. The three animals shuffle diagonally up the slope, their movements deliberate but weary. They have come from elsewhere but the sow has been here before, though her memories of it only make her want to move farther on.

She stops as abruptly as the rain. The cub closest to her bumps his head against her hind legs and she swings around, demanding attention. Water bends the branches lower and spills off their ends so that, for the first minute, there is no sound but a chorus of pissing.

The she-grizzly slowly rises. Her nose stretched high, the tip of a shaggy antenna. When she is standing at her full height, towering ten feet over her cubs, she swivels her head and takes in so many small sniffs that, when she exhales, it comes out in a grunt. With eyes closed she holds herself still. Her nostrils stretched wide, tasting the new, almost undetectable breeze from the south.

The sow recognizes something in it that her cubs have never smelled before. The odour of a danger equal to the burnt-butter stink of men.

She smells smoke.

THREE

.

As she steps toward him, Miles notices how the child's knees poke out below the hem of her dress, one and then the other, like turtle's heads. It's been so long since he's seen a girl of her age in a dress that it looks like a costume to him. Among the details he's lost hold of in the last few years are holidays—what dates they fall on and whether the Raven Nest Grocery will be closed on account of it. Because of this, and because of the dress, Miles has an idea that the girl is about to pull a pillowcase from behind her back and demand "Trick or treat!"

The Welcome Inn drinkers lift their heads to take a measure of the newcomers, studying the woman and girl without the reluctance to stare that one finds elsewhere. All of them notice how the woman's eyes don't move about the room. Instead, she raises her chin half an inch and peers straight ahead. It may be a way of seeing into the dark, or a gesture of confirmation, or fearlessness. Whether reflex or signal, she steps forward with her face lifted to them, which allows everyone to note the length of her neck as well as the colour of her eyes, green as quarry water.

The woman and girl breach the invisible circle usually afforded the fire supervisor and stand within handshaking range, though no hand is offered. Miles inhales and takes them in. A flavouring of citronella insect repellent and sweat.

"Rachel," the woman says, pulling the child forward to stand in front of her. "This is Miles."

The man with the scarred face and the girl in the strawberry dress nod at each other, once, at the same time.

***

.

If forest firefighters are asked why, among all the kinds of physical labour a person might do for money, they chose this particularly wilting, occasionally life-threatening work, the answer offered more than any other is that they love it. More odd is that if they are then asked to substantiate this love, they will have little, if anything, to offer. Most end up shrugging. Always the same shrug, one that makes it clear that there is no single reason they could state and at the same time believe to be true.

Miles thought he might have been slightly different on this count. He loved the job no less than the other men and women he has worked with, but he believed that in his case he could take a stab at explaining why.

"Fire isn't like us," he would tell Alex when she asked what he saw when he came closest to the flames. "It never forgives."

Sometimes, when he watched how a low, desultory smoker would tiptoe far enough along to touch off a dry thicket, Miles could see himself in the orange spirals, his own hunger devouring the arthritic limbs. He had heard fires described as cruel but he never saw them that way. What he recognized instead was how they were destructive only because they could be, the flames liberated by perfect indifference. Even before he was burned, he had this same talent himself.

This is why he'd come to this place out of all the end-of-the-world places he could have run to. There was nobody here that he knew, to remind him of who he was. Nobody he'd made a promise to or ever would. And there was fire.

For a while, though, he considered other options. For the better part of his first year on the road, driving from prairie town to prairie town across Saskatchewan, the Dakotas, Montana, Alberta and back again in a flat, pointless circle, he thought about bartending. He was spending most of every night in bars at the time anyway, and could see himself on the other side of the divide, pulling the taps and free pouring the rye, keeping an eye on the loudmouths and, when need be, directing the worst of them out the door with the end of his boot. There wouldn't be much trouble on his shifts, at any rate. He found that the scars did a lot to maintain order all on their own. There was a warning in the marks on his cheek that common, hayseed pugilists had to take into consideration. But even with all of these qualifications, Miles knew he wouldn't last a week. It wouldn't be the job, but the temptation to talk. He might be invited to barbecues or bowling tournaments or waitresses' rented rooms, and be asked questions that, over time, he would allow himself to answer.

For these reasons, Miles knew that if he wanted to run away he'd have to come back to fires. To his surprise, this was fine with him. Even after what had happened he still loved them, his dreams recalling the purposeful digging at the feet of a blaze he'd arrived at early enough to contain at least as often as the Mazko River blowup, the one fire he had ever been caught in. Alex knew all of this about him. It was the only clue that, once he was gone, she believed might lead her to him. And now it has.

"Have you been here the whole time? In this town, I mean?"

They are the first words either of them has spoken since they walked out of the Welcome Inn. The sun had not yet surrendered to the reach of the hills, and there was enough light left in the evening sky to blind them. For the first few minutes the three of them could only shuffle, stunned, through the gravel streets.

"Ross River," Miles says.

"That's it. I saw the name on the sign."

"Five years."

"You must like it."

"Five years isn't that long."

"It isn't?"

"Not so long that you have to like where you spent them."

Alex and Miles walk with their heads down, the girl running ahead and back again like a herd dog, circling behind and nudging their calves. They take the road down to the river, past the tiny, unpainted church, with its steeple of shining aluminum. Beyond

it, they find the path through the empty lot where Lloyd's Gas &
Tackle once was. Miles glances up at the one remaining pump
standing crooked, its glass face cracked, and sees it as a bespecta-
cled man struggling to his feet after a beating.

When they reach the banks of the Pelly they watch the lengthening curls and peek-a-boo whirlpools of the current. The water
heavy as oil, a glinting purple that conceals its depths. There are
no sounds except for the buzz of the first mosquitoes awakening
from the reeds, along with the river's gulps and spits.

In the absence of words, Miles feels the first tickles of the
moment's strangeness. It seems to him that the woman and girl
stand unnecessarily close, and a flurry of options occur to him. He
might fall to his knees and explode into tears. Beg forgiveness. He
might swing out his arms and knock them back.

All he can think of to hold off some show of madness is to keep
talking. He tells them of how, last summer, he had been standing
where they are now watching Margot play fetch with her dog,
Missie. Over and over Margot would throw a stick out, and each
time Missie would leap in, snatching it and cutting back to shore.
Once, Margot threw the stick ten feet farther than before. Missie
splashed into the swirls. This time, when she turned around with
the stick in her mouth, the current grabbed her from below. The
dog's front legs punched forward in panic but she couldn't break
free of the water's hold. Miles and Margot started out after her
only to see that she was already too far, speeding out of sight
around the bend behind the churchyard, down to join the Yukon
and, eventually, the delta that empties into the Beaufort Sea.

"Poor Missie," Alex says. "Poor Margot."

"It's terrible. Now she's only got Wade to follow her around."

Miles tries at a laugh, but it comes out in a messy sneeze. And
now that he's told the story of the drowned dog, he realizes it was
more grim than he remembered, and wonders if the girl might do
something awkward. But instead, Rachel cups her chin in her

palm, studying the site of the tragedy. When she turns to him her forehead is scrunched into serious ripples.

"We can't go swimming in *that* river," she says.

"I'd advise against it."

She shakes her head in regret. Then, in the next second, she snaps out of her grown-up considerations and sprints back up the road toward town.

Alex and Miles follow her past what Bonnie likes to call the Welcome Inn's courtyard, no more than a patch of grass with what, from a distance, looks to be a garden gnome stepping out of his lederhosen. They turn right, past a row of squat mobile homes, most with something left out in their front yards. A standing stepladder. A pickup truck raised on its rims, its hood agape. A Mr. Turtle wading pool.

They round the property of a cabin that appears to be made of nailed-together outhouses, all with grass growing high atop their roofs. Across the road, two boys sit side by side on a bench in front of a cinderblock building. Off to the side there's a swing set, along with climbing bars that could be a cage from which something has already escaped, and between them, a slide designed to look like a dinosaur's tongue.

"Can I go play?" the girl asks.

"Play away, kiddo."

"How old is she?" Miles asks once she has run off into the weed-riddled sand of the playground.

"Five and a half."

"Really?"

"How old do you think she could be?"

"I don't know. I guess I don't have much experience on what five and a half is. What they're capable of at that age."

"Rachel is capable of pretty much anything."

They crunch over the stones at the side of the road, watch the girl scramble up the ladder of the dinosaur's back and slide down its tongue. When she reaches the bottom she remains sitting on the aluminum lip. He tries to meet the girl's eyes but she's watching the two Kaska kids on the bench—Mungo's son, Tom, and one of his more-silent-than-most friends, Miles can see now. After a time of wondering what to do next in a second-rate playground while being observed by two teenaged Indian boys, Rachel abruptly runs around and up the dinosaur's back again. She pauses at the top and surveys the monkshood poking through the sand below. Then, with a regal salute, she plops on her bum and slides earthward a second time.

"There must be kids around here," Alex says, as though answering a question she had asked herself. "That looks like it could be a school, anyway."

"It is. And the library, town hall and RCMP detachment, all rolled into one. You're looking at civilization over there."

"Doesn't look like much."

"We're the shit end of the stick out here, I guess."

"Worse than anywhere else?"

"Worse than the towns whose native bands have signed the government land claim offers. Places that get to at least think about building a new school. Or a sewage system that can cut down on the number of times your bathtub fills up with what your neighbour flushed down his toilet five minutes ago." Miles looks down at his boots. "There's drugs here, and a lot of drinking," he says. "And I'm talking about the kids."

"Isn't there a counsellor or someone?"

"There's nobody."

"What about you?"

"I'm not paid to be a difference maker. It's not my job, it's yours."

"That sounded a little like contempt."

"You just heard it wrong."

Tom and his friend have slouched their way over to the playground's edge, where they stand with their hands in their pockets, asking Rachel questions that Miles and Alex cannot hear. The girl says something in return that brings goofy smiles to their faces.

"You still teaching?" Miles asks her.

"It's that or waitressing."

"You used to love it."

"I'm just tired. It's a lot to——" Alex lets her thought turn into a shrug.

"You're on your own?"

"As far as Rachel goes, yes."

"That can't be easy. And the kids you work with are even worse—*mentally challenged,* or whatever—it must be that much tougher to——"

"You're right. They'll kill you. You're helping and helping all day, and at the end of it, if you've done your job, they just need you more. You know?"

"Not really."

"No, you wouldn't."

From across the parking lot, Mungo Capoose strolls into view, his arm held over his head in a wave, as though Alex and Miles are a half mile distant instead of a hundred feet away.

"Where you off to?" Miles calls to him.

"Just following orders."

"What orders?"

"You wanted me to check on King, didn't you?"

Mungo grins at them. At Alex, anyway. Miles has forgotten that, in Ross River, Alex will appear not only as an obvious stranger but as uncommonly beautiful. For the first time, Miles acknowledges this as well. Green eyes, freckles, dark hair shining down the back of her neck.

"The fire office is the other way," Miles tells him.

"That I know. Just want to share a word with my son here."

Mungo keeps his eyes on Alex a moment longer, and when Miles glances to see if she is meeting the older man's gaze, he finds her smiling back at him.

"He seems nice."

"Nice? I suppose Mungo's nice. The sad truth is he's the best man on my crew."

"You've got friends up here, at least."

"I wouldn't go that far."

Mungo grabs Tom by the shoulders and gives him a shake. Tom's friend repeats whatever story he's already told Rachel and all of them laugh, with Mungo adding something at the end that brings another round of guffaws.

"She's good at that," Alex says.

"Good at what?"

"Figuring out strangers in a hurry."

"It's a hell of a skill to have."

"When you're on the road with just your mom around to keep an eye on you, it's a good thing to know who might be bad news."

"What do you mean, on the road?"

Alex takes a step forward so that she can look directly up into Miles's face. Her lips white, bloodless. He's certain she is about to throw her fist into his face and he spreads his feet apart to keep his balance when it comes.

"Four summers in a row," she says instead. "Looking for you."

Miles turns away. Over Alex's shoulder, he watches Mungo give Rachel a courtly bow, before taking Tom and his friend by the collars and pulling them off with him, squeezing the boys against his sides as they make a show of trying to escape his grip.

"I can walk you by where I live. I have a dog. His name is Stump," Miles offers in a rush.

"Rachel?" The girl runs up behind Alex, grinning. But when she looks at Miles, her face is instantly emptied of expression. "Would you like to meet a dog named Stump?"

"Stump?" She swallows, as though tasting the name. "Grumpy lump! Let's see Stump!"

***

Miles leads them past the prefab utility shed that once housed the radio station but now stands locked, the hastily painted CHRV-FM 88.9 sign over the door peeling away in rolls, the transmitting antenna bent to the side from kids using the shed as an observation tower.

"Can we hear it? On the radio in the truck?" Rachel asks him. No longer rushing ahead, the girl now lingers twenty feet behind Miles and Alex, kicking at stones that nip the backs of their ankles.

"They've closed it down."

"But when it *did* work, who talked on it?"

"Anybody that wanted to."

"So if it worked now, could I go on and talk?"

"There wouldn't be anybody to stop you."

Now that he thinks of it, Miles misses tuning in during his first year here, finding only static most of the time, but also unexpected treats. Bonnie reading from her grandmother's recipe box. Mungo playing the same side of Johnny Cash's *Ring of Fire* LP three times in a row. A bunch of preschoolers giggling for a half-hour straight. All of it reaching no farther than a two-mile radius of wilderness and perhaps a half-dozen others who may have been listening. There was a comfort in it, though. Sitting alone and having voices come to him. Confirming for whoever might be doing the talking or listening that they were here, together, even if what was being said and heard made no trace of difference in the world.

As they walk toward his cabin, Miles and Alex ask questions of each other for the girl's sake—Had Alex taken Rachel to see the dancing Gertie Girls in Dawson? Does Miles get a chance to go south in the winters?—but most of what passes between them comes in versions of the unsaid. No matter what caution they bring to their words, everything delivers both of them to the life they had discovered together, no greater in length than the time they have now been apart. They remember in the silence of shared understanding, two listeners tuned to the same voice. One that tells a story they already know but that surprises them anyway, leading them from what they had to what they lost, to Miles running away, to fire.

An afternoon rain has forced it underground. It hides beneath the surface, gnawing along roots far enough down to be untouched by moisture. The fire can find any number of hosts without ever showing itself to the world, living in oil shales, petroleum seeps or coal veins for weeks, even years. For now, tiny and unnamed, it allows itself to sleep.

A stethoscope placed on the ground would hear nothing, but a cheek could feel its warmth. In land like this, there may be a hundred such lazy fires for every square mile, more on the edges of swamps and bogs, where the fuels are rich but lie deeper. Most never awaken. They come to the end of whatever nourishes them and slowly suffocate, without a struggle, their hearts weak from birth. But this one is different. It was born with intent.

There. A white puff tails up from below, as though exhaled from an underworld cigarette. Another. Soon the smoke becomes a steady stream, broadening, clinging to the deadfall like morning fog.

Before it is extinguished, it will claim a land area greater than most national parks, leaving a lake of ash behind. It will turn bones to swan feathers. It will kill, and hide the bodies better than the most calculating assassin.

It will do all of this as though motivated by some idea of itself, by ambition, by hate. But as with all fires, it will have no desire but to live.

FOUR

Why Miles?

Alex has wondered this perhaps more than anything else. Why had she decided to shed all her shyness for that one sun-glowy, blue-eyed boy over all the others? Why *him,* sitting alone on the back fire escape of a Montreal walk-up at the first party of the new term, the weeks ahead of her fizzing with possibility, never mind the next year, the next five?

Sometimes she's sure it was his mouth that made her step out onto the fire escape on her own. Her housemate, Jen, a boy-crazy psych major from Massachusetts who liked to regard Alex as "*so* Canadian" (which meant, for her, an innocent who didn't stand a chance in the corrupt negotiations of sex), had asked where she was going when Alex had left her chatting up a pair of sniggering frat boys in the bathroom lineup, and Alex had told her, "I'm sure you can handle Beavis and Butthead on your own," and walked out into the cool night. It was his mouth that did it, she's almost certain. His lips fine but deeply coloured, a mark of delicate youth on a face she would have otherwise thought of as broad featured, even rough. She saw him through the kitchen window, noticed his mouth and wanted to kiss it, as she had wanted before, daydreamingly, of others'. What was remarkable about this boy's lips was that she wanted to kiss them first and then divide them with her tongue, slitting them apart as a blade opens an envelope, so that she could see what shape they'd make around his words.

"Have you ever tried to eat the stars?"

Alex is literally taken off balance. It's the heels she borrowed from Jen's endless collection jamming through the metal slats as much as his question.

"No," she says. "Maybe I've never been hungry enough."

"When I was a kid I would pick them right out of the sky. They had a taste, too."

"Were they good?"

"Oh yeah. *Too* good. My mom told me if I ate too many I'd start to shine."

Only now does Miles look at her directly, and Alex thinks that it's too late. This boy has already had more than his fill of stars.

Miles pulls a clear plastic sandwich bag out of his pocket and shakes it in the air. Inside, a cluster of withered caps and stems leap over each other as though in an effort to escape.

"What's that?"

"Mushrooms," he says. "I spent the summer out on Vancouver Island. Picked these lovelies myself. Very friendly."

"So, instead of stars, now you eat magic mushrooms."

"I'm always putting something in my mouth." He shakes the bag again. "Want some?"

"What do they do?"

"You mean you've never—?"

"No. I've never most things."

"That's okay. They basically take whatever mood you're in and enhance it, make you see beyond what you'd normally see."

"You're looking at me. What do you see?"

"A lot of things."

"Name one."

"I see someone who's wondering if she can trust this guy she's never met before, but thinks that she'd like to."

"Well," Alex laughs, pulling away before she could spoil everything by lunging forward to bite his lips. "I guess I'd better have some of those. You can't be the only mind reader around here."

Inside, the party gets suddenly louder, as though from a single twist of a volume knob. Alex can hear Jen squealing, pretending to be ticklish. A shattered glass receives a round of applause. The bass line from "Smells Like Teen Spirit" trembles through the kitchen window, entering the steel bones of the fire escape along with Miles and Alex themselves.

But nobody comes outside to interrupt them. Huddled close, their voices low and secretive, as though the simple facts they share are instead shocking revelations they had every intention of taking with them to the grave. They talk about the towns they were from, their majors, the four years that separated their ages (Miles was older), all without telling each other their names. Yet when they finally get around to introducing themselves, with a mannered, lingering handshake, they feel they already knew that they were Miles and Alex, and that speaking these words aloud merely satisfied a formality demanded of them.

"Have you climbed the mountain yet?" he asks her, and at first she thinks he is speaking figuratively, of some spiritual challenge he has already overcome that she hasn't even heard of. But in the next second she realizes he only means Mont Royal, the slope that rears up over campus and all of downtown, a patch of Canadian Shield in the middle of the city with an illuminated cross on top.

"I've worried that I'd get lost."

"I brought my compass," Miles says, tapping the side of his head.

Alex pulls off Jen's heels and clanks down the fire escape stairs after him, barefoot. Up St. Dominique, turning to catch their reflections in the windows of the Vietnamese and *churrasceira* restaurants on Duluth, north again past the musky, shivering nightclub lineups on St. Laurent. Alex wonders if it's the mushrooms that make her feel like she is levitating a half inch off the sidewalks.

They enter the park at L'Esplanade, emerging from the enclosure of streets into the expansive night. Alex can see the graphite outline of the mountain now, the white bulbs of the cross. When they move into the forest at the mountain's base they don't bother searching for a trail. "This way's up and that's where we're going," Miles tells her, dodging his way around maple saplings and warning her not to stub her toes on the larger rocks poking through the soil like half-buried skulls. Even though she can still hear the mechanical murmur of the city behind her, Alex imagines she is being pursued. Some wild thing—an animal or fire—hunts her on the slope.

At the crest, she scratches through a patch of burrs to find Miles lying on his back, panting. Alex looks behind her, expecting to see the grid of lights and the Olympic Stadium oval as she has in post-cards, but the trees block her view of all but strange flickers between the trunks, dancing like embers.

"It's bigger than you'd guess, isn't it?" Miles asks her, and she follows where he's pointing at the cross directly above them.

"And brighter."

"Bigger, brighter, better. That's the shrooms."

No, that's you, Alex nearly says.

Now that they are lying close they discover a comfortable silence between them. Miles finds Alex's hand and links his fingers through hers, a grade-school gesture of affection that disarms her nevertheless. They stay there, splayed out in the one piece of wilderness on an island of three million, until the first cold of autumn brings them to their feet.

"You guided me up here," she says. "Now you follow me."

Alex's apartment is a small 3 ½ over a bagel bakery. From the front window, the two of them look down on the street, where a line of assorted last-call drunks wait to get something to eat before the long stumble home. Even the curtains smell of coalfire and boiled dough from downstairs.

"It makes me constantly hungry," she says, pouring both of them glasses of ice water. "But I love it. So do the mice."

"Have you set traps?"

"Jen wants to, but I've been stalling. I know it's ridiculous, but my thinking is, they've got to live *somewhere,* right?"

"That's not ridiculous."

"Do you have mice?"

"No. But I don't have walls, either."

"Where do you live?"

"In my van."

"Don't you have friends you could stay with?"

"Some. But I've found a very picturesque parking lot. It's like they say: location, location, location."

In the morning, Alex awakens with Miles's arm wrapped around her, pulling her into his body. She remembers the delicate but insistent way that he took her clothes off under the covers, only to lie close, their whispers getting tangled in her hair. Sometime in the night they must have drifted into sleep, but she feels that even in their dreams they continued their talk, adding new confessions to the ones already offered, trumping each other's Most Embarrassing Moment and Worst First Date stories until her laughter shook her awake.

She turns over as quietly as she can, hoping to study Miles's face, but his eyes are already open. Alex lands her fingers on his shoulder and presses down, feels the muscle there yield to her. Her hand strokes lower and touches something stuck to him. A round button of fluff.

"What is that?" she says.

"What?"

"*That.*"

Miles tries to look over his shoulder but only Alex can see what's there. A furry grey circle the size of a dollar coin pressed into the skin. Alex pulls on the string attached to it and peels it off Miles's back.

"A mouse," she says, dangling it between them.

"A *flat* mouse."

"The poor thing. Snuggled up under the sheets one minute, and the next, the giant decides to roll over and *phwat!*"

"So much happens when you're asleep," Miles says, genuinely amazed.

Alex places the mouse on the bedside table. It's only then that she kisses his mouth.

When she bites, he doesn't pull away.

Jen moved out the next week. It wasn't supposed to be Alex, the naive Canadian, but Jen who found the cute older guy to skip class with for three days straight and spend all of them in the bedroom, living on sex, magnums of red wine and Thai take-out. The injustice was so intolerable she unhooked the shoe racks hanging on her walls and took a room in the all-girls dorm where she didn't have to deal with "shared bubble baths and bare asses running down the hallway all the time."

Alex and Miles didn't mind the mice, and though the apartment was small, it was, as Miles liked to point out, a good deal bigger than the back of a van. At first, they told each other it was an arrangement of convenience. For the first months, happy as they were, both of them found it easier to speak of their lease on the place over the bagel shop as the thing that brought them together, instead of something more truthful but overwhelming, like love or fate.

Still, they couldn't help themselves from making plans. Alex was taking education and, after some obligatory internships at special schools, discovered she had a talent for working with children with learning disabilities. Miles had to admit that Intro to Anatomy was the first course he'd ever taken where he saw the point behind it all, the practical link between science and people. He pored over textbooks with their painted pages of interconnected organs, arteries and bones, and could recognize not only the beauty in it but the ways he might fix them if the system failed or came under attack. Alex envisioned him as a surgeon. She told Miles he had all the natural skills for the job, which, in her mind, consisted mainly of a kind face and strong hands. Although Miles had never seriously thought of being a doctor before, within weeks she had persuaded him to apply to medical school the year after next. The University of Toronto was near the top of the field for both of them. The bagels weren't as good, but they figured they could handle just about any deprivation so long as they were together.

That summer, they sublet the apartment and Miles drove out west for the same job he had worked the past four years, taking a position on a forest firefighting crew in the British Columbia Interior. Alex joined him for the ride as far as Vancouver and found work at an East End daycare. They saw each other as much as they could, Miles coming down to the city on his breaks and Alex taking the eight-hour bus ride to Salmon Arm on Saturdays to spend the night with him before taking the bus back on Sunday morning.

On the return cross-country drive, in a Robin's Donuts parking lot on the outskirts of Moose Jaw, Miles gave Alex a ring he'd won from his foreman in a poker game.

"It's collateral," he said.

"You want a loan?"

"I want your time."

"I don't get it."

Miles placed his hands against the sides of Alex's head. She could feel them shaking.

"Next summer is going to be my last one working the fires. And when I come back, I want to give you something with a real rock in it."

"Are you looking for an answer now?"

"That's up to you."

Alex slipped the foreman's ring on her finger, a silver band with the name ROY on it in raised fool's gold. She turned it against her knuckle until the metal warmed her skin.

"It's not really my style. And it's way too big," she said. "But I'll keep it anyway."

***

They spoke frankly, always and right from the start, and best when of grave things, confessions, the conveying of bad news. For Miles, this involved the story of his missing father. A chemical engineer at the Nanaimo pulp mill who married Miles's mother, bought a modest house near the harbour, and on the day before his son's fifth birthday, left without leaving behind a note, an address, anything to suggest he was ever coming back.

Honesty was never an issue between them. They were truthful out of the need to be together, and plain talk came as naturally to them as desire itself. Before they knew it—and for the first time in their lives—they were speaking as man and wife.

Miles was accepted to the University of Toronto Faculty of Medicine and Alex took a position at the Arrowsmith School for learning disabled children in the same city. Three months separated them from their futures. For this final summer before the beginning of their new lives together, of true adulthood, of marriage, Miles headed west one last time to work the wildfire season.

His name is Tim, but everyone calls him the kid. Every attack team Miles has ever worked on has had a "kid," a nickname automatically assigned to the youngest member of the crew. But this one deserves it. He has the sort of face that is an indisputable foreshadowing of how he would look twenty, thirty, fifty years from now, and how even then, he would still be the kid. Round and shiny-chinned, his skin so flushed as to be an almost laughable display of good health. At first, Miles told himself to call the boy by his proper name, so that at least one of the crew saw that he was doing a man's job and deserved to be recognized for it. But by the end of the second week even Miles couldn't fight the obvious and called him nothing but "kid" from then on.

The fire camp Miles has been assigned to is about twelve miles out of Salmon Arm, at the petered-out end of a logging road. When Miles arrives, he is taken into the camp office, where the fire director as well as a rep from the pulp company sit on the other side of the room's single desk. Miles wonders what he could have already done that would justify being fired.

Instead, they make him foreman. The pay isn't much better than a crewman's, but the desk will be his, and use of the camp's only phone, which will allow him to call Alex in the evenings and catch her before she goes to bed, three hours ahead of him in the east. And he knows there likely isn't anyone in camp more knowledgeable than himself. Alex calls him a pyro-nerd. When he reads for pleasure, it's always scientific studies of how fire starts, how it lives, how it dies. Government "burn pattern" reports. Historical accounts of smokechasing disasters—Mann Gulch, South Canyon, Peshtigo.

"You have two things to take care of out here, Mr. McEwan," the pulp company guy says at the end of the interview, the only time he speaks at all. "The trees and the men. Just know that the company owns the trees."

"What about the men?"

"They're all yours."

Miles never thought of the crew as his, but he felt his responsibility as its leader at every moment, not so much a weight but something added to his blood to thicken it. It made it easier that Miles liked them, especially the kid. Another pyro-nerd in the making. Asking questions about the origins of pulaskis, the combination rake-hoes designed for cutting fireline in different ground conditions. Volunteering for the nastiest tasks—staying the night to keep an eye on spot fires extinguished the day before, axing a snag into pieces to see if the smoke had hidden inside it, manning the radio when everyone else opted to make a dent in the beer stocks. He did all of this not to seek approval but because he wanted to see how it was done. The rest of the crew liked him for this, too. Not only because the kid relieved them from unpleasant work but because he so plainly loved doing it. It was hard even to make fun of someone like that.

Miles also admired the way the kid could spend time with him without disturbing his thoughts. As a result, he spoke more freely with him than with anyone else on the attack team. Although Miles never brought up the topic of their friendship, he knew that this is what they had found together. Alex asked after him in every phone conversation they had. She always called him Tim.

"There's a pattern to every crewman's career," Miles remembers telling the kid on one of their long drives between watchtowers. "The first year you learn, the second year you complain, and the third year you actually enjoy yourself. There's almost never a fourth year."

"How long have you been doing it?"

"Five years," Miles says, laughing. "But I'm still learning. With fires, there's always something you think you know but don't."

What Miles neglected to add is that without fires to work on, there's not much to learn anything from. This year, June and most of July turn out to be curiously uneventful months, despite the above-average heat and string of eighteen days without rain. Aside from a handful of smouldering snags lit up by lightning, and a burning garbage can at a roadside picnic area fifteen miles to the south, the camp is fire free.

The crew spend the time inventing increasingly complex practical jokes, eating too much, pretending to be soldiers. Miles has experienced stretches like this before, though not nearly as long, and is coming to the end of make-work tasks. The two pockmarked pickups had been waxed into glittering auto show pretties. The cache's store of tools were sharp as butcher's cleavers, the other supplies hung upon hooks or lined in straight aisles according to an "attack priority sequence," just like the manual dreamed it might be. The bunkhouse was painted top to bottom four times, followed by a poll on each colour's aesthetic merits. By the middle of July, it was neon pink. A unanimous vote (Miles abstaining) determined it would stay this way for the rest of the season.

It isn't until the first week of August that they receive notice from a spotter plane of a smoker at the bottom end of a gulch funnelling down into the Mazko River, two hundred miles north. Miles had known that something was there for the past twenty-four hours, as the spotter had to pass the site twice to determine whether it was an actual fire or merely a "ghost," the mist that can rise in locations near water. The delay in identifying the fire hasn't allowed it much growth, though—the plane's last report was of a tight congestion of small spot fires, each one no bigger than the smouldering sticks left behind at morning campsites.

There is a tradition among attack teams of naming a fire they have fought on, large or small. Most of the time it arrives at the end, after mop-up is completed and some detail of the location or episode that occurred over the course of the job lends itself. But when they disembark from the helicopters in the lee of the smoke-fogged valley, the kid tosses a name out right away. The crew stand at the crest looking at the Mazko a half mile below and the four or five dozing spot fires where the gulch's walls meet. The slope down is steep, but they should be able to get to the fires and back up again without climbing gear or ropes. What will slow them are the loose pieces of shale scattered over the hillside, black diamonds of sharp armour like the scales of a serpent buried just below the surface. Although there is usually some debate surrounding an initial suggestion's merits, the kid's first try sticks without question. The Dragon's Back.

Miles is reluctant to touch the dragon's skin at all. It is one of the first principles of firefighting to avoid cutting line partway down a hill with the fire below. Better to come at it from the lower point and push it higher, the entry in this case being the banks of the river. But when Miles radioes the fire manager, he is told to continue down the slope and fight from above.

"Get a jump on it and it's simple as pissing in an ashtray," the manager says.

It's not in Miles's nature to argue, and his men are so bored with the disappointments of a fireless season that some are already side-stepping into the gulch, shouting jokes about taking long enough to make it down that they might be in line for some overtime. Miles, on the other hand, tells himself it will have to be quick. The longer they stay down there, the more chances there are to be surprised.

When their eyes begin to sting from the smoke, their cheeks freckled with ash, Miles looks back at the crest and judges it to be about four hundred yards up. Next, he does a size-up of what they have to face: a few spot fires, all more than twenty feet apart, licking at green stalks of cheat grass and fescue. Off to the side, a small patch of oak scrub stands untouched. They'll take the smokers one by one and get them early enough that they won't have to cut any fireline. Miles doesn't want to give it that much room to play.

"Split up in threes," Miles tells them. "Pick one and hot-spot it. When it's done, hustle on to the next. By noon, the sun is going to roast us like turkeys down here."

The day is already showing temperatures that are well above average, and the valley walls only contain the heat, the shale a million dark mirrors magnifying the sun on their backs. Still, for the first half-hour, the men go at their labours with something near joy, the simple pleasure of cutting the earth with the blades of their pulaskis singing up the muscles in their arms. They complain about the work when they aren't working, but now that they are, they bury the smoke in purposeful contentment.

The kid is the first to hear it.

Less a sound than its absence. Nothing like the silence that can sometimes visit a crew in the way a break in the conversations around a dinner table can leave a room in an accidental quiet. What the kid hears is not an interruption but an end. It makes him think of the project he submitted to his high-school science fair. A perfect vacuum. The demonstration involved sucking away all the air in an empty fish tank, an invisible violence taking place within. Now it's like he's inside the tank, looking out.

"The fuck was that?" he asks nobody in particular, but Miles hears the question. And now that his attention has been called to it, he can hear what the kid hears too. Unlike the kid, he knows exactly what it is.

"Let's move out!" Miles shouts, circling his arm over his head, directing the men up the hill.

For a time, they only look at him. They've just arrived, the spot fires not halfway to being buried. It seems the new foreman is something of a joker. One of the crew acknowledges Miles's gestures with a honking laugh, and the rest of the men except the kid join him in it.

"I'm not kidding. Take your shit and haul it on up."

"Quittin' time already, boss?" the first of the laughers shouts back.

"We're not quitting. We're pulling back. Right fucking now."

All of them look up at the sound of thunder. Shade their eyes with their hands, searching, but the sky remains a cloudless dome. The thunder rolls on. More a tremor in the atmosphere than something they hear, like standing over a pot of water coming to a boil.

A fire whirl. That's what the kid heard, what they can all hear now. A conflagration creating its own wind. But what terrifies Miles isn't the vacuum of a fire whirl but the fury that he knows must follow it.

He glances back to see the fire roiling up at them from the bottom of the gulch. At this distance, it looks to him to be a swarm of yellowjackets spewing forth from a rupture in the earth.

It's happened sooner than he had guessed. A blowup. The most feared event in fighting fires in the bush, but rare enough that most crewman's careers go by without seeing one. What begins as a series of spot fires sends hot, lighter air up, and the cooler, heavy air sweeps in to take its place, creating a kind of burning tornado.

The spot fires that had stood apart a moment before join together. Invisible gases rise into the air hotter than the white heart of a flame. The ground itself is ignited.

"Drop your tools!" Miles orders them, only now noticing that the men, including himself, have been slowed by the heavy pulaskis pulling at their shoulders. "Let go of whatever you've got! Now! *Now!*"

Most do. But despite his repeated command, a couple of the men refuse to release the grip on their shovels. Whether from an embedded sense of attachment or from shock that has seized their minds on nothing but the crest above them, Miles couldn't know. The rest of the crew, now sixteen pounds lighter and with the benefit of pumping both of their arms forward, are able to move at a quicker pace than before.

From Miles's broader perspective as last man back, he calculates that it still won't be enough. The men farthest ahead have already grown sluggish against the steepening hill face. At best, they're managing a couple hundred feet per minute. A fast fire will make triple that in forest conditions, and as much as eight hundred feet a minute in long, graded grass like this. Even faster if it's a blowup.

They're caught. A textbook firetrap, and he led them into it, allowed himself to be bullied by some shithead over a radio. Miles can do nothing now but will the men on, ordering one leg in front of the other in his head. *Go, go, go, go.* So long as he pushes them with these unspoken words he tries to believe they cannot fall.

There is no strategy to what they do now, nor could there be. Miles would be unable to find a single tactic in the wildland firefighter's training manual to help even if he had it in front of him. It is a foot race and nothing more. There is the fire, the crest, the closing yards between them. There is the searing muscles in the men's thighs, already cramping, reducing their strides to useless penguin hops. There is a window of time about to be shut. A situation that calls only for what Miles's first foreman used to call FEAR. Fuck Everything And Run.

From his position at the end of the snaking line, Miles watches and, in half-second evaluations, takes note of his various crew members' progress. Men he would have guessed to be the most nimble end up tripping over their own ankles, one falling chin first against the rock-strewn hillside and sliding helplessly backward. Another runs with his arms straight above his head, as though at gunpoint. None of them call out to each other. None of them scream. But the humanless quiet that results terrifies Miles more than anything else.

None are as slow as the kid. It's not his physical conditioning that works against him, as he is stronger than most, light and long-legged. It's that he can't help from looking back every five or six strides. No matter how brief his glances, simply turning his shoulders and blinking once against the rolling wall of flame is enough to break whatever speed he had worked up. When the kid's eyes return to the man ahead of him he has lost another five feet, and he must dig his toes in and start climbing all over again.

Because Miles won't allow himself to overtake any of the others, the kid slows him down as well.

Don't look at it! Miles is shouting at him, but the kid doesn't hear. He says it another three times before he realizes that the words are pronounced only as an idea within him. He works sideways across the hill to the kid's line of ascent and slams his palms against his shoulder blades. Every time the kid turns, he pushes again. *Don't look at it,* Miles says with his eyes, and this time, the kid gets it.

And then Miles looks too. He's astonished at the fire's speed. The conditions are perfect for it making a sprint like this—dried stalks of high grass, the accelerant of oak scrub at the bottom of the gulch, a slope for the flames to climb—but he still can't believe how it defies what he's ever observed of fire before, the way it turns gravity upside down. Now Miles can see that it's true what he's been told a thousand times. *Only fires and bears run faster uphill than downhill.*

Ahead, Miles can see the first figures making the crest. The fire is so close he can hear it—not its vacuum but its resulting explosion of flames. The whirl opened up and new air rushing in to fill the space in a metallic screech, a subway train grinding the rails as it goes too fast around a bend. The kid covers his ears.

The two of them are the only ones who remain below now, a little over a hundred yards short of where the slope levels and falls away into forest. It is close enough that Miles can see the individual fingers of grass at the top bending against the rush of heat. The fire will have burned the same blades to black wicks before they get halfway to touching them.

It is close, but Miles has noticed how his pace has slowed almost to a standstill, and the final ascent is far steeper than any other section of the hill. The other men have a chance of making it, so long as the fire is delayed on the crest. But even if they had wings it's too late for Miles and the kid.

Miles lunges forward and grabs the kid's arm, stopping them both. Without explanation, he slips his hand into his pack and pulls a fusee out. He lip-reads the kid's voiceless words—*Don't stop! Don't stop!*—but only raises his hand in reply. Miles ignites the fusee with the lighter he takes from his pocket. When it flares to life, he bends to touch its spitting mouth to the straw around them.

An escape fire. A small burning of grass lit before the main fire hits, so that the burned area—the "good black"—can be stepped into and, with their heads buried in the ashes, the worst of the fire may pass around them. It is a technique Miles has only read about. He remembers stories of turn-of-the-century natives saving themselves and any pilgrims who would join them, far out on the Great

Plains lit up like a prairie inferno. But there is no mention of escape fires in any of the current training materials, and for good reason. Miles knows that more men have burned in the good black than have been saved by it. But they will die if they run on, and die if they stand where they are. Miles decides for himself and for the kid. They will be an experiment.

Miles steps into the circle, the stalks still snapping and sending live sparks up his pant legs, and waves at the kid to join him. Just ten feet away, the kid stays where he is. Staring at Miles in an uncomprehending palsy of disbelief. Why is his foreman *starting* a fire when there already is one, a huge one, coming right at them?

For a moment, the two men meet each other's eyes through the smoke spiralling off the grass. The kid's effort to see the sense in what Miles has done plays visibly over his face. His throat seared shut, leaving all his questions to sit, heavy as marble, in his chest.

The kid is so close that Miles could grab him and try to pull him in. If the kid resisted, both of them would be caught outside the good black as the main fire hit. Still, if he holds on to the kid's wrist and falls back, it might be enough for them both to tumble down into the smoking ash and breathe. That's what Miles would tell the kid if he was lying next to where he is now. Breathe and stay low and bury your face in the charred soil where the pockets of oxygen might be and wait—

Behind them, the fire screams.

A shattering, human sound that sends the young firefighter scrambling a few feet higher up the slope. Though his voice doesn't reach his own ears, Miles can feel his shouts splitting his throat open.

He lifts his head from the ground to plead with the kid to come back and feels the first swipe of fire across the side of his face, tearing the shirt from his side.

I'm burning, Miles thinks.

A realization so simple it precedes understanding, precedes pain. But he doesn't lie down. Opens his mouth again to utter another wordless command and hears only the plasticky pop of his own skin.

He can only watch as the boy runs on. That, and make one last attempt to be heard. But before Miles can close his lips around his name, the kid is consumed by the rushing curtain of fire.

They keep him away from mirrors. Anything that can cast a reflection is hidden by the nurses. The chrome kettle in his room is removed, the curtains drawn at twilight when the glass surface begins to send back images of whoever may be trying to look outside. Even his cutlery is replaced with plastic knives, forks and especially the spoons, which, depending on the side turned to him, threaten to balloon or collapse the already distorted features of his new face.

For the first several days, the drugs keep him from knowing when they're taking off his bandages or peeling away dead layers of his skin. Morphine delivers him to a place well beyond the hospital room's beeping, bleach-reeking reminders that he is on a bad-news ward. The drip into his arm prevents him from caring about his injuries, how he might look if he ever gets out, about anything. Yet he remains aware of the events around him. The terrible food. A distressed-looking Alex with her hair tied in a bun (he hates it that way and thinks of asking her to let it down, but doesn't want to trouble her). His wish for something better to be on TV. Even the fire. He remembers trying to pull himself up the slow-motion slope, the unfamiliar sound of his own screams, the sight of the kid sucked back into the furious waves. He remembers it all, but it nevertheless feels second-hand, fictional, like the memory of a film seen years before.

The morphine leads him to a beautiful indifference. He loves the morphine. The days pass in rolls of gauze. Delicately applied and removed, the nurses forcing smiles, nearly constantly asking him *Are you okay?* He has no idea what *okay* would be under the circumstances, or what it ever was. *Yup,* he says. The last thing he wants is to hurt anybody's feelings. He just *yups* his way through his first three weeks in the burn ward, and holds Alex's hand with the one he can still move, all without a clue as to what might follow from here.

They pull back the sheet and leave him bare between dressings for a while now, to "get a little air on the business," as one of the nurses puts it. Although he's told not to, it allows him to feel the shape of the burn. From beneath his skin a shell emerges, rough as the edge of an empty tin. Not all of him, though. He has been split in two. The left side of his face is as he remembers it, but the right is a Halloween mask, all hardened latex and stray, unconvincing hairs. His hand continues down his neck, and he discovers that the half-mask comes with a half-bodysuit too. He strokes his chest from one side to the other. The line between the burned and unburned skin comes up hard against his fingertips, abrupt as the intrusion of the Rockies on a continental map. The east of him is smooth flatlands. The west, rows of jagged teeth.

Without warning, they pull the morphine out of his arm and replace it with a pair of Tylenol 3s on his breakfast serviette. The first thing he does is cry. It's the sight of the puny albino pills that does it. *These* are to be his new friends? He bawls so hard he can't catch his breath. Coughs himself out of bed, starts bawling again. The emergency bell that attaches his thumb to the nurses' station rings without pause, so that they close the door on him and let him wail himself to sleep. Even through his tears he's ashamed of himself, and makes some attempts at self-control, but then the image of the white pills returns to him, and it's all over.

When it comes, sleep is no better than waking. What's worse than the pain are the dreams. They start at different places, but all of them end with Miles running. There is no fire. What he runs from is invisible but explicit, human and not human, a creature with unfair advantages. *A vampire,* the voice-over of his dream tells him. One that pursues him through a grid of dark streets. Miles knows that he will lose the race but he rushes on, rounds another corner, hoping to find an avenue of light that never appears. Then, when the undead thing comes up next to him, Miles turns to see that it's the kid. Teeth bared, ravenous. The kid wrapping his mouth over Miles's neck. Ripping and swallowing.

When they release him from the hospital, the doctor gives Miles a pharmaceutical loot bag to take with him: tranquilizers, Tylenol 3s, steroid cream. Alex holds him by the arm on his good side, his steps slow and frail, head swimming. He can't tell whether the sensation of being helped along by his girlfriend makes him feel pathetically young or pathetically old.

They are asked to stay in town for a few days to participate in the coroner's inquest into the kid's death, although it's obvious to all that it's really Miles's trial. Fire is fire, and people who fight them get hurt from time to time. But the kid is different. His foreman stopped running from a fire to build one of his own and the kid had carried on up the hill. One rational decision, one irrational. If common sense determined rightful outcomes, the wrong man died.

The panel includes two of the managers who sent his team into the valley, and Miles tries to mentally hammer nails through their eyeballs as he listens to them ask their questions. They want to know how he could possibly justify his "grossly unorthodox defensive tactics." Miles calls it an escape fire. He calls it the good black. The managers call it unsound manoeuvres. His trial is one of semantics. They don't allow themselves to forgive him, but he can feel them wanting to. One says, "You were a good firefighter, Miles," and the past tense reddens the scar on his cheek.

In the end they do him the favour of coming up with excuses on his behalf. Miles wasn't much older than the kid himself, after all. The conditions were severe. Under the circumstances, it was hard to believe that only one man went down. Though his methods were well outside of acknowledged procedure, the investigators accept that Miles had done everything he could have done within his abilities and experience.

After, in a motel room in Salmon Arm with a NO ANIMAL SKINNING notice over the headboard, Alex and Miles lie side by side in the darkness, fully clothed, fingers locked over their chests like corpses. They talk about what they should do next. Neither of them can think of an option aside from what they would have done if the fire had never happened. They will leave in the morning for Toronto. Alex will take up her job at Arrowsmith's, and Miles will enter first year of med school. They will start again. Neither of them mentions the promise of marriage that Miles had made the year before.

They drive through the mountains, onto the high ranges of Alberta, across the cruise-control prairies, and over the humped spine of Lake Superior, all in a brooding near silence. Alex never asks about the fire, but Miles can sense her aching to. There's a buzz of vicious pleasure in refusing to help her open the topic, every hour of silence a greater punishment than anything he might think of to say to her. Behind the wheel, Miles takes an academic interest in his own anger. For instance, he would never have guessed he would resent Alex's sympathy even more than her curiosity.

The sight of Toronto shrinks them in their seats. Even the lake seems to pull back from the downtown towers. Its waves reluctant, perfunctory, the water the mottled grey of desert camouflage. They drive straight to the apartment Alex has found, a basement one-bedroom on Shaw Street, the only thing reasonably close to both her work and the university that they could afford.

"It's not rue Rachel," Miles says, looking up and down the street, the tiny front yards blurred with wrought-iron fences.

"It's different here," Alex agrees. "It's all different."

They unload their minimal belongings and, after one walk through the apartment, Miles tucks himself under the sheets of the futon and stays in the bedroom for the next week until classes start. Even then, he skips his lectures as often as he attends them. Instead, he drifts through the streets of the new city and feels its eyes upon him. He plays the game of trying to catch people staring.

Most of the time, his observers are quicker than he is. But when he snags slow ones, he sticks his tongue out and laughs like a serial killer and watches them scuttle away in what they think is fear, though he knows it's really shame.

His refusal to speak doesn't prevent Miles from tracing the growing shape of fury within him. Alex can see it too. It comes to the point that all she will allow herself to tell him is that she loves him, but even this gives offence. He interprets her simple, desperate words as a lie, something she repeats to convince herself of. It is impossible that Alex could feel the same about him as she once did. If he has been turned into a monster, won't their love have been similarly deformed?

More and more, Miles fears that if he stays with her, something as bad as what happened to the burned boy will happen to Alex. There is also the newfound worry that he might hurt her himself.

They make love only once after the fire. From the morning Miles was released from the hospital, over and over Alex had invited him to her. She had worn only the clothes he had most liked to remove, suggested massage oil backrubs, whispered dirty in his ear. Every time, Miles had declined. Finally, after she grazed her tongue across the back of his neck as he stood before a crackling frying pan in the kitchen, he had turned to her and said, "Don't you get it? I'm not interested in a mercy fuck," before returning to flip his eggs. She had not tried again after that.

What hurt her more than his rejection was the extent to which he was wrong about what she was asking of him. Mercy had nothing to do with it. It's true that she wanted to bring them together, if only for a time, as the open talk that they used to find so natural had deserted them. But her desire was real.

On this night, though, it is Miles who reaches for Alex. Aware of the sound of their own breathing, each clinging to the cold edge of their opposite bedsides, he had rolled over to bring his lips to her shoulder. Both of them are amazed at how even this tentative kiss revives something in them. Miles stays next to her, folding himself over her side. He wants to say a sweet word. Anything plucked from the standard vocabulary will do. But the mere thought of uttering any of them hurts his throat, like a bone caught halfway down.

They surprise themselves with the energy they find, a ruthless yearning. Everything they do is lingered over, repeated, another moment won against the long night. Despite this, they can sense an absence in each other's touch. The room's wintry drafts find ways between them, licking around the borders of warmth their bodies create.

Afterwards, they watch the flashing blue light of a streetcleaner tumble across the ceiling. This time it is Alex's turn to search for words and for everything she might say to strike her as laughably belated. It's not the fire that has come between them, she thinks, but an awareness of themselves. They never used to be self-conscious around each other, and this nakedness brought them an easy honesty, the gift of speaking without gain or penalty. Now they censor their thoughts as though someone is in the room with them, judging their appropriateness, their timing, whether they actually believe what they say or not. The streetcleaner's blue light retreats through the curtains.

Although she cannot tell Miles why she cries now, her back to him again, she knows it's because of this. Not the loss of words. Alex weeps for what they have found, the terrible discovery of what love prevents us from seeing as obvious. They have never been one, always two.

By the end of October, Miles stops attending classes altogether, spending his days in the laundry-strewn darkness of the apartment. Although Alex stocks the fridge with T-bones and leaves Mason jars of homemade spaghetti sauce for him in the freezer, he lives on delivery pizza and Chinese, the smelly boxes growing into a cardboard tower outside the bedroom door.

One day that is otherwise the same as the fifty that came before, Miles hears Alex unlock the front door and knows that something is about to change. She drops her keys on the kitchen table and the sound rips through the apartment like a crack of thunder. The storm is breaking and Miles welcomes it. He wants to stand tall enough for the lightning to find him.

"What's your plan?" Alex asks him, standing over the shadowy hump of his back under the sheets.

"I'm a man with no plan."

"Really? You look like you've got your crash-and-burn all figured out."

"No pun intended."

"I wanted to tell you something. If it makes any difference."

"I'm all ears."

"I'll never leave you."

"Hey! History's most broken promise."

"It's not history's promise. It's mine."

"You're a good girl, Alex. But not that good."

Alex crumples onto the end of the futon. She finds his cold foot sticking out and strokes the top of it, but it wriggles away at her touch.

"It's not your fault," she says.

"You're not the judge of that."

Alex leans forward and switches on the bedside lamp, which casts a tight circle of light out from under the shade. She can see Miles now. The covers pulled up to his chin, his hair a nest of greasy tosses and turns. His eyes blink against the forty-watt bulb as though he had just stepped into the midday sun.

"I'm right here," she says.

"You don't have to be."

"I'm telling you I *know* you."

"You have my apologies."

"Just listen, Miles. *Listen*. Even if you don't want to hear."

"Hear what, Herr Doctor?"

"You've always blamed yourself for what your father did, and now you're mixing that up with what happened in the fire."

"There's a nice logic to that, I admit," he says, tapping his chin. "It even seems to make sense. The trouble is, it doesn't. You keep looking for sense where there isn't any."

"So tell me, then. Tell me the senseless truth of it."

"The kid died."

"And?"

"The kid died."

"His name was Tim."

"I know his name."

There is no gesture Alex can think of that Miles wouldn't take as an insult. She disgusts him, although he assumes it is the other way around. If he said something first, something of his own, no matter how it might hurt her, it might be a way in. But he won't. He will reply, but not confess, not accuse. Her frustration knots its way through her shoulders, seizing her into a sculpture of pain.

"You're so angry and you don't even know it."

"You haven't done anything wrong."

"Not at me. You're angry at yourself." Alex pauses to take a new breath that will manage her next words at a lower register. "At your father."

"You can't be mad at someone you don't remember."

"But you can hate them. You can hate them easier for not remembering."

"Words of wisdom from Princess Nicey-Nice. What do you know about hating anything? You're too pure for that."

"Fuck you."

"I stand corrected."

"Everybody's capable of hate. That part's simple. The hard part is finding the strength to be capable of forgiving yourself, too."

"That's really *wonderful*. What section of the Hallmarks did you find that one in? Sympathy for Burn Victims? That would be it, wouldn't it? Right there between the Sorry for Your Amputation and God Loves You . . . Please Don't Overdose on the Sleeping Pills."

"Nothing is going to change unless you lose this whole sarcastic—"

"For Christ's sake, Alex! Love doesn't want to spend any time in a shithole like this," he says, pulling the sheet down and sitting up all at once. He frames his face with his palms and squeezes the skin into blotchy folds. "Love likes it pretty. It always has. Look at me."

"It's not about what you—"

"*Look* at me!"

And she does.

Alex sees a ghoul. For the first time, she recognizes Miles's scars for what they are. She sees their permanence, the wish she has that they weren't there, the memory of what he looked like when they weren't. It makes her gasp.

"You see? You *see?*" Miles is shouting at her, and she cannot reply because he's too close, too loud. And because the answer is yes. She sees.

She tells him of her doctor's visit in a note she leaves on the pillow next to him as he sleeps. It isn't long. Half a page of news listed in punchy headlines.

It's yours.

I'm going to keep it.

I still love you.

We'll talk tonight.

Much later, she wondered how long after waking it took for him to decide.

He packs in the morning when Alex is away at work. He can't face the rest of the apartment, so he starts with the bedroom essentials, stuffing a duffle bag with jeans, wool socks, half a dozen bedside-table paperbacks. Then he floats through the other rooms, holding framed photos of themselves to his eyes—kissing in the bleachers at a McGill vs. Queen's football game, dressed up and drunk at a friend's wedding—before putting them down again. He rattles through the piles of CDs but can't remember who bought which one for whom, and discovers he doesn't want to listen to any of it again anyway. They have collected so much meaningful garbage together that simply looking at it now makes him feel heavy, his veins pumping mercury.

He means to leave Alex a letter. In his mind he imagines an impossible document, at once less and more than an explanation or an apology or a cataloguing of his thousand unmanageable torments. Something along the lines of a thank-you note, or perhaps the obligatory sentence in an author's acknowledgements page expressing gratitude for all the help he has received but accepting all errors as his own. He even begins a draft, but it doesn't survive the first reading. No matter how much he keeps out of it, the words can't help referring to the kid, the gluttonous melodrama of his own self-pity. His second attempt is yet more minimalist, but ends up saying the same things with even greater force.

Miles can see the cruelty in leaving no trace of himself behind for her. It would seem intentional to Alex, one last, silent rejection, but he decides he has no choice. In the end he does nothing more than slide his keys under the door after pulling it shut.

FIVE

Miles has a dog with bad dreams. When he's home during the day he can hear Stump's sleep-muffled barks from the end of the bed the two of them share, the three-alarm *woo-woo-woomph!* associated with visitor warnings. Then something turns for the worse, and the terror that the dog faces brings out unfamiliar barks of distress, each distinct from the rest, as though he refuses to believe this could actually be happening to him, a good boy whose only fault is lifting himself to table edges to clean the plates once the diners have left the room.

Their arrival saves him from one such nightmare-in-progress. Without even the faintest pause, the dog pads across the brown shag of the living room and begins licking Rachel's face.

"This is Stump?" Rachel asks, the dog lapping at her laughter.

"That's him."

"Why?"

"Why what?"

"Why *Stump?*"

Miles has to think about this. It wasn't because any part of the dog was missing. Instead, his name came from the way that, when Miles first spotted him from the side of the road, an abandoned pup sitting on his haunches in a clearcut of forest a few miles outside Teslin, he was nearly the same size and stood with the same square, unmovable silhouette as the levelled stumps of lodgepole pine and tamarack.

"Stump!" Miles had called to him when he pulled over in his truck, and the dog had understood that this was his new name and came trotting over to have his side thumped.

"You're a Stump," his master said again, simply, as though Miles had finally discovered another living thing that was as much a Stump as he was.

"Because that's his name," is all Miles tells Rachel now.

Miles thinks of Stump as the Mr. Potato Head of dogs, his disproportionate features assembled with apparent malice, or perhaps humour. His nose as long as a ratter's (though he fears holes of any kind, and requires some coaxing to warm Miles under the bedsheets on hungover mornings). Oversized ears that stand rigid atop his head in a kind of victory salute. Eyes as dark and bulbous as chocolate chips. For all of these handicaps, Stump made friends easily, a talent due in no small part to his indiscriminate distribution of kisses, the pink waterslide of his tongue reaching out for the faces of all who know his name, scratch his silver goatee or simply bend within range. He is so generous with these compensations that some call him "handsome dog," although it is clear that handsomeness is about five crossbreedings removed from his present appearance. Still, he's not without his prejudices. He has never liked Wade Fuerst, for example. This for obvious reasons, even to a mongrel simpleton like Stump.

"Comfy," Alex says, running her fingers over the varnished log end tables and peering up at the oil painting of a wolf howling at a too-yellow moon over the wood stove.

"I don't need much," Miles says.

He leaves the door open behind him, but the air inside the cabin remains laden with a combination of uncirculated scents: the gamy moose steaks that Miles has been thawing and eating for his dinner four nights out of seven ever since Margot started dropping them off, the mildew of the hall bathroom that no amount of ammonia scrubbings could entirely get rid of. Now, with Rachel and Alex in the room with him, Miles smells the cabin as a visitor would, and he's embarrassed by what it says about his life. The bachelor's neglect. The sockfarty aura that likely follows wherever he goes.

Alex circles the room, stopping to pull back the curtains and looking out at the picnic table with beer bottles sprouting up around its legs like mushrooms, and beyond it, the wall of forest that borders the backyard and marks the end of Ross River itself. She puts her cheek against the glass and looks both ways, but the cabin is far enough from the rest of town that no neighbours are visible. Even here, Alex thinks, Miles has chosen to live on the outside of things.

"Momma! He's *following* me!" Rachel shrieks, walking backwards down the hall with Stump wagging after her.

"He sure is," Alex says, pulling away from the window to study the dining-room table next to it. A plate smeared with egg yolk, three half-filled coffee mugs, and at the opposite end, a chess board with a game laid out over its squares.

"Who are you playing?" she asks, picking up the white queen by her crown.

"My mother."

"She *lives* here?"

"No. She doesn't know that I'm here either."

"You don't visit?"

Alex places the queen down on the board again. There's a darkness under her eyes now that Miles remembers, clouds gathering over the crest of her cheekbones.

"I went down there once a couple years ago. It wasn't very—" He stops, shrugs. "I just think it's better if I stay up here."

Miles tries at a laugh but nothing comes out, so that there is only his opened throat for Alex to look down.

"How do you play?" she says.

"She sends me a postcard with her move on it, and then I send my move back to her. It's slow, but you can really think out the options. I've given her a post office box number in Whitehorse and they forward them up to me. There's less to worry about if nobody . . ."

"If nobody knows where you are."

Miles nods.

"The postcards are almost as fun as the game," he says, sensing that it's better to speak than not. "It's not easy finding something new in Ross River, once you've gone through the dog sled team and northern lights photos, and then the cards you can get anywhere on the planet, the bikini babes and the joke Yukon at Nights. I've been forced to make some of my own."

"Your own postcards?"

"Cut and paste. A photo of George Bush's head on top of Stump's body. The Welcome Inn with a Royal York letterhead underneath it. Arts and crafts."

"You make your own *postcards?*"

Miles can see that Alex is about to cry, and while he doesn't feel any particular sadness at the moment, he is more intensely humiliated than he can recall. Once more the smell of last night's moose steak reaches him and he is sure he cannot meet Alex's eyes again so long as the two of them remain in this room.

"The winters are long," he says.

Rachel is in the kitchen, opening and closing drawers that Miles knows contain little aside from rolling mouse turds. As she moves, Stump follows her, tapping his nails over the linoleum.

"Honey? It's time to go," Alex calls to her.

"Why?"

"Just come here."

Rachel trots into the living room and clasps her arms around Alex's legs, the dog plopping down in front, so that the three of them form an instant portrait.

Halfway through the current breath he is inhaling, Miles feels a wave of fatigue so great he thinks he might fall before he gets a chance to breathe again.

"You're going to need a place to stay," he manages.

"One with a shower would be nice."

"The Welcome Inn's the only place for fifty miles. Talk to Bonnie."

"And tell her Miles sent us?"

"If you want. But it won't bring the rates down any."

For Miles, the room is now a sickening carousel, rotating slowly, unstoppably, the different shades of brown carpet, furniture and panelling smearing together. He throws a hand out and finds the dining-room chair that his chess opponent would sit in if she were present.

"You have to go now," he says.

The idea of having to bend and slap the cheeks of a passed-out Miles on the floor of his dingy cabin makes Alex turn her back to him. She takes Rachel by the hand and strides out the cabin's open front door.

Even now, the solstice sun has not wholly surrendered to the night, so that the trees are cloaked figures against the sky. Alex has the strange sensation of being at once here and not here. Ross River. A name like a hundred others she has passed on signs hammered into the soil at town boundaries. It's impossible to believe that this place—*these* ragged power lines, *this* gravel street—is any different. She doesn't know what she expected of it, if she expected anything. All this time and she had never considered the place she would find Miles standing in, only Miles himself. What's more unsettling is that now she's standing in it with him.

It took less than an hour's walk through this weedy, broken-hearted nowhere to forget most of what she expected he would have become. All she's certain of is that he's in worse shape than even her most malicious scenarios. It's what allowed his talk of postcards and the sight of his big-eared dog to make a momentary dent. But even as she feels a brush of pity come and go, what remains is her desire to spray kerosene over the half of him the fire missed, toss a match his way, and watch. Not only for the pain it would cause, but to leave a tattoo that would forever mark his cowardice, his uncorrectable failure to the world. She has thought about this for longer and in greater detail than she would ever admit.

Alex is strangely glad to find that she still hates him. As much now that she's found him as she had the evening she'd come home to their empty apartment and looked for the note he hadn't bothered to leave. She's grateful that the sight of him has done nothing to alter her fundamental judgments. Her planned retributions.

What she hadn't seen coming is how much he frightens her. One of the things she hadn't told him about her past four summers was that a couple of the people she'd shown his photo to had recognized him, or at least had a story to tell. A mechanic in Dease Lake said the scars made him sound like a guy "way far up," one that had nearly killed a man for looking at him and asking if Halloween had come early this year. A hardware store clerk in Telegraph Creek claimed to have heard about someone with burns down one side of his face "like a line of shade" who hunted solo, living on grizzly meat and firing his shotgun at anyone who came within a half mile of his camp. Alex didn't believe these stories, nor did she dismiss them. She simply added them to the composite portrait she was assembling in her mind. One that took hideous shape as she added a murderous grin, jellied eyes, blood-soaked teeth.

The first summer had been something of an accident. A weekend drive out of the city after the end of term. She spent her first night in a creepy motel near the marina in Parry Sound, and found herself enjoying the creepiness, the foolish thrill of being a young mother on the lam. In the morning, instead of heading back, she turned north, then west. At lunch, she bought a half-dozen identical postcards showing a row of oiled men's torsos frying on a beach and sent them to the people who might be wondering where she'd gotten to. "I'm taking our show on the road," she wrote. "We'll be gone for as long as the credit card and Pampers hold out. Please don't worry." She signed each of them "Love, Alex and Rachel (a.k.a. Thelma and Louise)."

She bought a tent and sleeping bag in Dryden, a camp stove in Medicine Hat, matching toques for her and Rachel in Jasper. Even as far as Fort St. John she still wasn't looking for Miles in any concerted way. And yet, more and more, Alex found herself glancing through the windows of roadhouses, waiting for heads to turn her way in convenience store lineups, judging each town she passed through on its merits as a hiding place.

The next year, once school was out, Alex had plans to spoil herself for a change, a splurging on cheap good-for-you treats. She would catch up on the prize-winning novels she'd seen praised in the paper for their "affirming" and "meditative" qualities, start jogging again, plant tomatoes in her building's communal garden. To steal a few hours of freedom during the week, she enrolled Rachel in a daycare downtown. The girl's resistance, however, became apparent almost immediately. The daycare workers called with reports of her clawing at the fence around the Astroturfed playground. When asked to come inside with the other kids, she would only stare up between the surrounding buildings at the postage stamp of blue above.

The daycare people suggested it was homesickness, but Alex recognized the real cause of the girl's protest. After the long, indoors winter, Rachel had taken Toronto's warm sun as a broken promise. In the stifling evenings of their apartment, she would uncharacteristically cry, refuse favourite foods, fuss before being put down to sleep. She wanted *out*.

In the middle of June, overheated and underslept herself, Alex rented a car and took Rachel up to Algonquin. The idea was for the girl to sleep on the drive and be rewarded with a swim in one of the park's thousand green lakes. As soon as the hazy suburbs' brew-yer-owns, discount warehouses and twenty-four-screen multiplexes shaped like UFOs had given way to regrowth forests and grazing fields, the girl was quiet. Not asleep, but tranquilized, her fingers splayed against the car's window like an antenna receiving signals that had been unreadably scrambled in the city. Once at the park, Rachel's mood was wholly transformed. Alex hadn't realized how much she missed seeing her child smile, and how long she had gone without.

When they returned to the apartment two days later, it was

only to buy a used truck, pick up the tent and camping gear and leave messages with family and friends. They were heading west again. Looking back on it now, Alex sees the last thing she brought along as almost an afterthought. A photo of Miles she'd slipped in an envelope and stuck in the glove compartment.

She'd done it for Rachel. She'd done it for herself. She swung between these justifications from day to day, often between the hours. Both were true. Alex had vowed from the beginning not to keep Miles's existence a secret from the girl. And letting her see him at least once might help put some of her brewing questions to rest in advance.

Alex had her own dark wishes. More than anything, she wanted Miles to *hurt*. There was little she would be able to do all alone on this count. But with the girl, there might be enough left in him that could still be poisoned.

Yet now, as she walks with Rachel, her pink sneakers skipping over the stones, she feels the careful plans she'd devised shift an inch under her feet. Miles ran away. She chased him down. Other than this, all she's sure of is that whatever is going to jump out at her, she won't turn away from it. That's Miles's trick. Hers is to sink her teeth into the truth of a thing and not let go until she's tasted it.

"I like him," Rachel says.

"Oh yeah, baby? You like Miles?"

"Miles?" The child stops and stares up at her mother. "I like *Stump,* Momma. Stump licked *me*."

SIX

All of Ross River has gone to bed, though many, tonight, cannot sleep.

Some wonder about the woman and girl who had come all the way here only to walk with the fire chief around town like tourists with a guide. One sees an animal's eyes peering out from the closet. One wishes the self-pitying child's wish to never have been born.

Another cannot believe it was only this morning. Both his waking mind and dreams confirm it. Only this morning he was thinking the firestarter's thoughts. Whether he lies with eyes open or closed, he lives through the same hours. When he comes to the end he can only return to the beginning to live them over again.

He lies awake through the night, certain he can smell it. A lick of heat. Barbecued pine. Sulphur curling his nosehairs. A memory of fire in place of fire itself. He knows this even as he sits up all at once and fights to reshape his gasp into a yawn.

He assumed that creating the firestarter would be a convenience. A temporary alter ego that would allow him to return wholly to himself after he was finished with it, cut free like a booster rocket once gravity has been defeated. Instead, the firestarter clings to him. In fact, he can feel the beginnings of a struggle, another's hand on the wheel. It is still weaker than he. Thoughtless and mute. But it has a desperate tenacity he hadn't expected, an unmanageable weight. It threatens to take him down with it like a drowning dog.

He thinks of what he would give in dollar terms to sleep without dreams until morning. Starts at two-fifty and soon approaches everything he has.

It's not guilt. Not exactly. It's not yet worry, either. Tonight, what denies his rest is what the firestarter would say to him if it ever learned to speak.

SEVEN

Even from four miles off, during the few hours of a July night's darkness, the bear can smell Ross River before she spots the orange glow of its homes. Melted lard, yeast, the generator's dizzying fumes. All of it attracts her, so much stronger in its promises than the highbush cranberries and wild sweet pea, the only other food she can detect in the vicinity. They have been moving continuously for a full day without eating, and now hunger sharpens her senses as do the distant traces of smoke that have been pursuing them the whole time. She allows her cubs to rest, rolled back on their haunches, chewing at air. The three of them have made their way to the top of a rock outcropping that pokes through the treeline, midway up the slope of the Tintina Trench.

The sow has been here before. Last autumn, with her mate. It's how she knows that, in daylight, they could see the entire Pelly valley from where they are. Now, with the dawn only a blue thread atop the horizon, the killing ground is a field of shadow. Below them, the town throbs in electric flames.

She doesn't fear the people she knows to be there, but unless she has to, she will go no closer. It would be easy to push through one of the many breaks in the fence around the dump and feast on whatever spilled out of the piled bags she gutted. During the summer her mate stayed with her (far longer than other wandering, rutting boars), they would come here from time to time. The decision arose less out of necessity than as an addiction to the landfill's exotic pleasures. On the rare occasions that the dump manager came by to throw the beam of his flashlight over one of them, the other would bark from the opposite direction, diverting his attention. The beam leapt blindly in his hands. In seconds the sow and her mate would be through the fence.

But there is only the cubs with her now. They have never been close to people, and she wonders if their curiosity would cause them to pause, blinking at the light. She has seen this hypnotism used on other animals by hunters in the woods at night. No amount of barking could wake them once the dazzling bulb had captured their eyes.

They will not go closer to town. They will not run any farther away either. Over the other side of the range to the south is a river that, by now, will be running with easily scooped grayling and trout. And here, in the St. Cyr foothills, they are the only bears. Whatever food is available will be theirs without competition. She looks at her cubs. It will be another year before they will begin to make these calculations on their own, and for a moment, the thought of the time ahead exhausts her.

She lifts her snout and turns to the east in the direction they have come from. The cubs do the same. The oddly stringent smoke is still there. Stronger than the hour before. Though it hasn't moved, the sow feels that it wants to. And when it does, it will come this way.

In the morning, Miles stands in the shower until the hot water in the tank goes dry, and after it does, stands a while longer under the cold. It doesn't make him feel clean as much as raw, a layer of skin peeled off, leaving him tenderized. Sometimes it helps him to think. Today, the water draws all thought out of him, washing half-formed sentences down the drain. By the time he turns off the taps he'd be slow in coming up with his birthday, his postal code. When he steps out of the stall the only thing he recognizes is Stump's tongue licking his legs.

Beyond the bathroom window the morning sun is so bright it looks to Miles like the prolonged flash of some distant megaton explosion. And maybe it is. It is a summer of fire everywhere but here.

Even in a place as disconnected as Ross River, the images of disaster have found their way to him. On the TV hanging from chains in the Lucky China's ceiling, he has crunched and tartar-sauced his way through lunch while watching evacuations of famous ski villages and less-famous pulp towns on the lower mainland of British Columbia, the ruin of Washington State vineyards, flames licking against million-dollar glass cubes terraced over the hills of San Bernardino and the Simi Valley. Crews from as far as Ohio, Minnesota and Georgia have been dispatched to assist on the suburban infernos of Oregon and California. Reporters can't get through a story without speaking of it, with a grimness only half disguising their excitement, as "possibly the worst wildfire season in living memory." Every time they use the phrase, Miles can't help wondering whose living memory they're talking about. He's still alive. They should ask him sometime.

That the fires are so vast that smoke has been carried on the prevailing winds to redden the sun as far east as Winnipeg and St. Louis might surprise some of the experts, but not Miles. He has seen a summer like this one coming for a long time. Global warming. Continental drought. Fuel loading. The last of these being the biggest factor. After years of urban sprawl and "development" of what remains of the western forests, fighting fires has become more necessary in order to protect man-made values. The trouble is, the more smokers you put out, the more deadwood there is to blow up the next time around. Fire doesn't like being made to wait.

When he's dressed, Miles walks out to the main road and along the half mile to the fire office. The morning light continues to dazzle him, glinting off anything it can find, even the gravel, white as chalk. The rust-stained tin of the fire office looks as though it's been painted silver overnight.

Miles had expected the place to be empty, but King is already there, sipping at a mug of instant coffee. When Miles walks in he barely turns. Dreamy. That's what the kid is. Which makes him a little dangerous, too.

Patrick "King" Lear is this year's part-timer sent up from the University of Northern British Columbia's forestry management program to fill out the crew. He's not the worst that Miles has seen, a physically strong boy who obviously loves the bush and, like Miles, sees firefighting as a way to get paid for living in it. But there's an absence about King that made Miles at first suspect the kid was on drugs of some sort, one of the new kinds that make you rapturously amazed by everything. Now, he has come to believe that this is simply King's nature. What's worrying is that, on a burn site, it's not exactly the optimum mental state for your men to be in. Crookedhead may not be any better on the raw intelligence side of the ledger, and Jerry is always looking for a way out of the hottest or heaviest work, but at least their defects are predictable. With King, you can't tell when he might stop clearing deadwood or hacking out a fireline, hypnotized by the beauty of embers floating through a stand of aspens. Miles can only thank Christ that there hasn't been a fire of any substance for the length of his tenure as supervisor. They're good men. He cares for them more than he's comfortable admitting. But Miles would prefer to not see them tested by anything bigger than the bonfires of discarded mattresses they practise on out at the dump on Sundays.

"King," Miles says.

"Hey there, boss."

"You looked at the morning spotter reports?"

"Nothing."

"Not a thing?"

"It's almost weird. There's smokers in every district but ours."

"And the towers——?"

"Aren't seeing anything but a sunny day."

"How nice."

Miles looks at King and, for the first time, sees a younger version of himself in the hard brow, the blue, elsewhere eyes. He wishes he hadn't. And in a sense, he hadn't—King doesn't really look like Miles, not in the way you would ever confuse the two. It's only that King's self-containment, his distracted temperament that disguised something you might not want to get too close to, makes Miles think that those may well be the same impressions he leaves with others.

"I sent Mungo to check on you last night," Miles says.

"Three sheets to the wind, and *he's* checking to see if *I'm* awake."

"I wanted to get him out of the bar more than anything else. I was hoping that once he'd said hello to you, he'd find his way home to say hello to Jackie."

"You're a man with a plan."

"Always."

Miles says this and hears its emptiness in his chest.

"Speaking of plans, I was looking for you yesterday," King says.

"What for?"

"Wanted a sign-off on the pumper to do a training session. But you weren't around. The pumper was gone, too."

"I went for a drive."

"A drive?"

"That's right."

"It's just strange. It's a strange thing to—"

"Don't do this. It's not the right day."

King raises his hands in surrender.

"I'll be back in an hour," Miles says. "In the meantime, do me a favour and call the crew, get them out of bed so they can be here by the time I get back. Start with Mungo. He takes the longest."

"Absolutely," King says, returning his attention to the coffee mug on the table. "But there might not be anything for them to do when they get here."

"You never know in this business," Miles says, and slaps the kid on the back hard enough to make them both wonder if it was a friendly gesture or something else.

The Welcome Inn Lounge is empty except for Bonnie, who slams beer bottles into cases behind the bar, and Miles regrets coming in this way to look for Earl, the innkeeper. Bonnie pops her head up, a you're-not-going-anywhere grin on her face, and he knows he's about to be carpet-bombed with questions that a sour, bronchitic Earl would never trouble himself to ask.

"And how are you doing today, Bonnie?"

"Livin' the dream," she says, wiping her hands on her sweat-shirt. "Any fires this morning?"

"Haven't you heard? We're a smoke-free environment up here."

"A good one up in Dawson, a couple little farts down in Haines Junction, and nothing for us. That just isn't fair."

"It's a bitch, it's true."

"We don't get something soon and your boys are going to be under my feet next year even more than usual, asking to put it all on their tab. And you know something? I won't be able to do it. Those chuckleheads don't blow a candle out before winter and it'll leave you and Terry Gray as my only paying customers."

"We'll get our fire."

"It's not just me."

"I know all about—"

"It's like dominoes. You fellas lose your jobs and we'll all come falling after you."

"Don't worry, Bonnie. You've heard of a rain dance? Well, I did a little fire dance for us this morning."

"You did?"

"Oh yeah. Had smoke coming out my ass. You should've seen it."

"Maybe next time."

Miles glances toward the open back door, down the hallway that leads to the motel outbuilding. If he made a run for it right now he may not have to answer a single awkward inquiry. But he'll have to act quickly. Bonnie has placed her hands on her hips, elbows out. A gunslinger ready to fire.

"Is Earl around?" Miles asks instead of making a move, his boots stuck to the gummy floor.

"Need their room number?"

"You could at least make a *show* of minding your own business."

"Friends visiting?" she asks, pretending not to have heard him.

"They're people I know."

"Now that's a funny thing. When people I know come to town I have them stay at my place."

One night. That's all it takes. One night for not only Miles's life to take a serious turn toward the complicated, but for every citizen of Ross River to have heard about it. He can see this in Bonnie's bosom, of all things. Her breasts swelling high against the cotton in the pride of a job well done.

"It's a different situation from that," Miles says.

"Different how?"

"Listen—"

"I like her. Just so you know. I like the *look* of the woman. Sensible. And tougher than you'd guess, seems to me."

"Is that your female intuition talking?"

"Better. That's my bartender's intuition talking."

Miles laughs a genuine laugh, and suspects that his lack of sleep has left him giddy and vulnerable. But to his astonishment, Bonnie decides to let him off the hook.

"Go see Earl. You can talk to me about your fascinating life any old time."

"It's not fascinating," Miles says. "But one of these days, I'll tell you my whole boring story. You'll just have to promise to keep it between you and me."

"I'll make any promise you want. It's keeping those promises that gives me trouble, that's all."

As he does every time he sees it, Miles wonders where the hell the stone fountain in front of the Welcome Inn came from. A pot-bellied cherub pissing in spurts, which makes Miles think of his own private struggles, the prematurely enlarged prostate that bedevils his nights. He'd love to know the story behind it. This half-ton piece of Renaissance kitsch that somebody took the pains to haul up here and that Earl, a man who seems not to care a whit about others' comfort, plugs in every day that the temperature is above freezing. For the thousandth time, Miles makes a mental note to ask Bonnie about it the next time he sees her, and knows even as he does so that he will forget, again, as soon as the statue is out of his sight.

He climbs the outside stairs to the second floor, walks to the end of the outbuilding where Earl told him he'd put Alex and Rachel. ("Nice and quiet out there," he'd said, but Miles knew it was the room directly above the kitchen, and even though quiet, would stink of whatever daily special was lobbed into the deep fryer.)

Miles studies the cracks in the door's paint, waits for the whistle to leave his breath before knocking.

"Momma," Rachel calls out when she opens the door, wearing the same strawberry dress. "Miles is here."

"Good morning," he says, speaking over the sound of Alex flushing the toilet somewhere within the gloom.

"Where's Stump?"

"He likes to sleep in."

"He does?"

"Oh yeah. He's real big on the sleeping."

"Bet *I* could wake him up."

"Bet you could."

Alex emerges from the room's darkness to place her hands on Rachel's shoulders.

"Enjoying your stay?" he asks her.

"Aside from the gunk bubbling up the bathtub drain and the sheets that smell like chicken fingers, it's five star all the way."

"Mmm-mmm," Rachel says, licking her lips. "Chicken fingers!"

Alex is wearing a Clash T-shirt that Miles recognizes, the London Calling one with the sleeves cut off at the shoulders. It allows him to see how tanned she is relative to the white cotton, as well as the strength in her arms. He had not come here to admire her, or to indulge the nostalgia brought on by raggy clothes she hasn't gotten rid of, but he finds that he feels both. He makes the decision to fight these things directly. And if they break through his defences, he can't allow himself to be surprised.

"Momma?" Rachel says, craning her head back to face Alex. "Can I go outside?"

"If you promise to stay on the grass here, or in the back."

"I won't go far."

"It's not about far. It's about being where I can keep my eyes on you."

"I won't go far from your eyes."

Alex lifts her hands from the child's shoulders and she shoots out past Miles. There's a quaking in the wood as she runs away.

Miles stands at the door with arms folded high on his chest. He feels prissy and miscast, but now that he's here, he can't do a thing about it.

"Just leave it open behind you," Alex says, stepping back. "I like to listen for her."

He steps inside and can smell the steamy mix of soap and shampoo from Alex's shower along with the more historical traces of cooking seeped through from downstairs. He slides over the cigarette burns in the carpet, past the two single beds and rabbit-eared TV, to stand before the small window at the opposite end. It's bright outside but the light stops dead at the frame. Despite this, a

daddy-long-legs roams the other side of the glass, searching for a
way in.

"Why here?"

He turns. The room is much smaller now that the shadows have
pulled away to show the walls.

"The only other hotel's in Faro, and that's—"

"Not us. You. What was it about Ross River that made you stay?"

"The land is good. As good as any place in the Territory. And
the town is—" He stops to remember what he was about to say,
and realizes there's nothing there. "The town is nowhere," he goes
on finally. "I suppose it's somewhere for the people born here.
And for the Kaska it means all sorts of things, good and bad and
other stuff I don't have a clue about. But for me, it's the best
nowhere I was able to find."

"I knew that's what you'd be looking for."

"And that's how you found me."

Alex shrugs.

"I tried the easy ways first," she says. "But there was no phone
number under your name anywhere. I even tried looking up your
mom, but she's totally off-line, too."

"She got rid of her phone when she realized the only person she
has to call anymore is me. And we've already made our own
arrangements on that count."

"So what did that leave me with? Fifty thousand miles. I would
come to a road that ran off whatever road I was on and I'd follow it
to the end. When I couldn't go any farther on the last one I could
find—that's where I knew you would be."

"Nowhere."

"Nowhere's nowhere," she says. "Not when you're in it."

Miles doesn't agree—he's living proof that she's wrong—but
he doesn't contradict her.

"How long did you plan to keep it up?"

"This was it," Alex says, clapping her hands together once, hard.
An everybody-out-of-the-pool sound. "August first. Ten days

from now. Four seasons rolling from Eugene to Pink Mountain to Spokane and I'm finally ready to quit. Then you're right there. A bogeyman on a bar stool."

"It must have cost a hell of a lot. And your parents can't be giving—"

"To look for *you?*"

Alex releases a nasty laugh and sits on the end of the bed. The mattress screeches in protest. When she settles, however, her body is unnaturally still, as though something had switched off inside of her.

"A tent, a cooler full of hot dogs and bananas," she goes on, sliding her hands down the front of her jeans. "The rest is pretty cheap, really. Buy a used pickup at the beginning of the summer and resell it on Labour Day. The rest of the time it's driving and stopping. Showing a picture of you to everybody I meet, like a cop in a TV show. *Excuse me, ma'am, have you seen this man?* And they would look, and make a sad, oh-poor-dear face and shake their heads. I'd tell them to look again and imagine half his face scarred. Because it's weird, you know, but I never took a picture of you after you came back from the fire. Have you ever noticed that people only take pictures when they're happy? Anyway. *Anyway.* I'd show the old photo of you for a second time and tell them to add in a scar. Sometimes they wanted to help so much that they'd lie and say yes, they thought they saw somebody like that around last week. At the back of the pool hall, asking for spare change outside the liquor store—one of those places where you'd expect to come across the sort of person you wouldn't want to take a good look at. But I became an expert at detecting the sound of wishful thinking, and move on. Drive and stop and out comes the picture. *Excuse me, sir.* Drive and stop. When it got to the end of August, we'd turn around. That was it. That's the whole itinerary for four years running. Our annual adventure. The only summer holidays Rachel has ever known."

Alex stops now, a little breathless, and feels a blush heat her cheeks at how long she's spoken. It's been a while since she's talked to anyone aside from Rachel, and Alex knows that Miles can hear it as clearly as she can.

"I thought of changing my name," Miles says, turning to face the window again. "But I figured I didn't have to. For the natives, names are sacred. For the rest of us, we just feel better off not knowing."

"So it was easy."

"There was a time you couldn't get away from things as easy as I did. You were born someplace and you died there. If anybody asked who you were, you knew what to say. Your family name. Your church. Your trade. Nobody talked about finding or re-inventing themselves. You were only who you were."

His face has drifted so close to the window that his nose has grazed its warm surface, leaving a print behind. He pulls back an inch. Behind him, Alex waits for him to complete his thought, and only now does he realize he had one.

"It's different now, though," he says, and watches the patch of steam his words make against the glass. "People move around. Try whole new lives on for size."

"I guess that's freedom."

"Oh yeah. Free as birds."

"Is she there?" Alex asks after a time.

"I can see her," he says, and realizes he's been half watching Rachel for as long as he's been standing there.

Miles forces his eyes to focus. He looks out across the tall grass of the Welcome Inn's back lot to the yards of mobile homes beyond it. In one of them, a bunch of Kaska kids play on a trampo-line. Rachel is there, her strawberry dress lifting wide and sucking back against her legs with every jump. Miles is amazed how quickly they all have gone from introductions to holding hands, screaming in made-up terror. Without instruction they have worked out a pattern where only one pair of feet connect with the elastic tarp at a time, sending them into the air and the pink rubber bubbling up after until the next bare toes push it earthward again.

As Miles watches them he places three of his fingertips against his scar and draws them down. He does it so delicately that, to Alex, it appears that he is searching for something in the marks, reading his face like Braille.

"Do you have somebody here?" she asks, and her voice pulls his hand away from the burn.

"You mean like a girlfriend?"

"You can choose the term you'd like."

"No, I don't have somebody."

"I'm a little surprised."

"You shouldn't be. I'm not looking. And even if I was, there's nobody here to look for."

"There's that girl in the bar last night."

Alex isn't smiling, but her voice is. Viciously amused. Miles has forgotten it. The tone of accusation, mocking and inescapable.

"What girl?"

"The pretty one. The *only* one. The one who gave me the once-over and then burned her eyes right through your forehead when you walked out."

"Margot," he says. "She already lives with an asshole, she doesn't need two."

"From what I saw of her, I'm sure she thinks that's too damn bad."

"Listen to you. You're here for twelve hours and you've got everybody's secret motives all figured out."

"Not everybody's."

Outside, Rachel looks up at where Miles stands and raises both her arms in a jubilant wave. With a start, he realizes not only that she can see him but that she could for as long as he's been standing where he is.

"You must be lonely," Alex says behind him.

"I suppose it's a matter of getting used to something to the point that you don't even notice it anymore."

"Oh, it's still there."

"You're not telling me that you don't have guys sniffing around."

"I've gone out," she admits. "They come to *me,* you know? It's unbelievable. Pushing the stroller or wiping snot off Rachel's lip, wearing track pants and searching for the cheapest laundry detergent in the dollar store—they come to *me.* And not just the damaged goods, either. Some of them are cute, and/or rich, and/or sweet. Oh yeah, definitely, I've gone out."

Alex pauses now, arms crossed and her index finger tapping against her biceps as though taking an accounting of these men, summoning their positives and negatives to her mind. It takes her a while.

"It doesn't sound like loneliness to me," Miles says, and snorts.

"The test isn't whether you go out on dates, or have friends, or even get laid from time to time. The test is whether what's going on around you breaks your heart or not."

The idea of Alex being broken-hearted takes Miles by surprise. He had always thought of her as too lucky for real suffering. Who can know sorrow who has grown up white, semi-affluent, free of the multiple varieties of childhood abuses?

She could, of course. And he had been its cause. This comes to him as a belated revelation. After he'd run, and left her with his child—without a word, just as his father had—surely it was *she* who had the more valid claim to heartbreak than he. What did he *think* followed from his leaving? As unlikely as it strikes him now, he'd assumed a quick recovery. Once he was gone, she would have eventually come to realize her good fortune that he'd fucked off before he had the chance to do any undoable damage, as he certainly would have had he lingered on. Alex would be rid of him. But he would never be rid of himself. He calculated the latter as being the greater burden of the two.

He knows he's only being selfish with his victimhood, but he indulges this line of thinking for a moment. He studies Alex now and grafts onto her skin the veil of her fortunate youth. Home-video years spent in Stratford, Ontario, a leafy, postcard town of moneyed retirees, a repertory theatre, ball bearing factory and gift shops. Her parents still lived there. Retired now themselves but keeping up the family home, a Tudor monster on one of the broad streets of competitive landscaping and gardens in which beloved Labradors were buried.

Miles liked Alex's parents, but before he'd ever met them he'd developed an idea of them being smug and humourless Tories, and even the discovery that he was wrong couldn't stop him from needling Alex about them. The truth was he admired her father, the county solicitor who went to Harvard (and told deflating jokes about the place every time it came up), and his knockout wife, whom Miles got very confessional around and was half in love with. It was a home to spend Christmas in. Every December he and Alex had taken the train to the big cherry-smoke and Eggs Benedict house in Stratford, and every year he felt roughly awakened from a dream when it was time to go back. Alex always offered to go with him to Vancouver Island to stay with his mother over the holidays, and Miles would remind her of how much plane tickets cost at that time of year. But the real reason he didn't go back was to be with Alex's family instead. A home without missing people, the tinned-soup smell of unrecoverable losses.

Outside, the jumping game has turned into a kind of crazy tag, all the kids running around the trampoline and then back the other way, a Keystone Kops routine that ends with them piling up against each other.

Then, all at once, they turn their heads in the same direction. Someone that Miles can't see has called to them, and now they stand as he stands, waiting for whoever it is to come into view.

"Were you planning on saying anything to her?" Alex says.

"I don't think I was."

"I suppose the wording would be a little awkward."

"I wasn't worried about the words to use," Miles says, turning to her. "I just don't think what I might say would make any difference."

"I get it. You leave and let everyone else figure out why. Keep your mouth shut and you can pretend you're not a liar."

"She's not mine, Alex. Not in the sense that matters."

"And what sense is that?"

"Belonging to her."

Alex purses her lips, and with an abruptness that makes him stiffen, leaps up from the bed and turns on the TV. The room is shattered with studio audience laughter. She twists the knob, turning the channels, which offer nothing. The screen seething with black-and-white maggots.

"One channel, huh?" she says.

"That's one more than I usually get."

She keeps turning until the dial is back to where it started. Another round of false hoots and hollers.

"You know where she got her name?" Alex shouts.

"From the apartment. Above the bagel place."

"Very good! Not everything has been erased from the tapes."

"Nothing's been erased. That's part of the problem."

She lifts a cigarette pack from the bedsheets and lights one. She didn't smoke before. But Miles can tell it's not a new habit, either.

"I always liked the name of that street," she says. "*Rue Rachel.* There's a connection for me, I guess."

"Between me and her?"

"Between then and now."

He looks out the window and sees Wade standing among the trampoline kids. Addressing them with a face that shows nothing. And speaking not to all of them.

Miles watches Wade say something to Rachel and set his hand on her shoulder. It makes her wince. Not the firmness of his grip but its intent. Even Miles can see it. The girl's face squeezed tight with revulsion, the anticipation of an adult violence she has never been close to before.

Miles counts in his head and keeps his eyes on Wade's hand. It stays on the girl a full seven seconds longer than it should.

Just when he is about to run out the door, Wade releases his grip. Then he does something that holds Miles to where he is. Wade turns to look directly up at him, meeting his eyes through the window. An unseemly grin stretches over his face. Though he can't hear it, Miles imagines the chuckle Rachel must be able to hear.

As Wade leaves the circle of kids, he waves at the girl. She watches him go but doesn't wave back.

"You shouldn't have come," Miles says.

"I had to."

"I've got a life here. Half a life, anyway."

"There are some things people have to do."

"I know that."

"Then you understand why I'm here."

"And you'll understand why I'm telling you to go."

There's a silence so complete it sounds to both of them like a statement made by a third party, a confirmation of the impossibility that lies between them. Finally, Alex startles him by laughing.

"I'm just wondering if you were always such a pathetic coward," she says once she can find the breath. "I mean, we've both been working from the theory that the fire was the thing that got in the way, haven't we? But maybe it only brought out your full potential for being a useless piece of shit."

"Guess I always had it in me."

"And so smug about it too."

"I'm not proud of anything."

"Yes, you are. You even think that running from a pregnant woman makes you special. And doing it five years *before* your old man got around to it. Pity poor Miles McEwan! The Worst Man in the World!"

He sees that she's right at the same time he thinks of hitting her. What stops him is Wade. His hand on the girl. A promise of harm that Miles recognizes as a gesture he might have delivered himself—though, he used to believe, never to a woman or a child. If he hits Alex now, the last of the fading differences between him and Wade would be dissolved. And if he could do that to her, it might prove he could do it to a five-year-old, too.

"You should have kept her away."

"Oh no! I wanted her to see the fine, upstanding stock she came from."

"And now she can have nightmares about me."

"There's worse things." She splutters laughter again. "You'll see."

"Who are you doing this for, anyway? Her or you?"

"I don't think you get it yet," she says, now pulling on her cigarette so hard he can hear the crinkle of retreating paper. "I'm doing it for *you*. To leave you with something you'll always remember."

"Give it to me, then."

"You don't get to *keep* it. You just get to *look*."

Miles watches Alex exhale and sees her triumph through the blue smoke. The spillover of loathing finally permitted to show itself.

"You mean the girl," he says.

"She's seen you. You've seen her. But after tomorrow, never again. I'm pretty sure Rachel has the better chance of forgetting. But you? You'll always know that she's real."

Alex puts her cigarette out on the table next to the little TV.

"Right now you think you're a ghost," she says. "But ghosts have it easy. Floating around, feeling sorry for themselves. After today, I promise, *you* are going to be the haunted one."

She slaps her palm against the front of the TV and the sitcom noises instantly disappear, leaving the room even more uncomfortably muffled than before. Miles's hand involuntarily rises to his scar. Covers the worst of its fault lines with a joined pair of fingers.

"Still so scared," she says.

"I'm not scared of you."

"Not me. But you're so terrified of who you are you can't even look."

"You think—"

"No?" She takes two steps back from him and opens the closet door. On the inside, there's a mirror she angles so that Miles is reflected in full. "Feast your eyes."

He tries. But after the first unexpected glimpse of corrugated cheek, he can't keep his eyes on Alex, let alone himself.

She comes close again but doesn't lower her voice, so that he feels what she says as much as hears it.

"Not as many mirrors up here, I suppose. Well, let me show you a picture." Her breath hot on his skin as she looks it over. "Trembly chin, crybaby eyes that can't look at a woman straight. I don't know which half is uglier. Your burned-up face or the one that looks like it's already dead."

"I don't have time for this."

"What *do* you have time for, Miles? I'm curious. How you've spent the last six years is a real puzzle to me."

It just goes by, Miles nearly says. *Most of the time, you don't even feel it.*

Instead, he runs.

To get past her, he pushes Alex aside with more force than he intended, and she stumbles against the edge of the bed, nearly losing her balance. He thinks of apologizing but it's years too late for words of that kind. There is no choice for him but to leave, to get out into the air. With both his arms swinging in front of him, he lurches into the light of the open doorway.

She rushes to the door to watch him go. A stranger shuffling away with shoulders raised to cover his ears. Nothing he could do would prevent the next word she throws at him from getting through.

Yet what she ends up doing occurs outside herself. As Miles stumbles into the full sun of the courtyard, Alex raises her fist, aims an index finger at the back of his head, and fires.

EIGHT

That evening, Miles walks into the Welcome Inn Lounge through the same door Alex and Rachel had only a day before, and immediately feels that he should have stayed at home.

The entire fire team are there. Taking them in at once, Miles is reminded of how different the four of them look. Their ages (from King's twentysomething to Mungo's who-knows?-something), their headwear (Crookedhead James favouring an undersized Philadelphia Flyers ballcap, Jerry a skull-and-crossbones bandana), their teeth (King's full set on the one hand, Jerry's half-dozen can openers on the other). The shades of their skin, from sunburned pink to nutty brown. Aside from Miles, King is the only white guy on the crew, with Mungo a locally born Kaska, Jerry the mixed product of a long-gone prospector and his long-dead Tlingit wife, and Crookedhead a self-described "Indian combo platter," a descendant of Yukon Tutchone, Alaskan Haida, and "a shot of Irish, way back." While they couldn't look less alike in all of these respects, it doesn't prevent them from raising their heads in perfect unison when Miles opens the door. Each of them with the same wide-eyed look, one that makes it clear they had been talking about him up until the second he walked in.

Behind the crew's table, Bonnie waits for him to assume his position on the stool directly in front of her. Jackson Bader is here too, sitting alone. Although Miles finds it impossible that, even in Ross River, news of Alex and Rachel's arrival would have reached the Baders, the old man nevertheless glances at Miles with an indifference so perfect as to be taken for hostility. And worst of all, Wade is half in the bag. Playing pool by himself, bent to take a shot but weaving on his feet so badly he can't focus, let alone aim.

At the sight of Miles in the doorway, the big man's arms launch forward and the cue cuts under the nine ball, sending it flying off the table to roll onto the dance floor.

"Hey there, Miles," Mungo says, leaning back to pull an empty chair up to the fire team's table. "How about joining us for one?"

The invitation stops Miles. He has become so used to proceeding directly to his stool that the mere idea of doing anything else embarrasses him.

"Who's turn is it to buy?" he manages to ask.

"Jerry's. But seeing as getting twenty bucks out of him is like asking a stone to donate blood, I'll get it."

All of them know that Mungo is speaking of Jerry McCormack's truck. The two-year-old Ford he saw advertised in the *Yukon News* and has been aching for ever since. It's this month's justification for the lame excuses he comes up with to get out of paying for rounds. It's also why he's been asking every day about a fire.

"I left my wallet back at the trailer," Jerry says.

"The sooner you buy your Dodge, the sooner you find your wallet. Is that it?" Mungo says.

"It's a Ford," Jerry says.

Miles lets the door swing closed and falls into the chair next to Mungo. It's a whole new view of the room from down here. He scans the men sitting around him and returns their slight, almost imperceptible nods.

Bonnie unloads a tray of longnecks at their table, along with a Shirley Temple for Crookedhead James. People make fun of Crookedhead for a lot of things, but his refusal to drink since the day his girlfriend took off with their son is too proud a statement to be mocked by anyone. The arrival of cranberry juice or unspiked margarita mix is the one moment in a day he achieves something like nobility.

Miles knows that he's waiting for them both to come back. Crookedhead does little else but dream of the moment his runaway family walks in and finds him shaved, sipping orange juice instead of Jack Daniel's, a composed smile on his face. In the meantime, he sends them cheques. Half of what Crookedhead makes goes straight down to Chilliwack where his ex, his son and "some new fuckwad" have set up house. Everyone but Crooked-head knows they're never stepping through the Welcome Inn's door again. But instead of getting used to being alone, he keeps upping the amounts he sends south, an enticement for a second chance to come his way. It's Crookedhead's unspoken reason for needing a fire worse than any of them.

"Terry been in tonight?" Miles asks.

"Not so far," Crookedhead says. "He must be out at the lock-up, polishing his handcuffs."

"What do you want him for?" Mungo says, glancing over his shoulder at Wade, who continues to smash the balls around, muttering. "There's not going to be any trouble tonight."

Miles knocks down half his beer in a go.

None of the fire crew can summon a harmless, natural-sounding inquiry to their minds, so they remain silent, working to discern the words that Wade is, moment by moment, making more clear. Miles thinks of leaving, but knows there's nowhere to go. Whatever is about to happen will face him tomorrow if he refuses to face it today. He's found that malice cannot be escaped in a place like this. Better to sit where you are, finish your beer, and let it come at you. But as you wait, it's also wise to locate a little malice of your own.

"Hey, Miles!" Wade shouts.

"I have some real good advice for you," Mungo offers. "Go home."

"Why? I don't have any kids there to look after. Not like you. Or some other people in here."

Wade throws his pool cue onto the table and sidles over to where the fire team sit, his fists resting on his hips.

"Guess who I talked to today?"

Miles ignores him and takes another long drink that leaves his bottle empty.

"That little white girl playing with her little Indian friends. Sweet thing. I swear to God, she grows up half as pretty as her momma and she'll be a real treat in a few years."

"Sit down," Miles says, but it comes out as an inaudible squeak. Inside of him, he can hear a door opening. From behind it, a black oil spills and floods into an empty room.

"That's another funny thing about today," Wade goes on. "I walked up to have a word with that little girl and when she looked at me, damn if she didn't have her daddy's eyes."

"He's not worth the shit he's talking," Mungo says, but when he grips Miles's elbow, his hand jumps back, as though the skin he had touched was an open flame.

"Come to think of it," Wade announces, stepping closer, "I haven't yet met a dog who'd walk away from his bitch and pup. So what does that make you?"

Miles brings the empty bottle to his lips again and lets the last suds roll over his tongue. He notices Jackson Bader watching him, sucking a cigarette down to its filter. The old man wasn't smoking the other night. A secret habit, enjoyed only when the wife is tucked away. Miles can see that he's someone used to pursuing whatever pleasures strike his fancy, but that he has to hide them from at least one person in the world, otherwise they wouldn't be as pleasurable. Still, Miles thinks, it's taken a toll. The man has see-through skin, grey as a flake of ash.

"Where's Margot?" Miles asks, turning at last to Wade.

"What's she got to do with anything?"

"It's just that she's usually able to keep your head out of your ass."

Wade spits on the floor. He looks down to watch it evaporate, leaving only a faint white stain.

"The truth has a way of coming out, don't it, Miles?"

"You don't know a thing about me."

"I've seen liars before. And yellow bastards who put on airs. Goddamn if I don't know you inside out."

Miles can feel the electricity of his rage about to blossom, but before it can, he pushes his chair back and strides toward the door. On any other day, such provocations wouldn't have gone half as far as he's let Wade's go. Miles realizes that it's his summoning of the girl's face to his mind that calms him enough to walk away.

But Wade won't let him. With a feline howl, the giant throws himself on Miles's back as he crosses the door's threshold. Miles chokes against the fingers locked around his throat. He needs room. The railings on either side of the steps lock him in, and he bounces between them, the handles at the top tearing gashes through his jeans.

Since he can't haul himself forward, Miles decides to throw both of them over the railing and into the parking lot below. It's easy. With a lunge to the right they roll over, the grip released from Miles's neck.

They fall for what seems a longer time than possible. Both of them blink, once, at the sky. With black spots swooping into his vision, somewhere in Miles a voice notes how bright it is for this late in the day.

Then he hears something crunch and thinks it may be him. A rib, maybe. He hopes it's not his spine. The spine would be bad. The interruption of Wade's fists pummelling his face moves Miles's speculations to how he might flip over and engage his boots in the matter.

Wade is big, and his punches are not without force. But he's also drunk. This puts his aim off enough that he can't connect directly with Miles's nose, the magical knockout target. It also grants Miles the time between blows to roll out from under his attacker and keep going until he makes it into the middle of the road.

When he gets to his feet and sees Wade lumbering toward him, his arms already starting to swing at the air a full ten feet short of their destination, Miles has another of his visions of what is to happen next. And what he foresees is his beating Wade Fuerst into a weeping bag of pulp. It will be cruel, no matter that Miles took no part in starting it. It will, later on, make even Miles sick.

But for now, Miles allows the aperture for his anger to open wide within him, a dark current running out from his chest, down his arms. Somewhere behind him, Mungo is shouting—*Take it easy, there!*—but Miles can no longer hear anything but the rollicking blood in his ears.

With the first punch to his stomach, Wade doubles over and spews a six-pack onto the road. After a few seconds, the stream is cut off as abruptly as it was released. He coughs. A delicate *ahem,* swiping the back of his hand over his lips.

Then, so gently it might be mistaken as tenderness, Miles places an arm around the back of Wade's neck. But once he's held in place, all those who have rushed out of the Welcome Inn Lounge to witness the event can tell that Miles is only keeping Wade up so that, when the big man's legs go, he'll still be there to take what Miles intends to give him.

With his free arm, Miles starts a series of pumps to the gut. A half-dozen thuds in an evenly spaced sequence, all to the same location. When he's done, Miles takes a single step back.

Wade sinks, deboned.

Miles measures a step from where Wade has now lifted himself to his knees. His head wobbles until it sits almost straight atop his neck. Then, in a charge, Miles comes at him. Swings his boot into Wade's face. Before any other sound, there's the papery rip of skin where the lace clasps split his cheek.

Miles is aware of how easy it would be to kill this man. A little more time is all it would take. More of the same cracks to the sides of his head. Steel-toed kicks to rupture the tender parts inside. It wouldn't even make Miles tired.

It is only when Wade covers his bloodied face with his hands, whimpering, that the black door inside Miles is closed again.

He turns around and sees the mixture of horror and admiration on the faces of those who watch him. Only Jackson Bader keeps his eyes on Wade. Not out of sympathy but interest, a vague curiosity. It's the same expression he might have looking up at the sky and wondering if it will rain.

Miles bends to whisper in the fallen man's ear. "I know it was you."

"Yeah?"

"What they found out back of Mungo's trailer a few weeks back."

"That was practice."

"I saw you this morning, too. And if you go near her again, I'll make you choke on whatever teeth you got left."

Wade spits into his palm and squints, searching for bone. When he's satisfied that there is nothing there worth saving, he lifts his head and surveys the circle of onlookers, one by one. Miles might have expected to find some evidence of shame in his eyes, but there's nothing there, not even pain.

Wade turns his attention to the wet gravel beneath him. His nosebleed has stained the white stones with rust.

"This'll be your blood next time, gorgeous," he says, low enough that only Miles can hear.

"I don't think so."

"I do. Because I'm going to kill you."

Wade looks around him, his neck a raised periscope, his unswollen eye its glassy lens. A quarter of Ross River stands watching him. They wait for him to get up, but come no closer to help.

"While I'm at it, I think I'll kill all of you," Wade says, then turns to face Miles alone. "Your woman and little girl first. So you can see what they'll look like when I'm done."

Miles tries to tell himself that this is only a loser's empty threat. But something about Wade's tone sends a shiver of real fear through him. The big man digs his fingers into the stones, steadying himself, and when he mutters his words a second time—*fucking kill all you cunts*—Miles hears the hollow fury of a man who doesn't care anymore. About himself, about winning or losing, about any goddamn thing at all. No matter how many times Miles might beat him, humiliate him, better him in front of Margot and whatever audience might be on hand, Wade will keep coming back because he has arrived at the point of believing he has nothing left to have taken from him. As Miles has learned of himself as well as others, it isn't pride that makes a fighter truly dangerous, but the total lack of it.

Margot breaks through the circle. At the sight of Wade lying in the road, her shoulders drop.

"Jesus H."

"I'm sorry," Miles says, and she blinks at him for a second before looking straight down on Wade.

"Let's go home," she tells him, slipping her hands under his arms. Wade resists her help, but her grip is too strong for him to get out of, and he ends up wriggling against her like an overtired child.

"I'm sorry," Miles says again. "I didn't go looking—"

"I know it."

"Do you need somebody to check him over? I could run up to the nurses' station and see if—"

"Just leave us alone, Miles."

All at once Wade goes limp, his chin collapsed on Margot's shoulder. He whispers something in her ear and throws his arms around her, trying to find the right angle so that his feet might keep him up. With a grunt, Margot launches the two of them on their way. As they go, Wade strokes at her ponytailed hair.

Before they're out of sight, Jackson Bader steps forward and cups his hands around his mouth.

"I hope all this won't delay our departure in the morning," he calls out. "I paid for a week, and it's what I expect."

"You be here at eight, and so will we," Margot answers. "Both of us."

"Hell of a place," Bader says to himself, but loud enough for the others to hear.

Though he says nothing, Miles can only agree.

Wade Fuerst would agree, too. He felt he was in hell, anyway. Not an overheated cavern of sinners as he'd imagined, but a painful solitude he's found himself walking around in. It offered certain powers, though. A kind of magic that enabled him to actually do things that would have been no more than spiteful daydreams before.

Take that night just over a month ago, for instance. He'd watched Margot gun the truck out of the drive and knew where she was going. All he could see of her through the windshield was her hands on the wheel. Hands that he'd kissed, tried to put a ring on. Now they were locked tight, and he would never get them open again.

After she was gone, he walked over to the Welcome Inn and managed to get down seven bourbons before Bonnie asked him to leave, came back to the trailer to pick up his twelve-gauge and headed over to Miles McEwan's cabin with the idea of blowing a hole through his chest. It was the beginning of not caring, and even Wade couldn't have guessed how quickly he'd take to it. No rules, no deliberations. Overnight, he had been unleashed by the black liberties of worthlessness, and he figured he might as well try them out for size.

It was the middle of June. Late enough for true darkness to have settled over town, so that he felt he could stride along the edge of ditches and cut across yard corners with easy stealth. He made no effort to conceal his weapon or himself.

He padded over the uncut lawn in front of Miles's cabin and

peered into the crack between the drawn curtains. The lights were on. He slid the pump-action of the shotgun and felt the satisfying catch of the cartridge into the chamber. Without humour, he thought: *I'm really loaded now.* He had never much liked guns before, or at least he saw that he didn't have the gift for firing them, not in the way that born hunters like Margot did. Yet now, the weight of the Mossberg felt like a part of him, an outgrowth of his newfound destructive will.

He clicked the safety off and walked around the side of the cabin. The night air stirred and quieted, as though it had noticed his movements and waited to see what he would do next. A square of lamplight from the living room's window fell over the tufted grass. At the risk of being seen, Wade stepped into it and looked inside.

He was almost surprised to see Miles sitting at the table, peering down at a chess board. Wade had never played the game, but could tell it was in its final stages, the dead bishops and pawns lined up along the side. Who was he playing? Wade stood and waited for Miles's opponent to return from the bathroom or with a bowl of pretzels from the kitchen. After five minutes, he realized the guy was alone.

It would be messy, but he could fire a slug through the glass right now and, without having to aim, cut his target in half. Wade paused, if only to wonder at the ease of the task before him. He'd assumed there would be more steps involved. Breaking and entering. A stakeout. But, as it turned out, it could be as simple a thing as this. Shooting a man in his living room as he played chess against himself.

Now, so close to carrying out the act, Wade began to consider the context in which it would be performed, and deemed it lacking. A showdown was needed. The final exchange between rivals, a closing articulation of motives. But what *were* his motives? His hate was unfocused, generalized. It flowed by the easiest routes, indifferent to its direction, like rainwater after a storm.

Laughter echoed up the street behind him. A bottle clanking over gravel. Wade turned to see Crookedhead James and Jerry McCormack walking home and couldn't believe they hadn't seen him.

He slipped back into the darkness and felt it envelop him, the air cooling with every step. There was no moon. He would pass through the backyards of his neighbours, as unnoticed as a foraging coyote descended from the hills.

On the way back, a shadow slipped out from behind a darkened trailer and stopped directly in his path. Of a size that Wade had a sense of its weight before he could trace its outline. A shape he only figured to be a dog after meeting its eyes. Uncollared, silent, watching him come but refusing to move aside. One of the half-dozen sled team leaders that had earned the privilege to walk free of its kennel over the summer months, waiting for the return of cold, of snow.

The animal opens its mouth and the sight of its blue teeth brings him up short. It is only panting, or possibly smiling. But Wade interprets its ease in his presence as an affront, a challenge to his command of the night.

Without looking around to check if anyone is watching, he once more raises the shotgun's butt to his shoulder. The malamute stiffens its ears as though at a word it has heard before but can't recall its meaning.

Wade takes two steps forward and fires without stopping. Even the gun's kick doesn't slow him. He walks through the gap between the dog's halved body before all but one, asleep or awake, recognizes the crack as the sound of murder.

NINE

Not counting Mungo's attempts to sell hot dogs off his backyard barbecue after softball games, there is only one restaurant in town. Given these limitations, Alex and Rachel are surprised the next morning to discover that eating out in Ross River is an international affair. The two of them stand outside the Lucky China Buffet & Tavern, Alex reading aloud the claims of the sign over the door. "Serving 'China,' 'Canadian' and 'Whole World' Cuisine!'" she says. "There's got to be *something* in there we can eat."

"There's room over here!" Mungo calls to them as they walk through the door. Aside from his son, Tom, and a woman that Alex takes to be Mungo's wife sitting across from them, he is the only customer.

"Thanks," Alex says, ushering Rachel over to sit next to Tom and pulling out a chair for herself.

"These are the worst parts of my dysfunctional family," Mungo says by way of introduction. "My wife, Jackie. My son, Tom. The only one missing is my girl, Pam, and she's at the library, reading *books*. Heard of them, Tom? Those heavy things full of paper?"

"Ha," Tom says, and threatens to catapult a french fry at his father with his fork.

"Hello again," Mungo says, turning his attention to the girl.

"This is Rachel."

"She *looks* like a Rachel. But then again, I'd have said she looks like a Bob if you'd told me that was her name."

Alex and Rachel look over the menu, but Mungo tells them, "Just ask for two specials. You'll end up with what they've got too much of, no matter what you order."

Before the food comes, Tom and Rachel duck under the table to whisper stories to each other. Which leaves Jackie to ask where Alex has come from.

"Toronto," she says, surprised by the apology that finds its way into the word. "The other side of the world."

"It's all the same world."

"You're probably right."

"So what do you do on the other side of it?"

"I teach. Kids. Special kids. I'm a teacher," Alex says foolishly, and considers saying more to wipe away the blank expression on Jackie's face.

"You're a friend of Miles?"

"Not really."

"Miles keeps us in fires."

"You mean he fights them."

"She means he *finds* them," Mungo says.

"He doesn't *make* the fires," Alex says, with an irritation she hears but cannot contain.

"We're kind of superstitious around here, I guess," Mungo laughs. "We believe that, sometimes, people can make their own luck."

When the plates of scrambled eggs and bacon arrive, Alex lets Rachel eat her breakfast under the table with Tom. As she chews, Jackie tells Alex about the Ross River school, the computers in the library that had been delivered free from the manufacturer ("You know, so they could put a nice article in the corporate newsletter telling how they'd given some laptops to those glue-sniffing Eskimos") but that the kids had never been instructed how to use.

"Tom here can play video games where you blow the lungs out of Iraqis, and my husband has figured out how to look at porn from Sweden, but that's about it," Jackie says, patting Alex's free hand. "We're prehistoric. We're the goddamn Flintstones."

"Computers aren't everything. What's more important are people who want to get involved."

"Sounds like you're running for mayor. Mungo, do we even *have* a mayor?"

"I think we used to," Mungo says vaguely, sitting sideways with his head down, giggling along with Tom and Rachel under the table.

"Either way, Alex here's got my vote."

"I'm sure you don't need an outsider to tell you how to do things."

"Oh yeah, we can tie our own shoes. And you're right, there's smart people in this town. Committed people. All I'm saying is we can take all the help we can get. Or at least we *should*."

Jackie snorts to indicate a division of opinion on the issue.

"You planning on sticking around awhile?" Mungo asks, his head popping up from under the table.

"Not if I can find someone to take a look at my truck's transmission."

"You're leaving right away?"

"We only came to say hello."

"That's a lot of mileage for one word."

"There's nothing here, anyway."

"We're here."

"I'm sorry. I meant for *us*."

Mungo shakes his head, as though tossing a set of judgments from the front of his mind to somewhere in the back.

"Whatever you do, don't eat in this place tonight," he says to Rachel, crouched down so that his nose waggles six inches above hers.

"Why not?"

"Because I'm going to bring you something."

"A present?"

"Better," Mungo says, coming so close to the girl's face it crosses his eyes. "Moose burgers!"

Miles doesn't use his phone much. He's always found it strange to call people in Ross River, given that you could as easily stand on your front steps and shout your message into just about every living room in town. On this morning, however, he finds himself dialling the only number he knows by heart aside from his own.

"Mr. Bader?" Margot's voice. Tired, but ready for anything.

"It's me."

"Oh. Morning, bruiser."

"How is he?"

"Not bad enough."

"I called to apologize."

"I heard he was cutting pretty close to the bone."

"You know Wade."

"Less and less."

"What's that mean?"

"He's been strange lately. Ever since—"

"Don't."

"I'm just telling you. He's so angry. *Beyond* angry, so that he's in this weird trance a lot of the time. But you can tell there's something bad going on in there."

"Is he hitting you?"

"No more than usual. His heart isn't in it. I'm starting to think that smacking me around is just a way to kill time before he . . ."

"Before what?"

There's a pause so quiet that Miles wonders if they've been disconnected.

"He scares me," she says finally. Tries to laugh, but clears her throat instead. "Looks like you've got your hands full yourself."

"It's complicated."

"You don't say."

Miles can see her sitting at the kitchen table, her hair dripping from the shower, sipping at a jumbo mug of black coffee. She'll let Wade remain dead to the world until the last minute. And she'll let Miles hang on the end of the line until he comes up with something.

"I knew Alex at a different time, when I was a different person," he starts. He thinks of five different ways of beginning five different sentences and abandons each of them in turn. "Rachel, her little girl—I don't know her at all. They just showed up. And it's no good, Margot. It's no good."

"An instant family."

"They're not my family."

"Then why'd they come all the way up here? To ruin your day?"

"It's a formality."

"A woman doesn't spend that much time looking for a man for the sake of formalities."

"How do you—?"

"I spoke with her."

"You *what?*"

He can hear Margot take a sip, and the heat of the coffee passes down his throat as well as hers.

"I bumped into the two of them."

"What'd she tell you?"

"Nothing close to everything."

Miles stares down at his bare feet and thinks they look old. Bulging veins, gnarled toes, the smoothness given way to ugly bumps and ridges. If his feet look old, maybe he does, too. Perhaps that's what Alex has come to tell him. He's not what he used to be and it's time he woke up to the fact. Just look at those feet.

"I want you to do something for me," he says.

"I won't have time to make a steak delivery before I go."

"It's not that. I want you to radio in now and then when you go out on this hunt."

"And tell you what?"

"Where you are. That you're okay. You can get me at the fire office or in the truck. Will you do that?"

"Whatever you say," she says, doubt pulling at her words. "But I've got to tell you, you're spooking me a bit."

In the background there's a growling yawn, followed by bare feet thudding over linoleum. Miles wonders if Wade's feet have grown as unsightly as his own.

"I better go," Margot whispers, and he's about to say something more, something about a dream he had where everything went wrong, but she's already gone.

Alex and Rachel walk through Ross River with Mungo as their guide. Alex looks about her at the dishevelled cabins and corroded trailers and, not for the first time, feels that anywhere has the potential of being home. At the same time, she knows that such transience exists only in theory. It's the attachments that get in the way. Sometimes it is a place itself (she had friends at university who longed for their homes on the Newfoundland coast or solemn prairies with an intensity she had at first tried to dismiss as lyrical arrogance but in the end had envied). More often, it's people. A single friendship could be enough. A lover. Family, in any one of its nuclear, alternative or haunted forms.

Not that Miles could ever make a family out of Alex and Rachel. If anything, she believed that seeing him again was what had to be put behind her before she could begin to form a more permanent idea of family in her life, however that might be achieved. A new man. The contented resignation to single motherhood. Who knows? She had heard of farming communes made up of people like Rachel and herself, working together and sharing the food, the beds. Nothing would be ruled out in advance.

For now, she walks through another town that is not her home. One so alien and radiating defeat it counts as one on a long list of those that never could be.

But there is no question that it is Mungo's. He keeps telling her that he wants to show them what this place is all about, but after a while, she figures that their walk has no specific destination. It's the neighbours he wants them to meet. Tinkering under the hoods of trucks, playing tricycle smash-up derby, hanging laundry on lines sagging between cedar branches. Some say hello, though most refuse to speak. All of them stare.

That Mungo Capoose leads the parade makes it official. Government employed, a council member at the band office, second in command on the fire team. The sort of fellow you only respected more even as you laughed at him, his pincushion nose inflated with rye, his high-kneed walk. By the end of the hour Mungo has brought Alex and Rachel before half of Ross River's population. Judging by the mostly blank looks that have received them, Alex would judge their campaign a failure. Yet Mungo seems pleased.

"Not everyone is awake this early," he says, and Alex glances at her watch. Ten to noon.

Mungo leads them back to the Welcome Inn. It's the first time his face shows explicit curiosity.

"It's not my business, but I think I know Miles about as well as——"

"You're right. It's *not* your business."

"I'm saying he's broken, that's all. And that's a different thing from being bad."

"You want me to *forgive* him?"

Mungo looks at her, and sees something that makes him take a step back from her into the street.

"I was only——"

"You can't know the promises that someone's broken just by looking at him. And you can't ask someone to forgive what hasn't been done to you."

Alex smiles, but it's a mask. The girl comes running up to join them and she takes her by the hand.

"Thanks for the tour," Alex says, and starts back the way they came.

TEN

A day and a half later, Miles is in his truck, alone, heading out of town. His head emptied of all thoughts but one.

By the time he gets back, Alex and the girl will be gone.

He'd decided this was the best way to handle things only the night before, lying awake in his bed, trying not to think about the events of the preceding morning and afternoon. Even now, the day before only comes to him in painful snatches. His climb up Eagle's Nest Bluff with Alex and Rachel. The osprey flying over the river below. The handful of words he exchanged with the girl at the cliff's top that he's still trying to unscramble. Later. He'd get around to their strange hours on Eagle's Nest Bluff later, to sorting out the riddle of what he asked and what she answered over the interminable revisitations that were fated to be the rest of his life. He's just glad that, this time, he has a halfway believable excuse to make his escape.

As part of his duties as supervisor, Miles has to check on the handful of fire watchtowers in the region at least once each month. Two of them haven't seen him since June. A tour that should take him about three days. More than long enough to ensure that when he returns, nobody will be waiting for him.

He tries to credit himself for at least giving Alex a call before he left. But even that hadn't gone as he'd planned. When she answered, the idea of a no-harm-done goodbye strikes him as ridiculous, and in an instant he thinks of something else. As it passes his lips, he wonders whether he intended to say it in the first place.

"I was thinking," he says. "I'm going to be checking on some towers for the next couple of nights and, seeing what Earl is gouging you for, I thought you might want to stay here while I'm gone."

"Where will you leave the keys?" she answers without hesitation.

Miles knew they would go, had wanted them to go, yet had somehow counted on seeing the girl one more time before they did. Not that he has anything to say to her. He just assumed he would be given the chance to take a snapshot of her before she left. One he would conjure not with a lens but in his head. An ever-changing version that would age as he aged, so that she might be called upon if needed, far down the line.

"I'm terrible at this," he says with an idiotic chuckle.

"I don't know of anybody who's good at it."

"Well, then. I guess I want to thank you for bringing her here."

"Say her name."

"What?"

"She's like Tim. And your dad, Edward. Not saying their names doesn't make them go away."

He could argue with this, or simply hang up, because he's not sure that she's right, and even if she is, this kind of dissection is the last thing he needs. On any other of the preceding thousand mornings of his life, such prying would instantly push him into rage, and he waits for it, eyes closed.

"Rachel," he says. "Thank you for bringing Rachel."

They may mumble a farewell after this, they may not. He doesn't remember anything more, in any case. Miles hears the click at the end of the line and the world goes black, like standing in a windowless room when the bulb burns out. He's not afraid. It's a matter of getting used to it. You just stay where you are in the dark for a while until you can almost see again.

Is there a polite way to tell someone to shut the fuck up? This has been the primary question Margot has found herself mulling over on the forty-five-minute drive out of town and down the seldom used Lapie Canyon Road, listening to Elsie Bader chirp on about, well, about *what?* Sweet bugger all. A shower of touristy inquiries

and exclamations at "all the nature" around them that are so empty
of significance Margot can only guess the old woman has carefully
intended to speak without saying a single thing.

Margot checks the rear-view mirror every few minutes,
expecting Mr. Bader to take things in hand and stuff his bug shirt in
his wife's mouth, but he only pretends to sleep, his forehead leaving grease stains on the window. He's used to this, apparently.
And Wade, Margot knows, is so painkilled that, for the moment,
he is able to endure even this fresh hell.

Mungo's son is back there, too, having been brought along at
the last minute. She waved Tom over to her truck as she'd passed
him and Mungo giving Alex and Rachel a tour of the town and
asked him if he'd like to make a couple hundred bucks. The kid
had joined her in the bush from time to time in the past. He was
capable and, most important as far as Margot is concerned,
learned by example instead of asking dumb questions. Just the sort
of help she could use carrying the packs on a job like this. Tom is
alone in appearing amused by Mrs. Bader's running commentary.
He keeps a sideways grin on his face at any rate, though true to
form, offers no words of his own.

What's the worst thing about this woman? Margot wonders, and
knows the answer even as she asks it. It's that everything is "wonderful" to her. The word is so liberally sprayed through her mus-
ings that it makes Margot's teeth ache. By the time the truck pulls
over at the trailhead, Elsie Bader has singlehandedly managed to
bleach all the wonder out of the world. And not just the formerly
wonderful things one might discover on this particular morning,
but forevermore, as though her southern-fried burbles have veiled
what was in fact a sinister incantation, a black spell released into
the air.

Things are a little better once they start into the woods, though
Margot can tell the going will be slow. She could hear Mr. Bader's
laboured breathing within the first hundred yards. This, coupled
with his disturbing refusal to talk, has contributed to a pall being

cast over the hunting party before they put the first half mile behind them. It's obvious that Wade isn't about to be of much assistance, either. As a result, Tom shoulders more weight than any of them, though the kid doesn't seem to mind. Every time Margot glances at him he's keeping stride next to Elsie Bader. The two of them have become fast, if inexplicable, friends.

They stop early for breakfast. Mrs. Bader pulls all the food out of her pack and sets to laying out a lavish picnic of their rations. Wade starts a fire and puts a pot on for coffee before splaying out on his back, his arm covering his eyes. "I'll fix us a *wonderful* brunch in a jiffy!" Mrs. Bader calls out, and for the first time, Margot finds herself a little grateful for the woman's presence. The old lady's got pep, you had to admit.

Her husband, on the other hand, shuffles over to Margot where she stands out of hearing of the others, his complexion showing only slightly more colour than the bark on the trunks of birch that surround them.

"How do we get them to come to us?"

"We don't. We go to them."

"I read that they can smell us from miles off," he says, sniffing. "Why not just spray around something they like and pick 'em off when they show up?"

"It doesn't work that way. A bear smells us and goes in the other direction more often than it comes any closer."

"Unless they're hungry enough. Or if what they smell is fear."

"A bear doesn't smell fear. It smells *you*. To a bear, people are nothing *but* fear."

"That's funny. It's a view I subscribe to myself."

Margot doesn't laugh, because he isn't joking. Jackson Bader had been the president of the fourth-largest steelmaker in the Midwest over the twenty-five years that America needed steel more than anything else, more than Japanese computer engineering or million-dollar slogans brainstormed by Ivy League marketing brats. They were the last of the good times, as far as Bader is concerned, or at least the comprehensible times. The days when what was manufactured were hard things—cars, girders, missiles—instead of fluffball ideas. There were few better than he at what he did. And what was that? More than anything, his job was to put people in their place. He's aware of the accusations of coldness. Even he can't deny the sweeping layoffs, the unforgiving suppression of boardroom *coups d'état,* the union busting. But Jackson Bader would identify his principal talent not as heartlessness, but courage. He was among the rare company of men possessed of the true leader's capacity for making unpleasant decisions, the tough-loving patriarch able to hand down the punishments required in keeping an orderly home.

Even though they have lingered in the breakfast camp for a quarter-hour already, Bader continues to swallow air in gulps. To Margot, what's worrying is not so much his lack of conditioning—she's dealt with worse clients on that count—but that he seems to be fighting something within him. He breathes like a man who has forgotten how.

"Are you feeling all right?"

"Don't trouble yourself about me, Miss Lemontagne," he says, pronouncing it *Lemon Tang.*

"I just need to know if you can make it to where we need to go."

"You must have learned a thing or two about nature in your time out in this shit." He steps forward and grabs her forearm. Close enough that she can smell his breath. Wet straw and Pepsodent. "People got to take care of themselves, don't you think?"

"Get your hand—"

"So all you got to worry about is finding us some big footprints. How's that?"

Margot jerks her arm free. Without it to hold on to, Bader instantly shrinks. The brief show of strength is gone, and he's a bloodless old man again, spinning his head around to find his wife.

Margot watches him go and wishes her feelings about Jackson Bader were more consistent, a dislike on all fronts. But the fact is, there is something in the way he speaks to her that she can't help but be a little interested in listening to. It's there in the worldly gravel at the back of his throat: conspiratorial, teasing, letting her in on an indecent joke that she alone could appreciate. The effect he has on her puts Margot in the strange (but not entirely unfamiliar) situation of seeking approval from a man she has little respect for.

It may only be that he's a good-looking son of a bitch for his age. That's what Wade had said about Bader when he first showed up. Margot felt it was an accurate enough description. She *did* find Jackson Bader handsome, in the bullheaded way of grown-up GIs or college football stars. The slightly ridiculous Robert Mitchum squint. But it's none of these assets that prevent Margot from hating the old man. It's that he doesn't care *what* she thinks that makes her curious about him. He's come out here for a reason that has only a secondary relation to bringing down a Boone and Crockett grizzly, and she'd like to know what it is.

When Margot returns to the camp's fire, Elsie Bader asks another of her tour-bus questions.

"Margot! I was wondering how many bears there would be in the Yukon. Tom says he couldn't guess."

"Nobody knows the exact number. But most have it that there's twice as many grizzlies living outside of Whitehorse as there are people."

"Oh, Jackson!" Mrs. Bader exclaims. "We're *outnumbered!*"

Bader opens his mouth and shows his teeth. A store-bought smile of new dentures, vacant as an ice tray.

"It'll only make it easier for them to find us, dear," he says.

Miles's plan is to visit two towers, each about fifty miles apart as the crow flies. Normally, he looks forward to these tours—talking to the watchers who spend four months straight on their own doing little aside from looking out over the endless north, people who, like Miles, treasure their loneliness. He likes visiting the unmanned towers even more. He usually lingers on these trips, enjoying the fulfillment of responsibility while taking pleasure in being left to his own devices. But this time he keeps moving. The first tower is vacant, and he hopes to check on it and head out again before nightfall, sleeping midway between it and the next. It may not be so easy. Through the rear-view mirror, a black thunder-head pursues him.

When he parks a mile from the first tower and hikes in to its base, frigid drops are already slapping against his forehead. It makes the climb up the ladder chillier than he would like. He wishes he'd brought his gloves. The aluminum rungs bite through his palms. He makes himself confirm every new grip by sight.

By the time he climbs onto the deck, the thunderhead has become enormous on the horizon. Miles steps inside and closes the door. The wind whispers threats through the glass.

Even when fully functional, the only piece of operating equip-ment on hand aside from a radio is an Osborne Fire Finder, which hasn't been removed from this tower yet. Miles strokes its rotat-ing metal ring, the handle that turns its sight around 360 degrees to spot smoke from any direction. A solid, useful thing. As is the tower's only place to sit: a swivel captain's chair, its legs wrapped in layers of chipped-glass insulation. During periods of lightning, the watchers sit in this "safe seat," so that if a bolt strikes, the charge will pass through everything but them. Miles counts two zigzags touch the earth in the time it takes him to catch his breath.

He settles himself in the grounded chair and sends his mind out toward the approaching storm, circling over the crowns of black spruce. There is something in the spongy, coastal sky that makes him think of his mother, sitting alone in her rain-stained bungalow near the tracks in the south end of Nanaimo, studying the next chess move she will record on a postcard to mail to her runaway son. She would have the window open, letting in the intermittent whiffs of salt water, petrol and salmon emptied onto the docks. Now his mind has no choice but to stay with her. Floating over the town he grew up in and where his mother will be buried, trapped in a spiral of memory.

After his father left, Miles was a bad kid here. His crimes were soft-drugged, vandalizing, split-lipped. Yet they were serious enough to flirt with lengthy visits to juvie detention centres and to leave his mother in a state of near-constant worry. He's sorry about this as much as anything.

All this was before the fussily landscaped condos were built next to the port, before the pedestrian signals were outfitted with timers that count down from thirty so that the arthritic gentry could calculate the pace of their crossings for raisin buns at the "cappuccino bistro" where a bar called the Bucket of Blood used to stand. Miles looks down and sees that other things haven't changed at all. The cracked concrete snaking away from the harbour and falling past the Commercial Hotel. The twinkling of Fiesta Square Bowling's rotating F, towering over everything as though it was Nanaimo's principal claim, the promise it wished to beam out to the ships that might spot it as they found their way in from a furious sea.

It is this older version of the town that his father escaped from. One of the running men. Each with their own circumstances, brooding secrecy, self-justifying compulsions. The north is peppered with the sort of people that Miles believes his father must have been. He knows this because he's a running man too.

Why do they run? Miles is aware of the usual accusations. Cowardice, lust, wilful cruelty. But Miles believes that most of the time, these men are really trying to wriggle free from the constraints of who they are, the fixed particulars of identity. It's not some other, better life they seek, but the disappearance from life altogether. They run to escape the universal burden of selfhood.

Not that this allows him any sympathy toward others like his father. Miles may have run, but he didn't run from a child—at least, not one that he saw born and grow for the first five years of its life. Rachel doesn't count. He tries to tell himself this as the storm blows all around him, the tower wavering in the strong wind. Miles isn't like his father because he never left a child that he had spoken to, or held in his arms. He has gotten through the last few years on this slim distinction. Now even this has been taken from him.

With a split of thunder the storm engulfs the tower. The rain strikes the windows so hard he can see them shivering in their frames.

Miles lifts himself from the chair and stands on the steel floor. He kicks the door open and lets the rain drive in sideways, spraying the cobwebs from the corners and spinning the chair around on its pivot.

He can see the lightning getting closer. The last bolt struck a hilltop not a quarter mile away. He grips both his hands to the metal struts of the tower's frame and waits for the blackest cloud to find him.

Miles feels that a decision is about to be made, if not by him then by an unpredictable determination of fate. He wishes only that the storm tell him what to do. That, or flash-fry him into a pile of carbon and put him beyond decisions forever.

It comes in a rush, filling the world with shadows. The clouds tumbling lower until their underbellies could be touched with a raised hand.

Miles keeps his fingers locked around the steel struts. It occurs to him that if the lightning hits the tower, he won't be around to hear the thunder.

There is a full minute when he stands surrounded by grey sheets of mist. When he comes out the other end, the daylight blinds him. Miles looks back and sees the cloud curl up into itself like a jellyfish making its way to the surface, its hanging tendrils of rain already fading. There is a last growl of thunder, more bemused than menacing, before the storm blows north over the Nadaleen Range.

Miles collapses back into the chair and spins around. The fire didn't want him this time, either. He doesn't know what this means beyond the fact that he's still here, turning in circles, staring at the fields of green. But perhaps there is something even in that.

All three bears smell the hunters entering the woods. The sow had heard them, too, minutes before her cubs. Twittering laughter. The scrape of camp pots. Truck doors swung shut.

She scrambles higher and at first the cubs don't know what the hurry is. When she stops on the other side of a small ridge sprayed purple with fireweed, she turns them around to face the direction they have just come from. The hunters have come to a stop as well. The she-grizzly has the overwhelming feeling that they are close already.

The cubs pick up mostly on the delicacies they'd never encountered before in their lives—peanut butter, coffee, raisins. Each of these presents nose-puzzles to the young bears, questions of where food of this kind grew, how they might get close enough to the packs to have a snort inside. But the sow won't allow them any more time. She walks behind them now, pushing them up the foothills in a gradual ascent.

Only the sow knows that the pack carriers are hunters. This certainty comes less from an interpretation of scent than from experience: if a group of humans enter the woods a good distance from town, odds are they mean to kill something. The she-grizzly has seen her share of harmless hikers and campers, the ones who shimmy up the swaying trunks of eight-foot-high saplings at the sight of her loping along a game trail a hundred yards away. But she has never seen those sorts in this particular territory. There's little point in satisfying the itch of curiosity by going any closer. She has witnessed the penalty that such an interest will bring.

As now, there had been a group of them, four males and, unusual for human hunters, a female as well. The sow and her mate had come the night before for the treasures of the Ross River dump, and now dozed side by side on a mattress of grass halfway up the valley. The smell of sweat and chocolate woke them an hour before dawn.

The sow was in the first stage of pregnancy, milk-heavy and slow. Her mate stayed at her rump, calculating distances, launch pads for counterattack. The hunters were not fast, either. Yet there was a good tracker among them, one not fooled by the bears' switchbacks and creek crossings.

The sow's mate left her to track back to the hunters in order to mark their position. While he was gone, the she-grizzly lay down to gather her strength, her fur camouflaged among the brown bark of trunks. She wasn't frightened of the hunters. Although she had been tracked like this before, they had never gotten anywhere near close enough for a shot. But the tiny cubs she carries roll about within her, and she interprets their sudden movement as a warning.

As she waits, the she-grizzly hears footfalls in the bush. Careful, light, singular. Coming around in a big circle, taking a place somewhere ahead on the course they were travelling on.

When the hunter comes up against the direction of the breeze, the sow smells that it is the female, tracking alone. At the same time, the sow's mate joins her. They are now being stalked not only from behind but from ahead. It is also clear to the sow that her mate led the female hunter directly to them.

The bears strike off in a heading not of their own choosing, down deeper into the Tintina Trench, where the woods are thicker but with fewer outlets for escape. There are no more smells to inform them. As they run, the pregnant sow imagines she can feel her cubs clawing over each other, as though drowning inside her.

It is the female hunter who finally cuts them off, trapping them in a lunar clearing of chert rock. The sow sees her first. Standing upslope, the snout of the woman's rifle trained square at the she-grizzly's eyes.

Before the bears even have a chance to come to a full stop, the hunter notices the sow and boar's genders. She determines that these two must have been recently rutting, and that the sow is now likely pregnant. It makes the female hunter switch her aim to the sow's mate. The same steady bead on the flat front of his skull.

The male hunters break noisily into the clearing. All of them fall to their knees at the sight of the animals with one exception. A bearded man taller than the others, who waves his rifle in front of him. The sow focuses on his distinct scent. His skin a rank mixture of whisky and terror.

A couple of the hunters on their knees shout something, and the female replies in calm tones. The bearded man alone refuses to listen. He raises his rifle and, almost without looking, points it into the middle of the clearing. The barrel continues to flail around. Aimed from the hunter's own boots, to the bears, to a patch of indigo sky.

He fires and tries to run away at the same time.

The female hunter shouts something as the bearded man stumbles backwards. It makes him lower his rifle before catching the heel of his boot on one of the upturned rocks, flipping his feet out from under him so that he lands on his back. The gun spins from his hands, clattering to the ground outside his reach.

Everyone looks to the male grizzly. He has been gut-shot—the bullet blasted through the animal's intestines and out the other side. An injury that, for a bear of his size and age, is not immediately fatal.

The sow's mate blinks curiously at the exit wound. With hesitation, he tries to push his insides back in with his paw. When he decides to run, he trips over his bowels, trailing out behind him like pink rope.

When the female hunter fires a bullet neatly through a point two feet below the male grizzly's shoulder hump, something like soap pours out his nose. The bear watches the fluid drop to the stones, fascinated. He lifts his head to the female hunter and opens his mouth wide, less in threat than in the articulation of a thought that has suddenly escaped him. Discovering that he has nothing to say after all, he closes his mouth, blinking rapidly, and takes a single step toward his mate. The act of lifting his one paw from the earth undoes the animal's balance, and he falls heavily on his side. He inhales once, but the air passes straight through him and out the gaping hole in his lungs, making the fur around the wound dance in his breath.

The sow runs.

As she runs now. She thinks of the hunters that killed her mate as she urges her cubs up the same slope she ran across two seasons ago. The sow doesn't remember the details of the bearded man's face. But she remembers the woman, her long hair swishing over her back like a tail. She didn't see either of them this morning. But a sense that is neither sight nor smell tells her that the same two are among these hunters nevertheless.

She will move the cubs along steadily, stay high. The sow grunts in quiet hiccups that set the pace as they traverse what she remembers more and more as a killing ground. There is no doubt that these are the same trees, the same out-of-nowhere meadows she had crossed with her mate, running as hard as she could with the cubs sloshing inside her, their tracks a clear map in the rain-softened earth.

Unlike then, the soil they pound over now is relatively hard. And this time she knows who hunts them.

In Miles's experience, fire watchers come in one of two versions: the ones attracted to the job because they are unhinged, and the ones who become unhinged on account of the job. Ruby Ritter, the watcher at the Mount Locken Tower for the past three seasons, is likely both. It's why Miles likes her as much as he does.

"Pushing forty" is all she'll say whenever he asks her age, but he suspects she's been pushing against the same birthday for the last five or so. A bouquet of red pipecleaners atop her head, her skin freckled like a banana left too long in the sun. Divorced. She had never admitted this directly to Miles, but it was obvious all the same. The vague, historical references to a shared domestic life, the rolled eyes to introduce anecdotes started with "There was a man I knew once . . ." And she wrote. For as long as he knew her, Ruby was adding single-spaced sheet after sheet to a pile high enough to have required the decimation of half the forest she could see from her tower. It was the absurd arrogance of the writer in Ruby, the mad-scientist-like certainty that her bold experiment would change everything that made her obnoxious, comic and pitiable in equal turns. Any thoughts that Miles sometimes had about writing down his experiences in order to help sort them out were swept away by a single afternoon's visit with Ruby, and for that he was appreciative.

Miles climbs the tower's ladder, and when he pokes through her floor, Ruby is ready with a cup of coffee so strong it brings a syrup to his eyes.

"No way you're napping on the job drinking *this* stuff," Miles says, standing above Ruby, who sits straight in her chair. He can't help feeling like a barber readying himself to hack through her curls.

"Nothing gets by me."

"The boys are itching for something to work on, but it sounds like you've got nothing to help us out."

"I sees 'em, I don't starts 'em. But I could always send you guys out ghostchasing if you wanted."

"Standing around in a fog patch won't get us overtime either. Though I thank you for the offer."

She hasn't seen another human being in at least two weeks, and he hasn't been here longer than three minutes, and already Ruby is distracted, her eyes pulled to the accidental shrine she has set up for her magnum-opus-in-progress. Pencil stubs, highlighters, torn bits of jotted notes all guarding the monolithic slab on the table, noticeably higher than when Miles was here at the beginning of the season. He looks at the yellow tongues of Post-it notes sticking out of it like a series of staircases moving through the text, and hopes that, for her own good, this will be Ruby's last year on the job. *That's her brain over there,* he thinks. *That's Ruby's brain and it needs to get out more often.*

"How's the writing?" Miles asks her, as he might ask after "the elbow" of someone with their arm in a sling.

"I think there's been a breakthrough."

"Oh?"

"I'd been telling myself it was a novel. That it was *fiction,* y'know? But then I *realized.*"

She pauses dramatically, her upper teeth clamped on her lower lip. Miles will have to say something for either of their lives to continue.

"What did you realize?"

"It was all true!"

"Like an autobiography."

"More true than that. The *true* truth. The stuff that nobody can face straight on, because it's *too* true."

"I see."

"The world is nothing but a marketplace of falsehoods. But I'm free of that now. There's nobody to lie to up here."

"There wouldn't be much point in it," Miles concedes.

"It's going to blow them away," she says, letting her eyes gaze out the window, as though the forest was seething with acquisition editors, all shaking contracts in their fists and begging for a glimpse at the truth.

"You figuring to get it published?" Miles asks, as he does every time the topic of Ruby's book comes up.

"They wouldn't be able to handle it," she answers, as she does every time. "Besides, I'm not writing it for them."

"Who are you writing it for?"

"Myself."

"That's a hell of a small audience."

"Do I look like I care what other people think?"

Yes, Miles nearly says. *You look exactly like someone who cares what other people think. You care so much it's made you lose half your marbles and run away to live alone in a treehouse, writing a two-thousand-page letter to yourself.*

"I wouldn't know what you care about, Ruby," he says instead.

Miles looks out at what Ruby looks out at every day, and suddenly wants to leave. Not that he has a place in mind to go to. It's that, from up here, the rolling expanse of green makes him claustrophobic. So still and commanding, he can feel the time passing within him, the accelerated massing of age growing like fat around his heart.

"And how are *you?*" Ruby asks with visible effort.

"Just fine."

"You don't look it."

"No? Well, I guess I haven't looked fine for a while now," Miles says, absently cranking the Osborne Fire Finder next to him. "I just need a fire."

"It's on the way," Ruby promises, her voice already retreating back into her own thoughts, her book, the breakthrough she is willing herself to believe. "Don't you worry about it, Chief. I'll send a good fire your way real soon."

Miles makes his way back to his truck and tries to close his ears to the chattering trees. Poplar leaves brush together to form words in a language he can't understand but once could, a secret childhood code he has grown out of. He catches the gist all the same. The trees are judging him.

As he walks, he hears the distinct thump of human footfall behind him. He swings around to see who's there. Nothing. Before he continues on he spits, hoping to rid his mouth of the name he feels on the edge of speaking aloud.

He works to turn his mind to something else and comes up with his crew. Even out here, not an hour passes without Miles thinking about them. More and more they arrive in the form of a horrific vision, as four grinning corpses bolting up from shallow graves of ash. Other times he is visited only by their faces, enlarged on the screen of his closed eyelids, winking and whispering, sharing their knowledge of a crime he'd so far gotten away with. Yet when he tried to remember exactly what it was that he'd done, it slipped away, returning to the shadows like a fish that's caught sight of a glinting hook.

When he arrived as Ross River fire chief five years ago, his crew had every reason not to welcome him. White, first time in the Territory, parachuted in by the government pencil necks in Whitehorse. And he wasn't the friendliest guy they'd ever met, either. That nasty scar was the least of it. A distance they first read as arrogance, then contempt. Mungo alone made an effort, inviting Miles to join their table in the lounge, climbing up to the roof of his cabin armed with a hammer and a case of beer to help him repair a hole where the ice had pried up the shingles. In return, Miles had given them what he could. Not the openness that was beyond him but his loyalty.

If he had the authority to sign their cheques until each of their retirement days, he would. Miles is responsible for his crew's training and safety, but not their contracts. No amount of reminding himself of this saves him from the plain fact that some if not all of them will be without jobs next year if there isn't a fire to write up within the next couple of weeks. The government funding that is awarded to regional attack teams depends solely on how many smokers a particular crew had to chase. There was some forgiveness for "wet summers," but not a lot. Last year had already been a quiet one for Ross River. Time's up.

A pink slip wouldn't matter much to King. He was from Outside, on his way to a university degree, free of the attachments of skin or history. King wanted a fire as much as anyone, probably more. But if he was like the others of his kind Miles has worked with, he wanted it for the experience, the c.v. padding, the rush. Jerry, Crookedhead and Mungo, on the other hand, needed a fire to hold aloft their respective hopes for an almost-new truck, the return of a lost family, the survival of a cash-strapped community. If these positions dried up, there would be no transfers. Not for these guys, who clung to just the sort of term-contracts the budget cutters would love to see the end of.

Miles's situation is no better. If they closed down the Ross River team, he doubts that anywhere else would have him. There was the kid's death to darken his resumé. Worse, probably, are the rumours.

Drinks too much, I hear. And he's got a fuse so short you only have to look at him for it to go off. Knows fire, all right. But between you and me, he's a bad-luck kind of guy. Remember the Dragon's Back a few years ago?

It was for reasons like these that crewmen sometimes started their own fires. It didn't happen all the time, but it happened. Miles could only guess at the total number of smokers he'd cut line around that had been lit by a squirt of kerosene and a dropped match. Even within fire teams, off season or on, sober or drunk, arson was not a topic for open conversation. It went without saying that, caught once, you would never work in fire again. But there were also penalties that went well beyond having to find a new job. Fines. A criminal record. Prison time. Sometimes worse. Sometimes, people burned.

Despite this, no matter how severe the threat of discovery, crews will continue to set fires for as long as they are paid to fight them. There is overtime to claim, child support payments to catch up on, bottles to empty. The fire need not be anything serious, just enough to make the guys carry out the gear and put it to a day's work. A few hours spent lightening the load of the pisstank on your back could justify a new contract for a full year's salary.

There is another kind of firestarter, spoken of even less than the ones who do it for money. Years ago, Miles had worked with a guy in B.C.—Brad, he thinks his name was—who, the following season, was sentenced to nine years for starting what grew into a thousand-acre wildfire. Eight of those nine years were the result of his conviction not for arson, but manslaughter. On the last day before the fire was rained into submission, it had taken a crazed turn toward town that swept away a dozen homes, along with the lives of three crew members, trapped in a root cellar they had baked to death in.

Based on Miles's recollection of the guy—the silence he'd fall into staring into the camp barbecue, the awestruck surveying of even the smallest smouldering snag—Brad started fires for a satisfaction that had nothing to do with paycheques. By Miles's estimation, of the burns ignited by firefighters, nine-tenths are motivated by money, and the rest by pleasure in seeing the forest lit up like a giant birthday cake with your name on it.

When Miles reaches his truck he jumps into the cab and closes the door behind him as though he's being followed. After driving cautiously along the rutted access road for half an hour, he manages to push most thoughts of contracts and firestarters out of his mind. As a distraction, he allows himself to stop the truck to play one of his favourite games. Rolls the window down and lays on the horn. He laughs at the pathetic complaint that travels no farther than the first tangle of fallen trunks. But the laughter fails to bring him around, the sound coming up from inside him empty as the sound of the horn in the truck's interior.

More than anything, Miles feels awake. Everything around him overly alive to his senses, the volume cranked, colours bleeding. Even the dust suspended in the sunlit air of the cab crowds his vision. The thousands of square miles outside are no better. All the space he previously assumed to be limitless now appears two-dimensional, a shoddy stage backdrop.

It's at least six hours before sunset, but as he drives on into denser forest, what light makes its way through the branches above is only enough to create a dusky murk of shadows. Miles turns on his headlights for the first time in three weeks. The two cones of light excite the cloud of midges warming themselves over the hood. He flicks on the high beams, but it only brings the corner ahead of him into abrupt focus, the creeping brown veins that reach across the trail. Sound can't penetrate it. Light won't hold it back.

The truck comes into a turn and Miles gears down, slapping the wheel. He makes it, then feels his rear wheels sink into a soft rut. Kicks it into reverse. The engine cries at his stomped foot.

He lurches back, then forward so fast that mud sprayed up by the front tires slaps the windshield on its way down. Out, but now he's blind. He flips the wipers on and keeps gunning, preferring to risk being bumped by a tree to getting stuck again.

It takes three swipes of the blades for the glass to be cleared. And when it is, he sees a figure standing in the road ahead.

Miles drives straight at it. There may still be time to stop before hitting whoever is there, but he keeps his foot down.

With another blink, he recognizes who it is.

The kid's wearing the same fluorescent vest and green coveralls he wore on the Dragon's Back. Now, though, much of this has been burned away, so that he is a scarecrow patchwork of nylon and charred flesh. At the sight of Miles bearing down on him, the kid raises both his arms in an appeal for him to stop. His mouth opens—to call out, to take an overdue breath—and keeps opening, until his jaw hangs flat, a black plate against his throat.

For the first time, Miles considers stopping. A human figure stands in the road ahead, asking for help. By reflex, his foot drifts over the brake.

But comes down on the gas.

The truck finds drier earth and accelerates into the twenty-yard straightaway between it and the kid. Miles expects that, as he gets closer, the figure will disappear according to the normal means of ghostly departure, a blink-and-he's-gone or puff of smoke. Instead, he only comes into greater focus, his waving more furious.

The kid isn't there. But Miles can't stop himself from shutting his eyes.

There's a thump when he hits him. It's only one of the thousand rocks that fly up against the undercarriage on a road like this, but it comes at the same moment the front grille would have mown the kid down.

And keeps coming. The truck drifts on for a second or two and Miles can feel something being dragged along with it. Limbs caught in the axle. A pair of fists pounding against his muffler.

He skids to a stop and opens his eyes. For a time, he stares ahead and wonders if this is what losing your mind feels like. Embarrassing, more than anything. A slow slide into new and more foolish situations that cannot be avoided.

Miles checks the rear-view to see if the kid's body lies in the road. Nothing but fresh tire tracks bathed red in the glow of his brakelights.

"You should've remembered," Miles says aloud. "I never pick up hitchhikers."

He knew that seeing Alex and the girl would have its side effects. That the kid would be one of them is something of a curveball, but as far as he knows, this may well be the nature of shock, of grief. It likes to take you by surprise.

Miles drives on. The road here is no smoother than a dried-out river bottom, but he jolts along faster than he should. Twice, black stars cloud his vision from his head slamming against the cab's ceiling. His foot only pushes deeper. He's not sure where he's going, but for the first time in what feels like forever, there's somewhere he has to be.

ELEVEN

After breakfast, the hunters lift their packs and head out along the Trench's north-facing slope. There is something of a trail for the first half-hour, but Margot steers them off it, crossing first a squishy meadow, soaked by one of the hit-and-run showers of the last few days, before taking them into an endless stand of birches, the white trunks so close it tickles the backs of their eyes to look at them.

Margot walks in front, far slower than she's used to. She has to wait for Bader, followed by Tom and Elsie, and Wade in the rear, head down. There are frequent stops for Margot to consult her compass and pretend to study the ground for tracks, although she knows exactly where they are and that they will not yet find what they are looking for. The pauses are for Jackson Bader's benefit alone. Stooped over with his hands resting on his knees, a string of curses rising out of him like bubbles.

"Which way do we go to find the grizzlies?" Elsie Bader asks lightly as they enter the birches, as though inquiring after the location of the ladies' shoe section.

"First, we go to where they like to go," Margot says, falling back so that if the old woman insists on talking, neither of them will have to shout. "Then we try to find their tracks. But we have to be very quiet."

"Oh, of *course*. Quiet as Tom."

"Even quieter."

"Well, *I* certainly will be."

"It might be too late."

"Sorry?"

"They could be listening already."

"How do you mean?"

"The big bears, the ones we're after—they hunt us as much as we hunt them. I've seen some terrible things."

"Isn't that something?"

Margot decides to terrify the woman. In the name of ensuring her silence, Margot tells Mrs. Bader true stories about what bears can do when they put a mind to it. She starts with how when they attack, they rip your jaw out with their teeth, so that you lose the ability to bite them back. Sometimes, they drag unfinished kills to another location and bury them alive, to be returned to later. Even bringing one down with the advantage of a clear shot can be a flawed business. A gut-shot grizzly will run off and dig a hole in the ground. When you come to finish it, it jumps out of its hiding place and dedicates the last of its life to chewing through your legs, so that it might enjoy the consolation of watching you bleed to death next to him. Hit them in the hip and they walk on their front legs like a man doing a handstand. Hit them in the heart and they howl.

"Let's just say it's not a sound I'd care to hear again."

"Uh-huh," the old woman manages. And then, just one last thing out of her for the next hour. Its syllables cracked and tinny, a broken toy of a word. "Wonderful," she says.

Margot glances back at the others and notices Wade standing on his own off to the side of the trail. Even Mr. Bader has passed in front of him.

What she also registers is that Wade has his shotgun butt raised to his shoulder. His aim on the back of Elsie's head.

A joke. Yet Wade's crooked smile arrives only after he catches Margot watching him. Even from where she stands, she can see the exposed red tip next to the Mossberg's trigger. The safety is off.

By the time Margot makes it back to him, he has lowered the gun and is fishing in his pocket.

"What the fuck are you doing?"

"Just kidding around."

"That thing's loaded."

"It *is?*"

Wade looks down at the gun at his side and shakes his head. Then he opens his fist to show three tablets laid out in his palm.

"If you don't stop chewing on those you're going to drop before noon."

"I need them."

"And I need *you*."

"I'm hurting."

"Give them to me."

"I don't think so."

Wade takes a step and draws back his hand. It gives him the room to deliver a roundhouse to the side of her head if he chooses.

"Don't," she says.

Wade shrugs. Flicks all three pills into his mouth and swallows.

Whenever she hears someone say that people never change, Margot thinks that, among all truisms, this is the least true. In her experience, people changed, all right. They did nothing *but* change. Take Wade, for instance. There's no chance you'd ever confuse the man she had heart-drunkenly fallen for almost a decade ago with this wounded animal whose actions she could no longer predict.

A big kid off a cattle operation in Alberta, who had come north to bounce between fill-in jobs in the mines and government road crews, who happened to find himself playing blackjack at the casino in Dawson when Margot slid up onto the stool next to his. Until recently, Wade has figured this as a rare visit of good luck. What Margot keeps to herself is this original secret: she had been staring at the broad-backed boy with the wolf eyes, pale blue and wild, for nearly an hour before choosing the seat at his side.

"Looks to me like you've got a system," Wade had told her after watching her win—and himself lose—four hands in a row. She could feel him wanting to speak to her as soon as she brushed her arm against his when she threw her money on the table for chips.

And it was true that he wanted to say something to the beautiful Indian girl—a *woman,* undeniably, uncomfortably—that one of his hard-headed foremen might say. His search for words coupled with his excitement forced him into tapping for another card after being dealt an eighteen.

"Never had a system," she said. "I just go when I want to go. Stick when it feels good to stick."

"It's working for you."

"You should try it sometime."

"Playing by gut?"

"No," Margot said, winning another hand. "Doing what feels good."

She told him that she had a plan to start up a guiding business in one of the last of the "out there" towns, where she would attract the serious hunters and "none of this kayak day-trip bullshit." Wade offered his entire savings—just under two thousand—to become a partner. This was after only three days together, holed up in their room with the sloped floor at the Winchester Hotel, listening to The Band and Creedence Clearwater Revival covers tremble through the walls at night, and making love on the screeching bed in the afternoons. Margot remembers thinking that she liked this one more than she could explain. She had distinct thoughts speak themselves to her, clear announcements that had the bracing ring of insight to them. *This one's a gentleman,* she'd thought, and *Once he gets his hooks in me, he'll never quit.* It makes her angry every time she recognizes how one's own certainties can be dead wrong one minute and dead right the next.

Margot tries to forgive herself for her role in bringing on Wade's dulled eyes, the doubled gravitational pull on his bones, but she can never quite free herself of blame. He was beautiful once. Now, she's noticed that he's stopped looking at himself in the bathroom mirror. Instead, he brushes his teeth in the hall. Shaves in the dark.

And lately, even more troubling habits. Less than a week ago, right after dawn, she'd found him standing in his boxers in the yard, staring at the green hills as though waiting for a signal. And just yesterday afternoon, he'd been cleaning his shotgun in the living room when she passed on her way to the kitchen. As she opened the fridge door, the side glance she'd taken of him became suddenly clear. He didn't have his eye to the bore, peering down it to make sure it was free of obstruction as one is supposed to do. It was his mouth. Wade's lips wrapped around the end of the barrel.

When she'd run back into the living room, the Mossberg sat across Wade's lap. She was ready to confront him—he *knew* she'd seen him—but he met her eyes with a placid emptiness. Not the look of someone who means to kill himself. She'd caught Wade stealing a taste of what it is to be someone else. Another man's horror in the moment before being killed.

"You better get that," he said finally. Only then did Margot hear the dropped carton of orange juice glugging over the kitchen floor.

Margot tells herself that what keeps them together now is the business. It stopped convincing her a long time ago. The hunting trips have been managed by her alone pretty much since they started, and even Wade would admit that she's twice the tracker and three times the shot that he is. When she cuts away the bogus justifications for staying with a man she has come to fear more than love, Margot recognizes that what really keeps her with Wade is the memory of what he once was. She had been the only person present to observe the brief moment he was whole. Now she is this moment's guardian, carrying it with her, repeating it in her head as though a lost language and she its last remaining speaker.

In less than a minute of the broad strides she normally attacks the ground with, Margot resumes her position at the head of the line, climbing to the top of a soft ridge. There's no point in any more considerations of the past. Not out here, anyway. If there is a bear for them to take she's got to stay awake for all of them. Starting now. Because although she hasn't seen or heard anything big since entering the bush at the Lapie Canyon Road, Margot is halfway sure there's a bear close by. She may have lost confidence in her emotional intuitions, but her hunter's instincts are rarely wrong.

She heads another thirty yards up ahead of the others and raises herself on tiptoes, stretching her nose into the air as a bear does. Something new is there. It comes and goes so quickly she can't identify it, though she knows the regular texture of scents that makes up the forest at this time of year has been interrupted. It's not the grizzly they're looking for, either. It might only be a whiff of her own worry, the slightly bitter taste that foreshadows a headache. It could be something dead.

Margot lowers herself onto her heels and watches the hunting party make its way up the hill. The smell she caught is gone now, delivered on a fluke of wind. Something in the already fading memory of it makes her think of Miles. She knows it is the nature of smell to colonize whatever people or objects you leave near it. But it's too late to separate them now. Margot has summoned Miles's scarred face to her mind, and with it the air now carries the faintest trace of smoke.

Through the truck's bug-smeared windshield, Miles looks at his cabin and feels that it is someone else's. Perhaps it's that he's never really taken note of it before, not as he does now, tracing the wonky lines of its walls, the pockets of weeds sprouting out between the roof tiles. This is where he started from, but some invisible renovations have been done in his absence. His inclination to back up and surrender the property altogether is as strong as his desire to walk in and see what changes have been made inside.

He steps out of the truck and slides a hand over the hood as though calming a skittish horse. What's strange about the cabin, he realizes now, is that there is somebody inside. He has never seen the lights on from outside, never watched a shadow walk across the living room to the kitchen and return with plates in its hands. The simple observation that others are right now sitting in his home strikes him as an overwhelming intimacy. His scar burns in shyness.

When he walks in, Alex and Rachel are eating mooseburgers at the living-room table.

"Mungo gave them to us," Alex tells him.

"They taste funny," Rachel adds, though she follows this observation by taking a huge bite of the black meat.

Miles stands on the rubber mat by the door and watches them chew.

"I thought you'd be gone," he says to Alex.

"We would have been. But you're back a day early."

"I am?"

"We're packed and everything."

"You're right. I'm early."

"We could go back to the motel, if you want."

"No," Miles says, shaking his head at them. "It's too late for any of that tonight."

Rachel waves half her burger over her head, and Miles pads over to take the seat next to her. The girl slides her plate in front of him. The smell of the meat reminds Miles of his hunger.

"It tastes like the zoo," Rachel warns him, her voice lowered. "But it's pretty good."

Miles nods at her. Then he lifts the food the girl has given him and eats.

The sheet parts on the opposite side of the bed from where Miles lies half asleep. He wants so badly to be touched he doesn't mind if what slides in with him now is a creature of his own invention, a dream he's managed to bend into the shape of his need. It could be the ghost of the kid making room for himself and Miles wouldn't object. It is too late for him even to pretend that he could choose what contact he might be offered anymore, or whether it came from the living or the dead.

But the touch, when it comes, is warm. Smooth fingertips tracing the wings of his shoulder blades, flattening into circles over the whole of his back. Firm enough to build the always surprising heat that comes when skin moves over another's skin.

When he rolls over to stroke the back of his knuckles down Alex's neck, Miles feels the pulse there, a hard tom-tomming that fully awakens him. The clock radio reads 5:14 AM but there is light in the room. The first intimation of dawn creates a stencilling of his pants thrown over a chair, the paper lantern tied around the ceiling bulb, his boots yawning side by side by the door. He can see Alex, too.

At first, the sight of her naked body is too much for him and his eyes blink away. But when she draws closer she occupies his entire field of vision. As though for the first time, he takes note of Alex's face, the buckle of bone halfway down her nose, visible only in profile. It is one of the thousand reasons that bound him to her, years ago. He remembers this and sees her crooked nose as too good a thing to ever wish it was otherwise.

Their kisses are patient. Nothing will be missed. To Alex, Miles's lips taste the way they always had, something at once sweet and earthy, like black licorice. Without speaking, it is his tongue that tells her that it's really him with her now. She realizes that she has come to him for this. A confirmation that something essential remained in him that she could identify. A single, recovered detail that ran through the before and after of their lives.

Alex pulls the sheet back from Miles's chest and drops it on the floor. She takes the time to follow the map of his burn, long enough to let him know that she is unafraid. Miles allows her to study him. He spreads his arms out from his sides, turns his head to show the markings down his neck. When she balances herself on top of him, he wishes only that she stay there.

The idea of asking Alex why she is here passes through his mind.

The thing is that, even now, he wants to know. The comfort she gives him is so far beyond anything he deserves, he can't help but suspect she is leaving him with this so that he might know what he can never have again.

Tomorrow, he thinks. *She said they'll be gone by tomorrow.*

Through the veil of her hair he can see the morning shadows retreating under the eaves. Tomorrow is already today.

If it's a punishment she has in mind, he'll accept it. He will welcome her and the future on any terms it proposes. Miles steadies Alex's face in his hands, watches the green return to her irises in the growing light. There he finds the story of all that she's lost, the damage he's done, the versions of happiness she's imagined. And a mile farther down, he recognizes himself.

When Miles awakens, he's alone again. Alex had tucked him in when she got up, notching the cover under his chin as he imagines she does for Rachel on restless nights. The clock radio is blinking 7:15 AM—his usual alarm setting. He doesn't remember it going off but, judging by the way it's lying upside down next to his socks on the floor, he must have heard its hateful beepings and brought his fist down on the Snooze bar. It's the sort of thing he's done before. Usually, though, it's on account of several beers too many the night before, and not the continuation of a rare good dream. Already its details are rushing away. All he knows is that it had to do with flying. In it, Miles was a black-feathered bird, gliding over a spangled river. Although he couldn't see who flew next to him, he wasn't afraid because he wasn't alone.

Alex pushes the bedroom door open. She's wearing a bathrobe of his that he hasn't worn in years. It's so big on her and its plaid squares so bright and patchy she looks to have been halfway to putting on a clown suit before deciding to make coffee instead. She shuffles over the hardwood in bare feet and puts a mug down on the bedside table where the clock radio has left a dust-free rectangle.

Miles can't help staring up at her. She'd be warm inside all that bundled terrycloth. Her mouth would taste like sex and bitter grounds. He'd like to reach out and pull on the single knot in the belt around her waist. If he did, the robe would fall open like a curtain. Pink nipples and cocoa freckles in the morning's new light.

"Is Rachel up?"

Miles realizes that he's heard this question coming out of his mouth before he thought to ask it.

"Are you kidding? It's nearly eight. She's been running around with Stump the last three-quarters of an hour."

"I didn't hear you get up."

"I wanted to be out of here before Rachel came knocking."

He can hear Stump barking outside, a whoof of mock protest he hasn't heard from the dog in ages. The girl is giving him orders and he's doing his best to follow them. Miles tells himself to take the dog out more, maybe let him play with those kids around the trampoline. It's not fair to deny him the pleasure he can hear in those barks. Then again, maybe it's only Rachel he likes. People aren't interchangeable for other people. Why wouldn't it be the same for mutts?

"We've only slept together a few times," Miles says, once again surprising himself through his grogginess.

"Who?"

"Me and Margot. And it was a mistake."

"I would have thought that was nobody's business."

"It wasn't. But now it might be your business, too."

"Why?"

"Because of last night. I owe it to you to be honest, at least."

"You don't know a fucking thing about what you owe me."

Miles sits up on his elbows in retreat, the back of his head pressed to the wall.

"I'm just trying to talk to you," he says.

"And there's nothing to say. You ran away, I found you. You've seen her. Visiting hours are over. Time to get back to our real lives."

"I'm not sure what my real life is anymore."

"It's *this*," she says, shifting her eyes from side to side to take in the bedroom, the shape of his body in the bed. "Looks lonely, doesn't it? And it will be. But then, it's your home now. Lonely is where you belong."

All at once, Alex puts her mug down next to Miles's, pulls the belt away from her waist and drops the bathrobe into a fluffy circle around her feet. She can't stop herself from sneering. One last flash of satisfied vengeance.

She scans the floor for the clothes she shed the night before. Piece by piece she dresses herself, a reverse striptease that pains him to watch. Her nakedness taken from him in the slipping on of socks, the wriggling lift of underwear.

"There's still a couple things I need to have done on the truck," Alex is telling him. "So we'll be out of here first thing tomorrow instead of today."

"That's fine."

"We can stay at the motel."

"I'd rather you have the cash than Earl."

Alex is leaving him. It's what he wants, what he knows has to happen. To leave him like this, shrivelled and powerless, is why she'd looked for him in the first place. None of this stops his chest from filling with slushy weight, a pre-emptive mourning. He can see Alex zipping up her jeans, her bellybutton winking at him. He can hear Rachel's laughter through the glass. But Miles already feels both of their absences looming before him as though they are already gone.

The phone rings three times before Miles figures out what it is. When he answers his voice sounds drugged, his tongue thick.

"Hello?"

"Looks like our ship's come in."

The only way Mungo would be awake before noon is if he'd worked the overnight shift in the radio shack.

"The plane spotted it?" Miles asks.

"Not this time. It was Crazy Ruby, of all people. Put her pen down long enough to spy us some smoke."

"No chance it's a ghost?"

"The spotter did a fly-over and it's a *for-sure* hot spot. Looks like we're going to need your signature on a few forms."

"Call the others," Miles says. "I'll be down there in five minutes."

He sits up and notices his feet again, even uglier now, pale and cold looking after being stuck out over the end of the bed the past hour or two. And it would only have been that long, even less, since Alex had lain gently snoring next to him.

Miles suddenly recalls his own voice. Words spoken on another morning, another planet altogether.

So much happens when you're asleep.

"Sounds like you've got your fire," Alex says.

Miles realizes he's still holding the receiver and places it back in its cradle. Outside, Rachel is shouting sternly at the sky. *That's not very nice, Mr. Raven!* Alex stands fully dressed now, arms crossed. The fire has come and it's time to say goodbye. *Stump's not a dumb dog!* Soon he'll be himself again, the foreman with the bad-luck face, cutting line. It's all moving fast, like the river after the ice breaks in the spring. *You can be my friend too, if you want to, Mr. Raven.* It's going fast and he's caught in the current and in minutes the future will be here.

"It's the moment we've all been waiting for," Miles says.

TWELVE

"I think we might have got it early," Miles is telling Alex, unable to stop the tickertape of his thoughts. *Look at us,* he thinks as he blathers on. *The perfect pretend marriage. Hubby late for work and the missus searching for his socks on the floor.* "My guess is we'll have it under control within the first twenty-four hours, if it takes even that long. A couple of guys will have to sleep with it overnight. But Mungo sounds sober, and the rest of them can only be so hungover without him sitting at their table." *This is just what it would be like, isn't it? Someone to show your naked self to, and a stream of blah-blah-blah to swim along on.* "Ruby Ritter was the one to spot it. It's nutty as a squirrel's nest up in that tower of hers, but she's got a pair of the best eyes in the Territory." *I'm talking nothing but shit and I still can't shut up. That's Alex for you. The only person I'd pull the cork out for.* "I bet King is kicking his heels together right now! That kid's been waiting for a real-life fire to—"

"Miles?"

"—come along and shake us awake—"

"Miles?"

Alex has stepped forward to place her hands on the tops of his shoulders, and it is this touch, and not his name, that silences him.

"You have to do something."

"Name it," he says, losing balance, thrashing his trapped foot around within the maze of his trousers. "So long as it can be done within the next ninety seconds."

"That's all it'll take for you to say goodbye to Rachel."

"Sure, yeah. If it's so important to you."

"Funny you should put it that way," she says. "My thinking was that it might be important to *you.*"

Miles buttons his shirt, digs around the bottom of the closet for the fluorescent orange vest that must be worn on jobs, all in an effort not to meet Alex's eyes. As strange as seeing her again has made the last couple of days, he has accepted her as truly real only in the last ten minutes. Her voice, her body, even the dark-haired girl in the strawberry dress—all of it shrouded in the disbelief of a dream.

"You okay for money?" Miles asks, his head still lowered over the closet's piled sneakers and baseball caps.

"There's enough."

"Because I've got savings I don't plan to—"

"That's not why we're here."

"I'm just offering."

"And I'm just declining."

He finds the vest and slips it over his shoulders. The light glances off its reflective surface and throws orange juice over the bedroom walls. For a moment, Miles is shining.

"You're not going to be here when I get back," he says.

"No more, Miles."

"No more. No."

Rachel is still talking to the raven in the tree. He can hear her making sounds that might be words. Nonsense that means something only to her.

"She's waiting for you," Alex says.

What is the best way to leave? It's something he's given more thought to than most. From what Miles can tell, once the decision to run has been arrived at, it all becomes a question of style. A note on the fridge, a slammed door, a Frankly, my dear, I don't give a damn. The usuals. Miles has already tried the disappearing act. Now he's left with walking out to another fire with even less to say that might last or help or leave a print behind.

"She's waiting," Alex says.

***

He finds the girl outside the cabin, staring up into the treetops, listening to the strangely human mutterings of a raven that peers down on them both. Stump sits next to her, his tail raking the lawn around his rump. Rachel hasn't noticed Miles behind her. She hasn't looked anyway, though Miles can sense her awareness of an audience. As he comes closer he can hear her whispered replies to the raven. Squeaky croaks and groans in an unnatural mimicry of the bird's language.

Stump isn't scared of you, Mr. Raven, he hears her say. The bird struts along its branch in outraged response, clucking at her. *No, I'm not scared of you, either.*

"I hope that dog of mine is sticking up for you," Miles says.

Stump turns to him, head cocked. The girl doesn't seem to hear, although she and the raven stop their conversation at the interruption of his voice.

"You and that old bird seem to be having a good chat," he tries again.

When Rachel finally turns, he has a chance to study her face. It seems to Miles that she is touched by wildness. There is a feral bottomlessness to her eyes that makes him feel that they are constantly calculating his distance, resolve, the true intent behind each of his gestures. She's reading *him,* not what he says, which makes Miles think of her as possessing the most sharply intuitive of animal qualities.

"Mr. Raven has a lot of stories to tell," she says.

"Ravens always do."

Miles kneels before the girl, so close he can smell the soap on her skin. He searches for something to say, but it is Rachel who speaks first.

"We've looked for you so long," the girl says. There is no pleading in her voice, only the flat declaration of fact.

"Well, you don't have to look anymore. After this, you can stay in one place instead of hanging around lousy campgrounds and lumber towns with just your mom to keep you company, and you

can forget about this weird-looking man you've been hunting for.
Okay? You can go *home* now and not—"

He is stopped by the motion that Rachel makes with her right
hand. A swift swing toward his eyes that he takes to be an oncoming slap. But instead, the girl lands her fingers softly against the top
of his cheek, running them down the length of his scar, light as the
step of a spider. It makes him lose all his words. She seems to be
measuring him with her touch, both the ridges of his burn as well
as what lies beneath it. With her fingertips, the girl gauges
whether he is so far away he cannot feel what it is to be discovered
by another.

Nobody has touched his face since the fire, not even Alex. His
own fingers are numb as cigar butts when he strokes the burn. Yet
there is something in the girl's feathery explorations that sends a
pulse deep within him. As she continues down, Miles feels that she
is filling the grooves in his skin with a cool putty, leaving him
smooth.

It is her turn to ask the question he had attempted two days
before on Eagle's Nest Bluff, but that she now puts to him with her
hand alone.

Do you know who I am?

Miles doesn't answer. He kneels before the girl with the sun
thrown over him like a dazzling sheet, holding open the uglier half
of himself to be studied and touched as she pleases. The light
paints a bending stripe across her hair. He feels lean, beer-buzzed,
shameless. He'd nearly forgotten what sharing a secret can do.

She remembers this meadow. Ablaze with paintbrush and
Labrador tea, the slant of the valley's side showing itself in an opti-
cal illusion of gentleness. Under different circumstances, the bear
would see it as a field to linger in. There would be relief from the
roots and shale edges that rib the forest earth, and in their place
would be a thousand beds waiting to be made in the beardtongue.

More than broad enough to allow any wind they might have heard in the treetops to descend and curl about them, the sun warming the silver tips of their fur. But nothing can be permitted to slow them now. Today, as it was when she stopped here with her mate two seasons ago, it is the meadow's assets that worry her.

They could circle the open ground, staying under cover of the midget dogwoods crowded along the circumference, but it would take three times as long as a direct crossing. Although she is sure that the hunters have not closed any of the distance between them since morning, the sow is less certain about the female among them. At points over the last couple of hours, the bear had thought she could pick up the lead hunter's scent. It came from different directions each time, the sources so distant that it would require the speed of a hawk's wings to fly between them. The she-grizzly knows that she is only anticipating the female hunter's scent— recollecting it, creating it—rather than reading it in the air. She is making small mistakes already.

The bear stands at the green edge of the meadow and considers it afresh. To cross it, she and her cubs will be exposed on all sides.

She starts out at a full charge.

As they scramble after her, the cubs' initial honks of confusion become a terrified bleating. She tells herself to think of nothing but the simple thing. For now, it's reaching the far side of the meadow. She will comfort the cubs once they get there. But as long as the light makes them visible, she must keep her stride long, drawing the earth behind her with her claws.

She ignores the first screech from her cub. It's the voice of the bigger one, stronger but more timid than his brother. The sow assumes that his crying is only a renewed attempt to make her stop. She pounds ahead another hundred feet before the cub's second scream reaches her. This time, she hears the unmistakable shock of pain in it.

The she-grizzly skids and leaps backwards in a single motion. Her smaller cub has stopped next to the larger one, sitting up on his haunches. She tries to see if the larger cub is moving or not, but from where she is, he appears to be on his side. The sow whoofs a warning to whatever threat that stands, unseen, in the trees that ring the meadow.

When she comes upon her fallen cub, she expects to see him opened at the side as the gunshot had split apart her mate. She can't smell any of the hunters, but the female must have travelled faster than the sow had guessed. And now she's firing upon them from the shadows. From anywhere.

She's surprised not to see any blood in the grass. The larger cub mewls up at her and, using her paw as a spatula, she flips him over to his other side. Nothing stains, nothing seeps. The cub paws at the exposed pink of his jowls, whimpering.

Not shot, but stung. Around him, a thousand yellowjackets disgorge from the rupture in their nest. A giant paper egg that the cub had run over, having taken it for a mound of sand.

There is a moment when the wasps hang in the air between them, undecided. The sow feels a number of them settle between her ears, tickling the whiskers along her snout. Their wings so close she sees the world through a flickering filter of grey.

When she can be still no longer the sow takes a step back and, at first, the yellowjackets only follow her in the same drifting flight patterns, as though attached to elastic bands. With each retreat, the cubs follow. Only when a pair of wasps wriggle up the sow's nostrils does she bark. And then they sting.

The bear's voice excites the meadow into a flurry of motion. She rolls side over side in an attempt to crush the yellowjackets buried in the fur on her back, but they only jab at her belly instead. At the same time, the cubs run toward the end of the field, one high and one low, so that their pursuers are divided between them. The wasps kamikaze the bears' eyes. Buzz their bums.

By the time the she-grizzly finds her feet, her nose is swollen shut. It forces her to breathe through her mouth, now opened so wide that the yellowjackets plant stingers at the back of her tongue. The sun is clouded over by furiously dancing bugs. When she coughs, a handful of dead wasps spray out.

The shade blinds the sow before she realizes she's made it to the meadow's far side. She stops to find her cubs. The sudden cool of the forest calms the wasps. They drift up and away as though awakened from some hypnotic command to violence. Many float back into the meadow. A homeless stream returning to their broken nest to start building again.

The cubs come to her from opposite directions. A quick inspection shows them to have been more startled than hurt. The big cub in particular refuses his mother's attentions, shamed by his fear of so small a predator. She leads them on again, plowing a course through the hemlock.

Although her cubs' screams were not caused by any hunter's shot, it has reminded the bear that the chances of being found are far greater when they enter the broad canvas of fields, or the bare rocks above the mountain's treeline. They will have to shrink themselves from now on. Move unnoticed as yellowjackets do, instead of as three brown giants, visible for miles in open land. And like any prey, large or small, they must be prepared to sting.

It took more than an hour for the Ross River attack team to stir themselves from rye-soaked dreams, load the powerwagon with gear and head out of town toward the first real smoker of the season.

The men arrived one at a time. King first, eyes twinkly with excitement, followed by Crookedhead James, busily replacing a broken lace in his boot with the cord that hooked his VCR to his TV. And last, Jerry McCormack, pulling into the lot in the Ford pickup he'd gone ahead and splurged on the day before.

"Couldn't resist," Jerry said, beaming, as he stepped down from the cab.

"Thought you didn't have the money," Crookedhead pointed out.

Jerry shrugged. "I will now."

"You a fortune teller or something?"

"Just an optimist."

"Maybe your nose can smell smoke a day before Ruby can see it."

"It's only the smell of money."

Normally, Miles would take the opportunity to remind his crew that their response time was roughly four times longer than it should be, and that the crew cab's interior is a far more comfortable place when not smelling like it's been reupholstered with Welcome Inn beer mats. But instead he lets Mungo drive (a privilege nearly always reserved for himself) and sits in a denser silence than his standard, smoothing his hand over the map that will guide them down the Lapie Canyon Road four snaking miles, and another bushwhacking hike to the fire. On the rear bench, King sits sandwiched between Jerry and Crookedhead, the only one of the three with eyes open. More than open, Miles notes each time he glances back in the side mirror. Bedazzled, egg white.

"This is where Margot takes her clients, isn't it?" Miles asks as the road narrows and rises into the more crowded forest of the foothills.

"I'm not sure she works according to a system. Not as we would understand it," Mungo says, grinning the eroded ruins of his teeth out at him. From the moment they shook hands at the fire office this morning, Miles couldn't help noticing that the prospect of fire has lifted twenty years from the older man's shoulders and emptied the grey sacks atop his cheeks. "From what I can tell, that girl just wakes up and *smells* whatever she aims to shoot."

"Most of the time it's along here though, right?"

Mungo nods. "If it's a grizzly she's after. This would be it."

Miles lets another few minutes pass before pulling the receiver from the truck's radio and checking for Margot. If she's done what he asked her to do, she'll have her own radio open to calls. He'd put the chances of this at fifty-fifty.

When she finally answers, Miles can hear the depth of her

breathing, along with the wind that blows across the mouthpiece. The sound of distance.

"Hey there, Smoky."

"Wasn't sure you'd answer."

"You're in luck. I'm a mile ahead of the others. So we can talk in *private*."

Although her voice makes it clear that she's only joking, Miles reddens. Even Crookedhead pops open one of his eyes.

"You find any tracks?"

"Won't be too long."

"How do you know?"

"A girl knows these things."

Miles tries to remember what he wants to tell her, but it skitters away, so that the radio crackles for a time with him staring out the window at the sun, already high and enraged over the Anvil Range. The problem is that he really wants to be speaking to Alex. Not to deliver any specific message, but to hold her in place with words. With her, he would be speaking right now because, no matter what dribbled out of him, it would be understood.

"Where are you?" Margot asks.

"In the pumper."

"You got a fire."

"Looks that way. And not too far from you."

"A big one?"

"By all reports, no."

"Is that why you're scaring all the bears away? To inform me that you're going to stomp on a leftover campfire?"

"Just wanted to let you know that I'll have my radio with me if you need—"

"For fuck sake, Miles. When did you get so nervous?"

"I'm just keeping everybody's head up on this."

"Consider my head up."

"Miles?" Mungo reaches across the bench seat, gesturing for the receiver. "Is Tom there?"

"Margot? Mungo would like to say hello to his son."

"Tell him that Tom has been a total lifesaver," Margot says, her voice sucking away. "I don't know how we—"

"Say again?"

"What's wrong?"

"She's cutting out."

"Listen, Miles, I gotta go," Margot's voice returns, but faintly. "I've got *business* here, by the looks—"

"Repeat. I'm losing you."

"—maybe your fire—"

"Just give your position—"

"—scaring the big boys out into the clear. Drinks on me, Smoky. I've got a helluva *feeling* about—"

Miles's ear gulps shut against a wave of static. He could try her again, but she wouldn't answer. She's got *business*. Unless she contacts him, Margot's lost to him now. And the only way she'd call is if something got beyond her handling of it. Miles can't imagine what shape such an event might take, and doesn't want to.

"She's picked up something, hasn't she?" Mungo asks him.

"I'm not sure."

"That girl doesn't come out of the bush empty-handed too damn often. Not when there's money on it."

Behind them, Crookedhead returns to sleep with a rip of snoring.

"Don't worry about Tom."

"I know it," Mungo says, nodding. "Margot's good. The best."

"Then we'll just have to be good today too."

Bears don't leave tracks. Margot creates them. This is what a true hunter has to believe. That the animal is not discovered but summoned by will, a manifestation of her ability to envision her prey in such detail that it is obliged to exist.

She has walked on another mile after switching her radio off,

trying to clear Miles's voice from her mind. More than any creature, a grizzly is the hardest to create. She could turn from Wade
in the middle of a sentence and paint a moose standing at the edge
of a marsh, or coax a buck from an aspen grove while humming
the tune she heard on the radio that morning. But a bear of the
kind Margot works to bring forward now will not permit distraction. Margot can't worry about Miles, his fire, or the woman and
child who have come from Outside to find him. She needs to hold
the pencil in her mind now and draw. The hunter's art requires
silence, a standing apart. This is why she has hiked so far ahead of
Wade and the Baders. Why she stops and falls to her knees next to
a sprawling patch of saskatoon berries.

The tracks are there, just as she knew they would be. In the soft
earth of the bush's shadow, beneath the branches bent by something at once huge and cautious. A grizzly and her two cubs, travelling west. A seven-hundred-pound sow, maybe eight. Margot's
estimate is based on the largest set of claws she has ever traced
with her fingers. A bear even greater than the one she conceived in
her imagination. It is as though the animal has participated in its
own invention and wished itself a giant.

Judging from the huddled pattern of the tracks, the cubs follow
her closely. One slightly larger than the other, both two years old.
Margot is always sorry when there are cubs involved, even when
they are of an age to have a good chance of surviving on their own,
as she believes these ones to be. She never creates offspring for the
animals she summons. It doesn't stop them from appearing sometimes.

Though it troubles her, Margot is always awed by the realization that her authorship of the hunt, its story and outcome, is ultimately limited. She can make bears appear but cannot prevent
them from acting in unpredictable ways. Acknowledging this is
like prayer for her.

The smallest things can be the most splendid, in the bush as
much as elsewhere. Wild delphiniums stop her in mid-stride. A

gliding eagle surpasses her lushest dreams of flight. More than anything, she is humbled by children. Whether born of woman or
bear, they remind her that the hunter is not alone in being able to
choose between taking and creating life.

Miles knows that when they get as far on the road as the four-
wheel-drive will permit, and they roll out to strap pisstanks over
their shoulders and grab pulaskis from the flatbed, there will have
to be a smoke break. Nothing will get done—at least nothing
without Jerry and Crookedhead's constant complaint—until the
crew has huffed back a morning cigarette. It's a ritual that Miles
has come to see as a good-luck charm. Being superstitious in the
way of all firefighters, he grants them the two minutes it takes to
roll, lick the seam, clink open each of their lighters, and inject
themselves with the only nicotine they're likely to get before the
fire's mopped up. They've taught King how to roll his own along
with them, arguing in favour of bagged tobacco's freshness and
economy, not to mention that smoking filtered cigarettes is "like
trying to suck air through a tampon," as Jerry likes to put it.
Whenever asked why he doesn't share the habit, Miles tells them
he inhales enough monoxide working wildfires to last him a pack-
a-day lifetime. Nobody points out that Jerry, Mungo and King are
also firefighters and yet all of them smoke with grim dedication.
The truth is, Miles wants to keep whatever strength is left in him.
It's not that he has a special interest in living long. It's that if he has
to carry somebody out, he has promised himself to at least possess
the capacity to try.

"There it is," Mungo announces as he slams the powerwagon to
a stop. All of them pour out of the truck to get a better view of the
plume of grey. Then, right on schedule, all of them except Miles
pull sacks of Drum from their breast pockets.

"I like it," Jerry McCormack says.

"Like what?"

"A fire so close we can damn near drive the pumper up and roast marshmallows through the windows."

"There's still a walk ahead of us."

"I've had longer hikes to backyard outhouses."

"I guess we're just lucky," Crookedhead says.

"Lucky?"

Miles steps close to Crookedhead's face, glaring at him with an anger neither of them saw coming. He thinks that the man before him has been misnamed. For the first time, he notices it's not that Crookedhead's head is so crooked, but that his mouth is too small for the size of his skull. So small a thing, in fact, that it has trouble performing most of its basic functions—eating, yawning, spitting any distance beyond his own toes. Useless, really, except for talking. The man could jabber like a hand puppet with his undersized trap. At the moment, however, with Miles turned on him out of nowhere, his blab fails him.

"Just that, the fire—like Jerry said," Crookedhead stammers. "It's a good thing it's close."

"Arson. Is that what you mean by lucky?"

"Fuck no."

"Because if there *were* a firestarter, it would most likely be one of *us,* wouldn't it? We'd have it narrowed down to five right off the bat."

"Hey now," Mungo says, stepping between them but speaking only to Miles. "All the man's saying is that it's a good thing our first job is going to be a stroll to get to, that's all."

"That true, Crookedhead?"

"That's it."

"All right, then. If we're so lucky, let's find the goddamn thing and put it out."

By the time they march into the woods the afternoon has grown cloudless, gusty and hot. Under their boots, the dried toadflax crunches like bird bones. *A perfect day for a newborn fire,* Miles notes to himself. He considers the likelihood of the temperature surpassing forecasted highs, wonders how the wind is going to blow through the rest of the day.

He'd also like to know where his decision to start a pissing match with Crookedhead came from. *Arson. Firestarter.* He felt like a boy taking pleasure in speaking aloud the most foul of cuss words. And in a sense, it *had* pleased him. Watching the sleepiness drain out of Crookedhead's face be replaced by the shock of accusation.

What afflicts Miles now, though, is the idea that there's a bully living in him. A dirty fighter. A running man. A borderline alcoholic and mother neglecter. He'd admit to all of these and then some. But saying shit for the sake of saying it is a new vice altogether. And he can guess where it comes from, too. No matter how quick they put this smoker out, Alex and Rachel will be on the road when he gets back. It's the persistence of this simple fact that has raised the devil in him.

The fire turns out to be trickier to find than they first assumed. It's no farther than it appeared from the truck, but the character of the wind makes it seem so. Not strong, but shifty. It puts a new concern in Miles's mind. More than the dryness and availability of fuels, it is air movement that can make a fire go on a tear. The wind can also hide it altogether. "The old saying is a lie," he tells his crew every year. "Where there's smoke, there *isn't* always fire." The fumes will sometimes lie flat and crawl for miles away from the flames, so that when an attack crew arrives in a smoke-filled valley they find only smog.

Miles leads them, hacking through the kinnikinnick and alder saplings, tying orange trail tape to branches every hundred feet or so. He keeps his eye on the twisting pillar of smoke but, within five minutes, he has looped them back to where they started.

All of them notice the cut branches. Sharp breaks high enough up that they were unlikely to have been made by passing animals. Bushwhacking.

The fire crew meet eyes. In silence, it is decided to leave it alone. Someone was here. One of them, or someone else. But the implications of speaking this aloud, out here, would be unstoppable. They can see and think and conclude what they like. But words would tie all of them to something they might rather remain free of.

"It's straight that way," Miles says, pointing his chin. "It won't get us turned around twice."

Miles is right. In less time than it took them to discover that their initial course was mistaken, he delivers them to the smoker. A fairly innocuous business, by the looks of it. Low flames crackling through the regrowth of a small clearing, maybe a hundred and fifty yards end to end. It's been here a while, judging from the blackened soil and the near-complete exhaustion of the fuels within the clearing's borders.

The crew look around and find that they're somewhat higher here than the surrounding forest, which exposes them to more air. The elevation, together with the tall, carbon-hardened snag in the centre, suggest a lightning strike. But there are a couple of things about the site that put it slightly outside the everyday. For one thing, all of them know there hasn't been a lightning touch this close to town in the last month. For another, the burning that has already occurred has been unusually intense. Every step the crew take creates a high-pitched crinkling of charcoal, the roots and deadfall not just burned but cooked halfway to glass. And there's a lot more smoke than a fire of this size would normally send up. Darker, too.

None of them remark on any of this. An involuntary round of coughs acknowledges the sore throats they've got coming tomorrow.

"Gentlemen," Mungo says, taking the first dig at the fireline with his pulaski. "Allow me to introduce you to our contract extension."

***

Along with a course of direction, speed and identity, tracks will sometimes also tell a story. Margot looks down on the papery nest, the flattened grass, the furious digging of claws, and reads the tale of the yellowjackets versus the bears. Given the signs of struggle under her boots and the breadth of strides over the diverging tracks that race across the clearing, it's clear to Margot who won. The only thing she's curious about is where all the wasps got to.

She finds a stump aproned with soft lichen and settles with her back against it, lays the Remington alongside her leg. Sleep lingers nearby, darts closer and retreats, like wolves at the edge of a fire. It is no match for Margot's alertness when she is this close to finishing a job. She keeps one hand on the rifle. With the other she shields her eyes and studies the trail exit that Wade and the Baders will eventually emerge out of.

For a drifting second, Margot wonders what she's doing here. Then she remembers.

Over the past few years, she has become aware that what she sells these people isn't the beauty of the last true wilderness on the continent. It's not even the thrill of hunting an animal that, theoretically at least, could do you harm. Instead, Margot is in the nostalgia business. Most of her clients see the land between here and where Alaska reaches into the Bering Strait as an especially convincing theme park. The killing is only a small but essential part of the experience. Even the most politically defensive hunters know that the days of having anything of interest to blow away in the woods—even these woods—are being counted down. The big game that Margot leads them to used to number in the hundreds of thousands and over a habitat that would include all the land west of the Mississippi. It's why the state flag of California has a grizzly bear on it, even though they had been blasted into extinction there some decades ago. It's also why putting a hole through the skull of a moose or deer would mean little to a Jackson Bader. There were too many of those beasts still around to provide the necessary element of tragic poignancy to the moment, the bittersweetness that came with taking down one of the last of its kind. Today's trophy hunters aren't even especially interested in the trophy anymore. What they want is to play their part. And for $8,990 (U.S.) over ten days (local taxes and gratuities not included), Margot was prepared to sell them their walk-on roles in The End of the World.

Here they come now.

As Tom and the Baders make their way up to her, Margot can't help seeing them as an odd family: the distant father, his aging wife and their adopted Indian son. While this illusion requires Jackson Bader only to be himself, there is no doubt that Elsie Bader has taken to the boy. Tom is perhaps a full foot taller than she, yet he bows close, holding her arm as they step over a patch of loose rock that threatens to take her feet out from under her.

"I thought you'd gotten *lost!*" Elsie Bader exclaims as she comes upon Margot, her lips puffing out from sun-swollen cheeks. "And then I thought, 'She can't be lost! She's our *guide!*'"

"I went ahead on my own."

"You sure as hell did," Wade says.

The first thing Margot does is unstrap the radio from her waist and hand it to Wade. Simply carrying this connection to the Outside is a far heavier burden to her than the Remington and forty-pound pack on her back. And she doesn't want to haul thoughts of Miles around with her anymore, either. She can feel him worrying about her from wherever his fire is and it strikes her, in turns, as irritating, touching and a cause for concern greater than the bear itself.

The weight of the radio tugs at Wade's arm. Margot would say he's lost all of what remained of his colour in the morning if it weren't for the presence of Jackson Bader, who started out crispy skinned and white as a hospital sheet and now appears to have achieved an even more ghastly pallor. He turns Margot's mind to the way a filleted halibut looks displayed on a bed of ice in the

Raven Nest, one with an ON SALE! warning flag jabbed in it. Slippery, nearly translucent. A yellow taint creeping into the bleached flesh.

"You find anything?" Bader shouts up at her.

"I believe I have."

"Jackson, *please*. Sit here a minute," Mrs. Bader pleads even as her husband is folding himself down in the grass, his breathing a reedy whistle. When he disappears from Margot's view she could mistake him for a snake hissing through the wild sage. "You don't mind if we all take a little break, do you, Wade?"

"Not me."

"You've found tracks?" Bader asks. The words escape him low and fast, little more than a muffled cough. He sticks his head up so that it hovers amidst the grass like a half-deflated balloon.

"Been following them for a while."

"Them?"

"A female. And two cubs."

"How big?"

"We won't know until we see her. But she's leaving tracks the size of dinner plates."

"So why are we stopping?"

"Your wife asked."

Mrs. Bader blanches.

"Jackson, can't we just have a drink of water and catch our——?"

"Five minutes," he says.

Bader slips down into the sage once more. There isn't even the sound of his breathing anymore. But when his wife unscrews the top of her canteen, the old man gulps and gulps.

Margot isn't sure they can afford the time, but she'd rather let a bear slip out of range than have a client drop dead on her a full seven miles from the truck. She studies the far end of the clearing at the point where the tracks re-enter the bush. It always thrills her to follow an animal without seeing it, the knowledge that it was *here* before it moved on to the as-yet-undiscovered *there*.

Sometimes, she can feel their presence more in the contour of their footprints than when she takes her knife to their skins.

She notices Bader's hand flapping over the grass. She walks over and is mildly surprised to find him grinning. Unfriendly, intent, flirtatious.

"She's a prize one, isn't she?"

"It's a large bear."

"How far?"

"Bit of a ways. But we might sight them by the end of the day."

"You find them, and I'll bring them down," he says, wagging his finger at her, as though reminding a child of contractual terms, an agreement to let her go outside to play once she's tidied her room.

"Not the cubs. It's illegal. And I don't plan to let——"

"Your five minutes are up," he tells her, and struggles to his feet.

She considers reminding him that she wasn't the one who needed to pull her lungs out of her throat, and that he's not the one leading this party, and could never be, given that he couldn't track a horse through wet cement.

Instead, she watches him go. Wade, Tom and Mrs. Bader watch too. The old man walking straight from the waist up but with jellied knees, carrying himself over the clearing like someone who has awakened in an alien landscape and now strikes out for home on a path he's only guessed at.

"Shoo, you little devils!" Elsie Bader squeals, jumping from the handful of yellowjackets that have come by for a sniff at the sweat at the back of her neck. "You'd think I've been dipped in honey."

"We'd better go after him," Wade whispers in Margot's ear.

"He's a funny one, isn't he?"

"A laugh a minute."

"Jackson! Just hold *up* there!" Mrs. Bader calls to him, her voice close to breaking. Margot can hear not only the woman's fretfulness but her dependency, the loss of bearings that comes at the same instant her husband slips into the forest's shadow. It may be a version of love, for all Margot knows.

As they proceed across the meadow Margot considers telling them about the bears and the yellowjackets but decides not to. She's the one who has willed the bear into being, after all. What befalls the animal now can be viewed as her doing as well. No matter who pays, who shoots, who keeps the bones for souvenirs, this is her hunt. She will hold on to its secrets for herself.

THIRTEEN

It has been a dry summer. Dry even by the subarctic's arid standards, and with little meltage from the shallowest snowpack the Territory has seen in the past eight winters. Only now, in late July, have the rivers risen to normal levels. That's why it's so strange Miles and his crew haven't had a smoker to fight until now.

It's also why this one is as noisy as Chinese New Year's. The crack of bursting deadwood makes Miles think of bones breaking. He coughs on the smoke, and the fire seems to hear him. The flames' reckless celebration of a moment ago is hushed to a whispered sizzling. Then, apparently not finding much threat in the five men who have come out of the woods looking half-beaten already, it snaps away even louder than before, popping knots out of pine trunks like half a dozen .22s.

"Jerry. Crookedhead. King. You guys start the line here," Miles orders even as the others are pushing the branches at the clearing's perimeter out of their faces. "Mungo is going to help me cut this snag in the centre. Work fast, and we won't miss last call at the lounge."

Everyone knows this is an empty incentive. They will stay at the fire until it is mopped up, every last wisp of smoke buried or drowned by sprays from the five-gallon pisstanks the men will empty onto the fireground well into the night. But the simple idea of finally having a job to do and a reward at its completion sets the five of them to their assignments with a fury.

They start by pacing out the fire's borders, a quick size-up to best decide where to lay the fireline down. Miles directs Jerry, Crookedhead and King to the head, an arm of flame inching toward where they'd first entered the clearing. They're to be the back breakers. Pressurized hoses and airdrops and parachute smokejumping rarely come into the actual work of forest firefighting. Not up here anyway, where the roads are too few to get a pumper near enough to use, the air resources too far away, the bush too unpeopled. Most of the time the job involves what King, Crookedhead and Jerry do now. Grave digging. Ripping the spadeheads of their pulaskis down to the subsoil and raking away any needles and leaves within a two-foot-wide trench around the site. What makes it exciting is the aspect of a race. If they win, when the fire reaches the line it will have nowhere to go.

Within the proposed fireline, however, stands a second concern. A flaring twenty-foot-tall lodgepole pine, dried white and spinning coils of smoke. If its internal temperature gets too high, the trunk will explode, sending a hundred new firebrands out over the line. They'll have to fell the snag before it has the chance.

Miles steps into the fireground with the chainsaw held across his chest. With every step, the ash swirls up to his waist like hellish confetti. Despite his boots' thick soles his feet cook instantly. He hears Mungo cussing behind him, an incoherent compounding of swear words that is his partner's trademark. *Assholemotherfuck.* And then, as they reach the greater heat at the base of the snag, *Shitpiss.*

It's Mungo's job to stick the wedges into place, but also to watch for falling widowmakers. Whoever handles the chainsaw never has enough time to notice a branch collapsing on him. Mungo lends Miles an extra pair of eyes, ones that always look up.

Miles straps a Nomex shroud over his mouth and nose. Even before opening the furnace door with the first undercut, he can feel the snag throwing heat against his chest. He cuts into the wood and it births sparks into his face. Miles staggers back, but steps in almost immediately to further the cut. It takes a full minute of retreat and attack before he's able to kick out the slab. As soon as the backcut is exposed, Mungo stands by with the wedge. When there is enough room, he pushes it into the kerf and knocks it in place with the broad side of an axe.

"All right," Miles shouts over the idling saw. "Now step away so—"

Mungo bodychecks Miles's words out of his mouth. Both men stumble away from the snag held in each other's arms. They turn at the same time, cheek to cheek, to see a fifty-pound branch pocked with embers fall to where Miles's bootprints are still visible in the ash.

Before Miles can thank him, Mungo advances on the trunk again and hammers in another wedge. In a moment, the snag topples altogether. Miles opens the gas on the chainsaw, bucking the fallen tree into two-foot pieces with Mungo following behind him, dousing them with foam. Through the process, Miles keeps waiting for a break to say something, but Mungo doesn't stop long enough to let him, and when the snag is entirely dismembered, they both go to help the rest of the crew cut fireline. Miles had almost forgotten how it goes. You trust the men you can, and when they save your life, you get back to the job so you can be in a position to save theirs the next time around.

By the end of the first hour, the rising sun along with the radiant heat of the fire sweats the adrenaline out of them. Miles realizes not only that he is probably too old for this but that all of them are. Except for King, of course. Yet the advantage of the kid's youth is consistently undermined by his reveries. He could go like hell for forty minutes at a time but then, the next time you checked, he'd be frozen with his spade stuck in the earth, studying the way a breeze passes fire from one spruce crown to another.

Like now, for instance.

After Miles has cut his line far enough to join where Crooked-head's started, he raises his head to find King standing straight, his pulaski leaning against his leg and one hand over his brow to block the sun. The kid's eyes jumping between the flames. It holds Miles where he is for a moment, too. Not the fire, but the look on King's face. The same look he'd seen years ago when he caught

Brad sitting rapt by the orange tongues of a barbecue. It was only a year before the guy started a bigger one all for himself.

"King!" Miles shouts, and the kid turns to face him. Only now does Miles notice how King's entire frame is trembling.

A second later, the kid is at work again. Eyes down, the pulaski blade stirring the earth. Miles can't see his face anymore, but he does his best to believe it is as it was before. Just another grave digger, burying smoke.

They pause for an early lunch of packed rations—tins of flaked ham, a block of cheddar, saltines—all of it seasoned by an airborne peppering of ash. The fire seems to watch them as the men set the food atop their knees. But when they start to eat, the flames take the opportunity to skip ahead to the fireline. Antennae of clear gas measure the raked ground. Orange hairs the height of Popsicle sticks crop up along the line in both directions.

It's still a small blaze. Almost all the fuels within the clearing had been devoured, and when the team completes a line around it, it will die of starvation. Even now you could stomp the whole business out with boots if you had a dozen more pairs. A half-hour of rain would leave it a hissing patch of mud.

And yet Miles can't help marvelling at its defiance, the way it travels low and fast to find a way out. He knows a fire is incapable of thought. In fact, it irritates him when others think of them as possessing distinct personalities, as hunters see a human face in the animals they kill. Miles has called such thinking "pyropomorphic" in his notes. It's mysticism, as far as he's concerned. Which makes it stupid at best, and at worst, unsafe.

Still, even Miles can't help thinking that certain jobs, maybe one out of every hundred, are different. Chaos fires.

Fighting fire is like war, Miles recalls his first foreman telling him as he swallows his one and only bite of cheese. *You're either totally in control or totally out of control.*

Even as the men drop the food from their laps and jump up to defend the line, a sudden wind from the east—then the south, then the north—breathes life into the flames.

"It's going for a run," Crookedhead James says, a spoonful of ham dropping from his mouth.

The fire eats only the ground's flashiest fuels—needles, grass nests and cones—and ignores the trees, travelling faster than it possibly could if it stopped to consume everything in its path. The attack crew stand for a moment with forearms resting on their tool handles to watch it run white tubers over the soil. In less than two minutes, it has skittered a circle around the end of the fireline they'd started on and is free.

"Fast little bugger," Jerry McCormack observes.

"No good standing here cooing at the thing," Mungo says, already running back fifty feet and raking out a new line of deadfall. "Drop the lead out and give me a hand over here!"

They try. A hasty effort at a second line that all of them recognize won't work even as they bend to the task. After five frenetic, useless minutes, they stop again as the fire breaches the ground they would have cut if they had another hour.

"It's coming," King says, more in wonder than fear.

"We've got slopover all over the place," Jerry confirms.

They keep digging at the second line only to remain busy while Miles decides what to do next.

"This isn't going to come close," he says finally.

"We can radio in for an air show," Mungo says. "Dump half the Lapie River on the thing. See how it likes it."

"Take too long to get here to make a difference."

"Let's stay at it."

"I didn't say we're quitting yet."

"What else you going to do? Try a backfire on it?"

"Why not?"

"The wind was weird for a second there."

"But it seems steady now. We burn out these last pines here and it might waltz right into its own black."

"How do we make sure our own fire doesn't come round on us?" King asks.

"We do it fast."

As Mungo, Jerry, Crookedhead and King cut a third fireline, this one a short semicircle around the straggling pines, Miles pulls the fusees out of his pack to ignite the backfire. He tries to tell himself that this isn't desperation but a balance of risks. If it doesn't work, the fire they set now will join hands with the main fire, giving it a hundred yards for free and a boost of speed at the same time. On the other hand, the backfire could still burn away the fuels standing in the main fire's path in time, denying it an escape route. Miles knows it will all depend on the wind. One more dust-up like a minute ago and it could turn round on them like a stampeding herd.

When they've finished cutting a rough containment line, Miles touches the fusees to the sagewort on the other side.

"Stand away!" Miles orders them, but when he glances over his shoulder, the men are already running from the heat of the back-fire. Only Mungo stays with him.

"Let's move it!"

Mungo's voice awakens him from the briefest of dreams. One second he is lighting the backfire and feeling the new flames singe his cheeks, and the next he's leaping off the edge of Eagle's Nest Bluff with Rachel holding his hand as he goes. Both of them gliding over the river with an osprey slicing the blue ahead of them, teaching them how to dive, how to use the currents to rise again without effort.

For a time, the five of them stand wild-eyed and panting. Already, the grass backfire is racing toward the larger burn, skipping over the feathery tops of the foxtails.

"Would you look at that," Crookedhead James says. "Like a baby running to its momma."

It's only as they watch the backfire spread across the last green in the clearing that Miles points out they haven't given this job a name yet.

"The Comeback."

"What's that?" Jerry says, cupping his ear to hear King's suggestion. But Miles heard it the first time.

"The Comeback Fire," Miles announces. "It's a good name."

"Yeah," Mungo says, slapping King on the back. "You've got the gift, kid."

Miles hears the strain in Mungo's voice, a tone halfway to sarcasm. It's probably only exhaustion, the mangling of words that must pass through a scorched throat. But for a second, as the men watch their backfire join and double the fire it was meant to extinguish, it makes Miles wonder about secondary meanings. Does the kid have the gift for naming fires or for fighting them? More than either of these, Miles hopes he possesses the gift of surviving them.

The day is warm, but it's the light that assaults him. Nothing like Kentucky, or anything he'd had beamed down on him in the South, either back in the days when there was an ozone layer or in the present when he's been told there isn't. And he could take the heat. Not that he's been out in it much these past twenty—Christ, has it been forty?—years of office followed by rec-room cocoonage, when his only exposure to unrefrigerated air was the dazed walk from the Lincoln and across whatever parking lot he found himself in. Still, he was born in Alabama. What his daddy called the devil's sauna. He could recall summers so hot the dog would rather shit on the floor and take a whipping than go out into the yard to do his business. Hadn't slowed him down a bit. Jackson Bader has never fainted in his life, not from the sun or any other damn thing, and he has no plans to start now. Not in *Canada,* anyhow.

It's the light up here. He's not showing any burn—the wide-brimmed Tilley he picked up at the airport and Elsie's near-constant sunblock slatherings have taken care of that—but it hasn't stopped him from being cooked alive. The *light*. Pure, stark, true as heaven.

He'd heard that July days up here were long. What he hadn't been warned of was the terrible brightness of the dusks. High noon didn't mean a thing in the north. It was the sun's coming-at-you-sideways five-to-nine shift that forced his eyes shut and pulled the plug on his legs, so that he could only stumble on, radioactive and blind.

Not that he's complaining. Not that he's saying a word. Elsie asks him if he's all right on the quarter-hour and he grunts her away. The Indian kid seems to be looking out for her now, which is just dandy with Jackson. As for the barfight loser, he's got his own troubles. And the guide knows who's signing her cheque, so what does it matter if he doesn't feel so good? They're tracking a big Kodiak and it's close. He paid more for the new Winchester slung over his shoulder than the mahogany cabinets in last year's kitchen reno, and he's used both to the exact same degree. Not a once. But that's about to change.

He walks on after the others. There is nowhere to look where the brightness hasn't laid the world bare. It's a funny thing, but goddamn it if he doesn't miss his own shadow.

With every sting between her claws or on the moist puck of her nose, the bear feels whatever advantage she might have started with in the morning racing away. Not only do the human hunters pursue them now but so do a handful of yellowjackets. Circling, blinding, chainsawing in her ears. A few of them using her mouth as a fountain, licking at the saliva that foams around her chops. She is thankful that the wasps have elected to focus all of their punishments on her and leave the cubs alone.

The wasps have come with her so far because she is carrying them. Deep in the fur at the top of her back, a queen has colonized the hump of the bear's shoulders.

The sow would like to stop and roll onto her back, wriggle over the blades of loose shale so that her tormentors would be sliced into a thousand twitching bits. She'd like to drown them by running over the crest and down to the river, crouching in the cold water until their striped corpses bobbed on the surface. She'd like to howl in self-pity. But there isn't the time to stop now, and a mountain crossing would leave them fully exposed to view for miles around. Even complaint is barred to her.

She counts each new sting as a provocation. In time, the hunters and the yellowjackets become parties to the same offence. There will be an end to running, she knows. And when it comes, the bear is glad that there will be something left in her for them.

FOURTEEN

She has been looking for the bear so long—not just the past ten hours but for as long as she has hunted, and possibly longer than that—that when it looms out from behind the snarled end of an uprooted spruce it is the embodiment of her whole imagination. Nothing about the animal is unfamiliar to her. Margot watches the bear enlarge as it humps in her direction and has each of its physical details confirmed one by one. The four nipples hanging from her underbelly, shiny and round as the ends of dull pencils. The way she breathes through her mouth so that her incisors are exposed in a glinting overbite. The becalmed eyes that suggest disguised madness.

What wind there is cools the sweat on Margot's cheeks, blowing her scent behind so that she remains undetected. At the same time, the air delivers whiffs of the animal's fur to the back of her throat from a hundred and fifty yards away, allowing her to taste the grizzly's cologne of wet straw and peat. Margot lowers herself until she is lying flat behind a bush of wild huckleberries. The bears' tracks had led her higher onto a broad rockslide. It is early evening. Maybe seven, maybe eight—Margot considers checking her watch but her arm insists on staying where it is. The time doesn't matter in any case. It is the beginning of the long end of a clear July day.

Although she couldn't see anything at first, it was this place that told Margot she had caught up with the bears. Now her hand rests on the stock of her rifle, but she makes no effort to raise it. Wade, Tom and the Baders are still five minutes behind her. She pulls her arms in tight and digs her chin into the sphagnum moss carpeting the ground in an effort to disappear. Her goal has nothing to do with deceiving the bear. Not for the first time, Margot wishes to be here and *not* here, a state beyond invisibility. She'd give all she has to see how a wild thing as fine as this moves without it being hunted or watched.

Margot has dreamed of this bear. Not as a vague objective or trophy weight, as a bear *like* this one, but the bear coming at her in this exploding moment of particularity, as unmistakable as identifying one's own child among others in a crowded playground. If she thinks hard enough about it, all of Margot's dreams have had this animal lurking around the edges, sometimes taking an active role but more often standing just offstage as a threat, a savage angel. A magnificent silver-tip no less than eleven feet from snout to tail. Every time the sow picks up her feet Margot measures her claws, and every time, she adds another inch to her estimate. Four, five, six.

All at once, the bear launches back on its rump and starts batting at the sides of its head. Margot can't help thinking that the animal is trying to jar a memory loose, just as Margot does with a smack to the forehead whenever she forgets to make a payment on her truck. The bear gives itself a beating that thuds against the rocky slope and echoes back, deep as the rolling approach of a thunderhead. Then Margot sees the yellowjackets. Spinning around in a tormenting carousel, faster and faster. The great forepaws flail about in an already flagging counterattack, useless as shaking your fist at the sun to stop it from shining.

It's only when the sow gives up on the wasps altogether that the cubs join her. A pair of two-year-olds, just as Margot had guessed from their tracks, but bigger than she pictured them to be. The smaller one might be a hundred and forty pounds, but its bigger brother has to be close to two hundred. They inch closer to their mother with uncertain steps, wondering if her rage at the yellowjackets might be redirected toward them if they approach at the wrong time.

Ten feet short of the sow, the two of them fall back on their rumps just as their mother had and raise their noses to the air. Already they know to be wary of open spaces, even when under the close protection of the she-grizzly. The cubs sniff for their pursuers first, then for food. Neither seem to be anywhere near. The breeze is light but remains steady against Margot's face. So long as Wade and the Baders keep their mouths halfway shut, the bears won't know they're here.

"Just like you said," a voice says, so close that Margot takes it to be coming from within her. "A big old Boone and Crockett."

Margot shifts her view from the rockslide to take in Jackson Bader lying next to her. For the first time since they stepped out of the truck this morning, the old man's breathing is steady. In fact, he appears not to be breathing at all. His eyes agog, a bloodshot map. She watches his trembling fingers wipe the moustache of salt from his lip.

"Where are the others?"

"Coming up. Your man Wade a bit behind."

"Let's wait for them. The wind's against us nice. Take our time."

"She's beautiful, isn't she?"

For a second that nearly springs a laugh from her chest, Margot mistakes his remark as being directed at his wife, who joins them now on her hands and knees, with Tom sliding down next to her. But of course he means the bear. He doesn't even turn when Elsie strokes his back. Then Mrs. Bader sees the animals as well.

"Oh," she says.

For half a minute the four of them watch the cubs circle round their mother, standing on their hind legs to bat the yellowjackets from her flank. When she tires of this play the sow takes a long stride away from them, and shows the full length of her side to the hunters. But the cubs stay close, wriggling under her, so that the target appears as a single boulder balanced on the slope.

Without hesitation or instruction, Jackson Bader sets the butt of his rifle to his shoulder. The Winchester strikes Margot as too pretty

to be used. She has never seen a firearm so clean. Waxed, almost.
An artifact you'd see laid upon a velvet pillow in a glass case.

"Wait a second," Margot whispers to him sharply.

"Why?"

"They're too close together. And you're not even holding that
gun right."

"I got 'em."

"No, you don't. Not until I tell you, you don't."

"I got—"

Bader fires twice.

The shots' concussion lifts the old man clear from the ground.
He is in the air for less than a second but Margot is able to note
how every part of him twists away from the rifle as he goes, pushing it off him, as though a snake has come alive in his hands.

When he meets the earth again it lays him out in the shape of a
horseshoe. Too small for his clothes. The breath coming out of
him in little burps.

"Jackson?"

Margot hears Mrs. Bader's voice, though she's surprised she's
able to, as the ringing in her ears from Bader's gun snuffs out all
other sound. A whisper of perfect disbelief. The utterance that
comes before terror, before recognition, before the first tally of
how terribly things have changed. It's the only word she knows.

"Jackson?"

"Hold on. We need to—"

"Jackson!"

Mrs. Bader goes to her husband in a lunge so sudden that Margot
believes the woman intends to strangle him.

"Wade! We got some trouble here," Margot shouts. *"Wade?"*

A dial tone in her ears. An angry yellowjacket lands on the back
of her hand. Stings three knuckles in a row.

Without knowing why and before going to check on the old
man or even turning the other way to see if either of the shots had

found the bears, Margot picks up Bader's shining Winchester and pumps out the remaining cartridges, watches them roll between pads of lichen, and disappear. It's a light gun, all right. When she throws it behind her it tumbles bore over stock before clattering to the end of the avalanche chute. For a second, Margot, Tom and Mrs. Bader look down at where it has come to rest and are blinded by it shining up at them.

Bader's cough brings them back. It lifts his chest a full two inches off the ground before it crunches down on a bed of stones. After this, Margot sees a shiver run down the old man's back and out to the ends of his limbs. The tiny ripples scuttle under his clothes so that she expects to see a thousand ants rush out from his collar and sleeves.

"Where's Wade?" Margot asks Tom.

"Back there."

"Which way?"

"Took one look at the bear and just sort of—"

"He *ran?*"

Tom nods.

Another cough from Bader. Less forceful than the first, but with a wet rattle at the end.

In the next instant, Mrs. Bader has her hand in her waist pouch, searching. Speaks her husband's name again, this time as a lover would. Lies down to stroke the back of her hand over his cheeks.

"What's wrong with him?" Margot says.

"He needs his pills."

"What pills?"

"His heart, his heart, his *heart.*"

"What about his heart?"

"It was his birthday."

Although it will do no good, Margot considers striking the woman. Before she knows it, she has raised her hand at an angle to deliver a downward slap. Elsie Bader sees it and pouts.

"He wanted a bear for when he turned seventy," she says. Her face swollen. It's enough to lower Margot's hand. "He said he'd be okay so long as I came with him. It had been *so long* since he'd asked me for *anything*. I told him *of course* I would. I'd go anywhere he wanted me to. And I *would*. I—"

"Can you give him his pills now?" Margot interrupts, looking down at Bader as though calculating whether he could be folded up and stuffed in her backpack.

"He said he'd be *fine*."

"But he sure as hell isn't fine now. So can we slip him some of those—?"

"I can't."

"Why not?"

"Because they're *gone*," she cries. "The *hills*. Up and up and up. There's been too many *hills*."

Margot turns away from the Baders to look out over the killing ground. One of the cubs, the smaller of the two, lies still on its side. The other gut-shot but alive, limping in a dazed circle. The she-grizzly is nowhere to be seen.

"We've got to move."

"Can't we *wait?*" Mrs. Bader says, stroking her husband's hair flat against his head.

"He shot that cub. And looks to have done some damage to the other one, too."

"Where's the big one now?" Mrs. Bader asks, turning to look behind her.

"I don't know. But she's not going to stay away from her cubs long."

"Oh my God."

"It wouldn't be a birthday without a surprise, would it?"

Margot has pulled the Remington off her shoulder and pumped a cartridge into the chamber before she registers the sound of crunching steps approaching off to the right. She rolls onto her side and steadies the site on the dark shape slumping out of the brush twenty yards away. It's a poor position to shoot from, but she could hit a yellowjacket out of the air at this range.

"For fuck sake, it's *me*."

"Where were you?"

"Here."

"No you goddamn weren't."

Wade steps forward and only now does Margot lower the gun. He looks past her at the Baders, curled side by side on the rocks.

"Did you know about his pills?"

"His what?"

This proves it, Margot thinks. *I'm living with the worst liar that's ever had reason to tell one.*

"I think he's having a heart attack. That surprise you?"

"I saw him take something. I didn't know what."

"Thanks for letting me know, partner."

"I couldn't—"

"And then you run off at the first sight of a bear."

"I backed around to get a different angle from up in the alders."

"Really? I didn't hear you shoot."

"It nearly ran me over. All I could do is try to get clear. And then you've got your rifle pointed in my face."

Margot stands and notices that the injured cub has disappeared from the slide. From her new height she can make out the full shape of the smaller cub lying still. The spray of blood exited from the back of its head.

"There's nowhere to go but back the way we came," Margot says.

"I can carry him."

"You take one arm and I'll take the other. Tom, you help Elsie. We'll leave our packs here. They might slow her if she wants something to beat up on when she comes back."

She puts a hand against the back of Mrs. Bader's neck and the old woman spins around as though touched by ice.

"We'll take your husband. You just follow us close. Tom will be with you. You got that?"

"Oh, *yes*," she says, in the same tone she would use to accept an offer of ladyfingers with her tea. "Yes, yes."

Wade and Margot step to each side of Bader's body and yoke his arms over their shoulders. He emits a sigh that could be an expression of either resignation or pain. Margot counts aloud over top of it and, on three, they raise him to his feet. The toes of his boots dragging over the alpine blooms. Indian paintbrush, saxafrage, glacier lilies.

Margot lifts her head long enough to judge the treeline to be five hundred yards away. It will take them all the hours of the night and some of the morning to reach the truck. In the meantime, she will be grateful for the cover of the spruces, a net of shade between them and the hard twilight.

They don't even make it that far.

One of Bader's sighs turns into a word.

There.

They keep pulling him forward, but Margot is sure of what she heard. She lifts her head again. Fifty feet away, the she-grizzly stands astride the trail. Glaring at them with eyes pulled halfway back into her skull.

Margot releases Bader's arm. The doubled weight forces Wade to let go of him as well, so that the old man falls face first into an embroidered square of rosewort.

"The fuck?"

At the sound of Wade's voice, the bear takes a step forward, hackles raised. Swings her head low from side to side. *Like it's lost its contact lenses,* as Margot's father had put it on their first and only hunting trip together before the Mounties took him away for good. Margot had smiled as she thought she was expected to, but it was meant as a warning more than a joke. *When a bear moves like that, you get your gun ready. And if you don't have a gun, climb a tree.* Margot had asked what to do if there weren't any trees around. Play dead? The old bastard had laughed. *You won't have to play dead, girl.*

Even as she replays this loop of her father's voice Margot is reaching back to pull the rifle off her shoulder. The sow's head stops swinging. From somewhere behind her, Mrs. Bader states her husband's name once more.

The rifle's butt trips along the length of Bader's back on its way up into Margot's hands. Before it gets there the bear barks once and charges.

All of them pitch off the trail, slipping down the rockslide with knives of shale cutting the backs of their ankles. Wade lets go of his shotgun and it clatters ahead, disappearing in a snarl of saskatoon bushes. The grizzly covers the ground between them in three strides. If she stops, turns and heads down the slide she would be upon the four of them before they could find their balance. Instead, she keeps running.

Jackson Bader can only watch it come. The bear advances on him sideways. Taking her time. She allows him to appreciate her size, the futility of attempting anything now but the observation of her whims.

When she stops, she stands directly over him, blowing foul air over his face. It forces his eyes shut, but only for a second. Bader wants to see. He wants to touch, too. He sits up on one elbow, but the animal's chest is so high that even if he had the power to lift his arm straight up he couldn't reach its chin.

For a moment, the bear sniffs at the air over the old man, taking in whatever lifts off his skin. The deodorant he smeared on this morning. The deep-fried sweat. The powder from his gun's empty shells.

There might be time for Margot to take a shot, but something prevents her. Instead of trying to stop what she knows is to happen next, she feels only the need to prevent Bader's wife from seeing it.

Margot turns, expecting to see Elsie frozen behind her. And this *is* what Margot sees. Mrs. Bader's face at once blank and reflective of a hundred instantaneous, colliding thoughts. Fear is not among them.

"Elsie?" Margot says, reaching for her. But the woman is already turning away. Putting both her hands on Tom's shoulders and shaking him.

"This way," Elsie Bader says to the boy. "That first tree. Now run. *Run*."

Margot watches Mrs. Bader grab Tom's hand. It keeps them both on their feet as they scramble down the slope toward the treeline. Without pause she turns her back on her husband to guide her adopted son to safety.

The old man closes his eyes so as not to look directly down the bear's throat. It doesn't prevent him from smelling the hot gusts of its breath. Stewed berries, copper, rancid lettuce. It reminds him of the one and only time he stuck his head into Elsie's compost bin back home.

"No," he says.

Even now, the broken squeak of his voice fills Jackson Bader with regret. He should have said nothing. He wishes he could pull his shaking hands away from his face. Not to see what the bear is going to do to him but to show that he isn't afraid. Yet not even his pride can stop him from begging.

"No," he says again, though he and the bear alone hear it this time.

The only resistance he is capable of is a jerking tremor in his legs. The bear comes close to sniff at a flailing boot. She seems to consider what she will do next from a number of alternatives. As she does, the boot glances harmlessly off her snout. It decides the matter for her.

With a grunt, she steps on both of Bader's legs until they are calmed. The bear drags her claws up until her front paws rest on his chest. When she finds her balance, the bear opens her mouth wide and lowers it over his.

There is a succession of pops that, from where Margot stands, sound like stepped-on bubble wrap. The bear is patient. When she pulls back, Bader's jaw hangs flat as a door knocker.

The pain is so stunning and complete it closes his throat to any noise that might escape it. The bear continues to stand on him, so that his protest is limited to a nearly imperceptible shake of his head. Aside from this, he can do nothing but blink. It puts a flickering screen between the present moment and the next, cutting the bear's motion into primitive animation. A flip book.

Through it, he watches the animal come down on him again. With a dip of its head, the bear takes the top of his skull in its teeth and jerks it back. There is a single, hollow crack. Even Bader recognizes it, though nothing can be felt where it occurs, nothing anywhere.

The bear grips him by the throat. In a fluid motion he is hauled into the air, his feet kicking over the rocks. When she sits back on her hindquarters, the sow rakes her claws down Bader's body. Each stroke carves off another inch.

Margot knows what is happening without looking.

Fifty yards down, Elsie Bader knows too. Yet she doesn't turn, doesn't stop pushing Tom up the black spruce they have come to. It is only when he is fifteen feet up and hugging the trunk after her whispered urgings—*Higher, Tom. That's it, higher*—that she allows herself to scream.

It brings Margot down to her. Directing Elsie Bader over to the spruce next to Tom's and lifting her up around the waist.

"Grab that branch there," Margot tells her. "That's right. Now *pull*. Up, up, *up*."

On the rockslide, Wade hasn't moved. He watches the bear turn its attention to Margot and Mrs. Bader and feels the moment as one that ushers in the unstoppable.

He waves his arms over his head. Calls the animal the same name, over and over. Above him, she still holds Bader in her jaws. Shaking him now. Parts of him fall off, slapping against the stones. Raggedy Jackson.

All at once, the sun brightens even more. The bear catches Wade's eye.

"You," he says.

The animal's only response is to commence another flaying of the old man's body. Within seconds, all she holds is a loose assembly of white ligament and bone.

He's not sure why he does it, but Wade comes at the bear. Six feet below it now, shouting with a courage he doesn't feel, has never felt. Only as the sow drops Bader and brings a forepaw back to swing at him does Wade realize his intent isn't to save the old man but to give Margot enough time to run.

The bear's strike is faster than any of the barroom roundhouses Wade has watched swing his way. Still, he has time to notice how the open forepaw looks like a catcher's mitt. One with blackened steak knives where fingers should be.

But in the sliver of time between the claws' coming and going, the bear misses him altogether.

And yet he's airborne.

His feet pedalling air like that time he got on the trampoline on his way home from the lounge before Terry Gray showed up to tell him to knock it off. It's only just before his back meets the rocks twenty feet down the slide that the first tingling in his chest arrives. His head rolls on his neck to deliver glimpses of sky, the jagged ridgeline. A musical staff of five neat cuts seeping through his shirt.

Elsie Bader doesn't stop screaming. She doesn't stop climbing, either.

"One more," Margot orders her.

It's been perhaps a minute since the last of Wade's shouts. At first, she thought it was she he was calling *bitch*. Then nothing. Too abrupt an end for Wade to have silenced himself.

"Hold it tight," Margot tells her. "I'm going to check on the others. Just *hold* it."

Margot scrambles back up the rockslide. The rocks screech under her boots. It seems to take several hours to get high enough to look down into all of the chute's ledges and dents.

She nearly steps on Bader before she sees that it's him. A coil that has already attracted a party of bottlehead flies. She looks away, scanning the treeline, the ridge above. Wade and the bear are gone.

Margot runs the length of the slide's treeline, calling out for him. She searches for a trail but there is no blood to follow, and the bear would leave no tracks behind on the shale. The only sign that Wade had been here at all is the radio. Lying a few feet from Bader's body, its casing split open and the wires gutted.

Mrs. Bader continues to scream.

Keep it up, Margot can't stop herself from thinking. *You can do the wailing for both of us.*

Not that it matters. Not compassion, manners, love or anything else. There is only where they are. She knows the place, but might as well be lost for all the difference it makes. Caught between the smoke in the valley and the daytime moon. A doll's face, sitting on the crest of the hills.

FIFTEEN

"It's coming," King says.

In the time it took Jerry McCormack to take a nervous leak against the tree nearest him and zip up again, the fire has nearly doubled in size. The other three could only watch how it was done. How they'd helped it.

At the same time King stepped back, Miles saw the backfire lose its initial speed, so that when the main fire joined it, their own blaze showed it the way out. Mungo was the only one to speak. *Buggernuts,* he said.

"It's coming," King says again, this time without his earlier wonder, only dread.

The five of them stand spellbound. It lasts a few seconds but feels much longer, like the time between being launched over the handlebars and your chin finding the pavement.

"Let's move it back," Miles says, waving them down the path that had brought them here. "King? Are you with us?"

"Where are we going?"

"A little walk. Pick up your tools."

"Fucksake, Miles," Jerry says, still unable to pull his eyes from the blaze. "Maybe we better just——"

"I'll tell you when to drop your gear, and it's not now. We are *walking* out of here."

Miles looks back into the clearing once more to gauge the fire's direction and speed. Already, the original fuel of ground cover within the clearing is being replaced by the lodgepole pines of the surrounding forest, and the resulting heat lashes out at them a hundred yards away. Miles watches how the flames are emboldened with oxygen the higher they climb. A crown fire. One that turns the trees into candles, red leaping from wick to wick.

"We can still handle this thing," Mungo says, putting his hand on Miles's arm.

"I doubt that. But it doesn't make a difference. We're leaving it. Come back before dawn when it's asleep."

"If we just—"

"We're going, Mungo."

Miles looks at him, and without another word, Mungo leads the way down the trail. He knows that Miles will be the last one back. If the fire is to catch any of them, the crew boss will be first.

Behind them, the fire proceeds at the highest and lowest extremes. As the crowns light up thirty feet over their heads, the forest floor thrums with a million small ignitings of timber lit- ter—shrubs, conifer reproduction, anything rotten or dwarfish. Mungo sets a pace that is as fast as walking permits while carrying pulaskis and pisstanks on their backs.

It isn't far to the truck. Miles would guess no more than half a mile. They should be able to make it without running so long as they don't lose the trail. That's why Miles won't let them go any faster than they are now. For the moment, the risk of panic and one of them cutting back into the fire is higher than its overtaking them. He hopes he's right about their distance from the truck.

Miles counts out every passing of a trail tape tag. He's pretty sure he tied five orange bows between the truck and the smoker, but right now, he's seen only two whip across his arm, fluttering like Day-Glo butterflies. Once, King turns his head to check on the fire's progress, but whatever expression Miles shoots back at him—or whatever the kid sees in the face of the fire—returns his eyes to Jerry McCormack's shoulders in front of him.

When they pass the third trail tape, Miles glances back himself. He can't see or hear the fire anymore, only feel it, a papery breath of heat that glues his lips shut. He looks straight up into the canopy to make sure the crowns have not yet ignited, and thinks he catches a flash skip across a patch of sky. But when he stops to confirm it, he sees that it was only the fourth knot of trail tape he'd spotted in his peripheral vision as it flapped by.

Even as the fifth tie smacks Mungo's shoulder, Miles wonders if they should break into a sprint. He doesn't trust this fire. The way it's faster than it has a right to be. The way it hides. Perhaps it has come around them in a circle that, at the last second, will cut them off from the road. Perhaps it's already there.

"The road toad!" Crookedhead shouts as pixels of brown paint and chrome assemble into the crew truck through the aspen leaves.

Miles hadn't noticed the gully they had come down when they started out from the pumper. A thirty-foot rise between them and the road. It adds an extra minute to the calculations Miles has already made in his mind. Two if they hang on to all their tools.

At the head of the line, Mungo hits the slope and it immediately bends him over, his hand clutching at roots to gain purchase on the grade. Jerry and Crookedhead fan out on either side of him. Miles watches the three men stiffen, fighting for every inch like beetles on a sand dune.

Then realizes there are only three.

He squints into the trees they have just passed through and sees that many of them are already hissing back at him. Directly overhead, the crowns wave orange flags.

Halfway up the gully, Mungo turns. Miles waves him on.

King, his lips say.

When Miles steps down to find the trail again it is dappled with cinders. Fireflies of ash lighting in the air, circling. Resting on his arm to bite through hair.

He drops the chainsaw. His arm tingles with the release of weight. Swings it forward to get the feeling back and decides the direction it accidentally points in will be the one he follows.

The kid must have cut off to the side when Miles was counting the last of the tags, which means he couldn't have gone far. But it needn't be far for both of them to be caught now. The trees sprouting heads to make a continuous rooftop of fire, leaving it nowhere to go but down. If it does before they're out, Miles knows he and the kid will suffocate before they burn. He can only pull in inadequate half-breaths as it is. Searing his insides like gulps of boiled water.

He keeps to the line he's struck on. Neither he nor King would be capable of speech in the airless heat, so he doesn't bother trying to call. If he doesn't catch sight of the kid he won't find him at all.

It occurs to Miles that maybe he's already passed him. King could be with the others at the pumper right now, joining them in the debate over how long they could afford to wait before being forced to drive on. If this is how it goes, he hopes at least that one of them will go down to pick up his saw. A Stihl 044 he'd oiled and sharpened back from the grave. He really liked that saw.

When he first sees the kid he thinks he's part of the fire. Standing in the middle of aspens with flames wriggling out from within the bark. His fluorescent vest marking him as a burning tree among trees.

Miles waves him over. The kid doesn't move. His eyes flicking between the treetops and his own boots, fascinated by the shrinking distance between them.

To get to him, Miles walks straight through a thatch of flames. On the other side, his bootlaces and sleeves bring some along with him. He doesn't bother trying to put them out. Instead, he circles behind the kid and knocks him forward with both hands.

They aren't following any particular route this time. Miles keeps pushing, and the kid's head keeps whiplashing back. They will make it to the gully and up to the road, or they will not. But Miles will not let the kid space out again either way.

"Over here!"

Miles hears Crookedhead James's voice before he notices that he and the kid are now on the slope. Mungo and Jerry come down to help them, but Miles flinches from their touch. It leaves the two men to take the kid by the shoulders and drag him to the top.

At the pumper, Miles looks back and sees the forest they have emerged from thicken with fire. They have to roll out of here. But first, he asks a question of the doubled-over King.

"Why would you do that?"

"What?"

"Hey, King?"

"Yeah?"

"Look at me."

The kid takes some time to raise his eyes.

Miles throws a straight jab to his mouth. So fast none of them are sure it's even happened, including the kid. All he can do is smack his lips, tasting the instant, coppery seep from his gums.

"Listening?"

King blinks.

"*Why* would you stop out there?"

"The fire. It was just *flying*—"

A forearm, hard, to King's chin. It snaps his head back to bounce off the pumper's roof rack and return to bobble atop his neck.

"Wake up." Miles hits him again before King can reply. "*Hello?*" A slap that turns his ear white, then red. "*Hello?*" The other ear. "*Wake* the *fuck* up."

"Okay."

"Okay what?"

"I hear you."

"That's good. Because the next time you fall asleep, I'm going to let you burn."

They drop their gear in the back and get in. Miles thinks of going back for the saw, but the idea of getting himself killed on account of King at this point only makes him more angry. He climbs behind the wheel and takes it out on the gas, roaring the engine until the hood almost jumps free.

After he's bounced them a quarter-mile farther away from the site, Miles gets on the radio. His first request is for an air drop. The denial from overhead comes faster than usual. All air support is currently committed to fires at Dawson, Haines Junction and Atlin. Given the remoteness of the Comeback Fire, and its relative smallness, they shouldn't expect a reconnaissance fly-over, let alone a water bomber, for at least the next twelve hours.

Miles checks his watch. A quarter past seven. He decides there's no point in all of them staying out here scrunched up in a crew cab until nightfall, when the fire might have settled down in the cooler temperature and they could have a chance of giving it a second size-up. He calls in to the RCMP office and asks Terry Gray if he can come out and take men back into town to get a few hours' sleep. Mungo requests to stay with the truck, but Miles pretends not to hear him. Instead, he tells Terry that there will be four going back and one staying. It's clear to everyone who the boss intends to remain.

Finally, Miles tries to reach Ruby Ritter on the radio. He wants to hear for himself what she spotted of the Comeback, but only static greets his repeated attempts at contact. Next, he calls Margot on her frequencies. There are any number of harmless explanations as to why neither of them are answering, but Miles refuses to believe any of them.

Alex wonders whose move it is. She stands over the chessboard with Stump's tail slapping against her leg and feels her own heart-beat quicken to match its rhythm. She guesses he's playing white.

At first, she thought of shifting his rook around and putting him in checkmate, so that when he returned he would understand that she had left him a message. It even crosses her mind to pick up one of the pieces—the white queen—and slip it into the pocket of her jeans as a souvenir. But without him in it, the cabin feels too empty, too much like a sad museum of his solitude for any playful riddles or thefts. She's not surprised that she misses him a little. It's how quickly the disoriented longing invaded her spirits that she hadn't seen coming. Watching him dress in the morning, talking about the fire as his voice squeaked with emotion he seemed unable to hear, his eyes electrocuted—she assumed that Miles would be so much worse off than she.

And it was true that, for the first hour after his departure, she felt only a dull, philosophical regret, at the same time entertaining optimistic calculations of the long-term good she'd done. It almost worked. Then she made the mistake of noticing his details. The musk of beer and woodsmoke rising out of the laundry hamper. The ancient bottle of mouthwash she'd heard him pull out from under the bathroom sink when he had gotten up in the night and returned to kiss her neck with minty lips. The coloured tissue paper, Magic Markers and scissors left on the kitchen counter that he used in making postcards. All she had to do was open herself to these bits and pieces to feel the blade go in.

What made it worse is that she had watched Miles and Rachel's goodbye through the bedroom window. The way her daughter had touched his face as though to protect him from further injury.

Alex had followed Miles as he stood up from Rachel, walked around to the front of the cabin and started his truck. When she could no longer hear the crunch of gravel under his tires, she told herself that this was the scene she had come here to witness. With this pantomime of farewell, all their loose ends were tied. Surely now, with no more than life's usual bittersweetness, the three of them could carry on knowing that all that could be done was done.

Then an alternative view arrived. It came hard and very fast. She was a fool.

She called Rachel and Stump in from outside. She cranked the living-room window open to let the birdsong in. She rang the guy Mungo had asked to fix the grinding in her transmission to confirm that it was ready to pick up. She ate a four-egg, Cheez Whiz and onion omelette. None of it could prevent her from finding herself here, scraped clean from the inside out, frozen over the chessboard.

"Momma?" Rachel says, having joined Stump in beating against her leg. *"Momma?"*

"Yes, baby?"

"Are we *really* going away?"

"In the morning. First thing."

"Why?"

"It's time to go home."

"Can we bring Stump with us?"

"Stump belongs to Miles, sweetheart."

"Can we bring Stump *and* Miles?"

"Nope."

"Why?"

"Because they belong here."

It's so simple, Alex thinks, and decides to pocket the queen anyway. It's so simple once you say a thing to see it as true.

Aside from running away, Miles had kept his other secret to himself until this morning. Over the last five years, he'd thought it might have been Ross River's only one. Now, he'd told Alex about Margot and him without needing to, without anything bargained for in return. It wouldn't change anything, of course. That Miles had slept with the black-haired hunting guide within the first month of arriving in town, and had continued to, at the ritualistic rate of twice a year since, wasn't even very interesting as a stray piece of gossip. What he didn't tell Alex was how what he had done came to turn another man's soul to ash. There are even times when Miles wonders if he has had a hand in two deaths, not one.

"It's Margot," she had said over the phone when she called. The first of the two times she ever has. "We met at the lounge last night."

Miles remembered. He had played darts with her boyfriend,

Wade, a friendly giant who insisted on paying for all their beers and who had a startling memory for jokes involving a talking frog in a Mexican whorehouse. Margot had come along later. Miles felt her staring at him, at his scar. What was unusual was how her staring seemed an expression of approval.

"I think I owe your boyfriend a few rounds."

"Wade's just happy to see another white guy in town who isn't a cop."

"I'll get him next time, then."

"Actually, I'm calling to ask if you'd like to come over."

"Oh yeah? What are you guys up to?" Miles asked, knowing what was coming next. Wade would be out of town. There would be no dinner, no party. It would be drinks, just the two of them.

"Wade's gone down to Whitehorse for the weekend," Margot said, reading her line almost precisely as Miles had written it for her. "One of his getaways with the criminals he calls his friends. Thought I could handle a cocktail myself."

"Just you and me?"

"You want to bring a friend?"

"I don't really have any."

"Boo hoo. Why don't you stroll down here and see if you can make a new one?"

Affairs were neither Miles's history nor his interest. The word itself had the whiff of mothballs about it, the festive promise—*a fair!*—failing to hide its musty compromises. What's more, they had never made much sense to him. While he could see why neglected husbands or wives might look elsewhere, those who came from outside to service those within always struck him as slightly pathetic, unpaid servants. And then there were the moral rationalizations he found wearying even before having to choose one and stick to it:

It was a dead marriage, so what difference did it make?

Wade was abusive and therefore didn't deserve loyalty.

They didn't mean to, but Miles and Margot had fallen in love.

He was certain the third option didn't apply. As for the first two, he didn't know near enough about Wade and Margot to invoke them. Not yet, anyway. And even if Wade had some cuckolding coming to him, Miles would never bring himself to see that he had to be the man to deliver it.

Then why did he (after shaving, the extra swipe of deodorant, the twenty push-ups grunted out on his bedroom floor) walk over to Margot and Wade's trailer, his scar aglow? At the time, he guessed it was for the simplest of the adulterer's excuses: Wade would never find out. But even as he knocked on Margot's door, he saw that the real reason lay elsewhere. According to some instinctual alarm clock within him, Miles had determined that it was time to take up the sort of barely sustaining sexual life he figured was his due. Rare and sad dalliances in other men's homes, holiday one-offs with lonely waitresses, none of them convincing enough to alter even the most uncertain perspectives. He thought that if this was to be the extent of his contact with women hereafter, he might as well start getting used to it.

"You looked like someone with a past," Margot had answered when he asked why she'd chosen him, and Miles knew that she was speaking of his burn.

He lay beside her, hollowed out, aware of little but the rolled-up socks on the carpet, the photos taped to the bureau mirror, the faint smell of sweat and unwashed hair on the sheets—everything that could be identified as Wade's.

"Everyone has a past," he said. "And you haven't even asked about mine."

"I don't need to. All I need for now is to know you can handle this."

"I'm not sure that I can."

The comfort he had taken in her was already gone. He had expected it would be easier than this. A year was a long time.

"I've never done this before, you know," she said. Although her voice was steady, a pair of tears raced each other down opposite cheeks. Miles waited to see which hit the pillow first. As he watched, he wondered exactly what she meant. Never slept with a man behind Wade's back before? Or just never here, in his bed?

On the walk back to his cabin, Miles wondered if Margot had tried to tell him that she had never fallen in love with someone she didn't even know before. It took only a moment to dismiss this possibility. What he found much harder to shake was the fact he had found love that way once himself.

SIXTEEN

In the north, everything that does not occur above the 60th parallel takes place Outside. It's as though the people who live on the other side of the territory's boundaries exist only in virtual terms, as the product of some computer program responsible for generating characters to play international politics, mall shoppers, screen gazers. The "millions of people" one hears about but, up here, can't quite be taken seriously.

What Miles wonders is if not being Outside automatically makes him Inside. Cranked back in the driver's seat of the truck a half mile from the Comeback as he is now, or set atop his stool in the Welcome Inn Lounge as he is every other night—do any of these situations qualify him as being part of anything larger than himself? He doubts it. You need to belong to something in order to stand within it, and Miles is a man who has been meticulous in maintaining his freedom from affiliation. No softball league shirt with a nickname ironed over the shoulders, no hunting buddies. The necessary give-and-take that comes with community is a privilege that he has squandered, and now it's only fair that he pull himself from the game, from fellowship, from all but the recollection of love.

Miles knocks the side of his head against the closed driver's window. He wants to think of something else. *Anything.* How he has been transported to the surface of Mars, for example. Outside, the air is aswirl in alien oranges, purples and blacks, as though from paintbrushes being stirred in water. The whole sky drained of blue by the combination of twilight and smoke.

After Terry Gray came to collect the rest of the crew and take them back to Ross River to sleep half a night in their own beds,

Miles spent the first hour on the radio, alternating between requests (all denied) for air drops and attempts (all failed) to make contact with Margot or Ruby Ritter. After that, he gave up and acted like someone trying to get some rest. Even faked sleep eludes him.

Outside. No matter where he goes now he will stand with his fingers poked through the fence, looking in. The life he has made for himself in Ross River may be paper-thin, anaesthetized, a method actor's sustained performance of indifference. But it did boast the single virtue of control. And what had it taken to throw him off? Not much, when you added it up. A mother and child he can lay only the most technical claims to. Less than seventy-two hours. A walk up Eagle's Nest Bluff with the kid, a for-old-time's-sake roll with his ex. Hello and goodbye.

He wishes for sleep. And it will come. It must. But for the time being, he feels too stoned to sleep. This is Alex and Rachel's fault as well. They're the ones who had pressed a needle to his neck and jacked him on a drug he hasn't felt in his blood for enough years to count as forever. A hallucinogen, for the most part.

Fear.

Just past midnight in Miles's spare room, lying on a fold-out cot with Stump snoring on the pillow next to her, Rachel dreams of falling through ice. Even as her bare feet slide through the cracks and a sensation closer to burning than freezing shoots up her legs, she is aware that it is really nighttime in Ross River, that her mother is in the next room with both of their backpacks zipped tight at the end of her bed. She is the little girl about to drown, and she is not. She dies and watches herself die at once.

Although she is afraid to open her eyes underwater in motel pools and campground lakes, she opens them in her dream and sees only darkness. She cannot read any sign of the hands she knows are thrashing in front of her, cannot make a guess at how deep it is. This is death. Only five years old but she can read a symbol as plain as this one. It is nothing but black. A simpler thing than emptiness.

Rachel knows she is not supposed to be aware of such grim realities, and this is why she keeps this dream a secret from her mother. It will upset her to know that her daughter is fated to die the same as everyone. Far worse than disappearing is the idea of leaving her mother even more alone than she was. It makes her fight against the water one last time.

The only light comes from the grey circle in the ice, an impossible body-length away now. All her efforts have managed to do is hold her in place against the current. When she finally surrenders, she watches her mother's arm come down through the hole. Her skin so green it appears hairy with fungus.

When the girl opens her eyes again she takes a gulp of Stump's exhaled breath. A mouthful of liver kibble and old socks.

"Momma," she says, and hears the word followed by a cascade of sobs. She runs from the room with the dog following her and jumps into bed next to Alex.

"Did you have a bad dream, baby?" she asks, folding the girl's body into hers.

"You were *alone,* Momma."

"I've got you with me now, though, don't I?"

"Yes."

"And I'm not ever going to let you go. Right?"

The girl thinks of revealing to her mother the terrible news of her dream, but can't bring herself to do it. The dark water is something she must keep to herself. Sharing it would be an obscenity.

"Rachel? Honey?"

The girl snuzzles tighter and, for her mother's sake, pretends to sleep.

***

After Terry Gray drops the men in front of the fire office, they throw their gear inside and stand in a circle around Jerry McCormack's new Ford, none of them ready to go home just yet.

"I've got some beer," Jerry says.

Everyone turns to Mungo. Seeing as Miles isn't around, this would leave him responsible for handling the big decisions such as these.

"Just one," Mungo says. "But only because I want history to show that Jerry McCormack paid for at least a single round of drinks this year."

They slouch over to Jerry's trailer in the weeds behind what used to be the radio station. He apologizes for the mess as they pile in, though the closed curtains and forty-watt bulbs he switches on hide most of what they sense must be lurking in the carpet and on the kitchen countertops. As they find places to sit, the plywood floor bends under the unaccustomed weight of visitors.

After Jerry brings in their drinks (three beer bottles clamped between the fingers of one hand, a glass of orange juice for Crookedhead in the other), they spend a long minute thoughtfully glugging and belching and sighing. In each of their heads, a number of opening remarks are considered and rejected.

"I've been meaning to get around to this all day," Mungo says after a couple of minutes, rises and walks down the hall.

"That fire," Jerry says when Mungo has shut the bathroom door behind him.

"What about it?" King says.

"A funny one, that's all."

"Seemed normal to me."

"They all *look* about the same. Once they're going."

"C'mon, Jerry," Crookedhead says.

"It's after hours."

"Let's just drink our drinks."

"We *are* drinking. And talking. I can do both at the same time on good days."

They take sips from their bottles. Little kisses that have less to do with drinking than waiting to see who will speak next.

"I shouldn't even be saying this," King says finally, and goes no further.

"Maybe not," Jerry says. "But you're not saying *anything* right now."

"Remember when I was going to call you guys to take the pumper out for a drill a couple days ago?"

"I could think of better ways to spend an afternoon."

"We couldn't go because it was out."

"So?"

"He said he'd been using it on his own. Taken it out for a drive. And when I asked about it, he just got really pissed. Like, no more questions."

"He's a strange guy sometimes."

"But the timing was weird, you know? Given the way things have turned out."

"A bit weird," Jerry says, nodding.

Mungo walks back into the living room, the toilet gurgling behind him down the hall. He looks directly at Crookedhead.

"What are we talking about?"

"King was saying how the chief took the pumper out for a drive all on his own a couple days back."

"That so, King?"

"It was a conversation."

"There's things a fire crew doesn't converse about."

"I didn't know."

"I'll forgive you for that. But I've got a feeling these two others here are setting a bad example."

"You've got to admit," Jerry starts, "it's sort of weird that—"

"I don't have to admit shit. I just want to finish my beer and go to sleep."

"It's not like we would ever *tell* anybody, even if we *knew* something, which we don't."

"Well, so long as we're being so open here in our little private circle, what about you, Jerry?"

"Me?"

"Funny how you're blowing air up everybody's ass except your own."

"Why would—?"

"I'll tell you why. Your goddamn Dodge."

"It's a Ford."

"You don't shut up about this truck that you're never going to afford if we don't get some major overtime, and then, just yesterday, there it is. That's got to be up there on the weird list."

"I got a loan."

"And *who* would lend *you* money?"

"We shouldn't be messing with this," Crookedhead moans.

Jerry turns on him. "Why do you say that?"

"Because we put the fires out, and that's *all*."

"What's the problem? What we're saying is just between us, anyhow."

"And that's four too fucking many," Mungo says.

"Fine. But about the truck. I didn't know about—"

Mungo takes a step toward Jerry McCormack's chair, leans forward and grabs him by the neck, his recliner slamming against the wall behind him.

"I'm serious," Mungo spits. "I'm really *very* goddamn serious about this."

Crookedhead starts to rise. A reluctant shifting that he hopes doesn't need to go further.

"Hey, hey—"

"So this is the *end*. Isn't it, Jerry?"

Mungo releases him. It allows Jerry McCormack to rub the blazing ring around his neck and nod his assent.

"Thanks for the beer," Mungo says, gulping back what's left in his bottle. For a second, Crookedhead and King stay where they are. But when Mungo makes a move, they read his intention for them to follow in the broad readiness of his back.

When they're out, Mungo looks back at Jerry, who has come to stand at the door. He considers saying something forgiving, a self-deprecating word to clear away the foolish minutes they had just spent, but decides against it. Their suspicions of each other had been there from the moment they stepped out of the truck at the site. Now, they have been released to the air, and nothing he might say will contain them.

Their sleep will be deep. Tomorrow promises twice the work of today. Mungo only hopes that the fire will occupy all of their thoughts until it is out. By then, what they spoke of in Jerry's trailer will be one more secret among the thousand others men like them have always carried.

It begins as soon as he closes his eyes.

At first, Miles thinks he's fallen into one of Stump's bad dreams. A dog's universal nightmare of being chased. Running uphill, his legs burning. The ridge a hundred yards ahead of him. He doesn't turn back to see what pursues him. It doesn't stop him from knowing. A bear. A great silver-tip gaining ground against the slope.

Don't look back.

A voice just off to his side, not his own. He remembers it, though. Remembers saying the same thing himself once.

Don't look!

There's less concern in the voice than amusement, a schoolyard taunt. And Miles doesn't want to look. Not at the bear. Even less at whoever runs next to him.

But he does.

He wakes so hard his forehead toots the horn when it slams against the wheel.

For a time, Miles sits staring ahead into the dark. When he glances down at the dashboard clock it reads 3:27 AM. It was 3:24 when he last looked. He was out for only three minutes but it was enough to take him straight to the climax of a nightmare. With it waiting there for him, there's no way he's going to try at sleep again.

He spills out of the truck and takes a few strides down the road. Around him, the woods are stilled by an insulating mist. He listens for whatever might have followed him out of the dream, but there is only a boneyard quiet.

Don't look.

"Tim," Miles says, and turns to look back at the truck.

He half expects to see the kid there, grinning behind the windshield. And for a second he does. Hands so white they look like butler's gloves gripped to the wheel. The nose burned clean off his head.

"Stop," Miles says aloud, and at the sound of his own voice, realizes that he's talking to it now. Begging the kid not to step out of the truck and come any closer.

"Stop it!" he says again. This time a command to himself.

A blink clears the kid away and replaces him with a pale mirroring of the moon against the glass.

Miles keeps walking. Although he can smell the caramelized resin in the air, what flames the fire sends up at the moment are obscured by the drooping spruce boughs. He doesn't need to see it. Miles can tell the fire is calm for the time being. He hopes that the three hours of genuine darkness afforded on this late-July night cools it down enough to take a nap.

Unfamiliar stars peek through the smoke. He looks up to count them and stops walking without meaning to. Whatever wind had been knocking the spindly lodgepoles together withdraws all at once, leaving everything in a lull of silence. Miles waits for the inevitable scrabbling of a hare or ground squirrel in the brush to start things up again, but nothing moves. He tries to take a breath but has forgotten how.

The screech drops him to his knees.

He covers his ears but it pierces through. Traveling down his arms, his back, until his entire body sings like a wineglass stroked around its rim. He hears it as a dying bruin caught in a snare. A girl encircled by fire. Her mother forced to watch her burn.

Miles looks to see where it comes from but it shifts away each time he thinks he's determined its source. A quarter-mile off, then from inside the truck, then streaking through the air directly over him. Constantly moving but unchanged in tone. One sustained scream shattering through the trees.

He sees it once it is still.

A glistening raven standing on the hood of the truck, glaring at him. For whatever reason, Miles is certain it is the same bird that Rachel was speaking to in the tree outside the cabin.

"What do you want?"

Now that it has his attention, the bird serenades him with an unsettling medley of its trademark noises: the old-lady squawk, the strangled gasp, the dripping faucet.

"Who are you?" Miles shouts at it, and realizes that this is the question he wanted the answer to in the first place.

The raven laughs.

Miles bends to pick up a handful of stones to throw at it, no matter if one of them shatters his windshield or not. But when he raises his head again and takes aim, the raven is gone.

"So you can fly now, can you?" Miles calls out into the trees. "Well, you should have flown up that hill when you had the chance. You hear me? You should have fucking flown like the rest of them!"

He's breathing so hard the smoke chokes him. Behind him, he can feel the first colours of dawn spilling over the hills.

On his way back to the truck Miles tells himself he will try the radio again or make another attempt at sleep, although he knows he will only sit there waiting for the crew to return, keeping watch for Mr. Raven in the pines.

He awakens in darkness unmistakable for night. Starless and close, a density he has never felt from any sky. There is also a weight on his chest that makes it difficult to breathe. He wonders if he is having a heart attack. Then he realizes that the heaviness is not on his chest alone but on all of his body. You don't feel a heart attack in your legs, do you? Your forehead? Your balls?

Wade tries to move and confirms his initial impression that he cannot. Prevented not just from getting to his feet but from lifting a knee, a finger. The recognition of his paralysis forces a cry from his throat. It comes out little more than a squeak. When he inhales, he tastes not air but earth and stone.

The bear has buried him alive.

He remembers lying twisted on the avalanche slide after the sow struck him. Her head swinging. When unconsciousness drifted closer he had welcomed it.

She had taken his arm in her teeth, dragged him over the shale and into the trees. The throbbing above his left wrist tells him this. Not far from where they started, he thinks, but it could also be miles. He doesn't recall her digging up the forest and piling it on top of him, but this is what happened. Margot had told him how they do it. It's how bears build a food cache. And in time she will return to feed on what she has stored.

He tries moving again and this time manages to unsettle some of the smaller rocks over his face. It sends a cascade of dirt into his mouth.

He sobs for a time, but it is something that occurs only at the perimeter of his sensations, like the pain in his arm. The longer he stretches the moments between blacking out, the stronger he feels.

She should have buried him deeper.

SEVENTEEN

In the salt-and-pepper haze that counts for dawn on a fire site, Miles leaves the truck to walk back the half mile to the Comeback. Or rather, the half mile from where it was the night before. Today, it doesn't take nearly so long for him to find it. Less than a hundred yards from where he had fallen to his knees at the sound of the raven's screech, stubby flames gnaw at the pine saplings.

Miles instantly calculates its rate of growth over the last twenty-four hours and concludes a worst-case scenario and then some. The Comeback has gone from five acres to five hundred over a quiet, cool, nearly windless evening. As for today, already a hot breeze lifts sand off the road and throws yellow fistfuls after the smoke. If the fire was fast yesterday, the next few hours are going to be another matter altogether.

Miles runs back to the truck and radioes in to the fire office in Whitehorse. At first, the dispatcher assumes she's misunderstood his estimates.

"It was an initial attack, Rank 3 situation at eighteen hundred hours yesterday, correct?" she says. Ally's her name. New this season. Miles summons the ounce of patience left available to him and uses it up in his next two words.

"That's right."

"Now it's a Rank 5?"

"It's quick, all right. And you're not too slow yourself."

"Once more," Ally goes on as though she hadn't heard his last remark. Miles can hear her scratching and rescratching notes on her Priority Report Sheet. "You're telling me you've got an uncontrolled wildfire within fifteen kilometres of significant values?"

"If by significant values you mean two hundred and forty human beings and a whack of perfectly good mobile homes, you're reading me right."

"Cause of fire?"

"What difference does it make?"

"Procedure requires a combustion source query in order—"

"Let's call it undetermined."

There's a silence from the dispatcher, and Miles assumes she's filling in another blank on the page. But then she says, "Meteorological doesn't have you down for any lightning strikes."

"You always believe weather forecasters?"

"This isn't forecast. It's what we've already recorded. Lightning-free in your immediate area for the past two weeks."

"I sat through a storm in Tower 28 the day before yesterday."

"But that's sixty kilometres from *this* fire's point of origin."

"Lightning had to have started this."

"But it *didn't*. And there's no campgrounds or cabins anywhere nearby. I'm looking at the topographical right now."

"Good for you."

"I need to ask. Could this be a firestarter situation?"

"Could be."

"It's just that the fire's progress is so accelerated, it's consistent with—"

"Look, put down whatever you want as the cause."

"I'm going to red-flag this file, you know. For recommended investigation."

"You can stick red flags anywhere you'd like, Ally," he says, his voice rising a menacing degree. "Just get me some help."

While he waits for the aerial report, Miles tries once more to get Margot on the radio. There's nothing on her frequency but a strange new interference he guesses to be the fire, or maybe the clouds he's noticed gathering to the southwest. Next he calls in to town and tells King to wake the team and bring them in, but to wait until they hear from him before coming out to the site. What Miles doesn't tell him is that he has a feeling that this fire is already past the initial attack stage, and that their suppression efforts are about to turn the page into search and rescue.

Within eighty minutes of his air request to Whitehorse, Miles receives word of the spotter's report. Even he is surprised by how far the Comeback has travelled through the night. Worse, it has decided to choose the most threatening directions to run in. Having cut away from the truck, the fire has now laid a quarter-mile wall of flames across the Robert Campbell Highway, the only road in or out of Ross River. The only other possible route for evacuation would be the Pelly, but even if every powerboat in Faro and Carmacks were sent upriver right now, it would take ten days for them to carry a couple hundred people out. What Miles also knows is that the current is far too strong and the water, even in July, is too cold to act as a safe zone. There is only a single option remaining. An air evacuation using the three Bell 206Bs Whitehorse can get their hands on.

"Nothing but 6Bs?" Miles asks Ally. "They only seat four, maybe five. It's going to take forever to get everybody out."

"It's what we've got," she says plainly, and he's forced to admit that, given the half-dozen other established wildfires that resources have been assigned to in the Territory, not to mention British Columbia, Washington, Oregon and California, there's no doubt she's telling the truth.

She outlines Whitehorse Overhead's plans to establish a base camp on the other side of the St. Cyrs, the closest flat area south of the mountains, the fire and where he is now. Miles knows the valley well. A broad table of green through which the Lapie River runs north and joins the Pelly, accessible only by the single gravel lane of the unmaintained Canol Road coming up a hundred and twenty miles from Johnson's Crossing. No significant values anywhere close by, except for moose and some of the most striking scenery the tourists never get to see. Along the fast-moving Lapie sprout three almost identical teardrop lakes that bulge out from its course like grapes along a vine. If required, air tankers could use any of them as an "oasis," a water source for scooping buckets up to drop around the town. Miles has to agree that it's a good place to situate an evacuation camp. It's also the closest you can get to town without being north of the range, an area that will soon be considered too high risk. If the fire races south toward the base, the hills' crest should at least slow it down, as the wind along ridgetops tends to soothe the flames for a time as they wonder which direction to go in next. For the next day or two, the Lapie valley should be safe. Everything north of the mountains, on the other hand, is dry tinder standing in the path of a firestorm.

"Have you called an air-vac on all the towers?" Miles asks Ally when he reaches her again on the radio.

"The ones we can get to."

"What about Ruby Ritter's?"

"We haven't had contact with Mount Locken since last night. And when we did a fly-over this morning, it was gone."

"What do you mean, gone?"

"The tower," Ally says. "The fire got there before we could."

Miles switches off the radio. He sees Crazy Ruby losing her grip on the ladder on her way down into the smoke. He sees her burned before she had the chance to wake up. But when Miles tries to summon a glimpse of Ruby alive, nothing comes to him.

He checks his watch. Quarter to seven. He'd hoped it was later. Before he looked he'd closed his eyes and willed time to jump ahead an hour, as it sometimes does when you're not thinking about it. When he opens them, however, the second hand is shuffling round the dial at its usual pace. He turns the keys in the ignition to illuminate the dashboard clock. Eight minutes earlier than his watch. Alex and Rachel probably aren't even awake yet, let alone on the road. Including them, this brings the number of evacuees to 242.

Make that 244. He'd almost forgotten the Baders. Why the hell isn't Margot answering him? Not that it matters now. Whether she is being stubborn by leaving the radio off or ignoring him as some kind of punishment, or if they've already been caught in the fire, it amounts to the same thing. With the air-vac scheduled to get underway soon, if they don't start back to town immediately there's a good chance they'll be left behind.

There's no more fighting this fire, not today or the next day or the next. It's all about getting out of its way. And Miles is the closest to it at the moment. He knows the area well without even glancing at the map. The job of locating Margot, Wade, Tom and the Baders logically falls to him. Within hours, the fire is going to have the Tintina Trench all to itself, and he's going to be the last one to look under the bed before closing the door.

"Is it as big as they're saying it is?" Mungo asks when Miles radioes in to the fire office.

"The spotter flew over it twenty minutes ago, so I'd say it's even bigger now."

"What crawled up its ass and died?"

"Maybe some fires wake up on the wrong side of the bed the same way we do."

"I'm a married man. No need to say another thing about *that*."

Miles likes this man. He briefly considers telling him this. Mungo has been his only real friend for the last five years and Miles has never even called him that to his face. He's been all the usual things that prevent a man from making the most basic pronouncements: too proud, too stupid, too asleep. All Miles can hope is that Mungo knows without him saying so, because, of course, he's not about to start now.

He tells Mungo about Ruby's tower going down, and for a moment neither of them say anything. When Mungo speaks next, Miles can hear the effort the man brings to keeping his voice from pitching into a desperate register.

"Tom's out there too."

"Margot will bring him in. And if she needs any help, I'm going to find her."

"I wish it was me going after them."

"We've all got jobs to do. Which brings me to a favour I need to ask. I want you to bring Alex in."

"Not a problem."

"Try my place first."

As he waits, Miles watches the smoke rub against the truck's windshield like fur. He puts his hand against the glass and feels the heat like sunlight, though the sky and all but the closest trees are shrouded by billows of grey. He should drive ahead a little farther to give himself a wider buffer zone but he doesn't want to lose the radio reception. This is what he tells himself. But there is something about having the growing fire at his back that excites him. It makes it his.

It's the third time he hears his name that he realizes that Alex has not been conjured by his imagination but is actually speaking to him.

"Miles?"

"You're still there," he says, failing to hide his disappointment.

"We were going to leave after breakfast, but the road's closed."

"It's going to be all right."

"The sky's gone dark. It's all orange and yellow and black."

"Like Halloween," he says foolishly, though it's true.

"There's so *much* of it."

"They're bringing choppers in to take you out."

"When are you coming back?"

"I have to find Margot and Wade and the hunting party first."

"Why you?"

"Because I'm already here."

"But how long are——?"

"Not long, sweetheart."

It's the pause they both leave after Alex's almost inaudible gasp that allows his mind to catch up with his tongue. *Sweetheart?* It wasn't an endearment he remembered using back in the days when he could speak them. *Baby. Darlin'. Honey.* And the homemade ones—embarrassing if heard in any ear but theirs—that came so naturally and assumed so many names. *Little chicken.*

Pickle. Sweet feet. But never sweetheart. One word so commonly thrown about that it was near impossible for a man of his vintage to speak without irony. But he'd done it. He'd called Alex sweetheart and he'd never been more sincere.

"I'll come back for you," he says.

"Please. You don't—"

"For both of you. I promise."

There's a silence between them that feels more intimate to Miles than anything they shared together the night before last in his bed.

"Miles?"

"I'm here."

"I'm going to go now."

"Okay. Right."

"So. This is Alex. Over."

"Roger that, Alex. Hey. You don't have to use that radio—"

"Miles?"

"Mungo?"

"She gave it back to me, boss."

"So she did."

"You have anything else you want for—?"

"No. I better start moving."

"It's a good idea."

He tells Mungo to make sure he gets the two of them on one of the first air-vacs out. He tries to hold on to the certainty that it won't come to that, that he won't be long, but it's already slipping away. This fire looks like it has the speed to spread over the whole Trench within the next twelve hours, which is the least amount of time he figures he'll need to find Margot and the others. He'll just have to be faster than that. To get the hunting party out, yes. But also himself. To make it back in time to be lifted up and carried to the two faces awaiting him on the other side of the blue hills.

***

There are so few buildings in Ross River and so much uninhabited, unnamed, unowned wilderness surrounding it, that it's surprising how much difficulty the fire team have in deciding where to establish the helicopters' landing site. The school parking lot? More than big enough, but the flagpole in the centre would have to be removed, and nobody can think of an easy way of cutting through six inches of steel to fell it (although Crookedhead James suggests driving Bonnie's old Chevy into it, "you know, like at the demolition derby," the proposal gets little airtime). The grassy acre by the riverbank? Flat, but with muddy patches so soft they suck the boots off your feet. The Welcome Inn's courtyard? Too tight. And besides, the pissing cherub would be impossible to move without a crane.

Although it is located at the edge of town and its home-run fence has been obscured by overgrowths of toadflax weaving through the chain link—so close it could make things a bit tricky if the fire ever ends up making it this far—they determine the soft-ball diamond to be the best place to act as helipad. In the end, this is Mungo's decision. With Miles out in the bush searching for the hunting party, the organization of the air-vac falls to the attack crew's second-in-command, or Mr. Capoose as Crookedhead calls him, once, before the older man levels a glare his way that lets it be known that he will stand for no more fooling, however mild.

Once the helicopter site has been established, King and Jerry set to work spraypainting a giant H in the outfield and erecting an orange windsock over the visitors' dugout. Mungo next assigns Terry Gray with driving around town and knocking on doors to wake everybody up. Within the quarter-hour people begin to spill out of their homes, squinting at their neighbours who have done the same, as though to confirm that they alone aren't the victims of an officially sanctioned prank.

"You in charge of this whole town now?" one of the bolder men shouts at Terry.

"Mungo's giving the evacuation orders."

"Where's Miles?"

"Mungo's the chief now, and that's all you need to know."

Everyone looks to each other to see who will be the first to make a crack about Mungo Capoose—or any of the Ross River fire team—being in charge of anything, but nobody tries it. The stink of burning pine tells them how serious this is. Under the circumstances, they'll sooner listen to Mungo than be the last ones in line for the free whirlybird rides.

Mungo already knows who's going to be first. As he runs back to the fire office from the softball diamond he listens for the thump of the helos coming in, but the air holds nothing but dead heat. When he stops at the door, all he can hear is his heart.

He reaches out an upturned hand as though checking for rain. Even in the time it takes him to catch his breath, a powdery layer of ash collects over the lines in his palm.

She's thinking of the fire. She's thinking of how she should have left yesterday. But more than anything, Alex is thinking of the moment, only a month ago, when Rachel was born for the second time.

It had, as one says of the most unforgettable things, happened so quickly. The end of May in northern Ontario, crushed ice rattling along the shorelines like marguerita troughs. They had stopped at the edge of Lake Wawa so that Alex could scour the phone book to find the cheapest room along the bleak motel strip off the Trans-Canada. She hadn't told Rachel to stay in the truck as, usually, the girl didn't look for trouble, her infancy free of tongues stuck in electrical outlets or stolen mouthfuls of Javex. But on this cement-skied Monday, she decided to trot away from her mother and leap, without a glance, into eight feet of chattering slush.

Alex covered twenty feet before the receiver thudded against the phone booth's glass wall, before she was aware of running at all. From somewhere above, a gull does the screaming for her.

As she comes to the pier's end, Alex slides with both arms in front of her as though stealing second base. The ice slowing the waves into twisting rolls.

When the top of Rachel's head bobs through the surface and slips below again, Alex knows that if she doesn't grab the girl this time there won't be a second chance. At first, all her fingers can find is a ponytail knot. Alex slithers back along the pier, gaining inches, but with Rachel's head still submerged. She will have to let go of the girl's hair to grab something she can lift all at once. When she releases Rachel's ponytail she wonders if it will be the last time she touches the girl.

There is a second when Alex is sure she is about to go over the side altogether. Her arms are in too deep to keep her balance. But she only reaches deeper yet, plowing through the oily cold.

When her hands find the girl, they lock around her chest. Now, when Alex rolls back, the girl ends up lying on top of her. Eyelids closed and bloodless.

There are other things Alex should do, and even at the time, she knows it. Turn Rachel over to get the water out of her lungs. Mouth-to-mouth resuscitation. Run back to the phone and stab 911 out on the sticky buttons.

But her daughter is cold. Alex opens her jacket and slides her inside.

She remembers singing to her, but not the song.

After a time, she watches Rachel's eyes open. Hot gasps against her neck. Not just alive, but born.

Alex watches Rachel breathe and sees her daughter in almost scientific terms. A link between elements. All along, she figured the main storyline of her life was made up of decisions, a series of deliberate actions. But there is only our connections to others that make any difference. Blood. Love. The shared experience of horror.

It is in this moment that Alex decides this will be the last summer she will look for Miles. It is also the moment she knows she will find him.

She is thinking once more of the blue of the child's skin when Mungo finds her still sitting in the fire office and tells her to get over to the softball diamond.

"We'll wait."

"What do you want to do that for?" he asks her, taken aback by the way she looks at him. A sweet thing. But hard all the way through, like rock candy.

"There's plenty of time. You've said so yourself."

"But Miles told me to—"

"You're wrong if you think I do what he tells me to." A pair of unflinching, it's-as-simple-as-that dimples appear at the corners of her mouth. "Unless you can get Stump out early too."

"The *dog?*"

"Rachel won't budge without him."

"They're not taking dogs on the helos."

"Not the *first* ones. But if we wait until later, they said they would."

"Who told you that?"

"Terry Gray. He radioed in after Rachel had a talk with him. She kind of went over both our heads, I guess."

"No shit."

"They said it would only be an extra half-hour or so. And if I tell her she can't take Stump, she might make a run for it. I'm not as quick as I used to be."

Mungo shakes his head. He can't stop smiling at Alex, her green eyes estimating his resolve as the rubbery thing that it is.

"You're a lot like my wife, you know that?" he says. "Both of you. Stubborn as wolverines."

"It's a little crazy, I know."

"You're not crazy. A blindfolded fool could see that. I'm just concerned for you and your girl's safety here."

"So am I. I'm only asking to wait a bit."

That's it, then. He's not through his first hour of being in charge and already he's got five people out in the bush somewhere, a town waiting to be airlifted in helos that haven't arrived, and now, a woman and her child are giving him orders.

"All right," he says. "But I get the window seat."

"And I'll buy the beers."

"I'm not sure if beer alone is going to cut it."

EIGHTEEN

The black bird follows him from the moment he parks the truck and strikes out on the trail. Flapping from spruce top to squirrel's nest, nodding at his progress. Miles reminds himself to be grateful that, so far, the raven is silent. If it is the same creature from the night before and insists on tagging along to wish him the worst, he would prefer if it would at least keep its mouth shut until noon.

Miles cuts up the hillside that rises from the edge of the Lapie Canyon, a weaving slash along the valley bottom that he can catch glimpses of through the aspen leaves every couple of minutes. From this distance, the white water of the river looks to him like a braid of blond hair being pulled through the forest. At every pause in the breeze the sound of the rapids reaches him, amplified by the canyon walls. It will be lost, eventually, as he goes higher. He stops to listen now with a hand cupped to his ear as though the water is offering him its last orders.

He can smell the smoke of the Comeback as well, but it is less threatening than at the site, now just one scent competing among others. Even through the blur of his worry, the fragrances of the bush lend him a cleansing energy. Blackberry. Pine. Toasted vanilla. In the deeper shadow offered by the Engelmann spruces, there is also the mineral whiff of water that has been filtered through earth and stone. It reminds him of quarry swims when he was young. A golden truant tanned head to toe by the end of June, cutting the chains that held NO TRESPASSING signs over mud lanes. A smell that isn't really a smell at all, nor a taste, but air in its purest state, deeply breathed. It both awakens him and invites him to sleep.

He catches sight of a lynx before it disappears into the under-brush, its tail snapping in farewell. He startles a family of ptarmi-gan into flight, fat and rubber-necked as dwarfish turkeys. A pair of eagles—one golden, one bald—share the sky.

With every hundred feet of elevation gain the vegetation shrinks around him. Underfoot, black earth and roots are replaced by mosses and the tiny blue and yellow faces of alpine flowers, a blanket of life over the rocks. The stunted trees refuse to protect him from the sun. Before him the north side of the St. Cyr range runs off to a horizon that, in the brightness, appears close enough to hook a finger over.

He can still be shaken by how beautiful this place is. From time to time he looks about him and feels something too large to be contained fisting its way up, a cry perhaps, or an explosion of tears, he's not sure because so far he's been able to choke off its escape. Even now the land can make him want to stop where he is and never move again. Just as often, it makes him want to run and keep going until the landscape collapses at his back.

Miles brings his eyes back to the trail and stops at the sight of the girl. Standing forty feet ahead, motionless but for the crosshatch-ing of shade over her dress, her skin.

She is no more real than the kid. But like the kid, she is there nevertheless.

He looks back over his shoulder. It gives Rachel a chance to dis-appear. When he starts up toward where she was, the shade has dispersed in the new breeze, her outline devoured by light.

Just like when he'd seen her on the day before he left on his tour of the fire towers.

He had been standing in his kitchen, slicing a cocktail-onion, sauerkraut and gherkin sandwich in half. His regular picnic menu on his solitary hikes up Eagle's Nest Bluff, the river cliff outside of town. (The fact is, he lives on stuff you have to stab out of a jar.) Just as he'd pulled the blade free he glances out the window over the sink and sees the girl. Her eyes too white. Her lips parted in what could be the beginnings of a snarl.

The squeezable mustard sits on the counter beyond his reach and he slides over to grab it. When he returns to the window, the girl is gone.

He wraps the finished sandwich and stuffs it along with a thermos of coffee into a knapsack. He's about to grab a couple of beers out of the fridge when there's a knock at his door.

"Rachel's run away," Alex announces when he pulls it open.

"You think she came here?"

"It's somewhere she knows."

"Yes."

"Yes what?"

"Yes, she was here."

"And you just let her *go?*"

I thought she wasn't real, Miles is about to say, but Alex is already rushing around the side of the cabin.

He trots out and watches her cross the high grass to the edge of the forest, calling the girl's name into the trees. He hears it three times before it occurs to him that he should look for her too.

Miles starts up a jog but, not knowing which way to go, ends up standing in the middle of the yard, his bare feet an easy breakfast for the mosquitoes. The light is so clear that it pushes his vision past its normal limits, drawing clean lines around individual willow leaves a hundred yards down the road. But no Rachel.

She couldn't have gone far. There wasn't time for her to accept a ride with anyone unless they were already idling in the road. And even if there had been, who would it be?

A millisecond process of elimination is all it takes for everything to change.

Wade could have driven his own truck out to join the hunting party, but turned back to town first. It would only have taken a second to grab the girl. Maybe he didn't even have to. They had spoken before at the trampoline. He put his hand on her shoulder. Perhaps she'd mistaken him for a friend.

A month ago, he wouldn't have thought Wade Fuerst capable of harming a child. With an instant certainty, he sees that he was wrong. What had Margot said about him? *Something bad going on in there.*

Miles slaps his pockets for the keys to his truck. Pulls them out and drops them in the grass. When he bends, the blood rushes to his head. Bites at air as he stands, and still nearly faints.

He makes a spastic run to the driver's-side door. Jams the key in the slot only to see that the lock is already popped up.

Miles throws himself in. For a moment, the panic freezes the backs of his eyes. The result is that, for a time, he can do nothing but stare at the girl sitting in the passenger seat. His heart bangs against his chest so hard he wonders if she can see his shirt move.

Rachel shrugs and pulls the seat belt over her chest, snapping it in place.

"What do you think you're doing?"

"Putting my belt on."

"I can see that."

"Momma won't start her truck until I do."

"That so?"

"It's the *law*."

The girl nods at him and smiles so sweetly that the sheer audacity of it makes him want to laugh out loud. But nothing changes on his face. She's a funny kid, that's for sure. But goddamn it if Miles is going to let himself smile back at a child who, in certain respects, might just be smarter than he is.

After an awkward, unavoidable invitation—awkwardly, unavoidably accepted—for Alex to join him, and following a suffocating hour's drive, the three of them elbow-to-elbow on the cab's bench seat, Miles turned onto an overgrown road that nobody would notice even walking by. The truck lurches over stumps, the patches of foxtail swooning under the front grille. When he comes to a stop, he cranks the parking brake and jumps out without a word, the dog following but glancing worriedly back at Alex and Rachel as they follow.

Only a couple hundred yards in, Miles stops. Behind him a narrow trail winds its way up an abrupt slope.

"Where's the river?" Alex asks him.

"You can only really see it from the top."

"*I* want to see it," Rachel says.

"You first," Miles tells the girl, stepping back to reveal the trailhead. He hopes she will refuse such a frightening ascent altogether. Instead, she starts on her way without a glance at either of them.

Halfway up the three of them pause for a drink. The trail has lifted them above the level of the tallest trees, so that valley after valley tumbles away in every direction, daubed blue with unreachable lakes. A new quiet envelops them. The scurryings and footfalls of the bush replaced by nothing but the movement of air.

"I'll wait here," Alex says. "You two go on to the top on your own."

With her announcement, Stump rubs against the side of her leg and plants himself there, refusing to go any farther if he has an excuse not to. Miles gives Alex a pleading look for her to come with him.

"Don't worry," she tells him. "Rachel's as tough as you think you are."

There's nothing for it but to follow the girl, who is already lifting herself up the much steeper incline. As the two of them continue on, he can feel his mind pressed between attention to his environment and his fear of it. It was like this the only other time he had come here with someone else.

Miles catches his breath, blinking up at Rachel's sharp outline against the sky. Why does he feel more dizzy looking up than down? It's always been this way with him, a kind of reverse vertigo. And to make matters more light-headed, he can see that the only thing maintaining the girl's grip is her left hand clinging to a poplar root, a spindly loop that comes out and returns to the earth like an ingrown hair. If Rachel loses her hold on it, she will either tumble back straight into him or miss him and fly past. She can't weigh much more than sixty pounds. But with a bit of velocity, the contact would likely be enough to send them both back into the last line of aspens. If the trees didn't stop them, they would fall five hundred feet into the pretty picture below.

Then, even as he calculates the odds of it happening, the root springs from the earth.

There is no time to do anything but note her hair, a dark splash against the dome of blue.

In the next instant, her back slams into his knees.

Although he expects to, he doesn't fall. His toes reach through his soles to dig a half inch into the shallow soil. No other part of him has contact with the earth. But it holds them where they are long enough for him to lean forward, pressing Rachel against the trail.

"Are you all right?" he whispers into the back of her head. He snorts out strands of her hair and it leaves the grape juice smell of her shampoo behind.

"Fall down go boom," she giggles.

"We should go back."

"We're almost at the top."

"It's pretty steep between—"

"I won't fall."

"C'mon—"

"I *won't* fall."

"How are you two doing up there?" he hears Alex call from below, but from her tone he can tell she hadn't seen the girl slip.

"We're *fine!*" Rachel shouts back.

She slides out from under him and continues up the last steep third, her hind end waggling back and forth like a goat's. Miles struggles after her. Although they aren't high enough for the air to be any thinner, it feels to him as though it is.

"We made it!" Rachel is shouting when Miles is still ten feet short of the crest.

"What can you see?"

"The river. Momma and Stump. You. Everything! I can see *everything!*"

Miles pulls himself up over the edge with Rachel tugging on his sleeves. The bluff's crest is a flat tabletop of moss and black stone, a near-perfect circle fifty feet across. At the same moment, Miles and Rachel collapse onto their backs in the centre, the freshened breeze drying the sweat on their skin.

"They call this place Eagle's Nest Bluff," Miles finds himself telling her once he's caught his breath. "That's the name the gold rush prospectors gave it when they came up that river a hundred years ago. But the Northern Tutchone—those are the Indians around here—they called it something else for a thousand years before that. Tś àl Cho An. Which means Giant Frog's Den."

Rachel appears to be only half listening to him, peering over the cliff's edge at the river that fires shards of sunlight up at them.

"I have a name for it too," she says finally.

"Oh yeah?"

"The High Chair."

"Why the High Chair?"

"Because it makes you feel like a baby. After you've been lifted from the floor. *Swoop!* You're up. And you can *see*."

The two of them sit there for a time without speaking. Miles is astonished to feel within Rachel the recognition that the land belongs to nobody, despite the different names we might attach to it. Land like this cannot be owned except in the moment we see our place in it, our brief and dazzled passing. Somehow, Rachel understands this even now, and as well as he does.

"Do you know who I am?" he asks her. He wasn't planning the question, but now that it's out, he finds that he really would like to know.

Rachel folds her brow into a mocking scowl. Her head shaking in the frustration of a teacher having to start again with an especially slow student.

"I *think* I do," she says. "Dumb-dumb."

Miles glances behind the girl at an osprey diving close enough over their heads he could have touched it with a raised broomstick. For a second it dives again, having spotted a fish jumping near the bank, then corrects itself when it confirms the prey's escape, floating back toward them on an updraft.

The girl has turned to catch all of this too. When the bird spirals higher and higher away downstream, she claps her hands at the show's graceful finale. She goes on long enough that Miles can only join her in the applause.

Do you know who I am?

Miles hears his question repeated between every smack of his palms. Not only was he guilty of failing to be either subtle or direct, but now he's not even sure if he's been given an answer. Perhaps the girl thinks of him only as Miles, the strange-looking friend of her mother's. Or perhaps she knows far more than this, and is granting him the adult favour of tactfulness. In either case, he cannot ask again. It would only make him appear more of a dumb-dumb than he already is.

Rachel and Miles watch the osprey shrink far down the valley until its black dot is washed out in blue. They'll have to start back down now. And yet for a time he remains exactly where he is, his eyes on the girl, trying to breathe deeper and slower so that time might slow and deepen along with him. For the moment, he feels that it is enough. It is more than enough for Miles to have heard her say that she knows him, and for him to believe it to be true.

***

There are places that hunters go to look for different animals, according to their habitat, the season and the rumours shared over outfitters' counters and barroom tables. Caribou a few miles up the Dempster in late autumn. Moose around Ibex valley pond-sides a month before that. For grizzly bears, it's places like this. Remote mountainsides with access to water, land uninterrupted by highways or logging for miles in any direction. This is where Margot would have brought the Baders. But from here on, Miles will have to look for the same bear sign that she would have fol-lowed, make the right guesses. Try to read Margot's mind.

After backtracking for half an hour and starting out on a steeper game trail for no other reason than it caught his eye when he first passed it, Miles enters an alpine meadow. He is no expert at such things, but it strikes him that the place has been the scene of some recent activity. The high grasses seem crushed in spots. Farther toward the middle, Miles nearly trips over a wasps' nest. A hole punched through its equator, leaving a roll of torn greys and black, a cast-off newspaper blown a thousand miles north. He nudges it with his boot, and what remains of its structure col-lapses inward.

He doesn't notice the morning chill until it is lifted from him. After several hours of hiking the sun leaps from its hiding place to beam directly down on the top of his head. Without taking off his firepack, he digs a hand into it and pulls out a chocolate-coated granola bar. Eating reminds him of how thirsty he is. He chugs a quart from his canteen before he can stop himself.

Granola and water. A full meal if he was on one of the crash diets he notices on the covers of tabloids at the Raven Nest's checkout. *Forest Firefighter Loses Twenty Pounds in Just 48 Hours!* He'll have to write in when he gets back. You never know, they might take him up as their cause. (*Next Week: The Miracle Facial That Hides His Nasty Scars!*) It would be a funny thought if he weren't so hungry. As it is, he can't allow himself any more food until evening. Without knowing how long he's going to be out here, he'll have to ration himself like he's got a hundred miles to go. And maybe he has.

Later in the afternoon he breaks through the scrub onto an avalanche slide. The heat doubles off the black rock around him so that he can feel it reddening his bare arms.

If he didn't kick the radio where it lay hidden among the stones he would never have noticed it. Despite its condition, he recognizes it immediately as Margot's handheld unit. Burst open from the inside as though the transistors and wires had grown too large for their plastic casing. Not dropped but torn apart.

Miles grabs his own radio at his belt, but when he clicks the power switch there is only a sorrowful pop. He shakes it as if it may be sleeping. Whether it's a dead battery or some other failure, it's about as useful now as the one smashed on the rocks at his feet.

"Asswhistle," Miles pronounces, and realizes he's borrowed one of Mungo's custom-made profanities.

For the first time, Miles raises his head to study the slide. Perhaps fifty yards ahead, he notices a pile of clothing surrounded by strips of red ribbon. There is also something in it that makes Miles squint. Shining rivulets running through the cotton like an emptied box of silver chains.

He walks on. His boots feel five sizes too large. Without anything changing in what he sees, a wave of nausea comes upon him so fast it forces hiccups from his throat. None of it stops him from shuffling closer to what he now sees is Jackson Bader's body.

Miles guessed right about the clothes anyway. The saggy jeans, plaid shirt and camouflage vest he remembers seeing the old man wearing only a couple nights ago in the bar. But the ribbon is in fact something else. Ripped cords of muscle. The silver Miles thought he'd seen only the glint of half-dried spouts of blood.

Without slowing his approach, Miles wonders if he is about to gag. The discovery of the grisly corpse—in films, in dreams—has trained him to expect such a reaction in death novices such as himself. The thing is, he feels fine. Or rather, he feels nothing at all. Is this shock? If it is, Miles is thankful for it. He is happy to look at what is left of Bader's body and, for this particular second, not have to calculate the implications.

An index finger—his, he realizes vaguely—skips down the ridgeline of his scar. With his other hand, he brushes a bottlehead fly off its flight path toward the end of one of Bader's toes. Something in the prickly contact between the bug and his skin opens Miles's senses fully to the scene before him. And there is the faint beginnings of a scent. One that strikes him as both remembered and new.

Instead of being sick, Miles collapses chin first on the rocks. The impact blows a cough out of him. When he's able, he crawls away from the body on hands and knees and doesn't look back again.

The hunting party had found their grizzly. But someone aside from Margot had done the shooting, by the looks of it. A terrible logic states itself: If a bear did this to one of them, it may have done the same to the others. That, or the animal is now hunting those who started out hunting it.

And then, a second later: *Maybe it's still here.*

Miles struggles to focus on the edge of a shale chip a foot beneath his nose and blocks all further speculations from his thoughts.

So. What's next?

But that isn't the right question. People who clean up messes for a living, people like him, need to know only one thing.

So. Who's left?

Miles lifts his head and, at this low angle, sees bootprints in the bent grass at the opposite end of the slide. The wrong way. Whoever's prints they are, they're going toward the fire. If he can't catch them in time and haul them back to Ross River to make one of the last air-vacs, they're going to run straight into the worst of it. That is, if there are any of them left to run.

Getting back on his feet is a puzzle that takes a full minute to solve. He stands and waits for his head to stop swimming. The wind grows stronger against his cheeks, stretches the clouds into translucent veils.

Far away, Alex and Rachel would be eating their dinner now. Miles hopes they've taken something out of his freezer or fried a couple more of Mungo's mooseburgers instead of throwing themselves on the mercy of the Lucky China's kitchen. He drags his hand through a patch of sage growing improbably on the rocks next to him and brings his fingertips to his nose. The whiff of savoury green is all that's on the menu tonight. It is enough to remind him of roast chicken, which is more torture than comfort. The mere thought of cooked meat, seasoned and rich in spitting fats, only expands the emptiness within him, and Miles nearly doubles over with a stab of longing. Not for food, but to be with the two of them again. To watch them eat at his table and, perhaps, have the girl raise her plate to him to be shared.

He spits and walks on. Higher into the foothills, his ears straining to discern a human cry for help from the mocking chatter of the raven that follows him through the treetops, as impossible to escape as the eyes of the moon.

When the two of them stop it is without a glance between them. For the next minute, it doesn't matter if the female hunter follows a hundred feet downwind. Too much has already occurred this day for them to be immediately concerned about what might be about to happen next. A short rest will help them decide.

The she-grizzly's surviving cub, the larger of her two, slumps his head against her belly and falls into an instant sleep. Just feeling the proximity of the warm puffs from his mouth draws an ache to her teats. The smaller cub was always the stronger feeder. He would shove his brother aside for the pick of the nipples when their mother lolled onto her back and allowed herself to be fought over, tugged at, slept upon. The larger cub gained his weight not through aggression, but by suckling longer, waiting his turn and then keeping his mouth on the sow until she slapped him off. Now they are both past the age of using her this way. And now there is one, where there used to be two.

The she-grizzly stretches down to plug her surviving cub's bullet hole with her tongue. When a wound is inflicted only from the cuts of thorns, the pressure of her licks can usually staunch the bleeding, and the natural antibiotics in her spittle can do the job of cleaning it. But the opening in the cub's side is too wide to be mended with her mouth. She brings her nose in close and sniffs at it. If another bear had attacked her cub, she would smell whether it was brown or black, its sex. Instead, the cub's flesh reeks of powder and lead.

She lets her cub snore a minute longer. He will not be able to go much farther, but she hopes that breaks like this can help fool his body into thinking it has had a full day's sleep. They allow her the chance to pull her strength together too. Since what happened on the killing ground she can barely feel anything but a hot ball in her chest, a furious concentration she knows will grow as it seeps into her fat, her bones.

At least the yellowjackets seem to have left her. As she raises her nose to read the air, only a single wasp buzzes around her head. The bear considers snapping at it and grinding it in her molars, but decides to let it return to her fur if it chooses. There is enough power left in her to carry one wasp over the mountain.

She wakens the cub, lifting him to his feet on the forklift of her claws. They continue up the slope. Around them, the trees become more stunted, the ground cover increasingly prickly shrubs in place of wildflowers. The end of the treeline can't be much higher.

The smell of smoke grows stronger behind her. Yellow fingers reach across the sky like the hand of a god preparing to turn the page. The fire is moving faster than she ever thought it would. It is likely a greater threat to them now than the hunters who may still be tracking them on their sideways ascent.

There is no solution aside from carrying on. Over the ridge and down the other side to the south, there is a stream where she can catch easy grayling and feed it to her cub. There, in the dappled shade of overhanging willows, she can wash out his wound in the current.

The cub looks back at its mother and takes another painful breath. He wants only to show her that he feels no fear. He will go as far as she pushes him to go.

Jerry McCormack tilts his head back to take in the sky and sees it as the smoke-curdled ceiling in the Welcome Inn on busy nights. A haze that lowers inch by inch with every exhaled breath.

"Anything?"

Jerry hears the question but requires a second to determine if it comes from outside or within.

"You mean the helos?" he says finally, bringing his eyes down to Mungo standing in front of him. "Not a one."

"It's the visibility."

"A bitch, for sure."

"How are the evac priorities?"

"We've got them sorted out pretty good. For now, anyway. We don't get some action soon, though, and people start wondering what they're doing standing in a field holding hands in groups of five."

Mungo glances over his shoulder toward the softball diamond, but even in the time it's taken him to walk over and find Jerry, the smoke has obscured it from view.

"Terry Gray wants us at his office," Mungo says.

"What about?"

"Not a clue. Got me on the walkie-talkie and asked if we had a spare minute. I figured we did, until the birds start coming."

"I'll get Crookedhead and the kid."

Mungo takes the long way to the RCMP office, down his own street, peering through windows into living rooms he knows to be empty. More than once he catches sight of a face pressed to the glass. Children that have been left behind. Ones he had just seen waiting for the first helicopters at the softball diamond. When he starts to see them in every window he looks at, Mungo breaks into a jog all the way to Terry's office.

"Where's King?" Terry Gray asks Jerry, who is the last one in, closing the door behind him.

"Nobody knows."

"Have you looked?"

"Been a little busy around here."

"I'll get to him later."

Mungo folds his arms over his chest. "What's going on here, Terry?"

"They've opened a file on this fire."

"Who's they?"

"The Mounties. Me."

"But you're the police. Isn't Forestry handling it?"

"Things have taken a turn."

"A turn."

"It's a criminal investigation now."

"What's the crime in a fire burning in a goddamn forest?" Jerry McCormack laughs, but it's uncertain, and dies before it has a chance to convince anyone.

"If there's a firestarter, there could be plenty. Arson, for one. It comes through town, and there will be property offences to add to the mix. And it's likely to get worse than that yet."

"Worse?"

"Homicide."

"I didn't know anybody was dead."

"Ruby Ritter hasn't made contact for over twelve hours now. They've made some assumptions on that down in Whitehorse."

This silences them. Through the walls, they can hear distant shouting from the softball diamond. Already, the ordered lines for the air-vac were breaking down, nervous flare-ups more than actual panic. But that will come.

"For fuck sake, Terry," Mungo says evenly. "Even if somebody started it, doesn't mean they meant to kill anybody."

"Maybe not. Or maybe it doesn't matter."

"Maybe you could tell us what you're talking about."

"If there's a death directly related to a fire, one that someone started because they wanted it to kill—that's second-degree murder right there. And even if it was for some other reason and the thing got out of hand, manslaughter is still on the table."

"I still don't see what we're doing here."

"They're asking for backgrounds on you guys. Habits, changes in recent behaviour, personal circumstances."

"Motives."

"That's right."

Mungo laughs.

"Not sure this is so funny," Terry Gray says.

"Depends on how you look at it."

"And how are *you* looking at it?"

"From over in the corner here, listening to you. Thinking that this is the first time you've ever sounded like a real cop, and that you're getting quite a kick out of it. So am I."

Terry Gray stiffens. For a second, even Mungo is sure he's going to hit someone. Instead, the Mountie rests his hand over the butt of his pistol in its holster.

"It's my job," he says.

"Fine. Then let us get back to doing ours."

"I'm only doing you the courtesy of letting you know. Because once this fire's out, it won't just be me asking you questions but some very serious suits who couldn't give a shit about doing you any favours."

"Okay. Consider us advised," Mungo says, saluting.

Mungo opens the door, expecting Jerry and Crookedhead to take the opportunity for escape, but the two remain where they are, staring at Terry Gray.

"What are you going to tell them?" Crookedhead asks.

"Why each of you might have dropped a match out there," Gray says.

"*Why,* do you think?"

"There's Jerry's truck. Your long-lost family down in B.C. And I understand that Mungo's girl wants to go Outside to college in a couple of years."

"You're talking about money," Mungo says. "Everyone in this town could use some of that."

"But you're the only ones who could make it off a fire."

"This is *bullshit!*" Jerry startles them by shouting. "*Anybody* could have done it. Drop a cigarette under a pine and if the rain stays off it for a day or two, *ka-boom*."

Terry Gray pushes himself off the edge of his desk. It forces Jerry back until he bumps against the wall.

"That how you did it, Jerry? Or did it need a little more help than that?"

"That your evidence? Jerry McCormack smokes?" Mungo says. "You might as well put half the Yukon on your suspect list."

"I'm not sure anyone in the Yukon is as edgy as you three right now. It makes you wonder."

"You're a godawful fisherman, Terry. Quit while you're ahead." Mungo swings the door open wider. Nobody yet moves to pass out of it. It forces Mungo to finish his point. "Just because we're the fire crew doesn't mean we're the only ones with something to gain from this. This smoker might end up keeping the whole town alive."

"I guess our firestarter would be quite a hero, then, wouldn't he?"

"We don't do heroes around here."

"But you'll take the overtime anyway."

"If it's coming to me."

"This is too stupid for words," Jerry McCormack says, his courage dimly flaring.

"Speaking of stupid, I wanted to ask you about that truck of yours," Terry Gray says, addressing Jerry without taking his eyes from Mungo's. "Who did you say you got that loan from?"

Jerry punches Crookedhead, a vicious jab in the shoulder.

"You *told* him?"

"I didn't say shit!"

"You say nothing *but* shit. Well, how's this," Jerry says, turning to Terry and pointing at Crookedhead. "This guy has been driving out of town on his own after the bar closes the past couple of weeks. Wandering around in the bush drunk as a donkey, crying for his kid and girlfriend."

"Who told you that? Not that it's true," Crookedhead says. And then: "What's wrong with going for a walk? I could say a lot more about you than you could ever—"

"Shut up," Mungo says, quietly, though all of them hear it just the same. "You've left out King and the chief."

"King isn't here," the Mountie says. "As for Miles, I'm not sure what I'm going to say about him yet. Any suggestions?"

"That's it," Mungo says, taking a step out the open door so that one of his legs is bleached with light, the other remaining in the room's shade. "Time's up. You know, Terry, I could have used my break for a cigarette. Now we might have to wait till tomorrow to have a smoke."

Jerry McCormack follows Crookedhead James out. Mungo goes after them, but not before he gives Terry Gray a look that he hopes makes his position clear. *Don't.* Not a threat. A request between friends. *Don't take this any further.*

Terry shrugs. An acknowledgement of his powerlessness in the matter, something Mungo knows well enough himself. Once the worst suspicions are made official, they are as impossible to stop as a fire picked up on the wind.

NINETEEN

It amazes him every time. The way the mountain treeline is so abrupt, the division between the last spruces and the rock as neat as the line between farmers' crops. Miles walks from one and onto the other. The unfettered wind buffets his chest. Looking straight up the incline, he can clearly see what has caused the burning in his thighs. The wavering path had appeared gentler under the camouflage of shadow. Now, the stretched-out colonnade of the St. Cyr hills reveals their steepness. Even his eyes encounter resistance as he pushes them up to squint at the distant ridge.

The trail ahead is little more than a winding staircase of rubble. Centuries of passing goat and Dall sheep have worn smooth hoofprints into the rock. If he's right in thinking Margot would have proceeded higher up after the bear attack, this is the way she would have come. He wishes he'd brought his binoculars. Out here, he could look for miles and spot anything that might be making its way over the mountain face.

For the first time, it occurs to Miles that Margot may still be hunting the bear. Whoever survived whatever happened on the avalanche slide would want only to escape. But if Margot is alone, she would be relieved of her responsibilities as guide and be thinking only as a hunter again. If this is the case, her route would be more unpredictable, determined by her prey alone.

Miles looks once more along the treeline pulled straight out in front of him, the forest spilling down from the jaw of stone like a green beard. From this height he can now see the almost solid wall of smoke that separates him from where Ross River would be to the north. Even in the few seconds he watches it surges closer, a grey storm dancing toward him.

When he turns to continue he notices a boulder rolling down the slope. Maybe a mile off. Unmistakably bumping over the stone, the only moving thing he can see aside from the smoke. Miles stops to watch it, expecting it to displace the smaller rocks around it, bringing on a whole new slide. He wonders if it will make enough sound for him to hear.

He waits a second or two before he determines that the boulder moves too slowly for the grade of the hill, staying at the same pace as when he'd first spotted it. He shields his eyes with his hand to sharpen its position.

The boulder is slow because it isn't a boulder at all. Something that isn't rolling downhill but walking steadily up toward the ridge.

He can see nothing of its details, but instantly recognizes that it could be neither Margot nor Mrs. Bader. There is an element missing from human locomotion, a push-and-pull between head and feet, that makes it clear it is an animal that walks on four legs, not two. The colour is wrong for a goat or sheep or even a dog. And the thing must be big if he can see it at all from this far off.

Miles adjusts his course into as straight a line toward the bear as the rocks permit. A fresh excitement opens his lungs. The sight of the animal confirms he's going in the right direction. Whether Margot is hunting it or it is hunting Margot, he will eventually come upon them so long as he keeps moving.

A broad gulch opens at his feet. He decides to go straight down and up the other side without taking the extra half-hour he guesses would be required to climb around the top of its cut. For the first twenty yards he manages to keep his balance. But with each step, his weight loosens the stones behind as well as ahead and the ground shimmies under him. He slides the last hundred feet on his ass, the pebbles lacerating the skin through his pants.

To reach the relative flat at the top of the gulch's side, he has to scramble up the incline using his hands as well as his feet, throwing gravel between his legs. When he gets there he lies on his back, as useless as a turtle flipped upon its shell.

He blinks ahead to locate the bear again, but the mountain has turned white with smoke during his time in the shadowed cleft. The only moving objects he can see now are three figures. No more than a quarter-mile off.

"Margot!" he shouts, or tries to shout. It comes out as a bubbly apology, the sound a person makes as they rush to the bathroom to be sick.

It's easier to get to his feet again and jog after them. As he goes, the peaks on the horizon seem to approach more quickly than the three figures in the middle distance.

Margot walks alone ahead of Tom and Elsie, the two of them clinging to each other as they go. It's unclear who is helping whom. But Miles can see by the way both sets of their shoulders weave side to side that if it weren't for the one, the other would fall.

Even as he sees the black smear of Margot's hair and Mrs. Bader's camouflage scarf around her neck, Miles finds it difficult to believe that there are people here, on this slope, with him. It is a place where you could only be alone. A grizzly on the opposite mountain, a herd of indifferent goats, yes. But not another stumbling soul.

"Margot!" he tries again when they are only a hundred yards up from him, and this time it comes out as he intended.

The three stop but don't turn. Miles keeps scuffling toward them, hands held out as if to catch them if they fall. As he comes close enough to see the trembling in their legs, he stops too.

Maybe they're dead.

This idea comes out of nowhere, but once it arrives, it bears the weight of certainty. The three figures before him are as dead as the kid. And now they have joined him in populating the bush with zombies.

"It's me," he says instead of touching them.

At the sound of his voice, Elsie Bader spins her head halfway round. The inside of her mouth a wet pocket in her bloodless face.

"Jackson?"

"It's Miles McEwan, Mrs. Bader. We've got to—"

"*Jackson!*"

The old woman's shivering turns into an unwholesome dance, a rubbery twisting that leaves her head still facing him. Miles can see no sense in it, or in her.

"Help me," Tom says.

Miles pries Mrs. Bader's fingers off Tom's shirt before the old woman slumps to the ground, her other hand still clinging to a sleeve.

"You alone?" Margot asks. He can't meet her eyes. He's never seen her look scared before.

"Just me."

"We found our grizzly."

"You sure did."

"But we're in some deep shit now."

"Well, I'm in it with you. If that's any consolation."

It appears it isn't. She makes no motion to welcome or dismiss him. Miles gazes back the way he's come. When only smoke shows itself there, he turns again and pretends to be absorbed by something over the others' shoulders. He runs his eyes along the rock horizon just a few hundred feet away. If Margot, Tom and Mrs. Bader have been struggling along in this bowl for as long as he thinks they have, there's no way they could have seen the bear.

"Bader took the shots," Margot says, her lips squeezed thin. "Killed one cub, gut-shot the other. Now she's up ahead somewhere."

"You're still hunting it?"

"I'll shoot her if I see her. But I'm just trying to get us to the other side. Find some water. Wait for a spotter plane. Or you."

"You saw me?"

"I *know* you."

Miles tells them his radio has been eighty-sixed. Because he didn't inform anyone of his route in advance, there would be no search and rescue for them any time soon. Not that there is much in the way of available air resources anyway. Every helo and bush plane within a day of Ross River would be working the fire or the air-vac for the next twenty-four hours, probably longer. If the four of them are going to get off this mountain, it has to be on their own.

Margot and Miles decide that their best option would be to continue up over the crest and down to the fire base on the south side. It will take all night. A difficult hike under ideal conditions, and something approaching impossible with little food or water and Elsie Bader to drag between them. And then there's the cold. At this elevation, the temperatures regularly sink to freezing within an hour of sunset. They will have no choice but to walk straight through the darkness. So long as Mrs. Bader carries at least half her weight, they have a chance of coming within a couple miles of the base by morning.

Far too late, he remembers to ask about Wade.

"Stupid bastard," she says, and he hears how close to emotion she is, thumping up beneath the ice of her closed face. "Today of all days he decides he's going to be the hero."

"He tried to save Bader."

"I guess that was the plan. But the old man was already——" She stops at a round of coughing from Mrs. Bader. "The bear gave him a hell of a swat, is all I know. When I went back to look for him he was gone."

"And he wasn't on the slide when I came through."

"You saw what she did?"

"I saw."

Miles feels Margot turn away from him. Ducking his head low, he wraps Mrs. Bader's free arm over his neck and lifts her from her knees. Without a word, he pulls her up the slope, the old woman's sobs turning to grunts of effort. Tom stays close on her other side. He can hear Margot shuffling after them, hiding her tears from his notice.

He closes his eyes against the last of the sun.

By morning, on the other side of the mountain, they will be waiting for him. It's all he can think of to make his body do what he needs it to. Their faces are all he can see whether his eyes are open or closed.

There are more people in the stands today than for the final game of last year's softball tournament. Ross River, the host community, had made it all the way against Mayo, mostly on the strength of Jerry McCormack's hot bat and some favourable umpiring from Terry Gray, who was assigned the task on the wrongful assumption that an officer of the law could be counted on to be objective. Half the Yukon seemed to be here, along with a busload of thirsty Alaskans. Before the game even started the visitors drank the Welcome Inn dry—something the locals alone hadn't managed after years of strong efforts. In the end, the home team lost. Hardly anyone noticed. For a day, Ross River had been visited by the carnival.

Now, the softball field is surrounded by those waiting to be taken out by air-vac helicopters that have yet to appear. Mungo Capoose circulates among them, trying to look busy, though in fact there is little to do now but wait. There is calm among the evacuees for the moment, though he knows it won't last long. When the first round of helos come and go, they will figure out how long it's going to take to clear all of them out. Then Mungo and the fire team will have some real crowd-control duties to tend to.

In the meantime, he searches for King. He hasn't seen the kid for the past half-hour. Before that, he'd noticed him off on his own behind the dugout, switching his view between the ashen sky and his boots. Now he's gone. Though Mungo has no specific task in mind for him, it would be nice to know where the hell the kid's gotten to. Probably off in the woods hugging a tree.

As he looks around he notices Alex's girl sitting on her own at the end of the bleachers, staring up at the backstop. Mungo walks toward her and waves, but she doesn't move her eyes. When he looks up he sees a raven chattering down at her. A series of *heh-heh-heh*s. The laughter of a cartoon villain twirling his moustache.

"Your mom know you're here on your own?" he asks when he sits next to her. The girl shrugs. "Where is she?"

"Mr. Raven doesn't like dogs," Rachel says, and for the first time, Mungo notices Miles's mutt curled up under the bench at the girl's feet.

"They're funny about who they like and don't like."

"Miles said they tell stories."

"They sure do. Never shut up. It's why there's so many Indian stories about them."

"Like what?"

"Well, let's see. There's one that has to do with a raven and fire. The world's *first* fire, back when the earth was cold," Mungo tells her. "Lightning started a smoker in a dead tree on an island in the middle of a lake. When they saw it, all the animals got together to try to figure out how they could bring a piece of the fire back to the shore so they could warm up a little."

"This is a long time ago," Rachel clarifies.

"Oh yeah. Spirit time. The first fire *ever*."

"When animals could talk."

"It weren't yesterday."

"So how'd they touch the fire without getting burned?"

"It's a myth. Things don't always make sense. And there's a million different versions of each one, so you can never know how the story's going to turn out."

"But you said there's a raven in it."

"There's *definitely* a raven in it. He was the first volunteer to fly over to the island and bring back a hot chunk of wood. But when he was circling over the tree, the smoke covered him in soot and turned his feathers black, the same as they are today. Like greased-up coal."

"He was white before?"

"That's what they say."

"He must be scared of it."

"The raven's not scared of shit, pardon my Dutch. He's a trickster. A shapeshifter. He can turn into different animals—snakes and bears and fish. Even people. Don't worry about him. He's not scared of a thing."

"*I'm* scared."

"That's because you're smart."

"Mungo's not your babysitter, honey," Alex says, coming around the corner of the bleachers smacking the bottoms of two apple juice bottles. When she sits next to them, she screws the cap off one and hands it to the girl, who gulps at it before opening her mouth wide and uttering a thunderous belch.

The three of them turn to watch the smoke rising over the hills at the town limits, a rope of knotted whites and greys and blacks. For perhaps an hour it has rested there, growing higher and shrinking again as though catching its breath. But for now, it doesn't advance any farther toward the town's apron of forest and buildings. The only remaining fuels for it to consume to the north.

"I don't see the fire. Only smoke," Alex says.

"The fire is always the last thing you see."

"But it has to come down here sometime."

Mungo studies the line of hills as though he'd glimpsed a familiar face in a crowd.

"Mungo?"

"Uh?"

"It's going to burn this whole valley clean, isn't it?"

"They'll get us out of here before it does."

As though in rebuttal, even as Mungo speaks, the fire bares its orange teeth over the crest. A dozen crowns fired in spontaneous fury that reminds Alex of telescopic images of the sun, the flares that reach out into space like yearning arms.

"Oh my God," she whispers. She reaches around Rachel's chest and locks her fingers together.

"The river's no good," Mungo says in answer to the question he knows Alex is about to ask.

"Why?"

"It's too high, too fast."

"But we could stand in it if we had to."

"Not for long," Mungo says with a sigh that tells Alex he's already tried it in his head. "That water is *cold*. If you stood up to your knees in it you'd buckle under within two minutes. Step in any further and the current will grab ahold and take you with it."

"*Look,* Momma," Rachel says.

Alex searches the riverbank, hoping the girl has spotted something that she's missed. "What, baby? I don't see anything."

"Not there. *There.*"

Alex swings around to where Rachel is looking. The raven, flapping off its perch on the backstop and toward the fiery ridge.

"It's so *fast,*" the girl says.

"That's right. It's a fast old bird."

Mungo and Rachel share a glance that Alex doesn't notice. He understands that the girl is not speaking of the raven, but the fire.

What a day, Mungo thinks. Not yet four o'clock and he's already made two promises, one to Miles, one to his girls. This from a man who learned early on that the best way to avoid disappointing others is to teach them to expect nothing of him. And now? Now he's marching across the infield to find his own family and offer a whole new round of assurances. He hopes that the night is long. Sleep is out of the question now anyway. Mungo has struck a deal with himself. He will let his eyes close only after he sees his word kept in every case he's offered it.

The only way she breathes is through her husband's name. Three times in the first hour alone Miles has to stop to shake Mrs. Bader out of a faint. She will be walking with him one moment—or rather, swinging her feet and kicking at stones as Miles hauls the rest of her in his arms—and then she goes limp. Her head lolls on his shoulder, lips gaping. It takes something different each time to bring her back. He sings to her, pulls her hair, shouts one of Mungo's profanities in her face. Once, he kisses her cheek. Every rasp of air she takes when she returns is exhaled as a word—*Jackson*—that enters Miles's ear and fills him with the grief the dead man's wife is too burdened to carry on her own.

They climb on into dusk, each glimpse caught of the ridgeline above less determined than the last by the thickening darkness. None of the thoughts Miles has can be shared:

He cannot carry the old woman to the top on his own.

The fire may already be waiting on the other side.

They will stop to sleep and never wake.

The bear will find them first.

Whenever he forces himself from his mind-pictures of Alex and Rachel, these are the only ideas he has. It leaves him to work his burning legs in silence. Why would he share these hopeless probabilities with anyone else? Elsie Bader has long retreated into a simplified world, a pillow fort that a child makes to protect herself from outside terrors. And Margot knows better than he all the reasons they will fail.

For the first few hours, Mrs. Bader's weight had numbed his arm to any sensation but occasional cramps. Now it's on fire. Miles wonders if his shoulder has been dislocated, though he can't look and doesn't want to touch it in case it has. The idea of trying to switch her from one side to the other promises new agonies he can't afford to risk. And judging from the way Tom's chin keeps falling against his chest, he's doing all he can to stay awake. Miles reminds himself that they are still trudging upwards. He will happily sacrifice an arm so long as they keep eating the slope, inch by inch.

He has been fighting to hold the old woman up for half an hour before Miles realizes they have reached the crest and are now sliding down the steep southern face. There is not enough time to enjoy even a moment's triumph. In the dark, the grade falls away in front of him so that he can't stop tripping forward into nothingness.

Margot is ahead of him now, farther down and maybe a hundred yards off to the right. He can't see her and she doesn't call for him. But Miles is sure she has fallen. He can hear her cough with each new impact, the rocks clattering under her limbs.

When Miles, Tom and Mrs. Bader reach the south treeline, he finds Margot leaning against a hollow snag. Something trickling down her cheeks catches the wink of the moon.

"You okay?"

"Yeah."

"Looks like you're cut."

"I'm fine. Just not much left in the tank."

"We're good, though."

"We're perfect."

"Because if we—"

"Save it, Miles. All right?"

He is about to apologize to her—for not reaching her sooner, for Wade, for being the tongue-tied oaf that he is—but his head starts to swim and he knows if he doesn't start walking again he will pass out here and now.

A blur of grey encircles them. All of the trees are dead, the branch ends dry and sharp, dirty fingernails lashing their foreheads. Spruce beetles. The trees strangled by an infestation that sucks the green out and leaves them a metallic monochrome. When a group stand together like this, it is as though the world has been bleached of all its colour.

A hawk owl quizzes itself high in the swaying top of a black spruce—*Who? Who?*—before flapping into the night to escape the answer.

The forest forces them into what feels like circles. Margot shoves her way ahead to look for a game trail to follow, but there is only a new knotting of trunks. Their breathing is so loud within the walls of trees it strikes all of them as the whisperings of spirits.

He can't decide when it was that he started hearing their breathing joined by another. A couple of times he stops long enough to listen for the thud of paws or footsteps, but there is only the waiting forest.

Yet each time he starts again, a hoarse in-and-out follows them. Sometimes it's close enough that, if he turned, Miles is certain he would meet its eyes.

"I hear the birds coming, Momma."

"Is Mr. Raven bringing his friends here?"

"No, Momma. The *big* birds."

Now that Alex has tuned her ears to it, she too can hear the helicopters whining over the hills.

"We're going soon, aren't we?"

"Soon, baby."

"And Stump's coming too?"

"We'll see."

"But Mr. Raven's *already* gone."

"He never liked Stump much anyway. I guess he just had enough."

"I guess," Rachel says. "Or maybe he has something to do."

All over the softball diamond, Ross River tilts its head back to see what shape their delivery is to take. To Alex, they look like two hundred people all searching for the night's first star.

TWENTY

The light toothpicks his eyes through the earth. Worm tunnels
that allowed him to breathe can now be followed to the surface.
He blinks up at a brown world nicked with blue. He had been so
cold overnight he dreamed he lay under ice, not soil. But just minutes after the sun's first crowning, the weight that holds him down
has already warmed. It feels like another's body on top of his.

Though he'd intermittently convinced himself of the possibility
of escape through the night, Wade recognizes that now he must
actually attempt it. It disappoints him in an abstract way that he
won't be able to. And he knows that if he lives on into the next
round of darkness, it will be bad. Even with his loss of blood and
lack of water, he figures it might take a long time to die down here.

Yet there is still the formality of an attempt before he can allow
himself to give up. He concentrates all of of his strength into his
right arm and pushes its fist into the largest of the gaps. It nudges
enough rocks aside to slide up to the elbow. The breeze against his
skin wakens him, as though his mouth had been freed instead of his
twiddling fingers.

His wounded arm is forced up just as easily. He uses the one
hand that works properly to pluck away the rocks on top of him.
With the other, he bulldozes the soil from over his face.

After what he guesses to be hours he sits up. Sends a finger
round his mouth to scoop out the gritty wads.

He's in an aspen grove. Up the slope to his right he can glimpse
the avalanche slide. The bear hadn't taken him far.

He holds his breath and rises. A nylon Lazarus.

The first few steps hurt as though he breaks a toe each time his
foot meets the ground. It helps once he tells himself it doesn't

matter. Pain has no consequence for him. He has come back, and this time all his suffering will be set aside to be tallied later.

He makes his way onto the slide and, for the first time, smells the smoke. Then sees it. A swerving haze, trying on shapes for itself.

Above him, he notices what's left of Bader's body. There is no reflex left in him—of sympathy, of aid, of revulsion—to slow his step.

The old man's dead, Wade thinks. *So was I once.*

It would have been a fifty-fifty guess which way Margot had gone, over the ridge to the south or back toward the truck. The fire makes it simpler. When he's climbed high enough above the treeline to look north into the valley, he sees mile-long arms of fire reaching across the trail they'd come here on. Whoever the bear didn't bury will be running the other way.

He stops and blows snot out one side of his nose. A plug of dirt from his grave comes with it.

Wade lowers his gaze from the old man's body to the rocks around his own boots. There, shining from within, is Bader's Winchester. Such a beautiful gun. He picks it up, puts his eye to the telescopic site. The crosshairs find individual stones in the pile he'd made digging himself out. Lifts it higher and he could touch the nearest flames, leaping from the spruce tops. Even he could shoot whatever he wanted to from a quarter-mile away.

He sidesteps to where Margot had emptied the rifle's cartridges and finds five. Loads them all.

Wade cradles the gun against his chest and walks on.

Alive, but less than he was. He carries less of what he remembered of being himself, anyway. His name. A place he started from and the story of how he got to where he is. The thousand laws and million sub-rules that condition his range of possible actions. Wade finds that all of this agrees with him. He can move with only one purpose before him, and that purpose could shift from moment to moment and it wouldn't matter. It's like being preprogrammed. A happy, empty robot.

He makes his way off the slide feeling only a niggling impatience. What he will do, he would like to do now.

But first things first. He will carry on higher along the hill face. He will let the smoke cover his progress when the trees can't. He will watch for anything that moves. And whatever moves, he'll kill.

Dawn sprinkles down on them. A seasoning of greens and mustards collecting over the dark lines of things. The cold has hardened the moisture on their lips into moustaches of frost. Everything is coated in a layer of see-through silver. When the full sun appears through the branches the ice melts so quickly Miles doubts he'd seen it at all. Water hangs off the pine needles like tears.

As the ground levels off, the trees give way to wide bands of scrub. Sagewort and wintergreen for the first while, a soft carpet of grasses. Soon, though, they are bushwhacking through harder stuff. Junipers, wild cranberries. Given that they don't know where they're going, it makes little difference to their progress. From what could be one of five directions, a woodpecker natters against the frozen bark.

Since the first signs of morning, Miles hasn't heard Elsie Bader speak her husband's name. He carries her full weight now. When he catches her with eyes closed, nothing he says or does can open them. He realizes, with a peculiar indifference, that he may be piggybacking a corpse.

Sometime before noon, he catches sight of a helicopter thudding south. Even though it's impossible from this distance, he tries to see what faces might be pressed against its windows. He almost tricks himself into meeting the girl's dark eyes.

"You figure it's going to the camp?"

Margot's voice surprises him. He had come to think he was alone.

Miles nods and follows Margot's boots. He makes it less than twenty feet before Mrs. Bader slides off his back.

She makes no sound on impact, eyes still closed, her limbs folded and soft. Kneeling, Miles looks at her face in the new sunlight. She probably has children somewhere. Married, busy, with families of their own. Pagers buzzing at their waists. Channel surfing.

His hands slide under her spine and come up easy. With a moan, Miles finds his balance with the old woman cradled in his forearms. He knows it's only the exhaustion, some symptom that shows he's come to the end. Whatever its cause, he smiles. It's the image he imagines the raven in the willows up ahead has of him that he can't help but find funny. A groom carrying his bride over a lost threshold.

The second, and last, time Margot phoned Miles was in the last week of May. When he heard her voice on the line he was expecting another indirect invitation to her bed, a smoky mention of Wade being out of town for the night. They had carried on their affair at this tentative pace, and it had proved enough to hold both of them to the lives they had started it in. Only Wade had changed. His drinking purposeful, his backhanded slaps leaving Margot with bruises she explained away as implausible accidents, if she spoke of them at all.

Wade knew. Not that he'd brought it up with her—not that he ever mentioned Miles's name—but even he had awakened to the meaning behind Margot and Miles' Welcome Inn glances. Not their desire, but a shared sympathy. An *Are you okay?* shot through the blue smoke.

Wade knew. Miles could see it in him. It was, in part, why when he heard Margot's voice on the phone he had a list of polite refusals already prepared in his mind. *It's not you, it's me . . . There's someone I'm just not over yet . . . He's a bastard, I know. But it still isn't fair to Wade . . .* He might use some or all of these, depending on Margot's willingness to accept them.

"I have to see you," she said. The words pure soap opera, yet their tone was spontaneous.

"Are you okay?"

"Probably not."

"Is it Wade? Has he been——?"

"It's not him."

"I was just on my way out the door," he said, and it was true. His pickle and Spam sandwich zipped into his pack, which was his picnic to be eaten on this year's first trip to the top of Eagle's Nest Bluff.

"Where are you going?"

"Just a hike," he said, and waited for Margot to let him go. Perhaps thirty seconds passed in silence. "Would you like to come?"

"Don't pick me up. I'll come there."

They said little on the drive. Margot kept her face turned from him, gazing out the window but without fixing her eyes on any passing feature. He knew it wasn't possible, but Miles felt as though she was angry at him and he was having to undergo the vaguely familiar exercise of wondering what he had done or said wrong. It had been so long since he'd been alone like this with a woman that he had forgotten the conversational rituals of intimacy—the meaningful pantomimes, the punishments of words both offered and denied.

They parked halfway in on the overgrown lumber road and hiked to the bluff's base. Miles assumed the role of guide, though the trail was plain to both of them. The day brightened as they climbed higher, as though they were stepping through the clouds. By the time they reached the plateau the sun left them patting their pockets for sunglasses they'd both left behind.

Miles hid the awkwardness of having nothing to say by pretending it took him longer to catch his breath than it did. Bending over with his hands on his knees offered him the added advantage of not having to look directly at Margot. She had been the one to follow him. It was her job to start talking. Yet he felt like it was he who had asked her to come all the way up here only to forget why.

He tried for an icebreaker. Something harmless. If he was really lucky, they might get out of this without any serious talk at all.

"It's a helluva view from up—"

"The thing is, I'm pregnant," Margot said. Then, after a sip of breath, "And no, it's not yours."

"Not mine," Miles managed to repeat.

"It couldn't be, right? We've been safe and everything."

"We were safe."

"I've made an appointment at the Women's Place down in Whitehorse for tomorrow afternoon. That's what they call it. The Women's Place. Like all they do is sell cosmetics."

"I'm sorry," he said, spreading his feet wider apart on the rocks, suddenly top-heavy. "This can't be an easy decision."

"I haven't even made it yet."

"What do you mean?"

"I thought it might depend on what you have to say."

"I'm not sure I have anything to do with it."

"Not if you don't want to, no."

Miles stood up straight, though the breathlessness had returned to him for real.

"Have you talked to Wade about it?"

"Last night. Which explains the bags under my eyes."

"What exactly did you tell him?"

"Everything. About me, about you. I dropped every bomb I had."

"Well. Well, well."

"You said it."

"I guess he was pretty upset."

"That's the thing. He wasn't upset at all. He went from being shocked straight to happy. No, *overjoyed*."

"Didn't he wonder if it's his?"

"I told him it might not be. Because the truth is, I was hoping deep down that he would hear what I had to tell him and leave. That I could push him away by using you. I know that's the chicken-shit way to go, but there you have it."

"People do strange things," Miles said lamely, but couldn't think of any other way of phrasing the thought in his head.

"Yes, they do. Like when Wade hears that I've been—he hears what I've got to tell him—and all he can do is start crying like it's the best news he's ever heard."

"Maybe it is."

"Maybe it is. So I do my best to rain on his parade. I tell him that if I have this baby, we could never be sure. Then he kisses me. And you know what he says? He says, 'Yes, we would. We'd be sure it was ours.'"

Margot turned from him, her hand shading her eyes as though she was trying to spot something she'd glimpsed moving in the valley below. When she spoke again her voice was even, though louder, her words blown back on the wind coming across the plateau from the west.

"He said he didn't care. About what happened with you, or anything else. We were having a family and that's what mattered. This is *Wade* we're talking about. And here he is being—I don't know—*noble*."

She stepped away but kept talking so that Miles had to follow her to hear. He stopped just over her shoulder. Close enough that he could smell her hair, her skin warmed from the effort of the climb, her rushing disclosures.

"Sometimes, just to get away, I go up to Dawson and do a little gambling," she said. "It's where I met Wade. I loved him from the first blackjack hand he lost. But at the same time, I knew we weren't a forever sort of thing. He's too simple. I can't spend all my life looking out for somebody like that."

"You don't have to tell me this."

"Yes, I do. And I have to tell you that I'm a good gambler, Miles. At the end of the night, I'm almost never down. I don't know how it works. There's no secret. Nothing but feel. Like when I first saw you."

Margot turned before he had a chance to step back so that her face was very close.

"If you say no to this, that's it. We can just be friends, or just be nothing at all. But I figured I had to put this in front of you."

"You're seeing things in me that aren't there."

"Maybe. But if I'm wrong, it's my time to waste, isn't it?"

He wants to say yes. Margot was wrong about him, he felt sure. She was pegging her hopes for improvement on a man for no better reason than she didn't know him as well as the man she was with. And if Miles had run once, there's no way he could say he wouldn't run again. But was it his job to refuse the good luck that came his way?

In the end, Miles's answer was his silence. He stepped back and his eyes turned away to slide along the Yukon's current below, the light popping off the green surface like camera flashes. He'd never been here with someone else before, and it was a mistake. The place had the same effect on others, apparently, as it did on him. It drew out the honesty we work the hardest to fool ourselves about, the things you can face only briefly for the pain of its light, like the sun on the river below.

"I hear you," Margot said after perhaps three full minutes.

"I'm sorry."

"You listened. Most wouldn't have done even that."

Margot stood, and Miles thought she was about to start down the trail to the truck, but instead she came forward and kissed him. Not forgiving or grateful or friendly. Not a kiss meant to communicate something else, but a real one, flavourful and promising. It let him know what he was going to miss. And when she pulled away, he already did.

"What are you going to do?" he asked.

"I'll have to dream on it."

She stopped and faced him. The last time she did before they made it back to town.

"When I first met Wade, I thought he was going to be the one to break me in two. But I was wrong. It was always going to be *me* breaking *him*. My guess is you have some experience of what that feels like."

Margot was already walking away from him before Miles saw what she meant, what she'd seen in him, and that she was right.

The great bird roars through the treetops, its song so loud and low it thumps straight through their skins. The sow leads her cub under the cover of an alder bough. If the bird sees them, she worries it will sweep down to pluck him up in its talons, as she has seen hawks do with marmots and moles.

Neither bear has heard a helicopter before. Nevertheless, when they spot it flying across a clear spot in the branches they both recognize it as a machine. Trucks, generators, bush planes. There is never more than a moment's mistaking these for a living thing.

Knowing what it is doesn't prevent the bears from being terrified. While the cub is startled by the range of noise it makes—from the guttural thrumming to the rotor's piercing whine—the sow fears what its arrival might mean. The way the bird circles, flying low and fast over the hillside. Searching for something. Given where they are, high on the killing ground and without any sign of other bears in the vicinity, it's probably them.

When it finally leaves, the cub is reluctant to follow the sow any higher. A minute farther up the slope and they will pass through the end of the treeline, leaving them plainly visible on the subalpine fields. The bird is likely to return. When it does, he knows it will hunt him sooner than his mother. And he is so tired. The desire for sleep has surpassed everything now. If he could only tuck himself against her belly through the rest of the day and the night, he will cross whatever mountains she wants him to in the morning.

The she-grizzly reads his wishes and dismisses them with another prod of her snout. As she does, she smells the cub's blood seeping through his fur.

She lumbers on and the cub follows. In her ears, she can almost translate the grinding echo of the helicopter into the rush of water in the creek on the other side.

There are only six left to watch it come.

Over the last several hours the air-vac has picked up Ross River bit by bit and dropped it on the south side of the St. Cyrs. At first, the job had gone slowly but more or less calmly—only a handful had attempted to jump the line, and had been ordered back to their places without the threat of force. The helos had come and gone in regular appearances, so that a rhythm of approaching and fading rotors established itself in the afternoon's fog.

The last twenty evacuees, however, had longer to wait. A strengthening wind made landings trickier, the pilots sometimes requiring three or more attempts before touching down. The sounds of engines had been replaced only by the call of names, the eruption of coughing fits.

The delay had made none more nervous than King. Right at the end the kid had showed up from wherever he'd been hiding, his face bloodless and slick. When Mungo demanded to know what he'd been doing, King claimed to be ill, a sudden stomach bug that had him bent over the toilet in the fire office. Mungo decided there was little point in voicing his doubts.

Now the kid and almost everyone else is gone. The remaining half-dozen wait for the wind to clear the sky over their heads. For the last twenty minutes, the yellow smoke has huddled at the edge of the trees around the softball diamond like a gathering army of sand. Now, all at once, it advances.

As it spouts through the chain-link of the backstop and runs the baselines toward the last evacuees standing by the bleachers, all but one of them step closer together. They brush against each other's shoulders so that, when the smoke passes over them, they won't be left alone.

"Stay where you are. The last two—"

"Pam?"

"Over here."

"I've *got* her, Jackie."

"Terry? Where's Alex?"

"Right beside me. But I don't—"

At first, they think their rising voices are consumed by a noise made by the smoke itself. A choir of sustained shrieks and grinding metal.

The five who remain together link arms and shuffle back from where they believe the helo is lowering. There is little room for escape. Ten feet from where they started, their heels hit the lowest plank of the bleachers. The men tumble back hard as the women plunge their hands through the smoke to pull them up. A gust from the rotors nearly lifts all of them off their feet, breaking their grips. The helicopter takes sudden shape. Its wind pins them against the planks.

Mungo blinks up and watches the blades lean toward him. Their rotation lends them a velvety sheen, like the LPs he used to play at the radio station before they padlocked the place. He is aware of motion all around him. A glimpse of Pam's bare arms, waving. Alex looking around in just-dawning puzzlement.

"Get down!" he orders them against his own inclination to reach up and test the sharpness of the blades.

With an upward suck of air the smoke is momentarily lifted away, forming a hundred-foot ceiling over the field. The visibility allows the helo's pilot to see how close he is to the bleachers and pull back on the stick.

But his correction is too abrupt, and the landing rails gouge into the grass. As the helo shudders back it leaves two snaking trenches in the ground. When it manages to settle it is directly on top of the pitcher's mound, so that its frame totters slightly, see-sawing even as the engines calm to an idling roar.

"Everybody okay?" Mungo is asking even as he guides them down to the first-base line. "Pam? *Pam?*"

He directs this at his daughter in particular because of the way she stares at the helicopter awaiting them, her arms stiff at her sides.

"Keep an eye on her," he directs Jackie, and steps back to the bleachers.

"The dog," Alex says as he climbs up to the step below hers.

"What dog?"

"Before the smoke. She was with him."

"Rachel?"

"Stump. The helicopter scared him. I think she went to bring him back."

"I'll find her," Mungo says, his voice even but his grip firm around Alex's elbow.

When all of them make it down to the grass they stand facing the helicopter. The pilot waves at them. They can lip-read his profanities through the haze.

"We'll have to go in two trips," Mungo says. "I want Alex, Rachel and Pam on this one."

"But Rachel's not *here*."

"I'm going to look for her. But if I can't find her right away, I want you out."

"I'm not leaving without her."

"You've got to do—"

Before Mungo has finished, the smoke doubles upon itself, blurring the ground from under their feet. Only now do they feel the burning in their eyes. When it half clears again, they notice the tears spilling down each other's cheeks, as though all of them have been caught in the same wash of unexpected emotion.

"It's getting messy here," Terry Gray says.

Mungo glances past the bleachers at where Rachel has most likely run. When he turns back to the helo, its pilot is repeatedly jerking his thumb up and down.

"It might take a minute," Mungo says, raising his voice and struggling to keep it flat at the same time. "So listen. I want Jackie, Pam and Terry on this helo."

"It should be you," Terry Gray says.

"Forget it."

"That's your wife and daughter—"

"I *promised* him," Mungo hisses, stepping close so that only Terry hears him.

He lays his hand on the top of Terry's arm. Pushes him away. The taller man stumbles without losing Mungo's eyes.

Even as the three of them climb aboard, the pilot is powering the engines up to their previous pitch.

It's at the same time that Pam pulls the door shut behind her that Mungo feels a weight against his leg. He looks down to see Stump squeezed between him and Alex. They both swing around at once. Through the grey, they watch Rachel slapping her palms against the dog's rump, pushing him forward like a farmer nudging a cow into its pen.

I found him, the girl's lips say.

When Mungo turns back to the helo he can see that Terry Gray has spotted the girl as well and is now fiddling with the door handle to get out. Before he can, Mungo throws both hands out flat like an umpire calling a player safe at first base.

Already, the landing rails are lifting from the pitcher's mound. The smoke curls around the ship, obscuring the passengers' faces in the windows. There is no time even to wave goodbye, if such a gesture had occurred to those either in the air or on the ground.

When they can no longer hear the departing helo, Mungo

directs Alex and Rachel back onto the bleachers. The smoke lowers and lifts off the softball diamond like skirts of lace.

"They're coming," he tells them, and in his voice he hears the false edge that comes with willing what one says to be the same as making it happen.

When Miles drops Elsie Bader onto a cot in the fire base's medical tent, the sudden release of weight from his arms lifts them high. Palms open, trembling. He looks like a born-again at a revival meeting.

"Is she alive?" he asks the medic, who stands stunned by their unexpected appearance.

"There's a pulse," he says finally, two fingers pressed to Mrs. Bader's neck. "How are you doing?"

"I think I've got one too."

"Have a seat."

"Me first," Margot says, stepping around them both to collapse into the chair the medic had offered. Tom follows, wearing the same mischievous grin Miles had seen him share with Rachel in the playground.

Miles looks around for something to sit on, a bottle of water, anything that might be of use. The tent is suddenly too small for him. Through his weakness, he feels himself swelling with nervous might. Even now, his raised arms have come only halfway down.

"Go," Margot says. "They're out there somewhere."

He nods. Margot puts a raised finger against her lips. When he can't think of any way of saying how glad he is that she is here, safe, he nods again.

Once he's out, the taste of smoke has intensified in Miles's mouth. His tongue fat against his teeth. He tries calling for Alex and Rachel but it doesn't come out right. Their pictures have been so vivid for him that assigning them names feels as though he is speaking of the wrong people altogether.

The base is small. Maybe half a dozen wall tents set up in a rough circle, three mowed helipads, a portable radio antenna stuck to the top of a four-by-four. At the north and south ends, orange windsocks wave disconsolately on aluminum poles. Around these structures, forty firefighters and the population of Ross River wander about, helping themselves to sandwiches laid out on a tarp and shaking their heads at the trick of events that had pulled them out of their lives to drop them here, in a meadow next to the third of the three Lapie lakes.

Miles catches sight of men he drinks with at the Welcome Inn. Bonnie waves his way and seems about to shout something but, when she opens her mouth, changes her mind. He moves through the transplanted town, absently patting the shoulders of his neighbours. Earl, the hotel manager. Then Crookedhead James and King, standing together. When the kid spots Miles he looks away, refusing to meet his eyes.

The two faces are nowhere to be seen.

He's running now. Circling through the same clumps of people, casting his eyes over their heads. He notices the way they watch him, his stumbling frame interrupting their conversations. Frightening them.

Terry Gray is the one who finally stops him. Miles is so tired that, now that he's still, he nearly buries his cheek against the man's chest.

"Where are they?"

"Listen, there are some—"

"Where *are* they, Terry?"

"It was your dog."

Miles waits for him to explain, but Terry Gray looks at him as though it should be obvious how Stump would play a determining role in a situation like this.

"Rachel," Miles says.

"Your girl went to look for him right when the helo we came

out on was landing. There was so much smoke and the pilot wasn't going to wait for—"

He pauses. Miles watches as his pupils blow up so wide the black eats all the colour around them. *Your girl.* He hadn't missed that part, either.

"It was Mungo's call," Terry goes on. "Alex wasn't leaving without her, and he wasn't leaving without either of them."

"What about the air-vac after yours?"

"It was lousy with smoke in there. And then there's the wind. Even as we were lifting off we could feel it knocking us around. The last helo turned back at the ridge. Our pilot told us we were lucky we didn't smash into the side of the goddamn mountain."

"Can't they go back for them now?"

"I keep checking, and they keep telling me it's no good."

A new thought skips across Miles's mind. "Is Ruby here?"

Terry shakes his head.

The helicopter engines whistle at them from the other side of the base but their rotors remain still. On standby. They could stay this way for the next six hours and not run out of fuel.

Without knowing where he's going or what he intends to do, Miles walks toward the idling helos. There is a vague notion that he will beat the molars out of the first pilot he sees, but even in his frustration, Miles knows it makes little sense and would do no good.

He makes it halfway before the fire director up from White-horse stops him. Miles recalls that he used to like Dennis Parks. Now, something in the forced sympathy and suspiciously clean-shaven jawline of the man determines that Miles has no choice but to despise him forever.

Parks is talking into his satellite phone and making a scribbling motion at Miles. The press want to know how the region's biggest wildfire story of the decade is shaping up, and Dennis Parks is their go-to spokesperson. Half the continent this side of the Rockies, from L.A. to Anchorage, is burning. Amidst the inferno, Ross River's drama has made network coverage. What's immediately needed is some punchy, front-line commentary for the supper-time news hour. Over the longer term, however, there will be an overwhelming demand for heroes. Dennis Parks has volunteered his name for all causes.

After a laughing goodbye, the director snaps the phone shut and returns it to his belt. Then he starts talking at Miles. His pink chin bouncing up and down.

"This Comeback Fire of yours is something else, Miles," Parks is telling him, eyebrows raised but with an admiring half smile, as though he's talking about a giant lake trout Miles has just pulled into their boat. "It's breaking all the rules, that's for sure. Definitely one for the history books."

"I couldn't give a shit about history right now, Dennis."

"I'm just telling you what we're dealing with here."

"I know what we're dealing with."

"Not sure you do."

"I was on initial attack."

"That's right. You were."

"What's that—?"

"Then it got away from you. And now it's doing what it wants. That's why we haven't been able to send a bird back in there."

"If you think I'm going to accept that as an excuse for you not doing your job, you're way off."

"I'm not—"

"There are still *people* in there. And you're telling me how *unique* this fire is. Like it's already over and there's nothing to do but explain why we couldn't have done more."

Parks looks over his shoulder and notices a dozen evacuees staring at them. The optics on an exchange of this kind leave something to be desired. He'd taken a professional development course in Vancouver at the start of the season entitled Controlling the

On-Site Public Relations Environment. So far, his handling of Miles McEwan would have gotten him a flunking grade.

There's nowhere for Parks to go but around the back of his truck. Miles follows him. Parks would ask him to sit in the cab, but he isn't so sure he wants to be in closed quarters with the Ross River crew chief at the moment. A growing number of onlookers still watch them through the truck's windows, but now that they're on the other side, Parks hopes they can't hear what they say.

"We're doing everything we can short of endangering our own men."

"Don't you think Mungo Capoose is already in danger? Last time I checked, he was one of our men too. Unless Indians count for less down at head office."

"I'm not listening to this shit."

"You don't have to. I'm going back over that hill and finishing the evacuation myself."

For a second, Miles is gratified to see real shock take hold of Parks's face.

"You're not going in there alone."

"Then come with me."

"The spotter planes are telling us it's a firewall between here and there. You're just being stupid if you do this."

"Call me stupid. Think of the satisfaction," Miles says, turning to go.

"We're investigating this one!"

It's enough to make Miles pause.

"Investigating what?"

"The *cause*. You called it in as unknown. But there's a whiff of bullshit to that, you have to admit. For one thing, there hasn't been a lightning strike at the site of the fire's origin for over fifteen days."

"Don't imply, Dennis. I don't have time."

"This fire was *started*."

"What's that got to do with me?"

"Everything, if you did it."

"So fire me."

"You're not following. It's a hell of a lot bigger than your job now."

Miles takes a step forward.

"What are you talking about?"

"A crew working the northern line found your friend Ruby."

"Where is she? They bring her here?"

"Nothing to bring. But she was a tougher lady than I would have guessed, I'll say that. Made it about ten miles from her tower on foot before the fire chased her down. Know what else? When they found her she still had that book of hers with her."

"No . . ."

"Holding it like a baby against her chest. The guys tried to pry it out of her hands but it turned to snow."

"No."

"The Mounties have been itching to start up a homicide investigation right from the start, and now they've got it. And by the time this is over, there's probably going to be a few other bodies to join Ruby's. You okay, Miles? You've gone all white. That's interesting. Because I wouldn't imagine an innocent man would look so—"

Miles lunges at Parks so fast the man doesn't have time to remove the grin from his face. His back slams against the truck's passenger door. It shatters the glass with a single crunch. Miles's palms pinned against his shoulders, holding him there.

"Whatever you're thinking, you're wrong," Miles spits at him, then steps away, leaving Parks free to come at him. But he only feels his hands around his back to check where the glass has pierced his shirt.

"I think your phone is ringing," Miles says.

Parks reflexively looks down at his belt and pulls out the satellite phone attached to it, flips the lid and reads its blank screen. By the time he looks up again, Miles is already walking away.

"You know why you got scars all over that face of yours?"

Miles only lengthens his stride. It forces Parks to scream.

"Because you're reckless. You've already gotten one man killed. Now you want to kill yourself so you can go down looking like some dumbshit cowboy. You know what? While you're at it, why don't you take along your—"

Miles pulls back the flap into the outfitting tent, and when it falls into place behind him it blocks out the director's words. There's a table piled with cardboard boxes, food tins, batteries. On the ground, clean pulaskis and pisstanks. He grabs only the most essential supplies he can find—a gorp mix of nuts and raisins, bottles of water, half a dozen Hershey bars—and stuffs them into a pack hanging on a hook. There would be a rifle in the locker, too, but he would need Parks to give him the key. Besides, Miles figures his only chance of making it through the fire now is to run it light.

When he's got the pack over his shoulders he walks across the open circle of the camp, straight back toward the crest the way he'd come. People watch him go, but he doesn't turn his head to see who.

"Miles? Could you hold up a second?"

He turns to see Jerry McCormack running after him, holding something out in one of his hands. More than this, Miles notices how his crewman, usually shy about nothing, avoids meeting his eyes.

"I'm in kind of a hurry," Miles says once Jerry has caught up with him but only stands there, repeatedly clearing his throat.

"It's just that I made something. This here. I was hoping you'd take it with you."

Miles looks down at the thing gripped between Jerry's fingers. A half-dozen Popsicle sticks tied together in their middles with string so that they form the shape of a star. Their ends stained a pale red.

"Christ, Jerry. I don't—"

Miles's crewman silences him by revealing the long string connected to the centre of the Popsicle sticks. Then he steps forward and loops it over Miles's head.

"They call it a *shutch*," Jerry says, still not looking directly at Miles. The strangeness of the exchange is not the only thing that's made Jerry awkward. It's that he can't stop watching the fire working its way over the hills in the distance.

"Are you serious?" Miles asks, and is sorry even before it's out. Jerry's face clearly shows he's being about as serious as he's ever been.

"I don't know much about it, really. But back when my people still did the traditional things, the shaman would take a *shutch* with him when he went into the bush. They say it carries the spirit of a bear. And when you wear it, you can pass through fire. I even saw it once when I was a kid. An eighty-year-old medicine man walking over live coals like it was shag carpet."

"Well, well. Something like that could come in handy," Miles says, fingering the Popsicle sticks against his shirt and feeling their rounded ends, still wet.

"It's supposed to be a bundle of twigs that's been dipped in the blood of a bear's tongue," Jerry McCormack says, shrugging. "Well, you know me, the guy who's always forgetting to bring his bear's tongue along. So I asked the cook over in the canteen if I could dip it in the blood left from some steaks he had thawing out on his cutting board. Looked at me like the crazy Indian I am, but he let me do it."

Uncertain what to say to this, Miles shakes Jerry's hand. A firm grip signalling agreement, a fair deal struck. The best that two men in a bad spot can do.

Miles carries on out of the camp and is soon walking under the speckled shade of trees once more. He thinks he can hear Dennis Parks, as well as maybe some others. Trying to pull him back with reason, prudence, a dose of sensible fear. Their voices no more sway him than the squawks of the raven following overhead.

TWENTY-ONE

If he had only kept moving it might not have happened. All he had to do was stay in the bristling present and he would have been fine. Instead, he makes the mistake of stopping. It's only for a second, but it's long enough to open the smallest crack and let the firestarter in.

It is the touch of the lighter that does it. A hand absently slipped into his breast pocket. Before he knows what he's doing he has pulled the silver casing out to sit face up in his palm, so that when he looks down, the New York skyline winks back at him.

He watches the rising pillars of smoke and asks a question of himself that he instantly recognizes as borrowed. A line from one of those "classic" rebroadcasts on late-night TV. Before his time. Something with POWs, British accents. A tragic misinterpretation of duty.

What have I done?

The thing is, he knows.

For the briefest of moments, the firestarter feels the urge to lay out the arc of his intentions to another, if not confess outright. Who would he go to first to be understood? The answer surprises him. It slips him out of his firestarter self and, for a moment, he is caught in between, disembodied.

He sees himself from outside his skin. A lost-looking man holding a lighter etched with a city he has never been to.

TWENTY-TWO

He has heard that, for some, the northern lights will sing. As he walks back up the St. Cyrs, Miles strains to hear them. If the light is capable of music, it refuses to play for him tonight. It offers strange company, nevertheless. He watches the aurora's thrashing and coiling and sees it as torn ribbons of thought. Light without shape, unless it is the shape of dreams. Sun dust. He knows this is what causes the sky to dance. Ions borne for years on the solar wind to fall against the atmosphere seventy miles above him. They will come no closer than this. Yet there is something in the way the wavering sheets stretch earthward that makes him think he might be able to tug them down if he climbed even the stubbiest tree.

Sometime after midnight the sky dulls, blackens, lifts its surface of stars to its usual unthinkable distance. The moon a flashlight searching for him through the trees. In the clearings, it is bright enough that he can see his breath.

For the first few miles, the cold air cleans his mind of voices. Now that they're gone, he realizes he's been listening to maybe a dozen ongoing monologues ever since he started into the bush after Margot and Elsie Bader the morning before. Miles is more than glad to have them shut up. Trouble is, the drop in temperature comes with a price. The muscles in his legs, his arms, the ones in charge of holding his head on its neck, have stiffened into wires. He feels poorly assembled.

Even as he's falling, he tells himself he's only lying down for a nap. His skull just misses the white rocks poking up all over the hillside and he pretends he planned it that way.

He has brought no blanket, and his firepack is without even one of the standard-issue paper sleeping bags used by crews who have to spend nights on mop-up assignments. He's forced to sleep where he's dropped. Coyote camping.

Through the night, Miles lets the mosquitoes land on his face. Yet his stillness seems to discourage the bugs from their feast, as though his flesh is less appetizing without the struggle of resistance. He dozes in snatches so brief that coming out of them causes him pain. There is always a distant howl, a thud, a snort of animal disgust to lift his head from the ground. The earth so dry it feels like newspaper clippings under his cheek.

From time to time, the air is flash-fried by the explosion of solitary pines. A million glowing coals on the ground around him are a crimson mirroring of stars. As a result, his dreams have no floors or ceilings, no discernible up or down.

The first hint of sunlight wakes him for good. He's reminded of how the arctic hills change colour through the day. In the moments before dawn, they emerge as an improvised line. Now, they are a sterilized green. Later they will sharpen further yet, the hoodoos a line of tortoise shells. In the evening, he will have climbed into their blues. It occurs to him that he might never see these transformations again.

After a breakfast of chocolate eaten as he walks, Miles comes upon a narrow creek. He watches it run, clear as gin. It commands him to cup his hands and drink. His mouth fills with frosted steel and juniper. He peers back along the course of the creek and sees how it has passed under the boughs of pines that, over the warm afternoons, have dripped traces of resin to flavour the stream.

He rounds a small pond in the shadow of an unnamed peak and sees a crosshatching of moose tracks a foot below the surface. Farther on, he turns to the right where there was nothing before and a great buck looks back at him. It cocks its antlered head as though puzzling as to how Miles appeared out of nowhere, just as Miles wonders the same about it. He expects it to plow into the bush as he has seen them do a thousand times. But this one stays where he is. Lowers his head and drinks, having made some instant assessment that has determined Miles as less of a threat than thirst.

As he walks on, Miles notices how the animals visit him without fear. He's heard that fire can do this. The detection of smoke has tamed wildlife that would otherwise refuse to be seen by human eyes. Today, the peace has been extended to Miles, an unarmed man walking alone, and therefore in as much trouble as any other living thing. A pair of magpies twitter advice and fly ahead from limb to limb as though blazing a trail on his behalf. The raven stays with him too. Its caws and gulps a self-amusing performance.

More frequently now he feels the presence of something else just behind him, or just ahead. Not the raven. Something that moves on legs as he does, but more surely. Jumping out of view when he swings round to look. He has heard its breathing over the last several hours.

Along with a new sound. In just these last minutes, he's certain he heard it clear its throat to speak.

He gauges his fatigue by the fury of memories it allows in. Blinks of colour he recognizes as people or landscapes or sunlit rooms only after they have been replaced with something new, so that he is constantly trying to catch up. The apartment over the bagel bakery in Montreal. The girl's bug-bitten knees. Alex, mostly. Not her face, but close-up parts he hadn't consciously thought of since he left. The moles atop the knobs at each end of her collarbone. The incisor that is the last tooth to be seen before she closes her lips, nipping the flesh each time. Eyelids bruised from sleep.

He works to hold these pictures in place. For as long as they linger before him, he forgets himself and only drifts closer to where he's going. But then the snapshots slip away and he's alone again. Unsure if he is being guided or pursued.

***

For the second time in the last twenty-four hours Miles crosses over the ridge of the St. Cyrs, and for the second time he notices it only once it has passed. The valley to the north is too great a distraction. Nothing, not Ross River or the Pelly or the contour of the basin itself, is visible for the fire. As he descends, it appears to race to meet him, the spits of flame reaching from every direction. If he could see a clear way through, it would be from up here. Instead, there is only a panorama of the valley's destruction.

Even before he reaches the fireline, the air is burdened with heat. The going is maddeningly slow. His boots send hollow knocks through the earth, as though he is walking on bare planks. More than anything it is the sun that weighs upon his limbs, masked in the curls of grey.

His exhaustion allows the worst thoughts to pass without the dread that would otherwise accompany them. He will burn in this fire. Alex and Rachel will burn. The pain the child will endure.

Miles can thank his mother for his ability to come up with the worst of these scenarios. For the second half of her life, she has lived for the narratives of everyday tragedy. Savage divorces, crib deaths, bright youths turned instant quadriplegics from dives into shallow water. The young Miles was brought up on the saddest gossip Nanaimo had to offer. He had always assumed it was her way of interpreting his father's leaving her. A terrible thing had happened in her life, and she sought some comfort in observing that she was not alone in being visited by terrible things.

At the time, it struck neither of them as a morbid preoccupation. As with jokes, it all turns upon the telling. Miles's mother made a point of relating her reports of misfortune with genuine sympathy and, more important, the promise of a lesson to be learned. Only now, winding his way down into the fire-filled Tintina Trench, does Miles recognize what this lesson was. All through his childhood she had been trying to tell him that the true price one pays for love isn't the possibility of heartbreak but its certainty.

When he comes to the fire Miles stalks its borders, searching for a way through. It appears that no entry point is better than any other. He knows that at the heart of a fire of the Comeback's size it would be hot enough to melt gold. Even trees of the subarctic's stature shoot flames a hundred feet skyward, and smoke three times higher yet. The fire gives every sign that its purpose is to drive all life out of its path. And he's looking for a way in.

The raven flies in a tight circle above a patch of disparate flames, the space between their red columns little more than double the width of his shoulders. For the first time since Miles noticed it following him, the black bird is silent.

There is no time to consider whether the trickster, in its quiet, is offering help or malice. Its intent can't be known in any case. Miles must move forward or allow the remaining channels into the fire to close forever.

He cuts around to the raven's position and strides between the flames. His fingers play over the *shutch* on his chest. He wonders whether his skin or the Popsicle sticks will burn first.

Wade walks through his own fire. Though it's all around him, he can only really feel its heat through the rifle's metal, the barrel searing the palm of his good hand. It's like he's already shot the things he most looks forward to shooting.

As he clumps farther into the trees, he replays the day just a few weeks ago when Margot had taken the truck down to Whitehorse. All she told him was that she was going to keep an appointment, though he knew what this meant, the decision that announced itself in the zipping of her overnight bag down the hall as he sat staring at the moisture stains in the living-room ceiling. He didn't try to stop her. When he got back from the Welcome Inn later that night he'd plugged a cartridge into his shotgun and walked round to Miles's cabin.

Later, after Jerry and Crookedhead had interrupted him, after he'd found a strange, near-sober calm after killing the dog who'd stood in his way, Wade had made it home, dropped the Mossberg on the sofa, and dialled the number to the motel where Margot was staying. He'd apologized. Two or three times in a row. Not for anything he'd done or not done, but for being who he was. It was more like saying goodbye.

"I'm sorry."

"Why do you keep saying that?"

"Because I am."

"You sound weird."

"I tried to kill him."

"Who?"

"Playing with himself. I mean, playing *chess* against—"

"Go to bed."

"But I'm not tired. I'm so awake it's got my goddamn head split open. *Ideas*. I got ideas right now that you would never—"

"It's gone."

"What's that?"

"It's gone, Wade."

A foul twist in his guts. The final voiding of whatever had held him to his routine of muttering barefoot around the trailer during the day, scoffing at the contestants on reality TV shows, getting methodically drunk within an hour of his stomach settling from the abuses of the night before—the fading outline of a life. Now even this was gone. That's what he'd heard in Margot's words. Not her refusal to carry his child, but her refusal of *him*.

What filled him in its place wasn't rage—not at first—but terror. Even he had never been truly alone before. He had been born without the gift for friendship, and before Margot, women seemed to discover something in him in the early going that warned them off. Yet even with these handicaps, his self-defeating habits, Wade Fuerst had always had someone to sit across from, whether a fellow crewman in an oil field mess hall, or his parents, or Margot. There would be no one now, though, and he was afraid.

He might have stayed in his fear, booze-addled and harmless, were it not for Miles. It wasn't his affair with Margot that struck him as unjust, but the fact that he had turned down what Wade would have given anything to accept. A family. Offered to Miles not once, not twice, but three times, the third just last week, when the same green-eyed woman and little girl he'd run from came to the end of the world to present themselves to him. To Miles McEwan, the only bastard he could say for sure was no better than him. This was what Wade found intolerable. It was beyond unfair. It was *wrong*.

Wade walks down into the valley with the fire, quicker than he, on each side. A moment ago he might have turned around and had a chance of escaping it. Not that he wanted to. He's past even thinking about getting out now, of fixing things.

That's the bitch about last chances. You never know that's what they were until they're gone.

For a long while, Miles isn't sure if he's alive or dead. He studies the hands of his watch, but they hold no meaning. He's lost the ability to read time as well as anything else, all of his language pulled away, leaving him erased and dumb. The black hands of the timepiece stare up at him, making some repeated point he hasn't the faculties to understand.

Inches from the tip of his boots, a marmot leaps out of the flames. The creature takes a last blinking look at the sun, at Miles, before running blind back into the orange grass.

Crispy critters.

This is what every fire crew he's worked on calls animals burned in wildfires. It's only funny, Miles realizes, when you're walking through a safe zone after it's all over, kicking at the hollow dead things that lie in the ash. Even then, it's a nervous laughter.

Inside, the smoke is the colour of an old penny. For the moment, the fire keeps to the crowns of trees. The flashes from the canopy above show through like sheet lightning. When the flames work their way down the trunks he will be there waiting for it. Glowing cinders land on his tongue.

Up close, fire sounds like rain. The scalding drops rip cigarette holes through his shirt. Soon there is more exposed skin than cotton to cover it.

He stops for a drink but spits it out before it reaches the back of his throat. His mouth tastes sick. An itchy coating over his gums that no amount of horking can get rid of. It makes him think that he's eaten a rotten salad, milky and rust stained. He picks his teeth for lettuce that isn't there.

When he starts again the burned kid walks next to him. Although he doesn't turn to look directly into his face, Miles can feel him there. A frigid aura finding its way through the heat.

"Why don't you turn into a bird again and fly the fuck off," Miles says, but his voice cracks, and the threat breaks into a whimper.

The kid steps closer. Licks his lips as though to whisper words directly into Miles's skull.

"No! You can't speak! I won't *let* you speak!" Miles nearly sobs, spinning around to throw closed fists at where the kid would be standing. Although he makes contact with nothing, he won't let himself look to see what's there.

He runs for the next fifty yards, but the smoke congeals at the top of his lungs. Still the kid walks just behind him. His breath now an audible rasp.

"Where are they?" he finds himself asking, over and over.

The kid answers by pushing Miles's shoulder forward. The same urgent clip that Miles had delivered to him years ago on the Dragon's Back. The only difference is that, this time, the bony hand knocks Miles into the fire instead of away from it.

He nearly steps on the baby's head. Its cotton dress sending up whiskers of smoke. The green eyes held open. Sparkling.

Miles picks the doll up, smooths the hair back from its face. The smoke obscures whatever lies more than twenty feet ahead of him, but he knows where he must be. He drags his boot through the ash and finds part of a spraypainted H in the grass. A few steps on and the outfield gives way to the sandy diamond, the white bases left plugged in the ground. He finds the backstop fence and leaves the doll leaning against it, arms outstretched, as though begging him not to leave.

Miles starts in the direction of the main part of town but, more than once, the haze turns him around. He's sure of his bearings only when he bumps into the trampoline. He smooths his hands over the elastic tarp and recognizes it as the one Rachel had played on. The girl turning to look straight up at him, sure he'd be there. This, of course, being several lifetimes ago.

The fire is part of the town now, sneaking onto the grass roofs of some of the cabins just beyond the road-maintenance compound. Although he can't see it from here, Miles figures it's even odds whether his own place still stands or not. The grass in the yards smoulders where shrapnel from exploding poplars has landed. Out back of the Raven Nest, rings of yellow rip up the wooden goalposts of the neglected soccer field.

He feels his way around a couple of corrugated tin gates only to find himself in another backyard. He recognizes it as that of a neighbour of Jerry McCormack, a guy known only as Toot, a trapper who keeps a team of huskies in town. In the winters, he uses them to run the length of his trapline. The rest of the time, the dogs stay in the kennels that Miles tries to find his way out of now. The huskies pace around him, their tails snug against their holes. The noise of Miles's footsteps sets them to howling.

He opens their cage doors. The dogs scramble out, looking to each other, to Miles, for direction. One of the huskies trots out of the yard, and Miles and the rest of the dogs follow it. For a second, all of them stop in the road and take an accounting of the situation. When Miles walks on, the dogs stay where they are, looking around for someone to put their harnesses on. Only a half-dozen strides later, when Miles looks back, the smoke has smudged out everything but the sound of their panicked whimpers.

Even as he turns to continue, the same smoke lifts all at once. An updraft that pulls the grey off him and leaves the world momentarily exposed.

He sees the familiar detritus of Ross River in an overwhelming particularity. The pickups outside their respective mobile homes, the flag snapping over the school, the pissing cherub—everything overstating its place, suffused with internal illumination. Miles has a sense of seeing something he was not meant to see. Private but perfectly natural at the same time, as when a child walks into his parents' bedroom to witness their naked lovemaking.

His feet guide Miles directly to the door of the Welcome Inn Lounge. He stands there for a second with his hand on the handle. The same spot that Alex and the girl had stood less than a week ago. His vision of the future had started with them here, on the line between inside and outside. Just one step from one to the other and everything changes. Like being born. Or burned. Miles isn't sure that it matters. If there's a chance that what you've decided to belong to lies on the other side, there is no choice but to open it and walk in.

TWENTY-THREE

They have waited too long. The fire has forced them into a direct ascent for the last three hundred yards to the ridgeline. With every second step, the she-grizzly glances up at the crest and sees her progress reduced to nothing.

Her mistake had been to travel sideways as long as they had instead of up and over. She stayed on the avalanche chutes and alpine meadows of the St. Cyrs' north face in an effort to put a buffer between herself, her cub and the rifles. Now, with the fire raging through the whole of the valley behind them, the sow sees that she had identified the wrong threat all along. There can be no chance of escape if her cub falls, no matter how many guns or wildfires pursue them.

The bear turns and, as though in confirmation of her thoughts, watches her cub collapse on the rocks. His legs stiff but still twitching, each limb yet to realize its estrangement from the earth.

He had been the bigger of her two, but now, on his side, she can see the ribs pushing against his coat. His teeth coated in white lather. He wants only for her to see how far he'd come and how hard he'd tried. How he still tries.

The sow lies down next to him, feeling the last of his breaths stroke her snout. Already, the hole from the hunter's bullet opens wide beneath him, as though his will alone had held the wound closed until seconds ago. The blood glues stones to their fur.

Even when the cub lies still the sow stays with him. Her nose a thermometer against his tongue, gauging how fast it goes cold. She inhales what's left of his living scents, etching him on her memory using tools more intimate than words. She will linger here until there is no trace of him left to be detected in his coat, the leathery cups of his ears, the different ground covers they have travelled recorded between the pads of his feet. She holds nothing inside of her but him.

He doesn't so much open the door as pass through it, Casper-like, his feet drifting over the floor in a pantomime of walking just as Mrs. Bader's had when he carried her over the mountain. But who carries him? Miles wonders if the kid is now in charge of his body as well as at least half his mind.

The first surprise is that there is more smoke inside than outside. The seething murk makes it impossible to squint farther than the first tables, the only beacon into the room's depths an electric can of Coors streaking over the Rockies. It's not that the lounge is on fire. It's that its circulation is so poor that once a smell or vapour has seeped in, it becomes trapped forever.

From out of the fog, an elfin shadow emerges. The cherub from the Welcome Inn's fountain. Uprooted and now walking alone, haunting the hotel it had served over its misplaced, chipped plaster life.

In the next moment the cherub puts on clothes, a pair of canvas sneakers. When Rachel steps forward Miles is glad, first, that he won't now have to make conversation with a naked chubby kid with a bladder problem.

"You're late," she says.

Miles picks the girl up and, to his own surprise, smells her. Roots his nose around her jasmine neck, her citronella hair, sniffs at what he recognizes as the Mountain Spring Fresh! fabric softener he keeps on top of the dryer at the cabin. The force of his laughter sets him rolling on the back of his heels. He wonders if kissing her cheeks this much will rub them raw.

Alex is next to appear. He watches her face take shape as she comes closer through the smoke. Its almond outline first, followed by the particulars. As he counts them off, Miles realizes that although the picture from his memory was accurate, her features strike him as new. The spray of freckles. The serious lips. The sensual bump of her nose. He has struggled against the full recognition of her beauty since she passed through the same doorway he has just passed through himself, but now he is too weak, too grateful, too angered by what small pleasures have been denied by his pride to not see her whole. Even after two crossings of the St. Cyrs he feels unworthy of the reward of letting his eyes linger on her this way.

After a moment, he lowers Rachel to return to her mother, but the girl stays where she is, rapping his leg with playful jabs. Against his other leg, Stump has arrived to lick the stains off Miles's pants in welcome.

"You came back," Alex says, and the obviousness of her statement draws colour to her cheeks so bright that, even in the lounge's gloom, Miles can see it.

She can map the distance he has travelled in the fallen line of his shoulders. Instead of erasing him, his exhaustion has translated his body's language for her. It has left him open, readable. His knees have begun trembling now that he has stopped walking, and Alex fights the urge to slip her hands under his arms and bear some of his weight.

She lets him stare. As both of them know, the price for holding still long enough to see is to allow being seen.

His eyes—the blue ridges, rust spots, the burst vessels against the white—tell her what drove him here from however far away he has come. For once, she sees not only all that's broken but the working pieces that remain.

It is Miles's turn to be kissed. Hard, and only once. But there's a message in it, too. Passed in the taste of salt on the other's lips.

When Alex pulls away, Miles feels the cracking of a grin that he can't set halfway right. He knows what he must look like, and how he will always carry a face like a car wreck to one degree or another, and he could care less.

"You came back," Alex says again.

Miles can only nod at the truth of it.

"There was supposed to be one more helicopter," she says.

"Terry Gray told me."

"When are they coming?"

"They aren't. Not until the visibility gets a lot better than what it is."

"We're going to wait for it?"

Miles looks past her shoulder. "Where is he?"

Mungo waves at him from one of the tables closer to the bar.

"What are you hiding from?" Miles says. "Wouldn't bother me if you took a beer or two out of Bonnie's fridge."

"Thought I'd keep my distance."

"I'm not sure anybody could make these two do what they didn't want to."

"I know it."

"So if I'm going to kick your ass, it'll be later, when I'm in the right mood."

Through a momentary tunnel of clear air, Miles can see him smiling his way. Then, at an abrupt turn in the older man's thoughts, the smile disappears.

"Tom's safe," Miles says. "So is Margot and Mrs. Bader. They're at the camp on the other side."

Mungo nods. Something tells all of them not to ask about Wade or Mr. Bader.

The four of them gather in the open doorway, standing in an expectant circle. They might stay this way longer if not for the howling of the dogs outside. Somewhere on the edge of town, the huskies have discovered the fireline.

"We have to go," Miles says, already leading them down the steps of the lounge and into the slightly fresher air of the parking lot.

From here he can see that, even in the time it's taken him to locate the Welcome Inn, the fire has formed a closer circle around the town. Alex and Mungo notice it too. For the first time since Alex led her down to the bleachers the day before, Rachel begins to cry.

"We can't wait for an air-vac. We're just going to have to get out the same way I got in."

"You got the truck through?"

"No," Miles says. "I walked."

This knocks any other questions out of them. What they couldn't know, he tells them. How he found Mr. Bader's body on the rockslide, how he came across Margot, Tom and Bader's wife hiking over the ridge of the St. Cyrs. How he came back.

With a single sniff, Rachel stems her tears. "How far is it?" she asks.

"I'm not sure. Maybe fifteen, twenty miles."

"Is that *far?*"

"Up and over a big hill. But you? I think you can do it."

Rachel nods. She steps around Miles and beckons to Alex and Mungo to follow. It strikes the adults that the girl is the most prepared to begin of all of them.

They walk quickly to the fire office with only the shrieks of Toot's dog team passing between them. From the supply room, they collect two small packs and fill them with water and rations. Mungo considers aloud the merits of bringing oxygen tanks, but Miles tells him to forget it. The added weight will slow them enough that being able to breathe for an additional twenty minutes won't make a bit of difference. The same goes for hard hats, gloves, the aluminum Shake 'n' Bake tents they could hide under if the flames overtake them. They are well beyond the faint hopes of safety gear.

They march along the main road out of town like hitchhikers waiting for the next truck to take them to Faro or Carcross. The names of these other one-bar, one-store communities feel as far away from them now as Paris or Tokyo. The road takes them to the maintenance sheds, where they find the first flames running in the ditches on either side. Another hundred yards on, pylons of fire reach up and over the salt pile.

Miles takes them in. Above them, a square of impudent blue opens over the inferno.

"Where's Stump?"

Rachel's question freezes them in mid-step. The dog had left the lounge at the same time as the rest of them but now he's nowhere to be seen.

"Don't worry about him," Miles tells the girl, gripping her by the shoulders. "He's got a nose for us. When he's done digging up the bone he doesn't want to leave behind, he'll catch up."

"Don't *lie!*"

She flicks his hands away with a single twist.

Then she's off. Arms pumping at her sides. The backs of her legs a blur of pink sunburn.

"Rachel!"

His voice stops her. She stays put even as he walks to where she stands.

"You've got to come."

"Stump?"

He considers another sweetened fabrication, but says nothing. All he does is look at her.

When he offers his hand, she takes it. Though neither mention it, both of them hear Stump's howl join the huskies' through the smoke as they go.

When they return to Mungo and Alex, Miles squints skyward to find the raven. Within seconds, the wind changes again and he is blinded by the stinging smoke. Miles is their sole guide now, and he doesn't know the way. But when he looks back at Mungo, Alex and the girl, he finds only trust in their faces.

***

He slows at the sight of a shoe a half-dozen strides ahead of him. Its human incongruity standing out against the unmarked hillside. Little of it remains but a white loop of canvas, blackened holes for absent laces. Wade bends to pick it up and it audibly crinkles in his hand. He brings it closer to his eyes and is able to make out the material's pattern of laughing penguins wearing bow ties and top hats.

It must have dropped from the girl's foot, but not long ago. And whether walking or carried, she would not be alone.

The tattered loops of the child's sneaker strikes Wade as the best luck to come his way in some time. For one thing, it provides him with the knowledge of where the three of them are, and that they are not far. It also promises an opportunity to put Bader's rifle to use before exhaustion or smoke claims him. Even in his condition, he should be able to catch up. And given the Winchester's range, he won't have to get too close, though he thinks he might like to. In Wade's experience, the real pleasure of the hunt lies in the unexpected ways the animal comes down.

He starts off again with something like elation, the world viewed through a shimmery film. He'd whistle if he could remember a tune. A salute to his second life, his *after* life, one destined to deliver the clear results that his first time round had denied him. It's a comfort to think that perhaps his true talent has been waiting for him all along. Here on the barren slope, in the daylight murk of the underworld, in death.

They run on coals red as chimney brick. Heat cuts through the soles of their feet, eats their toes. It removes all balance from their strides, so that they hobble forward on what feels like open stumps. On fires such as this, Miles has worked on crews who have risked being swallowed by a fast-moving line in order to take off their boots and pour the last of their water in to cool them. None of those were as hot as this.

He spins around to check on Rachel and catches sight of her sprinting legs, her one remaining playground sneaker. Only now does he recognize the little black cartoon figures on the canvas as penguins in tuxes. She runs in the middle of the line they have formed, behind him and Alex but ahead of Mungo. He considers picking her up, but he's not sure he could carry her for long, and for now, she seems to be managing as well as the rest of them.

They dodge around trees dripping sap like candle wax. Even as she runs, Alex watches as floating sparks land in the lichen hugging their trunks. The moss flares, then immediately extinguishes, using up all the oxygen around it in a flush. If there isn't enough air to burn tinder—she wonders almost idly, already losing connection to her thoughts—how much could there be for them to breathe?

Something grips them by the ankles, a loop of muscle that forces each of them to stop. Glued to their places in a marshy pond. One that may have been as much as a foot deep a week ago, but the heat has evaporated all but an inch or two in its centre. At first, they can only move their heads, scanning the soft edges, where panicked game have left a tattoo of prints in the earth. The water that seeps into their socks the temperature of stock left to simmer on the stove.

"My head," Mungo says. His voice so soft it's not really there.

"What's wrong?"

"I'm *upside down*. I think I'm—"

Mungo interrupts his own whispers by vomiting what looks to Miles like a quart of milk over his boots. When he's finished, the older man nods, as though it was an event he'd seen coming for some time. His face so evenly pale it appears powdered with icing sugar.

"Don't think about it," Miles says, not sure if this is good advice or not.

It's enough to send Mungo stumbling on again with the girl in front of him. Before he joins them, Miles steals a glance at the fire reflected in the marsh's water. Torches held by a thousand invisible marchers, making their way down in deepening circles beneath the surface.

"We're going in goddamn circles!" Mungo is shouting.

We're going where it wants us to, Miles says, but not even he can hear.

The fire closes tight all at once. A patch of foxtails embosomed in a dry creek bed lights up in front of them, fizzing like birthday sparklers. Miles urges the three of them back, but the same foxtails they just passed through are already alive with light.

Miles raises his arms to make them watch him. When he has their attention, he points into the seething foxtail.

And runs into it straight.

The girl watches him go. To her, he holds open a velvet curtain. One that has hidden a secret mirror-world from view.

The bear reaches the ridge of the St. Cyrs alone. From here, she commands a view over the killing ground and watches it being devoured. The town she knows to be down there cloaked by clouds that have fallen to earth. Nothing moves over the slope but a line of goats inching along the crest, uncertain which descent is the safer of the two.

Closer, her cub's body lies on the rocks. The scent of his death is already being picked up on the wind. She considers staying if for no other reason than to chase the scavenging eagles off when they come, but she has been moving for so long that her body demands to continue.

She starts down the other side to the south. Though the fire is evident in this valley as well, she can see a route linking corridors of green that will take her to the river. Half a day's travel, probably less. Once she reaches the cover of the treeline, she can finally disappear.

But the sow goes no farther this way. Instead, she climbs back to the ridge. Without pausing to read the air, she walks in the same direction she had come with her cub and toward the fire they had raced to stay ahead of.

Her head is empty of intent. Something awaits her here and there is only the need to meet it. A summoning, as it was when she answered the call to mate. Until an hour ago, instinct had governed every action of her life. Now she is guided by grief alone.

Inside the inferno, there is nothing but white noise. A hateful buzzing, like a swarm of yellowjackets spewing from their nest. They clap palms to the sides of their heads but the most persistent still manage to wriggle in, lancing their eardrums.

Snags fall across their course. Twice, a branch holds Alex beneath it, cooking her on the whitened duff. Smoke pukes from the tops of their trunks. Each time, Miles stops to help Alex and Mungo picks the girl up, as much to know where she is as to protect her from falling widowmakers. Miles lifts the branches back with his bare hands and feels the skin there curl away.

You okay? he asks her.

Alex looks above him, through him. He circles his right ear with an index finger. She shrugs, uncomprehending. If she can't feel the missing half of the ear she'd planted on the burning earth, he's not going to explain it to her.

There is only enough time for Miles to recognize that his next actions will be his last. After that, the wasps will take their time to feed on all of them. If he didn't know as much about what such an experience would entail, he might welcome, after everything, the rush of surrender.

From somewhere far off, he hears the cacophony of an orchestra running scales in different keys.

***

Some time—a click of fingers, a night's sleep—passes. It's impossible for Miles to guess. He feels nothing but the urge to cough.

Without turning, he learns that Alex and Mungo lie next to him. It's their touch that tells him. Brushing the sparking wisps off each other's clothing.

All of them but the girl.

"Rachel?"

Alex speaks her name with tentative recollection. To Miles, it sounds as though it is something she had been trying to locate for hours that has only now been returned to her. A town they had holidayed in, or an exotic vegetable she had once been served in a restaurant.

She turns to Miles and says it again. A storm builds in the dark crescents under her eyes. Runs fingers around her wrists as though checking to see if she wears a watch. All the while she is oblivious to the smouldering bald patch at the side of her head. Her long hair now falling over only one of her shoulders to reveal the black plug of her ear.

"Rachel?"

Miles takes a breath of updrafting carbon and holds it. Inside his head, a violin sings the note that all other sound must be tuned to.

Then, before he can bring his own name to his mind, he lifts himself to his feet and walks back into the swarm.

TWENTY-FOUR

She tries to follow him. When her arms refuse to rise she pounds her forehead against the soil and uses it for leverage. It gets her on all fours for a second before she collapses on her side, knees up. Her body has betrayed her and she considers ways of leaving it behind altogether. Flight, above all. What she wants is to search for her daughter from the air.

Alex lies curled in the toasted grass and thinks, again, how Rachel had changed everything. This is what they say about children. Before Rachel was born, she had been told to expect the worst. Still young then. Unmoneyed, abandoned.

And what everyone said had turned out to be right: there *had* been changes. They came so hard and without interruption she hadn't the time to resent them. It was simply her life. Her new, no-going-back-now life.

There may exist a kind of love that one recovers from, but Alex has never known it. She would go to both of them now if her body allowed her. Instead, she can only search the flames for their shadows and wait for the new everything to arrive.

He calls out the girl's name even as he knows she can't hear it. He can't hear it himself. And yet, somewhere not too far off, he feels the vibration of Rachel's voice. A wordless howl, lost in the shifting labyrinth of fire.

He remembers something that, even as it occurs to him, he feels there isn't the time for. He remembers it anyway. How once, years ago, he'd been picked from the audience to be hypnotized onstage at a nightclub some friends of Alex's had taken them to. It was supposed to be funny. The hypnotist had made others before him quack like ducks and sob like sissies at nothing at all. When he started on Miles with the *Look deep into my eyes* and counting backwards from a hundred, something about the encroaching deadness had made Miles feel as if he was suffocating. He'd snapped out of it and run back to his seat, waving his hands in the air when the hypnotist shouted at him to come back. It had gotten the biggest laugh of the night.

It is how he feels now. The fire is trying to put him under and he's not going to let it. There's something he's got to do. There's someone.

A breeze too high for him to feel passes through the upper leaves of an unburned clump of birches. He risks a glance against the heat. It looks to him like an audience clapping a thousand green hands.

Rachel listens to the fire as she runs. It makes a scary music. Jangling and mean. Fingers drawn over piano strings with a toy fire engine holding down the sustain pedal (her preschool teacher hates it when she does this). Music that's hard to get out of your head once it's found its way in.

She knows that Miles is here with her, moving but coming no closer. Once or twice, she thinks she's heard him calling. But that's not how she knows.

Little Red Riding Hood. She was lost in the woods too. Rachel doesn't wear the cape that the pictures in the book showed—and which Rachel begged her mother for—but when she glances at the skin on her arms she sees that it has turned the same colour. Aside from these details, Rachel's and Red's stories diverge. There is no grandmother's house. No wolf. Though there is the same anticipation of a bad ending.

The girl bats at the fire that reaches up her legs like dogs jumping for food in her hands. Dogs that bite.

She swipes her hand down her side and it comes away wet.

Maybe it's raining.

He swings his arms in circles. It's all Miles can do to search for something when he can't see anymore.

When he makes contact, he's not sure his senses have got it right. Was that skin? Or wood? Grabs for it again and finds the girl's arm. He knows because it's so small. Its pulse.

When he falls the girl lands on his back, knocking the breath out of him. Wherever he is, it's cool enough to open his eyes. Rachel's head rests next to his. All of her hair has burned off, leaving only her pincushioned scalp for him to stroke.

Miles looks about him but can't find Mungo or Alex. Something drops from his lashes into his eyes, stinging them more than the smoke. When he draws his finger across his lids and inspects what he's wiped away, he sees that it is blood. Not his, but Rachel's. The whole of the girl's right side has been burned. Miles studies her wound like a map, seeking the extent of its borders. As he looks at what shock prevents her from feeling yet, his own scar alights with pain.

"Miles!"

"Over here."

"How bad is she?" Mungo asks, looking down at the girl with an expression that answers his own question.

The girl whispers something in Miles's ear.

"Don't talk."

"He's in there."

"We're out of it."

"Not us. *Him,*" she says before blacking out.

"What's she saying?"

Alex kneels beside the two of them. The freckles on her cheeks conjoined into a purple birthmark.

"She's in trouble," Miles tells her.

"It was only a minute."

"It got her."

Alex pushes his arm away. She is too strong for him to shield her from seeing where the fire had touched the girl.

"Oh my *God*—"

"I'll carry her."

"She's *bleeding*. My baby's *bleeding!*"

"That's why we've got to move now."

Alex's eyes turn to glass. She's not here anymore and, for the moment, Miles figures this is better than if she were.

"You want me to take her?" Mungo asks, meaning the girl.

"I've got her."

"You sure? You don't look—"

"I've *got* her."

Miles places Rachel on the grass next to him and lifts what's left of his undershirt over his head. Using the sleeves as straps, he fits it as best he can around the girl's wound. Before he's finished, glistening polka dots have already seeped through the cotton.

"We have to run," Mungo says, not taking his eyes off the fire.

Miles holds the girl against his chest and struggles to his feet. The shakes invade his legs before his first step.

"Miles?"

"I heard you."

"That's good. Because this son of a bitch looks like it wants a race."

TWENTY-FIVE

The bear eats only to clean the ash from its mouth. When she discovers a thatch of buffalo berries growing next to a creek, she crackles inside and lies down. She picks the last traces of colour off the largest bush in less than ten minutes. The creek is close enough to roll over and drink from. Its water numbs her tongue.

Sleep sings around her like mosquitoes, but she resists its invitation. The work involved in stripping each branch of its fruit keeps her awake. She lingers long enough that, when she's finished, crimson juice drips off her muzzle.

She crosses the stream and the current pulls out stones embedded between her claws. Climbing up the bank, she lifts her head to see the mountains, the alders, the taffy clouds, all redrawn in sharper lines. Her nose returned to its flaring survey of whatever moves for miles around.

She cracks through a thicket of devil's club, and its thorns comb dead yellowjackets from her fur. When the ground opens up again, her feet sink into the cushion of a wide peat meadow. The fire has come closer even since lunch. An inky haze climbs five hundred feet above the larches that border the field. An elk stands with its hindquarters only a few feet from a spot fire, seeking relief from the bog's blackflies, choosing to be seared instead of bitten for a change. Where the runoff collects in pools, mallards and pintails fidget through the reeds.

As soon as she reaches the shade on the meadow's opposite side she picks up their scent. Not the same ones she'd met on the rockslide. Not the female hunter, but unmistakably human. A half mile off at the most. She can feel a weight lifting from her great shoulders, lengthening her stride. The hunt focuses her.

A plume of smoke rising from a log ahead signals that she may be cutting too close to the fire. As she passes, she sees that it is only a near-solid cloud of gnats evicted from a fallen snag. Loud as a buzz-saw. An echo of the fury in her own ears.

She moves with eyes closed. There are always the infinite shadings of brown and green and black to camouflage the truth of where a thing stands. But nothing could ever be confused with the candied odour she follows now. It fills the bellows of her lungs. Its taste so purely imagined that when she swallows, she swallows blood.

The three of them come into view through the birches. Following the same creek he does. Maybe two hundred yards away. He would have seen them earlier if it weren't for the smoke.

Wade tries to narrow the distance between them by running along the grassy bank, but the ground is too soft for anything more than the foot-sucking march he's managed for the last half-hour. It forces him into the trees. Here, he moves faster but struggles to keep a line on the creek between the trunks.

When he figures he's made up enough ground, he cuts back to the right to meet the creek again. Finds that his run in the trees had pulled him off course, so that now he's gained no more than a hundred feet on them. His chest hurts. He bends on one knee to clear his vision. Figures he might as well try to hit them from here.

The telescope fits his eye socket so snug it steadies the rest of his body. The lens flattens Mungo and the woman against the slope, so that their backs appear, touchable. He pulls the scope over each of them in turn and feels its crosshairs tickle between his own shoulder blades.

It's only when he gets to Miles that he notices the girl. Resting her head against his neck, looking back. Her eyes blink in short-circuited jolts. But in the brief seconds they stay open she reaches directly into him.

A funny idea introduces itself. He will put the first bullet through the girl's skull. That way, Miles will feel her drop from his arms before he turns to recognize what has happened.

Wade can hear the fire now, like a hundred sets of novelty dentures clacking in the grass. He doesn't turn to see how close it is. Pulls the site away from his eye long enough to slide a cartridge into the chamber. Aims for real this time.

When he finds them again they have progressed only another dozen feet up the slope, but the creek has led them to the left. Soon they will be half-hidden in the birches. Still good targets. But he can't afford to miss. He picked up five cartridges on the slide. It allows for only one mistake. And he'd really like to get all of them.

He holds the crosshairs square on the girl's crown. She's bald where it looks like the fire got her. The darkened skin makes it easier to hold his line.

The trigger is the gun's only metal that is cool to the touch.

Even as he slips his finger around its curve, a wave of smoke breaks through the trees. Rolls over the creek and whitens like froth against the hillside. Wade knows better than to lower the site. He waits for the smoke to clear. A small adjustment will bring them back.

But the gust that brought the smoke dies, leaving a bank of grey between them. Wade slides to the left and spots them again. Already in the birches. A snatch of swinging arm. A torn pant leg.

He lowers the rifle. Considers swearing, but none of the most common choices seem right.

He's more excited than disappointed, anyway. A three-minute jog farther along the creekside and he will be able to tap their shoulders first before separating them from their heads. It will be worth the trouble getting there just to see it with his own eyes.

She is all the way down to the creek's edge before she realizes they are coming to her. The human scents reach the she-grizzly on the same wind that pulls smoke up and over the St. Cyrs. It limits her sight to thirty feet in any direction. Not that this troubles her. She won't need to see them.

The bear makes her way into a stand of birches. If they keep to the bank, they will pass within three strides of her. She settles into the quack grass and waits.

They make their way along the creek they can't hear anymore. For a time, the noise it made was a constant shattering of glass. Now the flames' hisses and cracks stand alone. They look down at the water every few steps to make sure it's still there.

Miles at the head of the line, the girl in his arms. He doesn't want to lose Mungo and Alex in the growing smoke, but they will have to move faster if they have any chance of making it to the ridge before the heat steals their air. His compromise is to make them chase him.

The tall grass mixes with willow saplings that bend against their legs. Off to the side, the bush cuts in close to the creek, so that the space they keep to now is narrowed to the width of a single lane. Up ahead, the creek turns away into thicker stuff. They will have to keep going straight after that without any guidance but the steepening slope.

They are startled by movement next to them. Something heavy enough that they can read its footfall through their boots.

"Bitchpricks," Mungo says, spinning around.

"Don't run. Not until we're sure it sees us."

Even as Miles speaks there is movement again from the bush. Closer than any of them would have guessed the first time. The dull thud of weight on the same roots the three of them stand on. They wait for the animal's grunt. But there's nothing but the stilled green all around them.

If they are to continue on their present upward route, they will have to pass just to the right of the sound's source. Miles waves them on. But when he steps forward, Alex stays back with Mungo, the two of them paralyzed.

"I've heard about you, big lady," Miles is saying, under his breath at first so that only Rachel and whatever waits in the shadowed layers can hear. Slowly, his voice grows louder. Speaking like a fool into the forest as he passes, though the forest quiets to listen nevertheless. "Seems you've had a bad couple of days. It's a shame, it really is. But we've got nothing to do with any of that. We don't have a gun. See? No hunters here. Just fire walkers. Like you."

A kicked stone off to their left brings their eyes to a new shape standing outlined against the greater darkness behind it. Human but only in that it may have been so once. Its body so humpbacked and soiled it could only be a replica of a living thing, a sewn-together collection of graverobbed limbs. Staring at Miles and coughing dirt past its lips.

"Hel-*lo,*" it says.

Wade's voice, but also not Wade's. Then Miles notices the rifle. Jostling around but pointed at his chest more than not.

"You found us," Miles says.

"I tracked you."

"Well, you're out now. You're okay."

"Okay?"

"You can put it down."

Wade follows Miles's eyes and finds the gun held in his own hands. When he looks up again, his face is a mask of stagy innocence. A *You-mean-this-little-thing?* pout.

"I don't think I will," he says, and firms his cupped grip under the barrel. Holds it steady on Miles.

"What are you doing?"

"Wait and see."

"Whatever you're thinking, you don't have to do it."

"No. But I *want* to."

Wade's arm snugs around the rifle's butt. Although his target stands no more than fifteen feet away, he puts his cheek deliberately to the metal. One eye shut, the other peering down the scope into the valleys and ridgelines of Miles's scars.

Miles takes a step toward him before he remembers he carries Rachel in his arms.

There is a pause that all of them understand the same way. Wade isn't hesitating, but savouring the moment of being taken seriously.

Miles turns and crouches at the same time, shielding Rachel with his back. It's only after he's closed his eyes that Miles sees Wade's lips trembling into a smile.

There's a clink. A suck of air.

Something hard hits the top of Miles's left shoulder and burns through to the other side. As it passes it rings against bone. The same sound that reaches through the windows of his cabin from the softball diamond when the heaviest hitters catch one full with the aluminum bat.

He flies. So does the girl. Sprung from his arms, her limbs powerless to find a way to break her fall.

He is spinning around to push himself up before the girl even begins her rolling disappearance into the long grass. Throws himself at where he thinks Wade was standing a second ago. Arms windmilling.

"Stop!"

He hears Alex's shout over the buzzing in his ears as though from a great distance. At first, he interprets the word as the announcement of a broad concept, something requiring further explanation. Its implications spool out over the surface of his thoughts: Everything is about to stop. Must be stopped. They have been coming to a stop forever.

As he finds his feet under him, she shouts it again. This time, Miles hears its intended simplicity. What she wants him to see is Wade holding the girl by the collar of her shirt. His other hand tapping the end of the barrel against the side of her head.

"*Stop!*"

Miles falls to his knees.

"He hit you," Mungo says from somewhere behind him, and Miles looks down at where the bullet took away a piece of his shoulder.

"How's that *feel?*" Wade asks.

"Like nothing," Miles says, and it's true.

"No? How about this?"

Rachel is too close to Wade's legs for him to fire down at her, so he pushes her ahead of him. Returns both hands to aiming at her crawling form. The end of the gun searching the length of her spine.

"Not her," Miles says.

"You know, I'm not such a great shot. I admit it. But I don't think I'm going to miss this one here."

"Wade—"

"Everybody got their eyes on the birdie? Good. Now *watch.*"

Miles comes at him in a hopeless run, all waving arms and twisted knees. There is too much ground between them for anything Miles does now to make a difference. Yet the fact that he stays on his feet, tripping forward, forces Wade to swing the bore around at him. He watches Miles loom and blur through the rifle's telescope as his hand pulls back the bolt.

Miles hits him with his bad shoulder first, but feels only a soft displacement, something come to rest where it shouldn't be. The contact is barely enough to test Wade's balance. Yet Miles clings to him, his boots dragged over the stones as Wade tries to step away. The two men hold each other without foot or fist coming free to land a blow, and for a second, the rifle is hugged between them, unwanted. Pointing at the ground. Under their chins.

The barrel tangles between their legs until Wade falls back. When he lands, the earth knocks out a sour breath that Miles, now lying on top of him, tastes against his tongue. When he puts his hands onto Wade's chest to push himself up, they come away sticky.

Miles gets to his feet and, at first, thinks he has left his right arm

behind on the ground. Yet he feels *something* where it used to be—
an unsustainable pressure, the filling of a thin-skinned balloon—
that isn't at all right. It reminds him of the rifle.

He bends to pick it up and beats Wade's grasping fingers to the
stock. Knocks him back with a dunt to the side of his head.

Miles looks back over the widening cleave in his shoulder and
sees Mungo lifting Rachel from where she landed. The girl's eyes
batting open, pulling him into focus.

"Keep going," Miles says.

Yet all of them stay where they are for a moment. A calculation
based less on whether what they are doing is right than on whether
they can do it at all.

"You have to," he says to Mungo alone this time.

With an ache that has nothing to do with his shoulder he
watches Mungo start away with the girl in his arms. Her bald head
cradled in Mungo's palm and the rest of her hanging loose, not
much bigger than the doll he had discovered in the ash at the edge
of town.

Alex follows with her head turned back at Miles. He watches
her face shrink, grow vague. It takes less than a minute for the
smoke to swallow them all.

Once they're gone, the weight of the rifle quadruples in Miles's
hands. All around, the skins of the birch trees curl up like pencil
shavings.

"What now, gorgeous?" Wade says.

Miles looks down at him and sees a distorted version of himself.
It's not a resemblance but a recognition of some fundamental kin-
ship that has been there all along. Wade Fuerst could be his
brother. Or closer than that. A Siamese twin cut free.

"If I gave you this gun back, what would you do with it?"

"I'd shoot you in the face."

"Then what?"

"Then I'd do the same for your sweetie pies and Tonto up there."

"And if I kept it and just walked away?"

"I'd get it back."

"I believe you."

"You should."

Miles watches the first embers skipping over the creek a hundred yards down. He thought the narrow breadth of water might slow it down for a minute or two. Now he can see it would take him longer to jump over than even the slowest pitching flame.

"If we stay here we're both going to burn," Miles says.

"You think I give a fuck?"

"I guess not."

"That's right. You know why? I'm already dead. I'm a goddamn zombie. I just keep coming and coming."

"I can't let you do that."

Miles knocks the end of the Winchester against Wade's forehead. His eyes cross. Squints the rifle's black mouth into focus.

"I'm not scared," Wade says.

"It doesn't matter."

"*You* would be, though. If this was you."

"You're right. I would be," Miles says, and slips the bore past the kneeling man's lips. "But I'm not the one who's already dead."

The shot is close but the bear stays where she is. Even through the smoke, human scents are all around her. Some heading higher up. Some staying behind.

It's the smell that finally forces her to move. The sharp discharge of powder. Opened skin. Coming from down the creek, she knows. But as she pounds into the cover of trees, she feels it lifting up around her, as though exhaled from the earth itself.

Miles watches Wade's face spray out the back of his head. He hears the crack of the rifle only after he sees what it does. Wade leans forward, headless, as though trying to find what he'd lost in the grass at his knees.

Miles stumbles back to the creek's edge. When Wade finally collapses onto his side, his body is suddenly too close. It forces Miles to shuffle sideways until he has the room to turn his back on Wade.

When he looks up the slope he's glad that he can't see them. The fire is already circling around on its way up the last of the St. Cyrs, but maybe enough time has passed for Mungo, Alex and the girl to have made it beyond its grasp. He feels the force of the rifle's concussion in his legs. A gelatinous tremor he can't think his way out of. He realizes he'd dropped the Winchester immediately after firing it.

He tries at a run and finds it easier than walking. An effort not to put what he'd done behind him but to see if he can catch them before he falls.

She heard the bullet that hit Miles. A cottony thud like a punched pillow next to her ear. Then Mungo picked her up and she heard the other. But it isn't the gun that opens the girl's eyes now. It's what she knows is going to happen next.

Rachel can sense it coming closer without seeing it. Like her dreams of falling in dark water, she was born with a knowledge of the bear. The weight of the fat it carries. The pigeon-toed feet. Along with Mr. Raven, the sow is a character in a play she has anticipated before ever coming to this place. The farther north her mother took her each summer, the more specific shape the drama took. By the time they arrived in Ross River it was only a matter of waiting for the opening scene. Miles. The burned man. She had seen him in her sleep too. And not the smooth-faced photo her mother had shown her, but after his fire. A sad monster.

***

"Shush now," Mungo soothes the girl.

"What's wrong?" Alex asks, coming up alongside him.

"She's just being squirmy."

For a second, both of them watch the chase going on behind the girl's eyelids. It allows them to look at something aside from each other while they catch their breath. To not have to mention the sound of the shot.

They continue on side by side for another minute before they stop to look back for Miles. And he's there, hobbling through a patch of beardtongue. When he is close, he stops and looks up the slope.

At first, Alex thinks he doesn't meet her eyes because of what he's done. But it's something behind her he has settled on.

Alex turns in time to see the grizzly squeezing out from a tight stand of jackpole pines and onto the trail. She makes a quick guess at how far ahead it is. Fifty feet. Close enough that she can see the sow breathing through her open mouth, the gums smooth and shining as enamel. The bear swivels its head from side to side with surprising fluidity. As it moves, Alex sees that her eyes are brown, and not the unreadable black she had assumed. There is as much life in them as in her own.

"Back up."

She hears Miles through what could be tin cans connected with string.

"Get off the trail. Don't run when you do it. Climb the first tree that can take your weight. Do it now."

When Mungo starts, the bear stops swaying its head and stares at him. Takes a step forward. The mouth closes and opens again, closes and opens. Clacking her teeth in warning.

"She's not going to let me."

"Don't look at her. Alex, you too."

But Alex can't stop looking at the bear. There is an expectation that the animal is about to reveal its true opinions of them. No matter how terrible the performance of her hate—if hate is what has brought her here at all—Alex feels an undeniable privilege at being a witness to it.

There is this transfixing curiosity, but ultimately what prevents Alex from attempting escape is the immensity of the animal's need. She watches it breathe, the smoke rattling deep inside it, and knows it is alive for a single reason. They are equal in this respect, if none other. Alex would have quit long ago—searching for Miles, running from the fire, holding back the tickling urge to scream—if it weren't for a prevailing imperative to hang on to. We survive not for ourselves, but for others. And now she watches the bear and tries to read its justification for coming as far as it has.

"Momma?"

Alex sees the child clinging to Mungo's neck. Eyes darker than the bear's, fighting not to let her mother blur away.

"It's all right, honey."

"Momma?"

"Mungo's got you. You hang on to him tight, okay? I'm going to be right over here," Alex says, stepping off the trail as she speaks.

The animal watches the three of them retreat with an almost detached interest. Although Miles still stands on the trail, it appears not to notice him. Instead, it watches Mungo fight for a grip on the lower branches of a spruce, one hand snapping around above him and the other propped under Rachel. There are a number of boughs sturdy enough to support their weight, but dozens of smaller twigs form a barrier around the trunk, pushing down on Mungo's head each time he tries to jump up. The bear studies their efforts. Panting, teeth bared.

"Hey there, big lady!" Miles addresses it, trying to turn its attention away from Mungo and Alex, who is now scraping the bark off the aspen she hugs.

His voice draws no more than a glance from the bear. It returns its attention to Alex. Miles realizes that, as he was speaking to it, he'd been looking into its eyes. It has prevented him from noticing that the bear is on the move. Dragging its claws over the settled ash.

"*Now,* Alex."

The bear charges as Alex's feet leave the ground. Its weight pounds the earth so that a low drumroll pushes out through the porous wall of trees. Every time its front paws meet the earth, it whoofs.

If it struck at half this pace it would be enough to crack the aspen in two. But as it enters the bush it is forced to weave around other trees first. It slows the animal so that, when it meets the aspen Alex has climbed, its impact is little more than a nudge.

The bear sighs. Looks up at her feet, still kicking at the bark. It could rise up on its hind legs and yank her down without stretching.

"*C'mon!*" Miles is screaming now. "What about me? Take a step this way and I promise you, I will—"

The bear spins around. The return of her eyes on him leaves Miles gasping. He looks away to see Mungo and Rachel struggling through a dead patch halfway up the spruce, the top swaying wildly. When he swings back to the bear's position, it's already on the trail.

The bear remains focused on Miles alone. It lowers its head so that its chin hovers inches off the ground. A sprinter awaiting the crack of the starter's gun.

None of them hear it. But when the grizzly comes, she comes as though in flight.

Miles watches her skin rippling under her fur, reaching forward. It enlarges her even more.

From somewhere behind and above, Rachel shrieks.

Whether it is the pitch of the child's voice or the way Miles shakes his hands in front of him but stands his ground, the bear stops. Close enough that Miles need only lean forward to touch its nose.

The bear blows spit. White bubbles over his boots.

The echo of Rachel's scream now a school bell rattling miles deep in the valley. Each time Miles inhales it fills him with a new undercurrent of the bear's odour. Straw. Fermented berries.

He can hear Mungo still scrabbling at the spruce's bark. Without turning his head away from the bear, Miles slowly backs up to join him.

"Get up there," he whispers when he stands beside Mungo, holding him around the waist with his good arm to give him a boost.

"I can't do it."

"Just hug it tight and I'll push you."

When Mungo and Rachel have made it up as far as they can go, Miles finds his own tree and tries to pull himself up using only one arm. The bear walks over to get a better view of his struggles. He swings for a moment before hooking his bad elbow over the lowest branch. Uses it to winch his feet off the ground.

He presses his cheek to the bark. The bear moves between their trees, snorts the air beneath their dangling feet. When she has confirmed which of them remains, she sits. Looks down the slope to watch the fire coming up at them. All of them do. An audience stilled by the same dancing forms.

TWENTY-SIX

They might have already figured out it was him.

He's not sure how, whether by a witness he was unaware of or evidence he was fool enough to leave behind, but in any case, he blames the firestarter. Not only for doing what he did but for failing to protect him from the consequences.

All the firestarter had to do was carry the memory of what was done, yet it is too easily distracted even for this simple job, and leaves him with himself more and more. In fact, he thinks the firestarter may be leaving him for good now. A creation meant to *do* things, not weigh them, not rationalize their harm. The firestarter is gone and he is alone with the knowledge that he will never be what he was before.

It didn't matter what he'd meant the fire to accomplish. Not now. This was his real crime, more fundamental than the incidental destruction, worse even than the killings. He had been guilty of thinking he could determine the intent of fire simply by igniting it with his own intent. It was an offence to nature. In a different time, according to a different religion, it would be the sort of thinking to anger gods.

Now they were coming for him. Not for the firestarter, not an excuse stuffed with straw, but him.

He'd been wrong to think he could divide himself as he'd tried to do. A man may be capable of any number of things, but even the most surprising of these only confirm the truth of who he's been all along.

TWENTY-SEVEN

Don't look.

Below them, the bear whoofs. Pacing between the trees they cling to, knocking her head against their trunks as she goes. Even this much of her weight pulls white roots from the ground.

Bears are like bumblebees. If you ignore them long enough, they go away.

Miles sends mind-messages out to the girl. It is only an excuse to stay where he is with his eyes closed a moment longer. But he's convinced that she can hear him anyway.

You're still looking, aren't you? Cheater.

The scaly bark leaves smears over the length of his scar. Lipstick kisses.

I'm going to count to three and open my eyes. If I catch you looking, you're in big trouble. Got it? One, two—

Miles opens his eyes. He finds Rachel immediately, awake in Mungo's arms. And she is looking. Not at the bear, but at him.

He looks away. The bear is still there, waiting for them to come down on their own. That, or weaken and fall. It would be a game they might have a chance of winning if it weren't for the fire, now charging uphill toward them, less than a hundred yards away. Miles had almost forgotten about it. After Bader, after Wade, after his long march there and back and nearly there again over the St. Cyrs—he had earned a slice of time in which all of it could be misplaced. He'd hugged the tamarack and breathed its cologne of green tea and tarragon and thought of nothing.

It was Rachel who had brought him back. The girl sending out messages of her own.

She's not leaving. Like a whisper in his ear, but closer. *She's waiting for us, isn't she?*

Don't look. Bears are like bumblebees.

From his elevated position, Miles can see the end of the treeline. After that, the ridge is only another couple hundred yards farther through the high grass, although the last ascent is at a much steeper grade.

"We have to go," he says.

His words halt the bear. She looks up at him, head cocked.

"Is it gone?" Mungo asks.

"She's here. So is the fire."

"It's coming up all around us."

"I'm going down first," Miles says, directing his words to the bear as much as to Mungo.

"Rachel?"

"Mungo's got her, Alex. Okay?"

"Okay."

"Just drop after I do. I'm the last back. Mungo, are you sure—?"

"I can take her."

For a time, nothing happens. Even the orange cinders falling about them hang suspended.

It's Miles's hands. They won't let go of the branches that hold him against the trunk. *One more thing.* He has to speak to his fingers directly before they loosen their grip. *After this, we're done. I promise. Just let me go.*

He watches his white knuckles turn pink. The return of blood down his arm brings the first real flare of pain to his shoulder, and with it, Wade's face. Coughing on the rifle as it was slammed against the back of his throat. His eyes laughing.

Miles hadn't paused. When he knew Alex, Mungo and the girl could no longer see him, he'd squeezed off the shot without having to tell himself that it was the only way, that six years of practised nothing had brought him to this.

This could have been you.

He'd read Wade's mind as he reads the girl's now, and this is what he wanted him to know, the thought he found so funny with a gun in his mouth. And Wade had been right.

Miles watches his fingers lifting away from the branch, so that he wonders what's holding him up at all. In the same instant, there's a sound like ripped denim. His boots scraping two lines of bark as he falls.

When he hits the ground his arms swing out for balance but he's already on his back. The bear watching him.

Oh, what a big lady you are.

The grizzly comes forward until she looms over him. Her nostrils recording him in swift, audible sucks.

And what a big nose you have.

Without looking back at the bear, Miles gets to his feet and limps a few steps higher.

He waits to hear the bass tremor of the animal's charge, to feel its skull knock the last air out of him. It makes him go farther than he intended. He's supposed to stand here, act as a distraction for the others. Instead he's stumbling away.

Again, he has to speak to his body to make it stop.

It's not about you. Nothing matters now but what you do for them.

Miles skids on one foot and nearly loses his balance. It turns him around to face back down the trail. The grizzly hasn't moved. For now, the clown show he's putting on is too good to miss. Her teeth displayed in a malicious smile.

"Now, Alex," Miles says.

In his peripheral vision, he watches her shimmy down without hesitation. She doesn't look back. As she walks past him, he hears the tin whistle of her breath.

The bear stretches its neck to look around Miles at Alex putting distance between them on her way up to the ridge. Takes a single step forward. Alex hears the animal's movement and stops.

"Miles?"

"Go."

"But you're—"

"*Go.*"

Alex starts up again. Her departure from the circle of trees momentarily confuses the bear more than enrages it. What appeared to be a smile is gone, at any rate. In its place the sow curls out her lower lip as though savouring a taste of delicate flavour in the air.

Miles hears the snap of dead branches. A *fucknuts* spoken under jagged breaths.

"Mungo?"

"Just got to get my arm out of—"

As Mungo drops, he keeps one arm around the girl. Presses her to his chest and leans back to protect her from impact.

The ground punches a word out of him. "*Oh,*" he says, and lies still.

The bear throws itself around to face them, its front paws scratching loose rocks aside. The noise of Mungo and Rachel's fall has started a process in her mind that had been stalled in their time in the trees. Each of the animal's breaths is a little bark, so that it sounds like she is mumbling to herself.

Mungo bends up at the waist. He didn't think he could move at all, but he's rolling over, using his free hand to push off from the pine needles he'd landed in and the other to hold Rachel close. When he makes it to his feet he starts out after Alex.

The bear lowers her chin. A short grunt escapes her. Quizzical, considered. Her anger has returned. All of them can see it. It's in the way her eyes have been emptied. The three of them look into her and, for the first time, see nothing at all.

The bear leaps. When she lands, she holds her snout a forearm's length from Mungo's face. Slowly, so he can see everything that it means, she opens her mouth wide.

A hot breeze gusts up the slope. The flames passing from crown to crown. Lighting the candles.

Into this silence that would be total were it not for the cracking of the fire rolling up at them, Rachel makes a sound so small only Mungo and the bear can hear it.

"No," the girl says.

Not pleading, not a reflex of terror or denial. She says it more as an acknowledgement of something already shared between the animal and the girl. The concluding word in an ongoing conversation.

The bear examines her. Traces its eyes down the length of the seeping burn on her side.

As slowly as she'd opened it, the sow closes her mouth. With the heat of the Comeback pressing on the back of his neck, Mungo steps around the bear and keeps going.

Although all his legs want to do is carry him back up to join them, Miles forces himself to remain with the bear. He knows he has to because he tells himself so out loud.

"It's got to be you, Smoky. So just hang around with the big lady here awhile. Looks like there's going to be some pyrotechnics in a minute. Should be one hell of a show."

The bear has turned around to listen to him. The loose skin over her eyes drawn up, incredulous.

"Sure wish we had some marshmallows," he tells her. "I'd have shared them if I did."

A standing sleep comes over him. His vision narrowed so that all he can see is the bear.

She is beautiful, Miles thinks, though not in the usual sense. A mystery not in the shape of her thoughts but in their irreducible simplicity. There is nothing within him to match the fineness of the bear's mind.

All he can do is return the memory of the girl's fingers on his cheek. He lets the animal read his scar with her eyes as Rachel had with her touch. And as he does he feels the relief, the unexpected buoyancy that comes with being known.

TWENTY-EIGHT

He hears his name and it sounds odd to him. A measure of distance. Not a man, not him. The voice that speaks it far away, as though to illustrate what his name truly means.

When he can't hear Alex anymore, he awakens.

Everything has changed. The bear is still there. The fire. The blur of smoke. Yet his brief sleep has added design to the world. A visible code he stands a chance of figuring out.

The bear's eyes, for instance. Miles can see colour in them again. Something that he recognizes in the sow, a sharing of base priorities. The things that, when applied to animals, go by the name of instinct. The survival of children. Revenge. Mercy.

Of these, Miles doesn't know which he sees. All he knows is that the bear is letting him go. He steps back and her only response to his movement is a doleful grunt. He hobbles away up the hill. Tells his legs to reach farther.

Alex and Mungo turn to watch him come, but he waves them on. They bend to stroke their fingers over the slope once more. Now he can see Rachel. Her chin on Mungo's shoulder. The only one of them who looks back and meets the eyes that stare after them.

The animal appears so small to her now, a fuzzy outline against the towering trees, their height doubled by top hats of flame. Smoke cascades over her, shading her from view.

Before she disappears completely, the animal turns to face the oncoming fire. Her head pitched high as if recognizing something in the flames.

Though she tries, the girl can't see what the animal sees, whether it is her cubs, her mate, something remembered or dreamed. In any case, it's not meant for her. Even Rachel, a child, knows that love is a kind of secret. One kept from yourself as often as from others.

The bear sits up on hind legs as she does to detect a distant scent. If her own secret lives in the fire, it is about to be revealed.

Every few seconds the smoke parts to let them look through at the ridgeline above. Close enough to see the shaved edges of individual rocks sitting on the crest. Past it, a blue sky so rich in colour it appears as an upturned lake. Then the smoke closes and the world is taken from them again.

Orange strings have made their way through the grass. Now they branch off in both directions, connecting with other strings on their way up, so that it builds a narrowing web around them. It forces their line of ascent into zigzags.

Only fires and bears run faster uphill than downhill.

The adage returns to Miles now, as it had on the Dragon's Back. The difference is that, over time, his memory of his run with the kid had been obscured by bit-by-bit revision, the layered varnishings of denial. Now there is no buffer to hold the fear at a distance. All the mirrors he has avoided looking into since he was burned have been turned on him, so that everything in the moment—Mungo's and Alex's backs struggling against the slope, his arms rubbering between them, the fire coming round on all sides—is cast back in a thousand reflections.

More than anything, he'd forgotten the noise the wildfire makes. It strikes him as both familiar and otherworldly. The voice of madness. An immense choir of despair, deafening and tuneless. Within it, Miles can pick out a handful of sounds he's certain he hears but, at the same time, knows he couldn't. Stump's bark. The clacking of the bear's teeth. A chainsaw biting into the side of a snag.

Ten feet higher, Mungo runs with Rachel held against him and feels every part of him grow w :aker except for his arms. The weight of the girl reminds his muscles of carrying his own kids when they were little. It's the way a child gives itself to its carrier that he finds impossible to forget, its exquisite trust. Tom had been the clingier of his two. Hard to believe given how faraway the boy has become. Now it is Pam who comes home from school to reward her father with unasked-for kisses, and Tom who barely turns his head at the shouting of his name. So what's it prove? Nothing, Mungo thinks, aside from the fact that you can't tell a thing by the way they are when they're small as this. A necessary deception. But what he finds funny about it is that, no matter the complications and defiance that show up over time, it is ultimately just as simple to love them now as then.

Alex feels the girl's weight too. A thrumming cord of sensation that makes her glance over with every third stride, only to be surprised each time not to find her hand holding on to the child's.

Rachel sees all of this as it happens and more. On each side, tunnels open and close in the smoke like a swallowing throat. Through one, she sees a white timber wolf with its tail and ears singed off. Through another, a sheep with spiralled horns lying on its side, legs thrashing.

Then, in a single surge, fire crests over their heads.

It takes Mungo's legs out from under him. When the girl meets the ground, she tumbles backwards through the brittle mountain avens, so that she is out of his reach before he recognizes she's gone.

Miles watches but doesn't stop. As Rachel rolls back at him he lowers his good right arm and snags her around the waist. With another three strides, he throws down his left and hooks Mungo's elbow.

The pain forces Miles to let him go. Yet the contact is enough to force Mungo forward, caught between falling and crawling on hands and knees. The two men bump together and swing apart like homeward drunks.

Miles scans up at what remains of the slope. There is still grass ahead of them that must be crossed. The web of flame runs through most of it now, working back to devour the patches it bypassed a minute ago.

He stops and puts Rachel down. The girl totters on splayed feet but manages to stand on her own. She watches as Miles slips a hand into his firepack and pulls a fusee out.

"What are you *doing?*" Alex asks him, but the question sounds as though it is addressed to a different context altogether. It means as much to Miles as when he catches an isolated phrase as he spins the tuner knob on the radio.

He ignites the fusee and walks with it held at his side, tracing a fifteen-foot semicircle with his boots.

Miles has never really considered why the kid—why *Tim*—had run on instead of joining him, and he gives the question no more than a passing thought now. Impulse, probably. The plug-your-nose-and-jump decision that isn't really a decision at all.

He looks down at Rachel and holds his hand out to her. Without explanation or coaxing, without a word between them, the girl takes it.

Alex attempts another question, but the dry air steals what's left of her breath. The interruption is long enough for her to forget what she wanted to know. She walks into the circle with the flames burning through her jeans. Arms outstretched, feeling for the girl.

Left alone, Mungo looks back at the main fire. Its radiance holds him in its path. He might stay where he is to observe its next wondrous innovation, but Miles's hand is on his shoulder, shaking him.

Mungo turns. All he can make out are the words Miles shapes with his mouth.

Come in.

An invitation. One that the woman and the girl have already accepted. He glimpses them there before a wall of smoke blows in to cut them off.

Come.

He walks inside. Blind but certain where he is.

Miles motions with his hand for the others to lie down close to the smouldering ground but they are already there. Each of them digging at the earth around their faces, scrabbling at the shallow earth.

The breath Miles took when he first lay down demands release. He coughs it out and takes another, fighting the reflex to gasp. It doesn't help. The new teaspoon of air shrieks through his chest. Frantic now, he digs until his nails rip from the ends of his fingers. Then his teeth. Chewing for air in the soil.

He has to tell the others something. A number of things. All of them essential, though he can grasp no more than one at a time. Once announced they are instantly forgotten, so that he loops back on them randomly, like a doll that speaks a handful of phrases when you pull the string in its back.

Don't look up.

Miles lifts his lips from their hole, his head bobbing up and down, as though in prayer.

Remember to breathe.

Keep your head down.

Don't look—

In the next instant, their heads are filled with thunder.

Before the darkness takes them, they feel each remaining strand of hair curl against their scalps. It almost tickles.

TWENTY-NINE

When it stops, it stops all at once.

The grass an explosive but short-lived fuel so that, within a minute of its passing, the fire is already leaping up to the crest of the slope. It wavers there for a time. The wind bats at it, stretches it thin, holds it still. Soon the flames shrink to campfire size. Dwindling tongues lashing at the sky.

Miles can't know how long he's been watching the fire die on the ridge. Lying with his chin held up on a burnt nest of Labrador tea, moving his eyes left to right and back again along the slope's abrupt horizon. Past it, the smoke lifts higher, rising fast as balloons released from a child's grip. Some of it distant enough to have lost the lines that gave it shape, when faces or castles or birds could be seen in the swirling grey.

Rachel is under him. He hasn't moved since losing consciousness, so that his back remains arched over her. The *shutch* still hangs around his neck, the bound Popsicle sticks now resting against the girl's shoulders.

He's been waiting to feel her move. Something more powerful than dread prevents him from rolling over to look. If he can only feel her wriggle against him, he will do, he will say—he will what? All that's left is what he has done, and what he will do next.

At first, the earth refuses to let him go. His knees and palms are glued to the black grass. He has to rock his weight from side to side to loosen its grip. After a couple of tries, he's able to drop on his shoulder.

He pulls the girl to him, scooping his fingers into her mouth to clear it of dirt. Shakes her but her eyes don't open.

Please. A dry crack in his throat.

The girl lies still. Her limbs loose, ill-fit in their sockets. He arranges her into human shape.

Please.

Though the fire has taken the hair from her head, her lashes remain long. Fine curls resting on the tops of her cheeks.

"Rachel?"

Only when he speaks her name does she awaken. When she can breathe without fighting for each gasp, she blinks up at Miles. Her hands reach for him and he holds her to his chest. The only point of contact is his scar to her lips.

Next to them, Mungo rises a foot off the ground. Alex's head squeezes out from under him. She coughs charred bits of twig from her throat. Even as she does, she stretches out her arms. Miles lifts the girl from his chest and lays her on Alex's.

Around them, the ground squeaks like melting ice.

He tries to stand but his legs won't accept the weight. It forces him to crawl past the two of them to reach Mungo. The clothing on his back is gone. Not just burned but stripped away. His shirt, his pants, even the heels of his boots all vapourized by the fire. Miles drags himself closer and kneels over the body. He can see how the flames had lingered over him. Its strokes have left his skin as delicate as dried tobacco leaves. Miles slips his hands under his ribs and rolls him over. Now he is clothed again. Eyes open but goggled all the way around.

He passes his hand over Mungo's chest, trying to smooth the creases in his shirt that have been hardened with the baked salt of his sweat. Something slips away from his touch inside the breast pocket. When he pulls his fingers out they hold a square of blackened steel.

Miles scratches the carbon off with his fingernail. Gradually, a city emerges. The cluster of familiar towers on a narrow island, the great bridges mooring it in place. With another scratch the words are revealed to confirm it. *New York City.*

He rubs Mungo's Zippo clean against his sleeve. The silver

catches what light it can find through the lingering smoke and shines back at him. He flips up the cap. It ignites on the first try.

Miles snuffs the flame and slips the lighter into his own breast pocket. Then, as best he can, he covers the body with a layer of ash. Shovelling it with his palm, sprinkling it like white pepper over his face. With each handful Mungo disappears beneath a grey hill. It's not a burial Miles wants to effect, but a shroud.

When he turns to Rachel and Alex again they are both watching him. For a time they can do nothing but take in each other's shape to confirm that they are actually here. Risen from the million burned wicks of grass to lounge propped up on their elbows. Taking in the view. Sitting like picnickers on the side of a hill, a circle of good black where a blanket would be.

THIRTY

Already, just weeks after the Comeback Fire had burned itself out, patches of fireweed rise from the fields of ash. The hills outside of town that used to stand in varied shades of green and blue now loom as scorched humps, prickly with violet stubble. In the spring, the first saplings will compete for the light.

Miles tells Rachel about this, about his favourite things in this place as well as those that appear in his unsettled dreams. Sitting on his lap in the cabin's backyard. Their eyes alert for ravens.

And then they find one that had been there all along, perched on the end of a branch too thin to bear its full weight. Its head jerking from left to right before finally fixing on Rachel and Miles sitting directly under it. The bird pulls its wings in tight like a cape.

"Will the boy ever come back?" Rachel asks, now studying her toes swishing through the grass.

"What boy?"

The girl reaches up and covers Miles's scar with her palm. He leans into her touch so that she need only whisper to be heard.

"The one who lives in the fire."

"You saw him?"

"No," she says. "But he *talked* to me. He told me which way to go."

Rachel shivers. It is the second weekend in September. The days curling up, the overnight frosts leaving pearly lace over the windows. Miles should go inside and zip the girl into a coat, but instead, he lifts his fleece pullover and tucks her legs inside. Another minute. With winter about to tumble over them any day now, he steals what light he can.

Miles can feel the map of the girl's scar pressed against his chest.

He is already so familiar with its shape he can read it even when hidden beneath a T-shirt. At the hospital, as soon as he'd seen it emerge from under the bandages, he told her it looked like an island, and she'd demanded to know more. Was there buried treasure there? Toys? Did any bears live in the woods? Miles's hours by Rachel's bed were spent racing to make up stories to satisfy her appetite. When she wasn't pulling fictions out of him, she was asking for the truth.

He answered her questions about scarring and what it feels like to have others "look at you and think you're gross." He told her things about his own recovery he had never told anyone. Admissions of fear, humiliations, the loss of vanity. It exhausted him, but seemed to inject the girl with bubbles of strength. A fair trade, as far as Miles was concerned. He was prepared to give her anything that might shorten the time between the next skin graft and the day they would let her go home.

"The boy helped you get out of the fire?" Miles asks.

"No, dumb-dumb. He helped me find *you*."

Miles is less shocked than becalmed by the girl's words, as though some long-held suspicion had now been confirmed. If she could see and hear *him* when he was a ghost, why not others?

"So," she says, tapping his Adam's apple with her forefinger.

"So what?"

"Will he ever come back?"

"I don't know. I think he might be gone for good."

Rachel nods absently, her mind already shifted to new concerns. Then she lifts her hand from Miles's face and, without looking up herself, points at the branch where the raven had been perched, now swaying from the force of its silent launch. When Miles looks for it, the bird is nowhere to be seen in the sky ahead or behind.

Alex steps out the back door and follows Miles's and Rachel's eyes.

"It's getting darker," she says.

And it is. Dusk pours over them like chalk powder. When the night comes it will grow as long as the day itself, then longer still, blotting out the light until there is only a dull wash of grey over the noon hour.

On one of the days at the hospital, the first that Miles noticed the retreat of light from the evening sky, he had tried to ask Alex if she would consider letting him return to the Outside with her and Rachel. She had interrupted him by shaking her head. He assumed she was preventing him from greater embarrassment by stopping his suggestion dead in its tracks. And of course, she'd have been right. Alex and Rachel weren't bounty hunters. They didn't come here to bring him back. He was about to thank her for saving him from making a fool of himself when she told him she had her own plans to reveal. She and Rachel both.

"You've already talked to her about this?" he asked.

"It's a joint submission."

"When? I mean, when did the two of you talk?"

"Even you fall asleep sometimes."

They had decided they'd like to try staying on in Ross River for a trial run. The girl had asked to and Alex, cautious of a child's stated wants, was prepared to entertain an experiment. Like the teachers before her, she would accept only a term contract at the school. All three of them would be here at least until Christmas. After that, they'd see. They'd see.

"You can have the cabin," Miles had offered immediately.

"That's nice. But we'd like you to be in it, too."

"Me. Oh."

"We'll take the spare room, and you can stay in yours. See how it goes."

"How it goes."

"Miles? Are you all right?"

He was shaking so hard the metal tips of his chair legs squeaked like mice over the tiles.

"I'm good. I just don't remember what this feels like."

"You're scared."

"No. Not scared," he said, gripping the armrests as though riding out a spell of turbulence. "Just a bit happy, I think."

His cabin, like all the remaining buildings in town, had been fattened by a layer of cottony ash, but was otherwise untouched. They were lucky. Nearly half the homes had been torched when the fire roared through. The Welcome Inn's outbuilding was a pile of black timber, but the lounge was open for business within hours of the authorities allowing people to return. The school, library and RCMP office were gone, along with the Lucky China and the fire crew's radio shack. Jerry McCormack's trailer was among those that were razed, and he had moved in with Crookedhead James until he could, he said, work out the insurance, though it was clear he'd never paid for insurance of any kind in his life and that the two men would continue as housemates for some time to come. Everyone without a home moved in with someone who had. Government offers of temporary relocation went unanswered. Even in the devastation, there was a shared sense of not wanting to miss anything. All of Ross River, and not just an unfortunate fraction, would have to start over again.

The Comeback had continued to burn two full weeks after human survivors and remains had been lifted out of it, and in the end laid waste to some twenty thousand acres of forest. But they were anonymous acres, distant and unpeopled, and therefore of little importance to the outside world. The wildfire season burned on here as elsewhere, but it was noted only for its curiosities, its bite-sized human dramas.

The handful of reporters who'd made the trip north to cover the story had moved on well before the dead had been buried. Stump had been first. From her hospital bed, Rachel made the funeral arrangements. She asked Miles to fill a jar with ash from where the four of them first entered the fire on the edge of town and bury it in the yard behind the cabin. "That's where we talked," she told him.

Miles took the next day off from his burn unit vigil to drive up to

Ross River. In the leaden field beyond the road maintenance sheds, he scooped an empty mustard bottle full of what was once the forest, Toot's husky team, the rooftops of half a dozen mobile homes, along with Stump's powdered bones. Alone, he dug a hole down to the permafrost and dropped it in.

It was only when he walked back into the kitchen that he felt it. The scraps from Alex and Rachel's interrupted breakfast before the air-vac—milk-sodden bran flakes, curdled coffee, a slice of toast with a moon bitten out of one corner—lay abandoned on the counter. The chess game in the living room that, even from where he stood, he could see was missing the white queen. He couldn't tell which was the trigger, but some combination of commonplace details brought the dog to him. Not any mere presence, either, no passing chill or creak of the floorboards. It was Stump slapping the back of Miles's legs with his tail. His trademark request for a second helping. Automatically, Miles bent to lift his dish off the floor. Before he could reach it, the wagging tail was gone. He told no one about it. Still, when he returned to Rachel's bedside the next morning, he had the impression the girl knew all the same.

They found some of Wade's teeth not far from Bader's Winchester, along with a scattering of other bones, the ones buried deep enough in ash to avoid the worst of the heat. They gathered what they could and flew it down to his family's place in Alberta. There had been a memorial service of sorts for him in town, right in the Welcome Inn Lounge.

"It's a funny thing," Margot had started her eulogy, delivered from behind the bar, a plywood pulpit. "If Wade's spirit is in this room with us today—and I believe it is—it would be the first time he's been in here, night or day, without a goddamn drink in his hand."

There had been a dreadful pause. It was Margot's face that held them in suspense. Deadpan at the best of times, and inscrutable when she was really trying. But on this occasion, even she couldn't hold it. A smile forced up the edges of her lips and, at the sight of her bared teeth, the place exploded in laughter, a communal shriek that concluded only after the minute it took for Jerry McCormack to blow his nose dry. All of it triggered by the first excuse for release they'd had since the fire, for something to express in public other than empty mumblings of *Damn shame* or *Helluva thing, helluva thing.* It took everyone by surprise. Of all people, it was Wade Fuerst they were grateful to for offering this release.

"Didn't think you'd come," Margot said to Miles afterwards.

"I came to say I was sorry."

"What's with you and apologies? Wade was like that too. All his life he's only doing what he couldn't stop himself from doing, and the whole time he's saying 'I'm sorry.'"

"This is a little different."

"Because you shot him?"

"If you want to hear it someday, there's a lot I could——"

"I know what happened."

"The Mounties sent you their report."

"They did, but I didn't read it."

"Then who have you been talking to?"

"I don't need to talk to anybody. I know because I shared his bed. Because I was the one stupid enough to think I was doing him a favour by staying with him."

Miles turned his shoulder to the rest of the room.

"Most of it is true," he told her. "But there's more to what I did than what the police found out."

Margot raises his chin with her finger.

"I told you, Miles. I already know."

She had left him to get herself a drink, and Miles had slipped out the door, uncertain whether he had just been forgiven or cursed. For most of the weeks that followed he stayed down in White-horse with Rachel in hospital. But only the day after their return to Ross River, Margot had come by the cabin to drop off frozen moose steaks. Alex invited her in but she declined, saying she was only there to make sure the three of them didn't starve until the Raven Nest opened up again. Miles had watched her from inside. Handing over the bag of steaks like some living thing they were being entrusted to care for. She may not have seen him standing there for the shadows, but he believes she had. Margot offering them part of an animal she had killed herself, a gift that showed the necessary violence in staying alive. Miles ate the meat that night and tasted in it Margot's assurance that he need never speak of what happened with Wade on the slope, not with her.

A much larger gathering than Wade's memorial took place later the same week at Mungo Capoose's funeral. Jackie wanted it at their house and not at the church by the river because her husband had "never set foot in any barn with a cross on it," and there was little point in starting now. The whole town came. A cross-cultural celebration that flipped between The Grateful Dead on the stereo and tribal drums, a speech by Jerry McCormack in English and a myth told by a band elder in Kaska. As the evening went on and the beer coolers emptied, the event took the form of a kind of First Nations wake, with dancing mourners spilling out into the yard and lighting a bonfire that began as a spontaneous means of staying warm but was later generally recognized as a poignant memorial to the deceased. At midnight, Crookedhead James brought over a couple of tents from the fire office. When the flames cooled, twenty guests slept outside, refusing to let the night end.

Earlier that night, Miles had given Tom his father's Zippo. There had been little ceremony about it, as the boy discouraged conversation at the best of times, and had been tearless but especially silent in the days after the fire. Miles had made an empty remark to fill the moment that he immediately regretted, something about how now maybe Tom might have the chance to visit New York himself, the city etched on the lighter that had been with Mungo all these years but that he had never come within an eight-hour flight of. But Tom had nodded and rubbed his thumb over the towers the same way he had watched his father do since he was old enough to take notice.

Not long after this, Tom had started visiting Miles at the fire office. Ostensibly, it was on his mother's orders to get out of the house and quit joysticking away entire days in front the computer. But soon, Tom started asking questions about the crew's equipment and how fires were fought. The two of them came to form a language of mourning using hose pressures, shovel types and fire history.

"The pulaski was named after a ranger who saved thirty-nine firefighters back in the Big Blowup of 1910. Led them into a mine-shaft and told them to lie down and breathe dirt. When the fire hit, one of the men panicked and tried to run out. But Ed Pulaski took out his pistol and told him he'd sooner shoot him dead than watch him burn. Now *there* was a guy who knew fire. Just *look* at this thing. Perfect for digging line and putting out spots," Miles would tell the boy, the two of them hacking at the earth behind the fire office. "Your dad knew fire, too. He would've come up with this if Ed hadn't gotten to it first. Knew how to use one, that's for sure."

"He was good?" Tom would ask. Not because he doubted the fact but to have it repeated.

"He was the best," Miles would tell him. "Next to *me*, of course."

It amazes Miles how unreadable he'd found Tom only days ago—how unreadable others still find him—and the future he can see in the kid now. Miles will recommend him for the training program in a couple of years, if Tom wants him to. A born firefighter. All bound-up intensity, a longing for escape and the desire to do something at once good and understandable. The same mischievous glint in his eyes as his father. An indication of humour that, under hard circumstances, could be translated into courage.

Dennis Parks and two government officials arrived to conduct a preliminary investigation into the cause of the Comeback Fire.

The Ross River attack team were interviewed first, one at a time, the little church by the river turned into an interrogation room. They asked about the crew's whereabouts on the days before the fire's discovery, the potential motive each of them might have had to light a smoker of their own. Little was revealed, as little was known. Miles was subject to the longest sessions, answering the same questions over and over about taking the pumper out for a drive around the time the fire would have been started, and whether he had any "special regrets" about losing the kid on the Dragon's Back years ago. Despite his frequent longing to lunge across the desk and take Parks by the throat, Miles remained calm. He told them he often took drives on his own to clear his head. His questioners nodded and looked doubtful, but it was all they could do. After a breakfast of Bonnie's sausages and eggs the following morning, all three of them were gone.

No one spoke of firestarters after that, though Miles knew that there was one, and who it was. A fire started not for money, he felt sure, but for the town itself. A reason for the few who found themselves at this end of the road to stay.

Miles's certainty on this count was based not on evidence but on instinct, the small shifts and compensations you can sense in someone you know well enough. He told no one except Alex. There were a dozen good reasons not to pursue further disclosures than this, and only one to compel him: every fire has to be started somehow, and knowing the Comeback's cause would advance the completeness of the official record. Miles was prepared to let the paperwork show another checkmark under Cause: Unknown. He'd keep everything else to himself. Alex and Miles both.

It wasn't the only secret between them now.

The doctors had recognized the injury to his shoulder as a bullet wound, and the police had been called to his hospital room to ask about it, and about Wade Fuerst. It was Miles's first day of consciousness after twenty hours of morphined sleep, and he had yet to speak to Alex or anyone else. There could be no planned corroboration with her in advance, and he knew that whatever version of events he told them now would be vulnerable to not only the physical evidence he'd left behind but Alex's—and perhaps even Rachel's—statements. So he told the truth, up to a point. Wade had tracked them after the bear attack, picking up Bader's rifle along the way. When he came upon them, he had shot Miles in the shoulder. A struggle followed. The gun spinning between them. When the stock hit the ground it fired, taking Wade's head off his neck.

Alex told them the same thing. The easiest and most credible fabrication had occurred to both of them without discussion. As to Wade's motive, Margot confirmed Miles's speculations. Wade had been a betrayed man. Denied not only his woman but the promise of a child, a family. Everyone in Ross River had been witness to his attacks on Miles. Things had escalated to gunplay. A set of circumstances hardly unfamiliar to the police.

In his truck parked on Whitehorse's Main Street, on a shared break from Rachel's bedside, eating takeout sandwiches off their laps, Miles told Alex what she already knew. There was no forgiveness. No oath of secrecy. It was as it had been between them. All they were trading was the truth. And now that it was shared, they saw how it might be carried.

Rachel shivers on Miles's lap again. From the cabin's back step, Alex watches the girl curl up inside his sweater, almost disappearing completely except for the top of her head that glows pale where the regrowth hair has yet to blanket her scalp. Alex smooths her own returning strands over her flame-bitten ear. Soon it will be hidden. Not for the first time she thinks that, no matter what happens, the three of them will carry the mark of fire. In plain view or not, its shape will be known among themselves.

She listens to Miles telling the girl it's time to put her coat on, followed by Rachel's reply of groans, and hears it as the performance of an already old routine. Miles turns to Alex and she can make out his shrug, his helpless *What-can-you-do?* look through the twilight. Even before she laughs she is aware of how awake she feels in this place. Not sleepless or nervy, but open to all signals, her senses keen-edged as she imagines the bear's had been.

The temperature drops another degree. It's time that all of them put on another layer before the party. It was Miles's idea. A welcome-home barbecue in honour of Rachel's return from hospital. All the simple, backyard rituals would be performed. Scorched patties and bottles stacked like logs between the fridge shelves. A gathering of friends to watch the night come on.

They will soon be here. Jerry and Crookedhead, the last members of the attack team left in town (King had taken off for the new term at university), Margot, Tom, Terry Gray and Bonnie. All of them except Margot would be seeing the inside of Miles's cabin for the first time.

Before he lifts Rachel in his arms and walks back into the cabin, Miles has another of his premonitions. What he envisions is nothing special, but its pleasures haunt him even before they have passed. They will eat too much, and tell stories they have all told before. Miles will be the first to notice the northern lights. He will sweep his hand over the underbelly of sky as though it is this gesture alone that creates the trailing curtains of spectral green. The aurora will fall close enough that even the adults will consider reaching their fingers up to touch it. For a painless moment they will allow themselves to remember. Runaways. Fire. They will draw their circle of chairs tighter around the barbecue's warm ashes, quiet now, their faces flushed by the unspoken truth that they are among the lucky ones, people who know where they are and that they belong.

ACKNOWLEDGEMENTS

First, thanks to my editors, Iris Tupholme and Julia Wisdom, as well as Anne McDermid for her early insights and enthusiasm. Readers of drafts along the way—David Rittenhouse, Sean Kane, Leah McLaren, Shaun Oakey, Lorissa Sengara—also offered helpful responses and encouragements.

During my time in the Yukon, I received counsel, stories and companionship from many friends and near strangers alike. For setting my mind on fruitful paths, I must acknowledge in particular Jackie Bazett, Belinda Smith, Al Macleod, Julia Finlay and all who have worked to establish the Berton House Writers' Retreat in Dawson City.

For his Kaska and Northern Tutchone translations, I am indebted to J. T. Ritter, Director of the Yukon Native Language Centre at Yukon College, Whitehorse.

Finally, I am grateful to Heidi Rittenhouse for riding shotgun the whole way.